DEALING

IN

FUTURES

DEALING

IN

FUTURES

STORIES BY

JOE HALDEMAN

VIKING

VIKING
Viking Penguin Inc., 40 West 23rd Street,
New York, New York 10010, U.S.A.
Penguin Books Ltd, Harmondsworth,
Middlesex, England
Penguin Books Australia Ltd, Ringwood,
Victoria, Australia
Penguin Books Canada Limited, 2801 John Street,
Markham, Ontario, Canada L3R 1B4
Penguin Books (N.Z.) Ltd, 182–190 Wairau Road,
Auckland 10, New Zealand

First published in 1985 by Viking Penguin Inc.
Published simultaneously in Canada

LIBRARY OF CONGRESS CATALOGING IN PUBLICATION DATA
Haldeman, Joe W.
  Dealing in futures.
  1. Science fiction, American. I. Title.
PS3558.A353D4 1985   813'.54   85-3359
ISBN 0-670-80635-8

Acknowledgment is made to the following publications in which some of the stories in this
book first appeared: *Alien Stars*, Baen Books, edited by Elizabeth Mitchell: "Seasons";
Amazing: "You Can Never Go Back"; *Analog:* "A !Tangled Web"; *Dark Forces*, edited by
Kirby McCauley: "Lindsay and the Red City Blues"; *Destinies*, edited by James Baen: "The
Pilot"; *Magazine of Fantasy & Science Fiction:* "Manifest Destiny"; *Omni:* "No Future in
It" and "Saul's Death"; *Playboy:* "Blood Sisters" and "More Than the Sum of His Parts";
Pulpsmith: "The Big Bang Theory Explained"; *Thieves' World*, edited by Robert Asprin:
"Blood Brothers"; *Twilight Zone:* "Seven and the Stars."

Printed in the United States of America by
The Book Press, Brattleboro, Vermont
Set in Century Schoolbook
Designed by Robin Hessel

CONTENTS

DEALING

IN

FUTURES

INTRODUCTION

When I put together my first short story collection, *Infinite Dreams*, the publisher asked that I introduce each story with a note about how it came to be written. I complied and, as here, had them put the notes in a different typeface, so those who wanted to get straight to the stories could easily slip by the blather.

That book produced more letters from readers than most of my novels have and, to my surprise, as much of the mail was about the blather as about the stories. I suspect that's because so many science fiction readers write the stuff themselves, or would like to, and so have a special taste for confessional bookchat.

One reader came up with an interesting observation, noting that I obviously had to pull my punches in the introductions sometimes, because telling all would have given away the ending of the story. He suggested that in the next collection I write afterwords instead, so I wouldn't have to work under that constraint.

The only problem with that is that there are villainous people, like myself, who always flip through a collection and read the introductions first, and we would probably do that even if they were afterwords instead. But the notion started me thinking, and I came up with a compromise that resulted in the way this book is put together.

This collection is arranged as a continuum, each story having an afterword that blends into the introduction of the next story. Yes, it's a cheap trick, an attempt to keep sucking you into the next story until you've read them all. But sometimes the relationships between the stories are interesting—and besides, you paid for all of them. Might as well give them a try.

The novella that follows came to be written because of an odd coincidence. I accepted a one-year visiting professorship at MIT, to teach science fiction writing and one other course each semester. For the second semester I was handed "Reading and Writing Longer Fiction," which was a lecture-and-workshop course on the theory and practice of writing novels and novellas. Novels, fine; I'd written a dozen and had even studied some of the theory. But of the theory of the novella I had read only one mercifully short essay by Henry James, and I hadn't actually written one of the little devils in at least ten years.

(When literary folks talk about a novella they usually mean anything that's too long to be considered a short story but isn't long or complex enough to be a novel. Commercial writing makes the further distinction between the novelette, a long story that's less than 17,500 words long, and the novella,.which can run up to 30,000 or 40,000.)

People who write for a living don't write many novellas. They demand at least as much work as the equivalent wordage of a novel—usually rather more—and pay perhaps an order of magnitude less. Magazine editors have little enthusiasm for them because they take up a third of the magazine but only add one title to the table of contents. So even if you can place one, it goes for a low rate of pay.

I was in a bit of a quandary. Teaching instinct, and to a certain extent conscience, told me that if I was going to make my students write novellas, I should sit down and write one myself. But my baser practical instincts were telling me that I'd be an idiot to invest a couple of months' work in a piece that would only bring a few hundred bucks.

This was where coincidence struck. The day after I learned I was going to teach the course, I was sitting in my office scratching my head over the dilemma, and the phone rang. It was Betsy Mitchell of Baen Books, asking whether I would like to write a novella for the book *Alien Stars*, a collection of three novellas on the theme "conflict with aliens." I recovered from synchronistic shock just long enough to ask for more money—the freelancer's primary conditioned reflex—and she said she'd check and call back.

That phrase sometimes means you've blown the deal. I'm no more superstitious than the next writer, which is to say that if somebody stole my lucky coffee cup I'd have to look for another line of work. Face it, the last time an editor had called asking for a novella was 1972! This was a portent. The Muse had sent me a sign and I had rejected her.

But she called back—Betsy Mitchell, not the Muse—agreeing

to my terms, so I immediately got down to work. And discovered I had a real problem.

Some of the most perfect stories in our language are novellas: *Heart of Darkness, The Ballad of the Sad Cafe, The Short Happy Life of Francis Macomber*. In science fiction we have such gems as *The Marching Morons, Universe, Flowers for Algernon*. But if they stand out as gems, it's at least partly because their companions are such mundane gravel. Most novellas are either bloated short stories or amputated novels. I had to stay away from those two traps.

To further complicate things, it seemed to me that most good novellas have a prickly kind of singularity about them—that is to say, it's impossible to make useful generalizations about what makes them stand out. (It *is* possible to make useful generalizations about the novel and the short story.) I had set myself up for a real job.

I'll spare you a description of all the theoretical considerations that went into the piece. Suffice it to say that I've written novels (adventure novels, anyhow) that took less time and effort than *Seasons*. Novellas are *hard*.

The perverse thing is that I'm itching to write another.

S E A S O N S

Transcripts edited from the last few hundred hours of recordings:

Maria

Forty-one is too young to die. I was never trained to be a soldier.
Trained to survive, yes, but not to kill or be killed.

That's the wrong way to start. Let me start this way.

As near as I can reckon, it's mid-noviembre, AC 238. I am
Maria Rubera, chief xenologist for the second Confederación expedition to Sanchrist IV. I am currently standing guard in the
mouth of a cave while my five comrades try to sleep. I am armed
with a stone axe and flint spear and a pile of rocks for throwing.
A cold rain is misting down, and I am wearing only a stiff kilt
and vest of wet rank fur. I am cold to the very heart but we dare
not risk a fire. The Plathys have too acute a sense of smell.

I am subvocalizing, recording this into my artificial bicuspid,
one of which each of us has; the only post–Stone Age artifacts
in this cave. It may survive even if, as is probable, I do not. Or
it may not survive. The Plathys have a way of eating animals
head first, crunching up skull and brain while the decapitated
body writhes at their feet or staggers around, which to them is
high humor. Innocent humor but ghastly. I almost came to love
them. Which is not to say I understand them.

Let me try to make this document as complete as possible. It
gives me something to do. I trust you have a machine that can
filter out the sound of my teeth chattering. For a while I could
do the Zen trick to keep my teeth still. But I'm too cold now. And
too certain of death, and afraid.

4

My specialty is xenology but I do have a doctorate in histori-cultural anthropology, which is essentially the study of dead cultures through the writings of dead anthropologists. In the nineteenth and twentieth centuries, old style, there were dozens of isolated cultures still existing without metals or writing or even, in some cases, agriculture or social organization beyond the family. None of them survived more than a couple of gen-erations beyond their contact with civilization, but civilization by then could afford the luxury of science, and so there are fairly complete records. The records are fascinating not only for the information about the primitives, but also for what they reveal of the investigating cultures' unconscious prejudices. My own specialties were the Maori and Eskimo tribes, and (by necessary association) the European and American cultures that investi-gated and more or less benignly destroyed them.

I will try not to stray from the point. That training is what led to my appointment as leader of this band of cold, half-naked, probably doomed, pseudo-primitive scientists. We do not repeat the errors of our forebears. We come to the primitives on equal terms, now, so as not to contaminate their habit patterns by superior example. No more than is necessary. Most of us do not bite the heads off living animals or exchange greetings by the tasting of excrement.

Saying that and thinking of it goads me to go down the hill again. We designated a latrine rock a few hundred meters away, in sight of the cave entrance but with no obvious path leading here, to throw them off our scent at least temporarily. I will not talk while going there. They also have acute hearing.

Back. Going too often and with too little result. Diet mostly raw meat in small amounts. Only warm place on my body is the hot and itching anus. No proper hygiene in the Stone Age. Just find a smooth rock. I can feel my digestive tract flourishing with worms and bugs. No evidence yet, though, nor blood. Carlos Flem-ing started passing blood, and two days later something burst and he died in a rush of it. We covered his body with stones. Ground too frozen for grave-digging. He was probably uncovered and eaten.

It can't be the diet. On Earth I paid high prices for raw meat and fish and never suffered except in the wallet. I'm afraid it may be a virus. We all are, and we indulge in dis-creet copromancy, the divining of future events through the inspection of stools. If there is blood your future will be short.

Perhaps it was stress. We are under unusual stress. But I stray.

It was specifically my study of Eskimos that impressed the assigning committee. Eskimos were small bands of hearty folk who lived in the polar regions of North America. Like the Plathys, they were anagricultural carnivores, preying on herds of large animals, sometimes fishing. The Plathys have no need for the Eskimos' fishing skills, since the sea teems with life edible and stupid. But they prefer red meat and the crunch of bone, the chewy liver and long suck of intestinal contents, the warm mush of brains. They are likable but not fastidious. And not predictable, we learned to our grief.

Like the Eskimos, the Plathys relish the cold and become rather dull and listless during the warm season. Sanchrist IV has no axial tilt, thus no "seasons" in the Terran sense, but its orbit is highly elongated, so more than two thirds of its year (three and a half Terran years) is spent in cold. We identified six discrete seasons: spring, summer, fall, winter, dead winter, and thaw. The placid sea gets ice skim in mid-fall.

If you are less than totally ignorant of science, you know that Sanchrist IV is one of the very few planets with not only earthlike conditions but with life forms that mimic our own patterns of DNA. There are various theories explaining this coincidence, which cannot be coincidence, but you can find them elsewhere. What this meant in terms of our conduct as xenologists was that we could function with minimal ecological impact, living off the fat of the land—and the blood and flesh and marrow, which did require a certain amount of desensitization training. (Less for me than for some of the others, as I've said, since I've always had an atavistic leaning toward dishes like steak tartare and sushi.)

Satellite observation has located 119 bands, or families, of Plathys, and there is no sign of other humanoid life on the planet. All of them live on islands in a southern subtropical sea—at least it would be subtropical on Earth—a shallow sea that freezes solid in dead winter and can be walked over from late fall to early thaw. During the warm months, on those occasions when they actually stir their bones to go someplace, they pole rafts from island to island. During low tide, they can wade most of the way.

We set up our base in the tropics, well beyond their normal range, and hiked south during the late summer. We made contact with a few individuals and small packs during our month-long trek but didn't join a family until we reached the southern mountains.

The Plathys aren't too interesting during the warm months, except for the short mating season. Mostly they loll around, conserving energy, living off the meat killed during the thaw, which they smoke and store in covered holes. When the meat gets too old, or starts running out, they do bestir themselves to fish, which takes little enough energy. The tides are rather high in summer and fall, and all they have to do is stake down nets in the right spots during high tide. The tide recedes and leaves behind flopping silver bounty. They grumble and joke about the taste of it, though.

They accepted our presence without question, placidly sharing their food and shelter as they would with any wayfaring member of another native family. They couldn't have mistaken us for natives, though. The smallest adult Plathy weighs twice as much as our largest. They stand about two and a half meters high and span about a meter and a half across the shoulders. Their heads are more conical than square, with huge powerful jaws: a mouth that runs almost ear to ear. Their eyes are set low, and they have mucous-membrane slits in place of external ears and noses. They are covered with sparse silky fur, which coarsens into thick hair on their heads, shoulders, armpits, and groins (and on the males' backs). The females have four teats defining the corners of a rectangular slab of lactiferous fatty tissue. The openings we thought were their vaginas are almost dorsal, with the cloacal openings toward the front. The male genitals are completely ventral, normally hidden under a mat of hair. (This took a bit of snooping. In all but the hottest times and mating season, both genders wear a "modest" kilt of skin.)

We had been observing them about three weeks when the females went into estrus—every mature female, all the same day. Their sexuality was prodigious.

Everybody shed their kilts and went into a week-long unrelenting spasm of sexual activity. There is nothing like it among any of the sentient cultures—or animal species!—that I have studied. To call it an orgy would be misleading and, I think, demeaning to the Plathys. The phenomenon was more like a tropism, in plants, than any animal or human instinct. They quite simply did not do anything else for six days.

The adults in our family numbered eighty-two males and nineteen females (the terrible reason for the disparity would become clear in a later season), so the females were engaged all the time, even while they slept. While one male copulated, two or three others would be waiting their turn, prancing impatiently, masturbating, sometimes indulging in homosexual coupling. ("Indulging" is the wrong word. There was no sense that they took pleasure in any sexual activity; it was more like the temporary relief of a terrible pressure that quickly built up again.) They attempted coupling with children and with the humans of my expedition. Fortunately, for all their huge strength they are rather slow and, for all the pressure of their "desire," easily deflected. A kick in the knee was enough to send them stumping off toward someone else.

No Plathys ate during the six days. They slept more and more toward the end of the period, the males sometimes falling asleep in the middle of copulation. (Conversely, we saw several instances of involuntary erection and ejaculation while sleeping.) When it was finally over, everyone sat around dazed for a while, and then the females retired to the storage holes and came back with armloads of dried and smoked meat and fish. Each one ate a mountain of food and fell into a coma.

There are interesting synchronies involved. At other times of the year, this long period of vulnerability would mean extinction of the family or of the whole species, since they evidently all copulate at the same time. But the large predators from the north do not swim down at that time of year. And when the litters were dropped, about 500 days later, it would be not long after the time of easiest food gathering, as herds of small animals migrated north for warmth.

Of course we never had a chance to dissect a Plathy. It would have been fascinating to investigate the internal makeup that impels the bizarre sexual behavior. External observation gives some hint as to the strangeness. The vulva is a small opening, a little over a centimeter in extent, that stays sealed closed except when the female is in estrus. The penis, normally an almost invisible nub, becomes a prehensile purple worm about twenty centimeters long. No external testicles; there must be an internal reservoir (quite large) for seminal fluid.

The anatomical particulars of pregnancy and birth are even more strange. The females become almost immobilized, gaining perhaps fifty percent in weight. When it comes time to give birth, the female makes an actual skeletal accommodation, evidently similar to the way a snake unhinges its jaw when ingesting large prey. It is obviously quite painful. The vulva (or whatever new name applies to that opening) is not involved; instead, a slit opens along the entire perineal area, nearly half a meter long, exposing a milky white membrane. The female claws the membrane open and expels the litter in a series of shuddering contractions. Then she pushes her pelvic bones back into shape with a painful grinding sound. She remains immobile and insensate for several days, nursing. The males bring females food and clean them during this period.

None of the data from the first expedition had prepared us for this. They had come during dead winter and stayed one (terran) year, so they missed the entire birth cycle. They had noted that there were evidently strong taboos against discussing sexual matters and birth. I think "taboo" is the wrong word. It's not as if there were guilt or shame associated with the processes. Rather, they appear to enter a different state of consciousness when the females are in heat and giving birth, a state that seems to blank out their verbal intelligence. They can no more discuss their sexuality than you or I could sit and chat about how our pancreas was doing.

There was an amusing, and revealing, episode after we had been with the family for several months. I had been getting along well with Tybru, a female elder with unusual linguistic ability. She was perplexed at what one of the children had told her.

The Plathys have no concept of privacy; they wander in and out of each other's *maffas* (the yurtlike tents of hide they use as shelter) at any time of the day or night, on random whim. It was inevitable that sooner or later they would observe humans having sex. The child had described what she'd seen fairly accurately. I had tried to explain human sexuality to Tybru earlier, as a way to get her to talk about that aspect of her own life. She would smile and nod diagonally through the whole thing, an infuriating gesture they normally use only with children prattling nonsense.

This time I was going to be blunt. I opened the *maffa* flap so there was plenty of light, then shed my kilt and got up on a table. I lay down on my back and tried to explain with simple words and gestures what went where and who did what to whom, and what might or might not happen nine months later.

She was more inclined to take me seriously this time. (The child who had witnessed copulation was four, pubescent, and thus too old to have fantasies.) After I explained she explored me herself, which was not pleasant, since her four-fingered hand was larger than a human foot, quite filthy, and equipped with deadly nails.

She admitted that all she really understood was the breasts. She could remember some weeks of nursing after the blackout period the female language calls "(big) pain-in-hips." (Their phrase for the other blackout period is literally "pain-in-the-ass.") She asked, logically enough, whether I could find a male and demonstrate.

Actually, I'm an objective enough person to have gone along with it, if I could have found a man able and willing to rise to the occasion. If it had been near the end of our stay, I probably would have done it. But leadership is a ticklish thing, even when you're leading a dozen highly educated, professionally detached people, and we still had three years to go.

I explained that the most-elder doesn't do this with the men she's in charge of, and Tybru accepted that. They don't have much of a handle on discipline, but they do understand polity and social form. She said she would ask the other human females.

Perhaps it should have been me who did the asking, but I didn't suggest it. I was glad to get off the hook, and also curious as to my people's reactions.

The couple who volunteered were the last ones I would have predicted. Both of them were shy, almost diffident, with the rest of us. Good field workers but not the sort of people you would let your hair down with. I suppose they had better "anthropological perspective" on their own behavior than the rest of us.

At any rate, they retired to the *maffa* that was nominally Tybru's, and she let out the ululation that means "All free females come here." I wondered whether our couple could actually perform in a cramped little yurt filled with sweaty giants asking questions in a weird language.

All the females did crowd into the tent, and after a couple of minutes a strange sound began to emanate from them. At first it puzzled me, but then I recognized it as laughter! I had heard individual Plathys laugh, a sort of inhaled croak—but nineteen of them at once was an unearthly din.

The couple was in there a long time, but I never did find out whether the demonstration was actually consummated. They came out of the *maffa* beet-red and staring at the ground, the laughter behind them not abating. I never talked to either of them about it, and whenever I asked Tybru or the others, all I got was choked laughter. I think we invented the dirty joke. (In exchange, I'm sure that Plathy sexuality will eventually see service in the ribald metaphor of every human culture.)

But let me go back to the beginning.

We came to Sanchrist IV armed with a small vocabulary and a great deal of misinformation. I don't mean to denigrate my colleagues' skill or application. But the Garcia expedition just came at the wrong time and didn't stay long enough.

Most of their experience with the Plathys was during deep winter, which is their most lively and civilized season. They spend their indoor time creating the complex sculptures that so impressed the art world ten years ago and performing improvisational music and dance that is delightful in its alien grace. Outdoors, they indulge in complicated games and athletic exhibitions. The larders are full, the time of birthing and nursing is well over, and the family exudes happiness, well into the thaw. We experienced this euphoria ourselves. I can't blame Garcia's people for their enthusiastic report.

We still don't know what happened. Or why it happened. Perhaps if these data survive, the next researchers . . .

Trouble.

Gabriel

I was having a strange dream of food—real food, cooked—when suddenly there was Maria, tugging on my arm, keeping me away from the table. She was whispering "Gab, wake up!" and so I did, cold and aching and hungry.

"What's—" She put her hand on my mouth, lightly.

"There's one outside. Mylab, I think." He had just turned three this winter, and been given his name. We crept together back to the mouth of the cave and both jumped when my ankle gave a loud pop.

It was Mylab, all right; the fur around one earhole was almost white against the blond. I was glad it wasn't an adult. He was only about a head taller than me. Stronger, though, and well fed.

We watched from the cave's darkness as he investigated the latrine rock, sniffing and licking, circling.

"Maybe he's a scout for a hunting party," I whispered. "Hunting us."

"Too young, I think." She passed me a stone axe. "Hope we don't have to kill him."

"Should we wake the others?"

"Not yet. Make us easier to scent." As if on cue, the Plathy walked directly away from the rock and stood, hands on hips, sniffing the air. His head wagged back and forth slowly, as if he were triangulating. He shuffled in a half-circle and stood looking in our direction.

"Stay still."

"He can't see us in the shadow."

"Maybe not." Their eyesight was more acute than ours, but they didn't have good night vision.

Behind us, someone woke up and sneezed. Mylab gave a little start and then began loping toward the cave.

"Damn it," Maria whispered. She stood up and huddled into the side of the cave entrance. "You get over there." I stationed myself opposite her, somewhat better hidden because of a projecting lip of rock.

Mylab slowed down a few meters from the cave entrance and walked warily forward, sniffing and blinking. Maria crouched, gripping her spear with both hands, for thrusting.

It was over in a couple of seconds, but my memory of it goes in slow motion: he saw Maria, or sensed her, and lumbered straight for her, claws out, growling. She thrust twice into his chest while I stepped forward and delivered a two-handed blow to the top of his head.

That axe would have cracked a human head from crown to jaw. Instead, it glanced off his thick skull and hit his shoulder, then spun out of my grip.

Shaking his head, he stepped around and swung a long arm at me. I was just out of range, staggering back; one claw opened up my cheek and the tip of my nose. Blood was spouting from two wounds in his chest. He stepped forward to finish me off and Maria plunged the spear into the back of his neck. The flint blade burst out under his chin in a spray of blood.

He stood staggering between us for a moment, trying to reach the spear shaft behind him. Two stones flew up from the rear of the cave; one missed, but the other hit his cheek with a loud crack. He turned and stumbled away down the slope, the spear bouncing grotesquely behind him.

The other four joined us at the cave entrance. Brenda, our doctor, looked at my wound and regretted her lack of equipment. So did I.

"Have to go after him," Derek said. "Kill him."

Maria shook her head. "He's still dangerous. Wait a few minutes; then we can follow the blood trail."

"He's dead," Brenda said. "His body just doesn't know it yet."

"Maybe so," Maria said, her shoulders slumping sadly. "Anyhow, we can't stay here. Hate to move during daylight, but we don't have any choice."

"We're not the only ones who can follow a blood trail," Herb said. He had a talent for stating the obvious.

We gathered up our few weapons, the water bladders, and the food sack, to which we had just added five small batlike creatures, mostly fur and bone. None of us looked forward to being hungry enough to eat them.

The trail was easy to follow, several bright red spatters per meter. He had gone about three hundred meters before collapsing.

We found him lying behind a rock in a widening pool of blood, the spear sticking straight up. When I pulled it out he made a terrible gurgling sound. Brenda made sure he was dead.

Maria looked very upset, biting her lip, I think to keep tears away. She is a strange woman. Hard and soft. She treats the Plathys by the book but obviously has a sentimental streak toward them. I sort of like them too, but don't think I'd want to take one home with me.

Brenda's upset too, retching now. My fault; I should have offered to do the knife. But she didn't ask.

I'd better take point position. Stop recording now. Concentrate on not getting surprised.

Maria

Back to the beginning. Quite hot when we were set down on the tropical mainland. It was the middle of the night and we worked quickly, with no lights (what I'd give for night glasses now), to set up our domed base.

In a way it's a misnomer to call it a "base," since we left it the next night, not to return for three and a half years. We thought. It was really just a staging area and a place where we would wait for pickup after our mission was ended. We really didn't foresee having to run back to it to hide from the Plathys.

It was halfheartedly camouflaged, looking like a dome of rock in the middle of a jungle terrain that featured no other domes of rock. To our knowledge at the time, no Plathy ever ventured that far north, so even that gesture toward noninterference was a matter of form rather than of actual caution. Now we know that some Plathys do go that far, on their rite-of-passage wanderings. So it's a good thing we didn't simply set up a force field.

I think the closest terrestrial match to the biome there would be the jungles of the Amazon basin. Plus volcanoes, for a little extra heat and interest. Sort of a steam bath with a whiff of sulfur dioxide added to the rich smell of decaying vegetable matter. In the clearings, riots of extravagant flowers, most of which gave off the aroma of rotting meat.

For the first leg of our journey, we had modern energy weapons hidden inside conventional-looking spears and axes. It would have been more sporting to face the Mesozoic fauna with primitive weapons, but of course we had no interest in that sort of adventure. We often did run into creatures resembling the Deinonychus (Lower Cretaceous period)—about the size of a human but fast, and all claws and teeth. They travel in packs, evidently preying on the large placid herbivores. We never saw fewer than six in a group, and once were cornered by a pack of twenty. We had to kill all of them, our beams silently slashing them into steaming chunks of meat. None paid any attention to what was happening to his comrades but just kept advancing, bent low to the ground, claws out, teeth bared, roaring. Their meat tasted like chicken, but very tough.

It took us nine days to reach the coast, following a river. (Did I mention that days here are twenty-eight hours long? Our circadian rhythms had been adjusted accordingly, but there are

other physiological factors. Mostly having to do with fatigue.)
We found a conspicuous rock formation and buried our modern
weapons a hundred meters to the north of it. Then we buried
their power sources another hundred paces north. We kept one
crazer for group defense, to be discarded before we reached the
first island, but otherwise all we had was flint and stone and
bicuspids with amazing memories.

We had built several boats with these tools during our training on Selva, but of course it was rather different here. The long
day, and no comfortable cot to retire to at night. No tent to keep
out the flying insects, no clean soft clothes in the morning, no
this, no that. Terrible heat and a pervasive moldy smell that kept
us all sniffling in spite of the antiallergenic drugs that our mod-
ified endocrine systems fed us. We did manage to get a fire going,
which gave us security and roast fish and greatly simplified the
boat-building. We felled two large trees and used fire to hollow
them out, making outrigger canoes similar to the ones the Maori
used to populate the sparse South Pacific. We weren't able to
raise sails, though, since the Plathys don't have that technology.
They wouldn't have helped much, anyway; summer was usually
dead calm. We didn't look forward to rowing 250 kilometers in
the subtropical heat. But we would do it systematically.

Herb was good at pottery, so I exempted him from boat-
building in exchange for the fascinating job of crafting and firing
dozens of water jugs. That was going to be our main survival
problem, since it was not likely to rain during the couple of weeks
we'd be at sea. Food was no problem; we could spear fish and
probably birds (though eating a raw bird was not an experiment
even I could look forward to) and also had a supply of smoked
dinosaur.

I designed the boats so that either one would be big enough
to carry all twelve of us, in case of trouble. As a further safeguard,
we took a shakedown cruise, a night and a day of paddling and
staying anchored near shore. We took our last fresh-water bath,
topped off the jugs, loaded our gear, and cast off at sundown.

The idea had been to row all night, with ten minutes' rest
each hour, and keep going for a couple of hours after sunup, for
as long as we could reliably gauge our direction from the angle
of the sun. Then anchor (the sea was nowhere more than ten or
twelve meters deep) and hide from the sun all day under woven
shades, fishing and sleeping and engaging in elevated discourse.

Start paddling again when the sun was low enough to tell us where north was. It did go that way for several days, until the weather changed.

It was just a thin haze, but it was enough to stop us dead. We had no navigational instruments, relying on the dim triangle of stars that marked the south celestial pole. No stars, no progress.

This was when I found out that I had chosen my party well. When the sky cleared two nights later, there was no talk of turning back, though everyone was capable of counting the water jugs and doing long division. A few more days becalmed and we would be in real danger of dying from dehydration, unable to make landfall in either direction.

I figured we had been making about 25 kilometers per night. We rowed harder and cut the break time down to five minutes, and kept rowing an extra hour or so after dawn, taking a chance on dead reckoning.

Daytime became a period of grim silence. People who were not sleeping spent the time fishing the way I had taught them, Eskimo style (though those folks did it through a hole in the ice): arm cocked, spear raised, staring at one point slightly under the surface; when a fish approaches a handspan above that point, let fly the spear. No Eskimo ever applied greater concentration to the task; none of them was ever fishing for water as well as food. Over the course of days we learned which kinds of fish had flesh that could be sucked for moisture, and which had to be avoided for the salty blood that suffused their tissues.

We rationed water fairly severely, doling it out in measures that would allow us to lose one night out of three to haze. As it turned out, that never happened again, and when we sighted land, finally, there was water enough for another four days of short rations. We stifled the impulse to drink it all in celebration; we still had to find a stream.

I'd memorized maps and satellite photos, but terrain looks much different seen horizontally. It took several hours of hugging the shore before I could figure out where we were; fortunately, the landmark was a broad shallow river.

Before we threw away the crazer and its power source, we used it to light a torch. When the Plathys traveled, they carried hot coals from the previous night's fire, insulated in ash inside a basket of tough fiber. We would do the same, rather than spend an hour each day resolutely sawing two pieces of dry wood together. We beached the canoes and hauled them a couple of hundred meters inland, to a stand of bushes where they could be reasonably well camouflaged. Perhaps not much chance they would still be there after a full year, but it was better than simply abandoning them.

We walked inland far enough for there to be no trace of salt in the muddy river water, and cavorted in it like schoolchildren. Then Brenda and I built a fire while the others stalked out in search of food.

Game was fairly plentiful near the river, but we were not yet skilled hunters. There was no way to move quietly through the grass, which was shoulder-high and stiff. So the hunters who had the best luck were the ones who tiptoed up the bank of the stream. They came back with five good-sized snakes, which we skinned and cleaned and roasted on sticks. After two weeks of raw fish, the sizzling fatty meat was delicious, though for most of us it went through the gut like a dropped rock.

We made pallets of soft grass, and most of us slept well, though I didn't. Combination of worry and indigestion. I was awake enough to notice that various couples took advantage of the relative privacy of the riverbank, which made me feel vaguely jealous and deprived. I toyed with the idea of asking somebody, but instead waited for somebody to ask me, and wound up listening to contented snores half the night.

A personal note, to be edited out if this tooth survives for publication. Gabriel. All of us women had been studying his naked body for the past two weeks, quite remarkable in proportion and endowment, and I suppose the younger women had been even more imaginative than me in theorizing about it. So I was a little dismayed when he went off to the riverbank with a male, his Selvan crony Marcus. I didn't know at the time that their generation on Selva is very casual about such things, and at any rate I should have been anthropologist enough to be objective about it. But I have my own cultural biases, too, and (perhaps more to the point) so do the Terran males in the party. As a scientist, I can appreciate the fact that homosexuality is common and natural and only attitudes about it change. That attitude is not currently very enlightened on Earth; I resolved to warn them the next day to be discreet. (Neither of them is exclusively homosexual, as it turned out; they both left their pallets with women later in the night, Gabriel at least twice.)

We had rolled two large and fairly dry logs over the fire before bedding down, orienting them so as to take advantage of the slight breeze, and the fire burned brightly all night without attention. That probably saved our lives. When we broke camp in the morning and headed south, we found hundreds of tracks just downwind, the footpads of large catlike creatures. What an idiot I had been, not to post guards! Everyone else was sheepish at not having thought of it themselves. The numb routine and hard labor of the past two weeks had dulled us; now we were properly galvanized by fear. We realized that for all our survival training, we still had the instincts of city folk, and those instincts could kill us all.

This island is roughly circular, about a hundred kilometers in diameter, with a central crater lake. We would follow this river to the lake and then go counterclockwise to the third stream and follow it to the southern shore. Then we would hop down an archipelago of small islands, another 80 kilometers, to the large island that was our final destination.

The scrub of the coastal lowland soon gave way to tangled forest, dominated by trees like Earth's banyan—a large central trunk with dozens or hundreds of subsidiary trunks holding up an extensive canopy of branches. It was impossible to tell where one tree's territory ended and another's began, but some of the largest must have commanded one or two ares of ground. Their bark was ashen white, relieved by splotches of rainbow lichen. No direct sunlight reached the ground through their dense foliage; only a few spindly bushes with pale yellow leaves pushed out of the rotting humus. Hard for anything to sneak up on us at ground level, but we could hear creatures moving overhead. I wondered whether the branches were strong enough to support the animals that had watched us the night before, and felt unseen cats' eyes everywhere.

We stopped to eat in a weird clearing. Something had killed one of the huge trees; its rotting stump dominated the clearing, and the remnants of its smaller trunks stood around like ghostly guardians, most of them dead but some of them starting to sprout green. I supposed one would eventually take over the space. After feasting on cold snake, we practiced spear-throwing, using the punky old stump as a target. I was the least competent, both in range and accuracy, which had also been the case on Selva. As a girl I'd shown no talent for athletics beyond jacks and playing doctor.

Suddenly all hell broke loose. Three cat-beasts leaped down from the forest canopy behind us and bounded in for the kill. I thrust out my spear and got one in the shoulder, the force of the impact knocking me over. Brenda killed it with a well-aimed throw. The other two checked their advance and circled warily. They dodged thrown spears; I shouted for everyone to hold their fire.

Brenda and I retrieved our weapons and, along with Gabriel and Martin, closed in on the beasts, moving them away from where the thrown spears lay. In a few seconds the twelve of us had them encircled, and I suddenly remembered the old English expression "having a tiger by the tail." The beasts were only about half the size of a human, but all muscle and teeth. They growled and snapped at us, heads wagging, saliva drooling.

I shouted "Now, Gab!"—he was the best shot—and he flung his spear at the closer one. It sank deep in the animal's side and it fell over, mewling and pawing the air. The other beast saw its chance and leaped straight at Gab, who instinctively ducked under it. It bounded off his back and sprang for the safety of the trees. Six or seven spears showered after it, but missed.

Gabriel had four puncture wounds under each shoulder blade from the cat's claws. Brenda washed them out thoroughly but decided against improvising a dressing out of leaf and vine. Just stay clean, always good advice.

We skinned and gutted the two cats and laboriously sliced their flesh into long thin strips for jerky. The old stump made a good smoky fire for the purpose. As darkness fell, we built another bright fire next to it.

I set up a guard schedule, with teams of three each standing three-hour shifts while the rest slept, but none of us slept too soundly. Over the crackle of the fires I was sure I could hear things moving restlessly in the woods. If they were there, though, they weren't bold enough to attack. During my watch a couple of dog-sized animals with large eyes came to the periphery of the clearing, to feast on the cat-beasts' entrails. We threw sticks at them but they just looked at us, and left after they had eaten their fill.

If my estimate of our progress was correct, we had about 30 kilometers of deep woods to go, until the topography opened up into rolling hills of grassland. Everyone agreed that we should try to make it in one push. There was no guarantee we could find another clearing, and nobody wanted to spend a night under the canopy. So at first light, we bundled the jerky up inside a stiff catskin and headed south.

As we moved along the river the nature of the trees changed, the banyans eventually being replaced by a variety of smaller trees—damn! Two of them!

Brenda

I wasn't paying close attention, still grieving over Mylab—actually, grieving for myself, for having committed murder. I've had patients die under my care, but the feeling isn't even remotely similar. His eyes, when I drew the flint across his throat—they went bright with pain and then immediately dull.

We'd been walking for about an hour after leaving the cave, picking our way down the north slope of the mountain, when Maria, in the lead, suddenly squatted down and made a silent gesture. We all crouched and moved forward.

Ahead of us on the trail, two adult Plathys sat together with their backs to us, talking quietly while they ate. They were armed with spear and broadaxe and knives. I doubted that the six of us could take even one of them in a face-to-face combat.

Maria stared, probably considering ambush, and then motioned for us to go back up the trail. I kept looking over my shoulder, every small scuff and scrape terribly amplified in my mind, expecting at any moment to see the two huge brutes charging after us. But their eating noise must have masked the sound of our retreat.

We crept back a couple of hundred meters to a fork in the trail and cautiously made our way down a roughly parallel track, going as fast as silence would allow. The light breeze was coming from behind us; we wanted to be past the Plathys—downwind of them—before they finished eating. We passed close enough to hear their talking, but didn't see them.

After about a kilometer the trail disappeared. We had to pick our way down a steep defile and couldn't help making noise, dislodging pebbles that often cascaded into small rattling avalanches. We were only a few meters from the bottom of the cliff when the two Plathys appeared above us. They discussed the situation loudly for a few moments—using the hunting language, which none of us had been allowed to learn—and then set aside their weapons in favor of rocks.

When I saw what they were doing I slid right to the bottom, willing to take a few abrasions rather than present too tempting a target. Most of the others did the same. Herb took a glancing blow to the head and fell backward, landing roughly. I ran over to him, afraid he was unconscious. Gab beat me to him and hauled him roughly to his feet; he was dazed but awake. We each took an arm and staggered away as fast as we could, zigzagging as Gab muttered "go left" and "right," so as to present a more difficult target. I sustained one hard blow to the left buttock, which knocked me down. It was going to make sitting uncomfortable, but we wouldn't have to worry about that for a while.

We were lucky the Plathys hadn't brought rope, as a larger hunting party in the mountains would have done. They are rather clumsy rock climbers (though with their long arms they can run up a steep slope very fast). One of them started down after us, but after a nearly fatal slip he scrambled back up.

We pressed our advantage, such as it was. To pursue us they would have to make a detour of a couple of kilometers, and at any rate we could go downhill faster than they could. It seemed likely that they would instead go back to their main group to report our whereabouts, and then all of them try to catch us in the veldt. On level ground they could easily run us down, once they caught our scent.

Maria, xenologist to the end, remarked how lucky we were that they had never developed the idea of signal drums. It is strange, since they use such a variety of percussion instruments in their music and dancing.

Such music and dancing. They seemed so human.

Our only chance for survival was to try to confuse them by splitting up. Maria breathlessly outlined a plan as we hurried down the slope. When we reached the valley we would get a bearing on the stream we'd followed here, then go six different ways, rendezvousing at the stream's outlet to the sea three days later; at nightfall, whoever was there would cross to the next island. Even at high tide it should be possible to wade most of the way.

I suggested we make it three pairs rather than six loners, but Maria pointed out that two of us really didn't stand a much better chance against an armed Plathy than one; in either case, the only way we could kill them would be by stealth. Murder. I told her I didn't think I would be able to do it, and she nodded. Probably thinking that she would have said the same thing a few days ago.

We stopped for a few minutes to rest on a plateau overlooking the veldt, where Maria pointed out the paths she wanted each of us to take. Herb and Derek would go the most direct route, more or less north, but twining in and out of each other's path so as to throw off the scent. Gab, being the fastest, would run halfway around the mountain, then make a broad arc north. She would go straight northeast for about half the distance and then cut back; Martin would do the opposite. I was to head due west, straight for the stream, and follow it down, in and out of the water. All of us were to "leave scent" at the places where our paths diverged the most from straight north.

A compass would have been nice. At night we'd be okay if it didn't cloud up again, but during the day we'd just have to follow our direction bump through the tall grass. I was glad I had an easy path.

Not all that easy. The three water bladders went to the ones who would be farthest from the stream, of course. So I had to go a good half day without water. Assuming I didn't get lost. We divided the food and scrambled down in six different directions.

Maria

Where was I? Coming here, we got around the crater lake without incident, but the descent to the shore was more difficult than I had anticipated. It was not terribly steep, but the dense undergrowth of vines and bushes impeded our progress. After two days we emerged on the shore, covered with scratches and bruises. At least we'd encountered no large fauna.

(By this time I had a great deal of sympathy for the lazybones minority on the Planning Committee who'd contended that we were being overly cautious in putting the base so far from the Plathy island. They'd recommended we put it on this island, with only 80 kilometers of shallow sea separating us from our destination. I'd voted, along with the majority, for the northern mainland, partly out of a boneheaded desire for adventure.)

What we faced was a chain of six small islands and countless sandbars, in a puddle of a sea that rarely was more than a meter deep. We knew from Garcia's experience that a boat would be useless. With vine and driftwood we lashed together a raft to carry our weapons and provisions, filled the water jugs, and splashed south.

It was tiring. The sand underfoot was firm, but sloshing through the shallow water was like walking with heavy weights attached to your ankles. We had to make good progress, though; the only island we were sure had fresh water was 40 kilometers south, halfway.

We made a good 25 kilometers the first day, dragging our weary bones up onto an island that actually had trees. Marcus and Gab went off in search of water, finding none, while the rest of us gathered driftwood for a fire or tried lackadaisically to fish. Nanci speared a gruesome thing that no one would touch, including her, and nobody else caught anything. Susan and Brenda dug up a couple of dozen shellfish, though, which obediently popped open when roasted. They tasted like abalone with sulfur sauce.

As we were settling in for the night, we met our first Plathy. She walked silently up to the fire, as if it were the most normal thing in the world to happen upon a dozen creatures from another planet. She was young, only a little larger than me (now, of course, we know she was on her Walk North). When I stood up and tried to say "Welcome, sister" in the female language, she screamed and ran. We heard her splashing away for some time, headed for the next county.

The next day was harder, though we didn't have as far to go. Some geological gremlin had raked channels across our path, new features since Garcia's mission, and several times we had to swim as much as 200 meters before slogging again. (Thank the gods for Gab, who would gamely paddle out toward the horizon in search of solid ground, and for Marcus, who could swim strongly enough one-handed to tow the raft.)

It was dark by the time we got to the water hole island, and we had lost our coals to an inopportune wave. We were cold and terminally wrinkled, but so parched from sucking salt water that we staggered around like maniacs, even laughing like maniacs, searching blindly for the artesian well that Garcia's records said was there. Finally Joanna found it, stumbling in headfirst and coming up choking and laughing. We all gorged ourselves, wallowing. In my case the relief was more than mouth and throat and stomach. At sundown I'd squatted in the shallows and squeezed out piss dark with stringy blood. That scared me. But the fresh water evidently cleared it up.

There were no more surprises the next two days of island-hopping, except the pleasant one of finding another water source. We couldn't find any wood dry enough to start a fire with, but it didn't get all that cold at night.

Late afternoon of the second day we slogged into the swamp that was the northern edge of the Plathy island. The dominant form of life was a kind of bilious spotted serpent that would swim heavily away as we approached. We were out of food but didn't go after them. Before nightfall the swamp had given way to rather damp forest, but we found dry dead wood suspended in the branches and spun up a bright fire. We dug up a kind of tuber that Garcia's group had identified as edible and roasted them. Then tried to sleep in spite of the noises in the darkness. At first light we moved out fast, knowing that in 30 or so kilometers the forest would give way to open grassland.

The change from forest to veldt was abrupt. We were so happy to be out of the shadow of it—funny that in my present situation I feel exactly the opposite; I feel exposed, and hurry toward the concealment of the thick underbrush and close-spaced heavy trunks. I feel so visible, so vulnerable. And I probably won't find water until I get there. I'm going to turn off this tooth for a few minutes and try not to scream.

All right. Let me see. On our way to the Plathys, we walked across the veldt for two days. Food was plentiful; the *zamri* are like rabbits, but slow. For some reason they like to cluster around the *ecivrel* bush, a thorny malodorous plant, and all we would have to do to bag several of them was form a loose circle around the bush and move in, clubbing them as they tried to escape. I would like to find one now. Their blood is sweet.

There's a Plathy song:

Sim garlish a sim garlish farla tob—!ka.
Soo pan du mairly garlish ezda tob—!ka.
Oe vairly tem se garlish mizga mer—!ka.
Garlish—!ka. Tem se garlish—!ka.

Translating it into my own language doesn't work well:

Sacar sangre y sacar sangre para vivir—sí.
En sangre damos muerte y sacamos vida—sí.
Alabamos la sangre de vida que usted nos da—sí.
Sangre—sí. Sangre de vida—sí.

Herb, who's a linguist, did a more accurate rendering in English:

Take blood and take blood for living—yes.
In blood we give death and take living—yes.
We worship the blood of life you give us—yes.
Blood—yes. Blood of life—yes!

But there is really no translation. Except in the love of sweet blood.

I've become too much like them. My human instinct is to keep running and, when I can't run, to hide. But a strong Plathy feeling is to stand in a clearing and shout for them. Let them come for me; let me die in a terrible ecstasy of tearing flesh and cracking bone. Let them suck my soft guts so I can live in them—

God. I have to stop. You'll think I'm crazy. Maybe I'm getting there. Why won't it rain?

Gabriel

Turned on the tooth while I sit by the water and rest. Maria wants us to record as much as we can, in case. Just in case.

Why the hell did I sign up for this? I was going to switch out of xenology and work for an advanced degree in business. But she came on campus recruiting, with all those exotic Earth women. They're just like women anywhere, big surprise. Except her. She is truly weird. Listen to this, tooth: I want her. She is such a mystery. Maybe if we live through this I'll get up the courage to ask. Plumb her, so to speak; make her open up to me, so to speak;

get to the bottom of her, so to speak. A nice bottom for a woman of her advanced years.

How can I think of sex at a time like this? With a woman twice my age. If somebody on a follow-up expedition finds this tooth in a fossilized pile of Plathy shit, please excuse my digression. If I live to have the tooth extracted and played back, I don't think it will make much difference to my professional reputation. I'll be writing poetry and clerking for my father's export firm.

I ran around the mountain. Collapsed once and slept for I don't know how long. Got up and ran to the river. Drank too much. Here I sit, too bloated to move. If a Plathy finds me I won't be a fun meal.

I was really getting to like them, before they turned on us. They seemed like such vegetables until it started to get cold. Then it was as if they had turned into a different species. With hindsight, it's no big surprise that they should change again. Or that they should be capable of such terrible violence. We were lulled by their tenderness toward each other and their friendliness toward us, and the subtle alien grace of their dancing and music and sculpture. We should have been cautious, having witnessed the two other changes: the overnight transformation into completely sexual creatures and the slower evolution from lumpish primitives to charming creators, when the snow started to fall.

The change was obvious after the first heavy snowfall, which left about half a meter of the stuff on the ground. The Plathys started singing and laughing spontaneously. They rolled up their *maffas* and stored them in a cave and began playing in the snow— or at least it seemed like play, they were so carefree and childlike about it. Actually, they were building a city of snow.

The individual buildings, *lacules*, were uniform domes built up from blocks of snow. Maria called them igloos, after a similar primitive structure on Earth, and the name stuck. Even some of the Plathys used it.

There were twenty-nine domes arranged in a circle, eventually connected by tunnels as the snow deepened. The inside of the circle was kept clear, the snow being constantly shoveled into the spaces between the domes. The net result was a high circular wall that kept the wind out. Later we learned it would also keep people *in*.

They had a fire going most of the time in the middle of the circle, which served as a center for their daytime activities: music, dance, tumbling, athletic competition, and storytelling (which seemed to be a kind of fanciful history combined with moral instruction). Even with the sun up, the temperature rarely got above freezing, but the Plathys thrived in the cold. They would sit for hours on the ice, watching the performances, wearing only their kilts. We wore leggings and boots, jackets, and hats. The Plathys would only dress up if they had to go out at night (which they often did, for reasons they couldn't or wouldn't explain to us), when the temperature dropped to forty or fifty below.

I went out at night a couple of times, but I didn't go far. Too easy to get lost. If it was clear you could see the ring of igloos ghostly in the starlight, but if there was any weather you couldn't see your own hand in front of your face.

The igloos were surprisingly warm, though the only source of heat was one or two small oil lamps, plus metabolism. That metabolism also permeated everything with the weird smell of Plathy sweat, which resembled rotten bananas. Our own dome got pretty high with the aroma of unwashed humans; Plathys would rarely visit for more than a minute or two.

Seems odd to me that the Plathys didn't continue some of their activities, like music and storytelling, during the long nights. Some of them did routine housekeeping chores, mending and straightening, while others concentrated on sculpture. The sculptors seemed to go into a kind of trance, scraping patiently away at their rock or wood with teeth and claws. I never saw one use a tool, though they did carve and whittle when making everyday objects. I once watched an elder through the whole process. He sorted through a pile of rocks and logs until he found a rock he liked. Then he sat back and studied it from every angle, staring for more than an hour before beginning. Then he closed his eyes and started gnawing and scratching. I don't think he opened his eyes until he was done working. When I asked him if he had opened his eyes, he said, "Of course not."

Over the course of six nights he must have spent about sixty hours on the stone. When he finished, it was a delicate lacy abstraction. The other Plathys came by, one at a time, to compliment him on it—the older ones offering gentle criticism—and after everyone had seen it, he threw it outside for the children to play with. I retrieved it and kept it, which he thought was funny. It had served its purpose, as he had served his purpose for it: finding its soul (its "face inside") and releasing it.

I shouldn't talk about sculpture; that's Herb's area of expertise. The assignment Maria gave me was to memorize the patterns of the athletic competitions. (I was an athlete in school, twice winning the Hombre de Hierro award for my district.) There's not much to say about it, though. How high can you jump, how fast can you run, how far can you spit. That was an interesting one. They can spit with great force. Another interesting one was wood-eating. Two contestants are given similar pieces of wood—kindling, a few centimeters wide by half a meter long— and they crunch away until one has consumed the whole thing. Since the other doesn't have to continue eating afterward, it's hard to say which one is the actual winner. (When I first saw the contest, I thought they must derive some pleasure from eating wood. When I asked one about it, though, he said it tastes terrible and hurts at both ends. I can imagine.)

Another painful sport is hitting. It's unlike boxing in that there's no aggression, no real sense of a fight. One contestant hits the other on the head or body with a club. Then he (or she) hands the club to the opponent, who returns the blow precisely. The contest goes on until one of them drops, which can take several hours.

You ask them why they do this and most of them will not understand—"why" is a really difficult concept for Plathys; they have no word for it—but when you do get a response it's on the order of "This is part of life." Which is uninformative but not so alien. Why do humans lift heavy weights or run till they drop or beat each other senseless in a ring?

Oh my God. Here comes one.

Maria

Finally, water. I wish there were some way to play back this tooth and edit it. I must have raved for some time, before I fell unconscious a few kilometers from here. I woke up with a curious *zamri* licking my face. I broke its neck and tore open its throat and drank deeply. That gave me the strength to get here. I drank my fill and then moved one thousand steps downstream, through the cold water, where I now sit concealed behind a bush, picking morsels from the *zamri*'s carcass. When I get back to Earth I think I'll become a vegetarian.

This is very close to the place where we met our first cooperative Plathy. There were three of them, young; two ran away when they spotted us, but the third clapped a greeting, and when we clapped back he cautiously joined us. We talked for an hour or so, the other two watching from behind trees.

They were from the Tumlil family, providentially; the family that had hosted Garcia's expedition. This male was too young to actually remember the humans, but he had heard stories about them. He explained about the Walk North. In their third or fourth year, every Plathy goes off on his own, going far enough north to get to where "things are different." He brings back something odd. The elders then rule on how powerful the oddness of the thing is, and according to that power, the youngster is assigned his preliminary rank in the tribe.

(They know that this can eventually make the difference between life and death. The higher up you start, the more likely you are to wind up an elder. Those who aren't elders are allowed to die when they can no longer provide for themselves; elders are fed and protected indefinitely.)

Most of them travel as far as the crater lake island, but a few go all the way to the northern mainland. That was the ambition of the one we were talking to. I interrogated him as to his preparations for a boat, food, and water, and he said a boat would be nice but not necessary, and the sea was full of food and water. He figured he could swim it in three hands of days, twelve. Unless he was chaffing me, they can evidently sleep floating and drink salt water. That will complicate our escape, if they keep pursuing.

I take it that the three of them were cheating a bit by banding together. He repeatedly stressed that they would be going their separate ways as soon as they got to the archipelago. I hope they stayed together the whole way. I'd hate to face that forest alone. Maybe I'll have to, though.

Before he left he gave us directions to his family, but we'd decided to at least start out with a different one from Garcia's, in the interests of objectivity and to see how much information traveled from family to family. Little or none, it turned out. Our Camchai family knew about the Tumlils, since they shared the same area of veldt during the late summer, but none of the Tumlils had mentioned that ten hairless dwarfs had spent one winter with them.

After two days of relatively easy travel, we found the Camchais in their late-summer habitat, the almost treeless grassland at the foot of the southern mountains. Duplicating the experience of Garcia's group, we found ourselves unexcitedly welcomed into the tribe: we were shown where the food was, and various Plathys scrounged up the framework and hides to cobble together a *maffa* for us. Then we joined the family in their typical summertime activity, sitting around.

After a few weeks of trying to cajole information out of them, we witnessed the sudden explosion of sexual activity described earlier. Then they rested some more, five or six days, and began to pull up stakes.

Their supply of stored food was getting low and there was no easy hunting left in that part of the veldt, so they had to move around the mountains to the seashore and a wretched diet of fish.

The trek was organized and led by Kalyym, who by virtue of being the youngest elder was considered chief for such practical matters. She was one of the few Plathys we met who wore ornaments; hers was a necklace of dinosaur teeth she'd brought back from her Walk North, the teeth of a large carnivore. She claimed to have killed it, but everyone knew that was a lie, and respected her for being capable of lying past puberty.

It was significantly cooler on the other side of the mountains, with a chilly south wind in the evening warning that fall had begun and frost was near. The Plathys still lazed through midday, but in the mornings and evenings they fished with some energy and prepared for the stampede. They stockpiled driftwood and salt and sat around the fire chipping extra flints, complaining about eating fish and looking forward to bounty.

We spent several months in this transitional state, until one morning a lookout shouted a happy cry and the whole family went down to the shore with clubs. Each adult took about three meters of shoreline, the children standing behind them with knives.

We could hear them before we could see them—the *tolliws*, rabbit-sized mammals that chirped like birds. They sounded like what I imagine a distant cloud of locusts sounded like, in old times. The Plathys laughed excitedly.

Then they were visible, one whirring mass from horizon to

horizon, like an island-sized mat of wriggling wet fur. Mammals schooling like fish. They spilled on to dry land and staggered into the line of waiting Plathys.

At first there was more enthusiasm than result. Everybody had to pick up his first *tolliw* and bite off its head and extol its gustatory virtues to the others, in as gruesome a display of bad table manners as you could find anywhere in the Confederación. Then, after a few too-energetic smashings, they settled into a productive routine: with the little animals milling around their ankles in an almost continuous stream, the adult would choose a large and healthy-looking one and club it with a backhand swipe that lofted the stunned animal in an arc, back to where the child waited with the knife. The child would slit the animal's throat and set it on a large hide to bleed, and then wait happily for the next one. When the carcass had bled itself nearly dry, the child would give it a squeeze and transfer it to a stack on the sand, eventually working in a smooth assembly-line fashion. The purpose of the systematic bleeding was to build up on the hide layers of coagulated blood that, when dry, would be cut up into squares and used for snacks.

Large predators were scattered here and there through the swimming herd, fawn-colored animals resembling terrestrial kangaroos, but with fingerlong fangs overhanging the lower jaw. Most of them successfully evaded the Plathys, but occasionally one would be surrounded and clubbed to death amid jubilant screeching and singing.

This went on for what seemed to be a little less than two hours, during which time the oldest elders busied themselves filling a long trench with wood and collecting wet seaweed. When the last stragglers of the school crawled out of the water and followed the others down the beach, there were sixty pyramidal stacks of furry bodies, each stack nearly as tall as a Plathy, ranged down the beach. We could hear the family west of us laughing and clubbing away.

(The statistics of the process bothered me. They seemed to have killed about one out of a hundred of the beasts and then sent the remainder on down the beach, where the next family would presumably do the same, and so on. There were more than a hundred families, we knew. Why didn't they run out of *tolliws*? For once, Tybru gave me a straightforward answer: they take turns. Only sixteen families "gather" the creatures during each migration, alternating in a rotating order that had been fixed since the dawn of time. The other families took advantage of the migrations of other animals; she was looking forward to two years hence, when it would be their turn for the *jukha* slaughter. They were the tastiest, and kept well.

By this time it was getting dark. I had been helping the elders set up the long trench of bonfires; now we lit them, and with the evening chill coming in over the sea I was grateful for the snapping flames.

Tybru demonstrated the butchering process so we could lend a hand. Selected internal organs went into hides of brine for pickling; then the skin was torn off and the yellow layer of fat that clung to it was scraped into clay jars for reducing to oil. More fat was flensed from the body, and then the meat was cut off in thin strips, which were draped over green sticks for smoking. Alas, they had no way to preserve the brains, so most of the Plathys crunched and sucked all night while they worked.

We weren't strong enough or experienced enough to keep up with even the children, but we gamely butchered through the night, trying not to cut ourselves on the slippery flint razors, working in the light of guttering torches. The seaweed produced an acrid halogen-smelling smoke that Tybru claimed was good for the lungs. Maybe because of its preservative effect.

The sun came up on a scene out of Hieronymus Bosch: smoke swirling over bloody sands littered with bones and heaps of entrails, Plathys and people blood-smeared and haggard with fatigue. We splashed into the icy water and scrubbed off dried blood with handfuls of sand, then stood in the stinging smoke trying to thaw out.

It was time to pack up and go. Already the rich smell of fresh blood was underlaid with a whiff of rot; insects were buzzing, and hardshell scavengers were scuttling up onto the beach. When the sun got high the place would become unlivable, even by Plathy standards.

We rolled up the smoked meat and blood squares into the raw scraped hides, which would later be pegged out and dried in the sun, and followed a trail up into the mountains. We set up our *maffas* on a plateau about a thousand meters up and waited placidly for the snow.

Someone coming.

Derek

I can no longer view them as other than dangerous animals. They mimic humanity—no, what I mean is that *we* interpret in human terms the things they do. The animal things they do. Maria, I'm sorry. I can't be a scientist about this, not any more. Not after what I just saw.

Herb and I were supposed to crisscross, going northeast a thousand steps, then northwest a thousand, and so forth. That was supposed to confuse them. They caught Herb.

I heard the scream. Maybe half a kilometer away. I should have run, knowing there was nothing I could do, but Herb and I've been close since school. Undergraduate. Were close. And there he—

Two of them had run him down in a small clearing, killed him and taken off his head. They were, one of them was . . . I can't.

I hid in the underbrush. All I had was a club there was nothing I could do. One of them was eating his, his private parts. The other was scooping him out, curious, dissecting him. I ran away. It's a wonder they didn't—

Oh shit. Here they come.

Gabriel

I think my wrist is broken. Maybe just sprained. But I killed the son of a bitch. He came around a bend in the river and I was on him with the spear. Element of surprise. I got him two good ones in the thorax before he grabbed me—where are their goddamned vital organs? A human would've dropped dead. He grabbed me by the wrist and slammed me to the ground. I rolled away, retrieved the spear, and impaled him as he jumped on me. He made a lot of noise and finally decided to die, after scraping my arm pretty well. For some reason he wasn't armed. Thank God. He was Embrek, the one who taught me how to fish. We got along so well. What the hell happened?

It was the first time it rained instead of snowing. All the music and everything stopped. They moped around all day and wouldn't talk. When it got dark they went wild.

They burst into our igloo, four of them, and started ripping off our clothes. Nanci, Susan, and Marcus resisted and were killed right there. One bite each. The rest of us were stripped and led or carried out into the cold, into the center of the compound. The cheerful fire was black mud now, starting to glaze with ice.

All the family except the oldest elders were there, standing around like zombies. No one spoke; no one took notice of anybody else. We all stood naked in the darkness. Kalyym eventually brought out a single oil candle, so we could be mocked by its flickering warm light.

The nature of the rite became clear after a couple of hours. It was a winnowing process. If you lost consciousness the Plathys would gather around you and try to poke and kick you awake. If you stood up they would go back to ignoring you. If you stayed down, you would die. After a certain number of pokes and kicks, Kalyym or some other elder would tear open the thorax in a single rip. Even worse than the blood was the sudden rush of steam into the cold air. Like life escaping the body.

Then they would feed.

We knew we wouldn't last the night. But the slippery walls were impossible to scale, and the largest Plathys stood guard at every entrance to the ring of igloos.

After some whispered discussion, we agreed we had to do the obvious: rush the Plathy who stood guard in front of our own igloo. The ones who survived would rush in, quickly gather weapons and clothing, and try to make it out the back entrance before the Plathys could react. Then run for the caves.

We were lucky. We rushed the guard from six different directions. Crouching to slash at Derek, he turned his back to me, and I leaped, striking him between the shoulders with both feet. He sprawled face down in the mud, and didn't get up. We scrambled into the igloo and I stood guard with a spear while the others gathered up things. A couple of Plathys stuck their heads in the entrance and snarled, but they evidently didn't want to risk the spear.

We weren't immediately followed, and for the first hour or so we made good time. Then it started to rain again, which slowed us down to a crawl. With no stars, we had to rely on Maria's sense of direction, which is pretty good. We found the caves just at dawn, and got a few hours' sleep before Mylab found us and we had to kill him.

How long is this phase going to last? If it goes as long as the summer or winter phases, they're sure to track us down. We may be safe inside the dome, if we can get that far—

Noise . . . Maria!

Maria

I might as well say it. It might be of some interest. None of us is going to live anyhow. I'm beyond embarrassment, beyond dignity. Nothing to be embarrassed about anyhow, not really.

The thing that was splashing up the stream turned out to be Gabriel. I ran out of hiding and grabbed him, hugged him; we were both a little hysterical about it. Anyhow he got hard and we took care of it, and then we went back to my hiding place and took care of it again. It was the first happy thing that's happened to me in a long time. Now I'm watching him sleep and fighting the impulse to wake him up to try for thirds. One more time before we die.

It's a strange state, feeling like a girl again, all tickled and excited inside, and at the same time feeling doomed. Like a patient with a terminal disease, high on medicine and mortality. There's no way we can outrun them. They'll sniff us down and tear us apart, maybe today, maybe tomorrow. They'll get us. Oh, wake up, Gab.

Be rational. This ferocity is just another change of state. They don't know what they're doing. Like the sex and birth phases. Tomorrow they may go back to being bovine sweet things. Or artisans again. Or maybe they'll discover the wheel for a week. What a weird, fucked-up bunch of . . .

There must be some survival value in it. Certainly it serves to cull the weakest members out. And killing most of the females before puberty compensates for the size of the litters—or could the size of the litters be a response to the scarcity of females? Lamarckism either way. Can't think straight.

At any rate it certainly can't be instinctive behavior in regard to us, since we aren't part of their normal environment. Maybe we've unknowingly triggered aberrant behavior. Stress response. Olfactory catalyst. Violent displacement activity. Who knows? Maybe whoever reads this tooth will be able to make some sense of it. You will excuse me for the time being. I have to wake him up.

Brenda

Maria and Gab were waiting for me when I got to the mouth of
the river. Gab has a badly sprained wrist; I splinted and bound
it. His grip is still good, and fortunately he's left-handed.
Maria's okay physically, just a little weak, but I wonder about
her psychological state. Almost euphoric, which hardly seems
appropriate.

We waited an extra half day, but the others are either dead
or lost. They can catch up with us at the dome. We have axe,
spear, and two knives. Gab turned one of the knives into a spear
for me. Two water bladders. We filled the bladders, drank to
saturation, and waded out into the sea.

The water seems icy cold, probably more than ten degrees
colder than when we walked through it before. Numb from the
waist down after a few minutes. When the water is shallow or
you get to walk along a sandbar, sensation returns, deep stinging
pain. It was a good thing we'd found that second water island;
only 10 kilometers of wading and limping along the wet sand.

We'd rolled up our furs and shouldered them, so they were
fairly dry. Couldn't risk a fire (and probably couldn't have found
enough dry stuff to make one), so we just huddled together for
warmth. We whispered, mapping out our strategy, such as it was,
and kept an eye out to the south. Though if we'd been followed
by even one Plathy we'd be pretty helpless.

Thirty kilometers to the next water hole. We decided to stay
here for a couple of days, eating the sulfurous oysters and regaining strength. It would have to be a fast push, going all the
way on less than five liters of water.

In fact we stayed four days. Gab came down with bad diar-
rhea, and we couldn't push on until his body could hold fluid. It
was just as well. We were all bone-tired and stressed to the limit.

The first night we just collapsed in a hamster pile and slept
like the dead. The next day we gathered enough soft dry grass
to make a kind of mattress, and spread our furs into a piecemeal
blanket. We still huddled for warmth and reassurance, and after
a certain amount of nonverbal discussion, Gab unleashed his
singular talent on both of us impartially.

That was interesting. Something Maria said indicated that
Gab was new to her. I'd thought that nothing—male, female, or
Plathy—was safe around him. Maybe Maria's strength intimi-

dated him, or her age. Or being the authority figure. That must be why she was in such a strange mood when I caught up with them. Anyhow, I'm glad for her.

Gab entertained us with poetry and songs in three languages. It's odd that all three of us know English. Maria had to learn it for her study of the Eskimos, and I did a residency in Massachusetts. Gab picked it up just for the hell of it, along with a couple of other Earth languages, besides Spanish and Pan-Swahili, and all three Selvan dialects. He's quite a boy. Maria was the only one who could speak Plathy better than he. They tried duets on the blood songs and shit songs, but it doesn't sound too convincing. The consonants *!ka* and *!ko* you just can't do unless you have teeth like beartraps.

The stress triggered my period a week early. When we fled the igloo I hadn't had time to gather up my moss pads and leather strap contraption, so I just sort of dripped all over the island. It obviously upset Gab, but I'm not going to waddle around with a handful of grass for his precious male sensibilities. (His rather gruesome sickness didn't do much for *my* sensibilities, either, doctor or no.)

We spent the last day in futile basket weaving, trying to craft something that would hold water for more than a few minutes. We all knew that it could be done, but it couldn't be done by us, not with the grass on the island. Maria did manage to cobble together a bucket out of her kilt by working a framework of sticks around it. That will double our amount of water, but she'll have to cradle it with both arms.

Thirty kilometers. I hope we make it.

Maria

We were almost dead from thirst and exposure by the time we got to the water hole island. We had long since lost track of our progress, since the vegetation on the islands was radically different from summer's, and some of the shorelines had changed. We just hoped each large island would be the one, and finally one was.

Alongside the water hole we found the fresh remains of a fire. At first that gave us a little hope, since it was possible that the rest of our team had leapfrogged us while Gab was convalescing. But then we found the dropping place, and the excrement was Plathy. Three or four of them, by the looks of it. A day or so ahead of us.

We didn't know what to do. Were they hunters searching us out, or a group on their Walk North? If the latter, it would probably be smartest to stay here for a couple of days; let them get way ahead. If they were hunters, though, they might still be on the island, and it would be smarter for us to move on.

Gab didn't think they were hunters, since they would've overtaken us earlier and made lunchmeat out of us. I wasn't sure. There were at least three logical paths through the archipelago; they might have taken one of the others. Since they could drink salt water, they didn't have to go out of their way to get to the island we first stopped at.

None of us felt up to pushing on. The going would be easier, but it would still be at least ten hours of sloshing through cold water on small rations. So we compromised.

In case there were hunters on the island, we made camp on the southern tip (the wind was from the north) in a small clearing almost completely surrounded by thick brambles. If we had to stand and fight, there was really only one direction they could approach us from. We didn't risk a fire and sent only one person out at a time for water or shellfish. One stayed awake while the other two slept.

Our precautions wouldn't amount to much if there actually were three or four of them and they all came after us. But they might be split up, and both Gab and I had proved they could be killed, at least one at a time.

We spent two uneventful days regaining our strength. About midday on the third, Gab went out for water and came back with Derek.

He was half dead from exposure and hunger. We fed him tiny bits of shellfish in water, and after a day of intermittent sleeping and raving, he came around enough to talk.

He'd seen two Plathys in the process of eating Herb. They ran after him, but he plunged blindly into brambles (his arms and lower legs were covered with festering scratches), and they evidently didn't follow him very far. He'd found the river and run out to sea in a blind panic. Got to the first water island and lay there for days. He couldn't remember whether he'd eaten.

Then he heard Plathys, or thought he did, and took off north as fast as he could manage. He didn't remember getting here. Gab found him unconscious at the water's edge.

So now the plan is to wait here two or three more days, until Derek feels strong enough for the next push.

Hardest part still ahead. Even if we don't run into Plathys. What if the boats are gone?

Gabriel

We didn't see any further sign of the Plathys. After four days Derek was ready to go. For a full day we drank all the water we could hold, and then at sundown set out.

There was only one place so deep we had to swim. I tried to carry Maria's water basket, sidestroking, but it didn't work. So the last 20 or 25 kilometers we were racing against the dwindling supply of water in the two bladders.

At first light there was still no sight of land, and we had to proceed by dead reckoning. (The Plathys evidently don't have this problem; they're somehow sensitive to the planet's magnetic field, like some Selvan migrating birds.) We saved a few spoonfuls of water to drink when we finally sighted land.

We went along in silence for an hour or so, and then Derek had a brainstorm. We were scanning the horizon from only a meter or so above sea level; if someone stood on my shoulders, he could see twice as far. Derek was the tallest. I ducked under and hoisted him up. He could stay balanced only for a second, but it did work; he saw a green smudge off to the left. We adjusted our course and slogged on with new energy. When all of us could see the smudge, we celebrated with a last sip of water.

Of course the stream that would be our guide uphill was nowhere to be seen. We stumbled ashore and did manage to lick enough moisture from foliage to partly allay our terrible thirst, though the bitter flavor soured my stomach.

We marked the spot with a large X in the sand and split into pairs, Brenda and I going one direction and Maria and Derek going the other, each with a water bladder to fill when one pair found the river. We agreed to turn back after no more than ten thousand steps. If neither pair found the river within 10 kilometers of our starting place, we'd just work our way uphill toward the crater lake. It would be slower going than following the stream's

course, but we could probably manage it, licking leaves and splitting some kinds of stalks for water. And we'd be less likely to
run into an ambush, if there were hunters waiting ahead. I wasn't
looking forward to it, though. Coming down had been enough
trouble.

We were lucky. In a sense. Brenda and I stumbled on the
stream less than two kilometers from where we started. We drank
deeply and jogged back to catch up with Maria and Derek.

We made an overnight camp some distance from the stream
and foraged for food. There were no fish in the shallows, and none
of the sulfurous oysters. There were small crabs, but they were
hard to catch and had only a pinch of meat. We wound up digging
tubers, which were not very palatable raw but would sustain us
until we got to the lake, where fish were plentiful.

It might have been a little safer to travel by night, but we
remembered how the brambles had flayed us before, and decided
to take the chance. It was a mistake.

As we had hoped, progress was a lot faster and easier going
up than it had been coming down. Less slipping. It was obvious
that Plathys had preceded us, though, from footprints and freshly
broken vegetation, so we climbed as quietly as possible.

Not quietly enough, perhaps, or maybe our luck just ran out.
Damn it, we lost Derek. He had to be the one in front.

Maria

We couldn't see the sun because of the forest canopy, but it was
obvious from the reddening of the light that we would soon have
to decide whether to make camp or push on through the darkness.
Gab and I were discussing this, whispering, when the Plathy
attacked.

Derek was in front. The spear hit him in the center of the
chest and passed almost completely through his body. I think it
killed him instantly. The Plathy, a lone young female, came
charging down the stream bed toward us, roaring. She tripped
and fell almost at our feet. Probably stunned. Gab and I killed
her with spear and axe. After she was dead, Gab hacked off her
head and threw it into the bush.

We waited for the rest of them, but she evidently had been
alone. Gab had a hard time controlling his grief.

When it got dark we pushed on. The stream was slightly

phosphorescent, but we relied mainly on feeling our way. A kind of fungus on the forest floor always grew in pairs, and glowed dull red, like pairs of sullen eyes watching us.

We made more noise than we had during the daytime, but there was probably little risk. Plathys sleep like dead things, and in this kind of terrain they don't post guard at night, since none of the predators here is big enough to bother them. Big enough to give us trouble, though. Three times we moved to the middle of the stream, when we thought we heard something stalking us.

The slope began to level off before it got light, and by dawn we were moving through the marshy grassland that bordered the crater lake.

We had unbelievable luck with the lake fish. Hundreds of large females lay almost immobile in the shallows. They were full of delicious roe. We gorged ourselves and then cut strips of flesh to dry in the sun. Not as effective as smoking, but we couldn't risk a fire.

We decided it would be safest to sleep separately, in case someone had picked up our trail. Like Gab, I found a tree to drape myself in. Brenda just found a patch of sunlight, arranged her furs on the wet ground, and collapsed. I thought I was too jangled to sleep, after Derek, but in fact I barely had time to find a reasonably secure set of branches before my body turned itself off.

Our survival reflexes have improved. A few hours later—it was not quite noon—I woke up suddenly in response to a slight vibration. One of the cat creatures was creeping toward me along another branch.

I didn't want to throw the spear, of course. So I took the offensive, crawling closer to the beast. He snarled and backed up warily. When I was a couple of spear lengths from him I started poking toward his face. Eventually I forced him onto too small a limb, and he crashed to the ground. He lay there a moment, then heaved himself up, growled at the world, and limped away. I went back to my branch and slept a few more hours unmolested.

Gab woke me up with the bad news that Brenda was gone. There was no sign of violence at the spot where she'd settled down, though, and we eventually found her hiding in a tree as we had. She'd heard a noise.

We gathered up our dried fish—that it hadn't been disturbed was encouraging—and killed a few fresh ones to carry along for dinner. Then we moved with some haste down along the river we had followed up so long ago. If all goes well we will be able to duplicate in reverse the earlier sequence: rest tonight on this side of the banyan forest, then push through to the large clearing; spend the night there, and at first light press on to the sea.

Gabriel

The sea. I was never so glad to see water.

The first boat we found was beyond use, burned in two, but the water jugs nearby were unharmed, curiously enough. It's possible some immature Plathys had come upon it and not recognized that it was a boat, just a hollow log that had burned partway through. So they may have innocently used it for fuel.

The other boat, farther away from the river, was untouched. If anything, it might be in better shape now than when we left it, since it has been propped up on two logs, hollow side down. It was dryer and harder, and apparently had no insect damage.

Unfortunately, it was too heavy for three people to lift; it had been something of a struggle for all twelve of us. We went back upstream a couple of kilometers to where Maria remembered having seen a stand of saplings. Stripped of branches, they looked like they would make good rollers. We each took an armload. It was dark by the time we got back to the boat.

It might have been prudent to try to launch it in the darkness, and paddle out to comparative safety. But there hadn't been any sign of Plathys on this side of the island, and we were exhausted. I stood first watch, and had to trudge around in circles to stay awake. A couple of times I heard something out in the grass, but it never came close. Maria and Brenda heard it on their shifts, but it left before dawn.

At first light we started rolling the boat. A good three hours of hard labor, since when the saplings got into sand they forgot how to be wheels. We dragged it the last hundred meters, one bonecracking centimeter after another. Once it was floating free, we anchored it and sat in the shallow water for a long time, poleaxed by fatigue. It was amazing how much warmer the water was here, just a hundred or so kilometers north of the Plathy island: volcanic activity, coupled with distance from the continental shelf drop-off.

We dragged ourselves back to the place we'd slept and found

that all our food was gone. Animals; the weapons were still there. Rather than start off with no reserve food, we spent the rest of the morning hunting. A dozen large snakes and seven small animals like *zamri*, but with six legs. We risked a fire to smoke them, which perhaps was not wise. One person guarded the fire while the other two loaded all the jars and then arranged a makeshift vessel in the stern, pegging the largest fur out in a cup shape.

Finally we loaded all the food and weapons aboard and swung up over the side (the outriggers kept us from losing too much water from the stern). We paddled almost hysterically for an hour or so, and then, with the island just a whisper of dark on the horizon, anchored to sleep until the guide stars came out.

Brenda

It was smart of Maria to pick a beefy young athlete as one of her graduate assistants. I don't think that she and I would have stood a chance alone, pushing this heavy old log 250 kilometers. We're all pretty tough and stringy after months of playing caveman, but the forced march has drained us. Last night I paddled more and more feebly until, just before dawn, I simply passed out. It's a good thing Gab was in the rear position. He heard me slump over and grabbed the paddle as it floated by. When the sun got too high to continue, he massaged the knots out of my arms and shoulders, and when I fell asleep again he was doing the same for Maria.

Perhaps we should have delayed our launch long enough to weave a sunshield. It isn't all that hot but it must have some dehydrating effect. And it would be easier to sleep. But Martin was the only one who could weave very well, and he—

Oh my God. My God, we left him for dead and I haven't even thought about him since, since we met up at the river mouth. Now we've left him behind with no boat. He could have been just a day or an hour behind us, and if he was we've murdered him.

Maria

Brenda suddenly burst into tears and started going on about Martin. I gave him up before we left the Plathy island. His route was a mirror image of mine and he was a much faster runner. They must have caught him.

I pointed out to Brenda that if Martin did make it to the coast of the crater lake island, he could probably survive indefinitely with his primitive skills, since it would be fairly easy for one man alone to stay away from the Plathys who occasionally passed through there. Surely he would be intelligent enough to stamp out a regular marking in the sand, easily visible from the satellite. Then the next expedition could rescue him. That fantasy calmed her down a bit. Now she's sleeping.

I'm starting to think we might make it. We have water enough for twenty days and food for half that time, even if we don't catch any fish. Admittedly it's harder to keep a straight course when the guiding stars are behind you, but it shouldn't take us twice as long as the trip south, especially if there are no clouds.

Once we get to the mainland and retrieve the modern weapons, the trek back to the base will be simple. And the year waiting inside the dome will be sybaritic luxury. Real food. Chairs. No bugs. Books. Wonder if I can still read?

Gabriel

Seven days of uneventful routine. On the eighth day I woke up in the afternoon and took a spear up to the bow to stare at the water. I stood up to piss overboard, which sometimes attracts fish, and saw a Plathy swimming straight toward us.

He stopped and treaded water about eight meters away, staring at me and the spear. I called out to him but he didn't answer. Just stared for several minutes in what seemed to be a calculating way. Then he turned his back and swam on, powerful strokes that gave him more speed than we could ever muster.

Could he tip us over? Probably not, with nothing to stand on. Once in the water, though, we'd be no match for one of them. My brain started to run away with fear, after a week of the luxury and novelty of not being afraid. He could approach underwater and pull us overboard one by one. He could grab an outrigger while we were sleeping and rock us out. He could for God's sake bite a *hole* in the boat!

When the women woke up I told them, and we made the obvious decision to maintain a rotating watch. I wondered privately how much good it would do. I suspected that a Plathy could hold his breath for a long time; if he approached underwater we might not be able to see him until he was right by the boat. Or one might overtake us in darkness. I didn't give voice to any of these specific fears. Neither of them lacks imagination, and they didn't need my scenarios to add to their own private apprehensions.

How much farther? I suspect we'll be making better time from now on.

Maria

I began to have a recurrent dream that we'd somehow got turned around, and were paddling furiously back to the waiting Plathys. This daymare even began invading my waking hours, especially toward dawn, when I was in that vulnerable, suggestible mental state that extreme fatigue and undirected anxiety can bring on.

So when in the first light I saw land, the emotion I felt was speechless apprehension. We'd been paddling eleven days. We *must* have gotten turned around; we couldn't have covered the distance in that time. I stared at it for half a minute before Brenda mumbled something about it being too early to take a break.

Then Gab also saw the faint green line on the horizon, and we chattered on about it for a while, drifting. As it got lighter we could see the purple cones of distant volcanoes, which put my subconscious to rest.

The volcanoes simplified navigation, since I could remember what their relative positions had been on the way out. It looked as if we were going to land 10 or 15 kilometers west of the mouth of the river that led to the base. The question was whether to alter our course off to the right, so as to land closer to the river, or go straight in and walk along the beach. We were safer on the water but terminally tired of paddling, so we opted for the short approach.

It was little more than an hour before the canoe landed with a solid crunch. We jumped out and immediately fell down. No land legs. I could stand up, but the ground seemed to teeter. For some reason it was a lot worse than it had been on the outward trip. There had been a little more wave action this time, which could account for that. It might also account for the good time we made: some sort of seasonal current.

Using the spears as canes, we practiced walking for a while.

When we could stagger pretty well unsupported, we gathered our stuff and started down the beach as quickly as possible. It would be a good idea to find the weapons and dig them up before dark.

Eventually we were making pretty good progress (though when we stopped the ground would still rock back and forth). The musty jungle actually smelled good, reassuring. We ate the last of the smoked snake while hungrily discussing the culinary miracles waiting for us at the base. There was enough food there to last twelve people for more than a year, a precaution against disaster.

We reached the mouth of the river before midday. But when we paced off from the rock to where the weapons were supposed to be buried, we got a nasty surprise: someone had already dug them up. Humus had filled the hole, but there was a definite depression there, and the ground was soft.

Dejected and frightened, we paced on to the next site, and it had also been dug up—but we found three of the exhumed fuel cells lying in the brush. The Plathys wouldn't know how to install them, of course. Even if, as now seemed likely, they had been watching us when we first buried them, they wouldn't have been able to find the hidden studs that had to be pushed simultaneously to open the camouflaged weapons. Even if they somehow got one open, they wouldn't know how to screw in the fuel cell and unsafe it.

We went back to the first site on the off-chance that they might have discarded the weapons, too, since ours weren't superior, in conventional capabilities, to what they would normally carry. That turned out to be a smart move: we found a club and a spear snarled in the undergrowth, still in good working order. (They'd been crafted of Bruuchian ironwood, and so were impervious to moisture and mold.)

We armed the two and confirmed that they worked. There were probably others hidden more deeply in the brush, but we were too tired to continue the search. We'd been pushing for most of a day, burning adrenaline. The two weapons would be enough to protect us while we slept.

Gabriel

Brenda woke me up delightfully. I was having an interesting dream, and then it wasn't a dream.

I had the last guard shift before dawn. Scouting the perimeter of our site for firewood, I almost stumbled over a slow lizard, about a meter long, and fat. Skinned and cleaned him and had him roasting on a spit by the time the women woke up.

After breakfast, we spent a good two hours searching the area around the weapons pit, spiraling out systematically, but didn't find anything further. Well, it was good luck we even had the two weapons. We were considerably better with spear, knife, and club than we had been when we landed, but probably not good enough for an extended trek through the mainland. Packs of hungry carnivores, even if no Plathys waited in ambush.

Combing the other site did find us two more fuel cells, which should be plenty. Each one is good for more than an hour of continuous firing when new, and none of them was half used up. We could even afford to use the weapons to light fires.

So we started off in pretty high spirits. By noon we weren't quite so springy. One long sleep isn't enough to turn night creatures into day creatures, and though walking is easier than paddling, our leg muscles were weak from disuse. There was a bare rock island in the middle of the broad river; we waded out to it and made camp. That consisted of laying down our furs and collapsing.

Brenda usually takes the first watch, but she couldn't keep her eyes open, so I did odds-and-evens with Maria, and lost. And so I was the one to see the first Plathy.

I was gathering driftwood for the night's fire. I'd been concentrating my watch on the nearer bank, the one we'd come from. No telling how long the Plathy had been looking at me, standing quietly on the other side.

Our side was relatively open; compact stands of bamboolike grass every 20 or 30 meters, with only low bushes in between. The other bank was dense jungle, which was why we avoided it. The Plathy was making no special effort to conceal himself but was hard to see in the dappled shade. I continued picking up wood, studying him out of the corner of my eye.

He was an adult male, carrying a spear. That was bad. If he had been a child he might have been on his Walk North, accidentally stumbling on us. An adult had no reason to be here except us, and he wouldn't be here alone.

I didn't recognize him. If he wasn't from the Camchai family, that probably meant they had enlisted the aid of other families, so we might be up against any number. But I couldn't be sure; even in social situations I often got individuals mixed up. Maria was good at telling them apart. I took an armload of wood back to the camp and quietly woke her up and explained what was happening. She walked over to the other side of the island, casually picking up sticks, and took a look. But he was gone.

We had a whispered conference and decided to stay on the island. They would have a hard time rushing us; the river bottom was too muddy for running. And their spears couldn't reach us from either bank.

She's taken over the watch now. Enough talking. Try to sleep.

Brenda

What a terrible night. Nobody woke me for my afternoon watch turn, so I slept almost until dark. Maria said she hadn't awakened me because she was too nervous to sleep anyhow, and explained about Gab seeing the Plathy.

When the sun went down we lit the fire, and Gab joined us. We decided to double the watch—two on, one off, one person with a crazer watching each bank. Maria curled up by the fire and tried to sleep.

They hit us about an hour before midnight, coming from Gab's side, the near bank. He called out and I ran over.

Spears falling out of the darkness. We had the fire behind us, and so were pretty good targets. Crazers don't make much light; we had to fan them and hope we hit someone. All the time running back and forth sideways, trying to spoil their aim. Maria woke up and I gave her the club crazer, then retired to the other side of the island, under Gab's orders: watch for an "envelopment." But they weren't that sophisticated.

No way to tell how many we killed. The spears came less and less frequently, and then there were rocks, and then nothing. When dawn came, pieces of four or five sliced-up Plathy bodies lay on the shore, any number having been washed downstream.

I wish I could feel guilty about it. Two weeks ago, I would have. Instead, I have to admit to a kind of manic glee. We beat them. They snuck up on us and we beat them.

Maria

We burned both crazers down to quarter charge. A little more than half charge on the two backup cells. But I don't expect any more attacks like last night. They aren't dumb.

So much for the First Commandment. We've demonstrated high technology. Some of them must have survived, to go back and tell others about the magic. But we had no choice.

From now on we'll have to assume we're being followed, of course, and be triply careful about ambush setups. That won't be a real problem until the last day or two, traveling with thick jungle on both sides of the river. Why did we have to be so cautious in siting the dome?

Well, it may turn out that we'll be glad it's where it is. What if they follow us all the way there? If they try to encircle the clearing and wait us out, the jungle will get them; we won't have to do a thing. Plathy skills work fine down on their friendly island, but up where the dome is situated a hunting party armed with clubs and spears wouldn't last a week. Free lunch for the fauna.

We have to push on fast. Islands like this one will be common while the river is wide and slow. We'll be fairly safe. When the jungle closes in on both sides, though, the river will become a narrow twisting cataract. No island protection but its noise might confound Plathy hearing, make it harder for them to ambush us.

At any rate, this is the plan: each day on the plain, cover as much ground as possible, consistent with getting a few hours of sleep each night. Rest up just south of the jungle and then make a forced march, two days to the dome.

Maybe this haste is unnecessary. If the Plathys were their normal, rather sensible selves, they'd cut their losses and go home. But now we have no idea of what's normal. They may harry us until we kill them all. That would be good for the race, leaving it relatively uncontaminated culturally. Bad for us. A few more engagements like last night and we won't have enough power in the crazers to make it through the jungle. Might as well stand by the river and sing blood songs to the hungry lizards.

Gabriel

Five days of no contact, but I can't shake the feeling we're being watched. Have been watched all the way. Now an afternoon and night of rest on this last island, and Maria wants us to push all the way to the dome.

Physically, I suppose we can do it. The terrain isn't difficult, since a game trail parallels the water all the way up. But the game that made the trail are formidable. They gave us plenty of trouble when there were twelve of us. And theoretically no Plathys.

(I wonder about that now, though. Surely someone was watching us back when we buried the weapons. How long had they been following us? They claimed that they never go to the mainland, except for a few brave Walkers, and of course they always tell the truth. About what they remember, anyhow.)

I haven't recorded anything for a long time. Waiting for my state of mind to improve. After the night of the attack I ran out of hope. Things haven't improved but I'm talking to myself to stay awake for the rest of this watch. I think Brenda's doing the same thing. Sitting on the other side of the island staring at the water, mumbling. I should go remind her to pay attention. But I can cover both banks from this side.

Besides, if they're going to hit us, I wish they'd hit us here. Clear fields of fire all around. Of course they won't; they learn from their mistakes, Maria says.

I'm being paranoiac. They're gone. The being-watched feeling, I don't know. Ever since Derek got it I've been a— I've been . . . loose in the head. Trying to control this—this panic. They look to me for strength, even Maria does, but all I have is muscle, jaw muscle to keep the screams in. When that one swam by us headed for the mainland I knew we were deep in shit.

Derek had religion. We argued long nights about that. What would he be doing now, praying? *"Nuestro Señor que vives en el cielo, alabado sea tu nombre. . . ."* Good spear repellent. I miss him so.

Nobody will ever find this tooth with its feeble beep transmitter. When they come back and find the dome empty, that will be the end of it. Not enough budget for a search through obviously hostile territory. Not enough resources on this planet for anybody to want to exploit it, so no new money to find our teeth. We'll pass into Plathy legend and be forgotten, or distorted beyond recognition.

A good thing for them. If there was anything of use here,

we'd be like the Eskimo anthropologists Maria talks about, recording the ways of a race doomed by the fact of recording. So maybe the Plathys will have another million years of untroubled evolution. Maybe they'll learn table manners.

I'm afraid of them but can't be mad at them. Even after Derek. They are what they are and we should have been more careful. Maybe I'm becoming a real xenologist, at this late date. Derek would say I'm trying to compose myself into a state of grace. Before dying.

It infuriated me that he always had answers. All I ever had was questions.

So two days' push and we're safe inside the dome. Food and cube and books and spears bounce off. Maybe I've read too much, written too much; the pattern seems inescapable. We're at death's door. Capital Death's Door. If we make it to the dome we'll break the rules.

Cálmate. Calm. Maybe I'm projecting, making patterns. Here there's only real things: cause, effect, randomness, entropy—your death is like the falling of a leaf, Derek said; like the leaf falling, it's a small tragedy, but necessary. If everything lived forever the universe would fill up in short order.

Mustn't blather. Reality, not philosophy. We rest so we can be alert. If we're alert enough we'll beat the jungle. Beat the Plathys that aren't there. It's all in my head. For the next two days take the head out of the circuit. Only reflex. Smell, listen, watch: react. React fast enough, you live.

Only I keep thinking about Derek. He never knew what hit him.

Brenda

Gab asked me to watch both banks for a while so he could give love to Maria before it got dark. Hard to watch both banks when I want to watch him. Men look so vulnerable from this angle, bouncing; a new perspective for me. I've never been an audience except for watching on the cube. It's different.

Admit I'm jealous of her. She's fifteen years older than I and shows it. But he wants her for his last one. That was obvious in his tone of voice. At some level I think he's as scared as I am.

If he thinks this is his last one he doesn't know much about women. Maria will let me wake him up when our shift is over.

If I can wait that long. I've watched him sleeping; he has the refractory period of a twelve-year-old. To be exact, I know from observation that he can do it twice and still get an erection in his sleep. No privacy under our circumstances.

Funny friendly sound, don't hear it like that while you're doing it—what was that? Something move?

Just a lizard, I guess. Nothing now. We've been seeing them the last two days on the jungle side, around dusk and in the firelight. They don't come in the water. What's going to happen tomorrow night, no island, no fire? Don't want to die that way, jumped by a pack of dinosaurs. Nor have my head bitten off by a sentient primitive. I was going to be a grandmother and sit on the porch and tell doctor stories and die with no fuss.

Why won't they attack? I know they're out there, waiting. If they would only come now, I could die that way. I remember the feeling, fifty or a hundred of them against the three of us and our two crazers. Not a fair fight, perhaps, but God it did feel good, holding our own, epinephrine from head to toe. This waiting and worrying. Light the fire.

Stack the wet wood around to dry. Gives me something to do while they're finishing up. Being quiet for the sake of my sensibilities, or theirs. Just heavier breathing and a faster rhythm of liquid sounds. I've followed that unspoken code, too; we haven't been all three together since the water hole. She's had him seven times since, to my four. To my knowledge. Why am I keeping score? They were made for each other. Iron man, iron woman.

I was in love once or twice and know this is something else. Not just sex; I've been that way before, too. Hysteria is part of it, but not in the old-fashioned womanish sense, the womb taking over. This is a certainty-of-death hysteria, to coin a category. It's different from just fear. It's like, it's like—I don't know. As if you had never tasted water before, or seen colors, and suddenly here is a cold spring or a rainbow. Minus the joy. Just something primal and unlike anything before. Does that make sense? We've been in danger God knows constantly for how long? Not the same. There was always hope. Now we're two days away from total sanctuary and for some reason I know we won't make it.

I remember from psych class a lesson about people who seemed to know they were going to die. Not sick people; soldiers, adventurers, whose sudden violent death seemed to resonate backward in time—they told their friends that somehow they felt that this was it, and by God it was. You can call it coincidence or invoke pragmatic causality—they were nervous and therefore careless and therefore died—but here and now I think there's more to it. Once I'm safe inside the dome I'll publish a retraction. Right now I feel my death as strongly as I feel the need for that man inside of me.

Maria

Somehow we lived through that one.

We'd been in the jungle for perhaps twelve hours, dusk approaching, when a lizard pack hit us, or two packs, from in front and behind. The trail is scarcely two meters wide, which saved us. The carcasses piled up and impeded their charge. We must have killed forty of them, man-sized or slightly smaller. Not a type we'd seen on the way down.

Were they intelligent enough to coordinate their charge, or is it some kind of instinctive attack pattern? Scary either way. Used up a lot of energy. If it happens a few more times . . . it happens. No use thinking about it.

At least the action seems to have been good for morale. Both of them have been radiating depression and fear since we started out this morning. Reinforcing each other's premonitions of doom. I shouldn't have let her go to him at watch change, or I should have admonished her to fuck, don't talk. It was too much like saying goodbye. I got that feeling from Gab too, last night, but I tried to reassure him. Words.

By my reckoning we have fourteen to eighteen hours to go, depending on how much ground we can cover without light. Decided against torches, of course. The Plathys don't normally hunt at night, but they sure as hell attacked us in the dark.

Natural impulse is to climb a tree and wait for dawn. That would be suicidal. The jungle canopy is thick and supports its own very active ecology. We can't take to the water because the current's too swift, even if we wanted to chance the snakes.

We'll stay within touching distance, Gab in front because he has the best hearing. Brenda hears better than me, so she should bring up the rear, but I think she'll be better off in the middle, feeling protected. Besides, I want to have one of the weapons.

Gabriel

Never another night like that. I wound up firing at every sound, jumpy. But a few times there actually was something waiting in front of us, once something that wasn't a lizard. Big shaggy animal that stood up on its hind legs and reared over us, all teeth and claws and a dick the size of my arm. He was too dumb to know he was dead, and actually kept scrabbling toward us after I cut him off at the knees. If we'd gone a few steps farther before I fired he would have gotten at least me, maybe all of us. The crazer light was almost bright in the pitch blackness, a lurid strobe. I used up the last of one fuel cell and had to reload by touch.

At least we don't have to worry about the Plathys. Nothing remotely edible could make it through a night like that without energy weapons.

When I mentioned that to Maria, she said not to be too sure. They were tracking us on the jungle side before. Not the same, though. This jungle makes that one look like a park.

Dead tired but moving fast. We're looking for a pink granite outcropping. Fifty paces upstream from it there's a minor trail to the right; the dome clearing is about half a kilometer in. Can't be more than a few hours away.

Brenda

There it is! The rock! Hard to . . . talk . . . running . . .

Maria

Slow down! Careful! That's better. Not a sound now.

Gabriel

Oh, no. Shit, no.

Brenda

They . . . burned it?

Gabriel

Spears—

Maria

Take his weapon! Get to cover! Here!

Brenda

I—oh!

Maria

So . . . so this is how it ends. Gab died about ten minutes ago, in the first moment of the attack. A spear in the back of his head. Brenda was hit then too, a spear that went in her shoulder and came out her back. She lived for several minutes, though, and acquitted herself well when the Plathys charged. I think we killed them all, thirty-seven by my count. If there are any left in the jungle they are staying there for the time being.

They must have piled wood up around the dome and kept a bonfire going until the force field overloaded and collapsed. It wasn't engineered for that kind of punishment, I suppose. Obviously.

Little of use left in the ruins. Rations destroyed, fuel cells popped by the heat. There's a toolbox not badly harmed. Nothing around to repair with it, though. Maybe if I dug I could find some rations merely overcooked. But I don't want to stay around to search. Doubt that I'll live long enough to have another meal, anyhow.

My fault. Eleven good people dead, and how many innocent savages, because I wasn't prudent. With that first abrupt life change, the frenzied breeding, I should have ordered us to tiptoe away. Another decade of satellite surveillance and we would have learned which times were safe to come in for close-up study. Now everything is a shambles.

Racial vanity is part of it, I guess, or my vanity. Thinking we could come naked into a heavily armed Stone Age culture and survive by our superior intelligence and advanced perspective. It worked before. But this place is not Obelobel.

I guess all I can do now is be sure a record survives. These teeth might not make it through a Plathy or lizard digestive system. I'll . . . I'll use the pliers from the tool kit. Leave the teeth here in the ruins. Buried enough so the Plathys can't find them easily. One hell of a prize to bring back from your Walk North.

I have only about a tenth charge left. Brenda used up all of the other before she died. Not enough to get out of the jungle, not even if it were all daylight. One woman alone doesn't have a bloody fucking chance on this world. I'll try the river. Maybe I can find a log that will float me down to the savannah. Then hike to the coast. If I can make it to the beach maybe I can stay alive there for a while. Sleep with one eye open. I don't know. Look for me there. But don't bother to look for too long. The pliers.

Sorry, Brenda. . . .

Sorry . . . Gab. Sweet Gab. Still warm.

Now mine. One jerk. Some blood, some pain. *Tem se garlish. !ka.*

To: Ahmadou Masire, Coordinator
      Selva Sector Recreational Facilities
      Confederación Office Building, Suite 100
      Bolivar 243 488 739
      Selva

From: Federico Santesteban, Publicity Director
      Office of Resources Allocation
      Chimbarazo Interplanetario
      Ecuador 3874658
      Terra

Dr. Masire:

I hope you will find the enclosed transcript of some use. Your assistant, Sra. Videla, mentioned the possibility of a documentary cube show to generate interest in the hunting trips to Sanchrist IV. Seems to me that if you inject some romance into this you have a natural story: sacrifice, tragedy, brave kids battling against impossible odds.

We could save you some production costs by getting a few Plathys shipped to your studio via our xenological division on Perrin's World. They have a hundred or so there and keep their

56

stock stable by cloning. You'll have to have somebody put together a grant proposal demonstrating that they'll be put to legitimate scholarly use. Garcia Belaunde at your Instituto Xenológico is a tame one, as you probably know. Have him talk to Leon Jawara at the PW Xenological Exchange Commission. He'll make sure you get the beasts at the right part of their life cycle. Otherwise they'd eat all of your actors.

I tried to pull some strings, but I'm afraid there's no way we can get you permission to take a crew onto the Plathy island itself. That's a xenological preserve now, isolated by a force field, the few remaining Plathys constantly monitored by flying bugs. You can shoot on the mainland, if your actors are as crazy as your hunters, or use the crater lake island. There are a few feral Plathys roaming there, though, so take precautions, no matter what the season. Use a restraining field if that's within your budget; otherwise, regrettably, the smartest thing would be to kill them on sight. Their behavior patterns become erratic if they're separated from family for more than a year.

The search party that followed up on Dr. Rubera's expedition could only find five of the tooth transmitters. There was no trace of Maria Rubera, or any other human remains.

A sad story but I think a useful one for your purposes. Gives your expeditions a dramatic historical context.

Let me know if I can be of further service. And by all means send us a copy of the cube, if you decide to go into production.

Your servant,
Federico Santesteban

There's a great temptation in science fiction writing to succumb to the Law of the Conservation of Backgrounds: having worked out a useful and interesting fictional "future history," you hate to throw it away after just one story. So you recycle it.

I've used the universe that lies behind *Seasons* in a half-dozen stories and two novels (*All My Sins Remembered* and *There Is No Darkness*), and it's one I tend to return to whenever a story demands a starfaring human civilization. The basic premise is that

way back in the twenty-first century the bases of political and economic power changed radically: America and Russia started slug-
ging it out and they brought Europe, China, and Japan down with
them. Africa and South America emerged more or less intact, so
when a practical faster-than-light drive was developed (by Hartford,
an Australian concern), it was a Spanish- and Swahili-speaking
"Confederación" that pushed out to the stars. Some of the stories
in the series, like *Seasons,* are rather serious, and some, like the
one that follows, are rather otherwise.

When you look at a story several years after writing it, sometimes it's difficult to remember what impulse caused you to start
the thing. That's not a problem with this next one. Another writer
made me do it.

In the late summer of 1981, Jerry Pournelle kindly arranged for
the Jet Propulsion Laboratory to invite a dozen or so science fiction
writers to come to Pasadena and watch Voyager 2's Saturn flyby
pictures as they came in. It was one of the most exciting things
that's ever happened to me. Every few hours—sometimes every
few minutes!—a picture would come in that set planetary science
on its ear. The scientists' enthusiasm was contagious; the very air
crackled with suspense, mystery, joy.

But they didn't have any beer.

So every now and then, when there was a lull in the data
transmission, we'd saunter down the hill to where Jerry had parked
his jeep, providentially loaded with iced beer, and stand in the hazy
California heat sucking long-necked Budweisers, talking about this
and that. Sometimes about science fiction.

The topic of *Star Wars* came up, and I expressed admiration
for the cantina scene; all those weird aliens sitting around drinking
noxious fluids, munching on raw meat, whatever.

Jerry was not so impressed. "Every science fiction writer has
written the aliens-in-a-bar scene a dozen times," he said.

Not every one, Jerry. I hadn't. So I did.

A !TANGLED

WEB

Your spaceport bars fall into two distinct groups: the ones for the baggage and the ones for the crew. I was baggage, this trip, but didn't feel like paying the prices that people who space for fun can afford. The Facilities Directory listed under "Food and Drink" four establishments: the Hartford Club (inevitably), the Silver Slipper Lounge, Antoine's, and Slim Joan's Bar & Grill.

I went to a currency exchange booth first, assuming that Slim Joan was no better at arithmetic than most bartenders, and cashed in a hundredth share of Hartford stock. Then I took the drop lift down to the bottom level. That the bar's door was right at the drop-lift exit would be a dead giveaway even if its name had been the Bell, Book, and Candle. Baggage don't generally like to fall ten stories, no matter how slowly.

It smelled right, stir-fry and stale beer, and the low lighting suggested economy rather than atmosphere. Slim Joan turned out to be about a hundred thousand grams of transvestite. Well, I hadn't come for the scenery.

The clientele seemed evenly mixed between humans and others, most of the aliens being !tang, since this was Morocho III. I've got nothing against the company of aliens, but if I was going to spend all next week wrapping my jaws around !tangish, I preferred to mix my drinking with some human tongue.

"Speak English?" I asked Slim Joan.

"Some," he/she/it growled. "You would drink something?" I'd

never heard a Russian-Brooklyn accent before. I ordered a double saki, cold, in Russian, and took it to an empty booth.

One of the advantages of being a Hartford interpreter is that you can order a drink in a hundred different languages and dialects. Saves money; they figure if you can speak the lingo you can count your change.

I was freelancing this trip, though, working for a real-estate cartel that wanted to screw the !tang out of a few thousand square kilometers of useless seashore property. It wouldn't stay useless, of course.

Morocho III is a real garden of a planet, but most people never see it. The tachyon nexus is down by Morocho I, which we in the trade refer to as "Armpit," and not many people take the local hop out to III (Armpit's the stopover on the Earth–Sammler run). Starlodge, Limited, was hoping to change that situation.

I couldn't help eavesdropping on the !tangs behind me. (I'm not a snoop; it's a side effect of the hypnotic-induction learning process.) One of them was leaving for Earth today, and the other was full of useful advice. "He"—they have seven singular pronoun classes, depending on the individual's age and estrous condition—was telling "her" never to make any reference to human body odor, no matter how vile it may be. He should also have told her not to breathe on anyone. One of the by-products of their metabolism is butyl nitrite, which smells like well-aged socks and makes humans get all faint and cross-eyed.

I've worked with !tangs a few times before, and they're some of my favorite people. Very serious, very honest, and their logic is closer to human logic than most. But they *are* strange-looking. Imagine a perambulating haystack with an elephant's trunk protruding. They have two arms under the pile of yellow hair, but it's impolite to take them out in public unless one is engaged in physical work. They do have sex in public, constantly, but it takes a zoologist with a magnifying glass to tell when.

He wanted her to bring back some Kentucky bcʌrbon and Swiss chocolate. Their metabolism parts company with ours over proteins and fats, but they love our carbohydrates and alcohol. The alcohol has a psychedelic effect on them, and sugar leaves them plastered.

A human walked in and stood blinking in the half-light. I recognized him and shrank back into the booth. Too late.

He strode over and stuck out his hand. "Dick Navarro!"

"Hello, Pete." I shook his hand once. "What brings you here? Hartford business?" Pete was also an interpreter.

—Oh, no, he said in Arabic. —Only journeying.

—Knock it off, I said in Serbo-Croatian. —Isn't your native language English? I added in Greek.

"Sure it is. Yours?"

"English or Spanish. Have a seat."

I smacked my lips twice at Slim Joan, and she came over with a menu. "To be eating you want?"

"Nyet," he said. "Vodka." I told her I'd take another.

"So what are you doing here?" Pete asked.

"Business."

"Hartford?"

"Nope."

"Secret."

"That's right." Actually, they hadn't said anything about its being secret. But I knew Peter Lafitte. He wasn't just passing through.

We both sat silently for a minute, listening to the !tangs. We had to smile when he explained to her how to decide which public bathroom to use when. This was important to humans, he said. Slim Joan came with the drinks and Pete paid for both, a bad sign.

"How did that Spica business finally turn out?" he asked.

"Badly." Lafitte and I had worked together on a partition-of-rights hearing on Spica IV, with the Confederación actually bucking Hartford over an alien-rights problem. "I couldn't get the humans to understand that the minerals had souls, and I couldn't get the natives to believe that refining the minerals didn't affect their spiritual status. It came to a show of force, and the natives backed down. I wouldn't like to be there in twenty years, though."

"Yeah. I was glad to be recalled. Arcturus all over."

"That's what I tried to tell them." Arcturus wasn't a regular stop any more, not since a ship landed and found every human artistically dismembered. "You're just sightseeing?"

"This has always been one of my favorite planets."

"Nothing to do."

"Not for you city boys. The fishing is great, though."

Ah ha. "Ocean fishing?"

"Best in the Confederación."

"I might give it a try. Where do you get a boat?"

He smiled and looked directly at me. "Little coastal village, Pa'an!al."

Smack in the middle of the tribal territory I'd be dickering for. I dutifully repeated the information into my ring.

I changed the subject and we talked about nothing for a while. Then I excused myself, saying I was time-lagging and had to get some sleep. Which was true enough, since the shuttle had stayed on Armpit time, and I was eight hours out of phase with III. But I bounced straight to the Hartford courier's office.

The courier on duty was Estelle Dorring, whom I knew slightly. I cut short the pleasantries. "How long to get a message to Earth?"

She studied the clocks on the wall. "You're out of luck if you want it hand-carried. I'm not going to Armpit until tomorrow. Two days on the shuttle and I'll miss the Earth run by half a day.

"If broadcast is all right, you can beam to Armpit and the courier there can take it on the Twosday run. That leaves in seventy-two minutes. Call it nineteen minutes' beam time. You know what you want to say?"

"Yeah. Set it up." I sat down at the customers' console.

STARLODGE LIMITED
642 EASTRIVER
NEW YORK, NEW YORK 100992
ATTENTION: PATRICE DUVAL

YOU MAY HAVE SOME COMPETITION HERE. NOTHING OPEN YET BUT A GUY WE CALL PETER RABBIT IS ON THE SCENE. CHECK INTERPRETERS GUILD AND SEE WHO'S PAYING PETER LAFITTE. CHANGE TERMS OF SALE? PLEASE REPLY NEXT SAMMLER RUN— RICARDO NAVARRO/RM 2048/MOROCHO HILTON

I wasn't sure what good the information would do me, unless they also found out how much he was offering and authorized me to outbid him. At any rate, I wouldn't hear for three days, earliest. Sleep.

Morocho III—its real name is !ka'al—rides a slow sweeping orbit around Morocho A, the brighter of the two suns that make up the Morocho system (Morocho A is a close double star itself, but its white dwarf companion hugs so close that it's lost in the glare). At this time of day, Morocho B was visible low in the sky, a hard blue diamond too bright to stare at, and A was right overhead, a bloated golden ball. On the sandy beach below us the flyer cast two shadows, dark blue and faint yellow, which raced to come together as we landed.

Pa'an!al is a fishing village thousands of years old, on a natural harbor formed where a broad jungle river flows into the sea. Here on the beach were only a few pole huts with thatched roofs, where the fishers who worked the surf and shallow pools lived. Pa'an!al proper was behind a high stone wall, which protected it on one side from the occasional hurricane and on the other from the interesting fauna of the jungle.

I paid off my driver and told him to come back at second sundown. I took a deep breath and mounted the steps. There was an open-cage Otis elevator beside the stairs, but people didn't use it, only fish.

The !tang are compulsive about geometry. This wall was a precise 1:2 rectangle, and the stairs mounted from one corner to the opposite in a satisfyingly Euclidian 30 degrees. A guardrail would have spoiled the harmony. The stairs were just wide enough for two !tang to pass, and the rise of each step was a good half meter. By the time I got to the top I was both tired and slightly terrified.

A spacefaring man shouldn't be afraid of heights, and I'm not, so long as I'm in a vehicle. But when I attained the top of the wall and looked down the equally long and perilous flight of stairs to ground level, I almost swooned. Why couldn't they simply have left a door in the wall?

I sat there for a minute and looked down at the small city. The geometric regularity *was* pleasing. Each building was either a cube or a stack of cubes, and the rock from which the city was built had been carefully sorted, so that each building was a uniform shade. They went from white marble through sandy yellow and salmon to pearly gray and obsidian. The streets were a regular matrix of red brick. I walked down, hugging the wall.

At the bottom of the steps a !tang sat on a low bench, watching the nonexistent traffic. —Greetings, I clicked and snorted at him. —It certainly is a pleasant day.

—Not everywhere, he grunted and wheezed back. An unusually direct response.

—Are you waiting for me?

—Who can say? I am waiting. His trunk made a philosophical

circle in the air. —If you had not come, who knows for what I would have been waiting?

—Well, that's true. He made a circle in the other direction, which I think meant What else? I stood there for a minute while he looked at me or the ground or the sky. You could never tell.

—I hope this isn't a rude question, he said. —Will you forgive me if this is a rude question?

—I certainly will try.

—Is your name !ica'o *va!o?

That was admirably close. —It certainly is.

—You could follow me. He got up. —Or enjoy the pleasant day.

I followed him closely down the narrow street. If he got in a crowd I'd lose him for sure. I couldn't tell an estrus-four female from a neuter, not having sonar (they tell each other apart by sensing body cavities, very romantic).

We went through the center of town, where the well and the market square were. A few dozen !tang bargained over food, craft items, or abstractions. They were the most mercantile race on the planet, although they had sidestepped the idea of money in favor of labor equivalence: for those two ugly fish I will trade you an original sonnet about your daughter and three vile limericks for your next affinity-group meeting. Four limericks, tops.

We went into a large white building that might have been City Hall. It was evidently guarded, at least symbolically, since two !tang stood by the door with their arms exposed.

It was a single large room similar to a Terran mosque, with a regular pattern of square columns holding up the ceiling. The columns supported shelving in neat squares, up to about two meters; on the shelves were neat stacks of accordion-style books. Although the ceiling had inset squares of glass that gave adequate light, there was a strong smell of burnt fish oil, which meant the building was used at night. (We had introduced them to electricity, but they used it only for heavy machinery and toys.)

The !tang led me to the farthest corner, where a large haystack was bent over a book, scribbling. They had to read or write with their heads a few centimeters from the book, since their light-eyes were only good for close work.

—It has happened as you foretold, Uncle.

Not too amazing a prophecy, as I'd sent a messenger over yesterday.

Uncle waved his nose in my direction. —Are you the same one who came four days ago?

—No. I have never been to this place. I am Ricardo Navarro, from the Starlodge tribe.

—I grovel in embarrassment. Truly it is difficult to tell one human from another. To my poor eyes you look exactly like Peter Lafitte.

(Peter Rabbit is bald and ugly, with terrible ears. I have long curly hair with only a trace of gray, and women have called me attractive.) —Please do not be embarrassed. This is often true when different peoples meet. Did my brother say what tribe he represented?

—I die. O my hair falls out and my flesh rots and my bones are cracked by the hungry ta!a'an. He drops me behind him all around the forest and nothing will grow where his excrement from my marrow falls. As the years pass the forest dies from the poison of my remains. The soil washes into the sea and poisons the fish, and all die. O the embarrassment.

—He didn't say?

—He did but said not to tell you.

That was that. —Did he by some chance say he was interested in the small morsel of land I mentioned to you by courier long ago?

—No, he was not interested in the land.

—Can you tell me what he was interested in?

—He was interested in *buying* the land.

Verbs. —May I ask a potentially embarrassing question?

He exposed his arms. —We are businessmen.

—What were the terms of his offer?

—I die. I breathe in and breathe in and cannot exhale. I explode all over my friends. They forget my name and pretend it is dung. They wash off in the square and the well becomes polluted. All die. O the embarrassment.

—He said not to tell me?

—That's right.

—Did you agree to sell him the land?

—That is a difficult question to answer.

—Let me rephrase the question: is it possible that you might sell the land to my tribe?

—It is possible, if you offer better terms. But only possible, in any case.

—This is embarrassing. I, uh, die and, um, the last breath from my lungs is a terrible acid. It melts the seaward wall of the city and a hurricane comes and washes it away. All die. O the embarrassment.

—You're much better at that than he was.

—Thank you. But may I ask you to amplify as to the possibility?

—Certainly. Land is not a fish or an elevator. Land is something that keeps you from falling all the way down. It gives the sea a shore and makes the air stop. Do you understand?

—So far. Please continue.

—Land is time, but not in a mercantile sense. I can say "In return for the time it takes me to decide which one of you is the guilty party, you must give me such-and-so." But how can I say "In return for the land I am standing on you must give me this-and-that"? Nobody can step off the time, you see, but I can step off the land, and then what is it? Does it even exist? In a mercantile sense? These questions and corollaries to them have been occupying some of our finest minds ever since your courier came long ago.

—May I make a suggestion?

—Please do. Anything might help.

—Why not just sell it to the tribe that offers the most?

—No, you don't see. Forgive me, you Terrans are very simpleminded people, for all your marvelous Otis elevators and starships (this does not embarrass me to say because it is meant to help you understand yourself; if you were !tang you would have to pay for it). You see, there are three mercantile classes. Things and services may be of no worth, of measurable worth, or of infinite worth. Land has never been classified before, and it may belong in any of the categories.

—But Uncle! The Lafitte and I have offered to buy the land. Surely that eliminates the first class.

—O you poor Terran. I would hate to see you try to buy a fish. You must think of all the implications.

—I die. I, uh, have a terrible fever in my head and it gets hotter and hotter until my head is a fire, a forge, a star. I set the world on fire and everybody dies. O the embarrassment. What implications?

—Here is the simplest. If the land has finite value, when at best all it does is keep things from falling all the way down, how

66

much is air worth? Air is necessary for life, and it makes fires burn. If you pay for land do you think we should let you have air for free?

—An interesting point, I said, thinking fast and !tangly. —But you have answered it yourself. Since air is necessary for life, it is of infinite value, and not even one breath can be paid for with all the riches of the universe.

—O poor one, how can you have gotten through life without losing your feet? Air would be of infinite worth thus only if *life* were of infinite worth, and even so little as I know of your rich and glorious history proves conclusively that you place very little value on life. Other people's lives, at any rate. Sad to say, our own history contains a similarly bonehungry period.

—Neither are we that way now, Uncle.

—I die. My brain turns to maggots. . . .

I talked with Uncle for an hour or so but got nothing out of it save a sore soft palate. When I got back to the hotel there was a message from Peter Lafitte, asking whether I would like to join him at Antoine's for dinner. No, I would not *like* to, but under the circumstances it seemed prudent. I had to rent a formal tunic from the bellbot.

Antoine's has all the *joie de vivre* of a frozen halibut, which puts it on a par with every other French restaurant off Earth. We started with an artichoke vinaigrette that should have been left to rot in the hydroponics tank. Then a filet of "beef" from some local animal that I doubt was even warm-blooded. All this served by a waiter who was a Canadian with a fake Parisian accent.

But we also had a bottle of phony Pouilly-Fuissé followed by a bottle of ersatz Burgundy followed by a bottle of synthetic Château-d'Yquem. Then they cleared the table and set a bottle of brandy between us, and the real duel began. Short duel, it turned out.

"So how long is your vacation going to last?" I made a gesture that was admirably economical. "Not long at these prices."

"Well, there's always Slim Joan's." He poured himself a little brandy and me a lot. "How about yourself?"

"Ran into a snag," I said. "Have to wait until I hear from Earth."

"They're not easy to work with, are they?"

"Terrans? I'm one myself."

"The !tang, I mean." He stared into his glass and swirled the liquor. "Terrans as well, though. Could I set to you a hypothetical proposition?"

"My favorite kind," I said. The brandy stung my throat.

"Suppose you were a peaceable sort of fellow."

"I am." Slightly fuzzy, but peaceable.

"And you were on a planet to make some agreement with the natives."

I nodded seriously.

"Billions of bux involved. Trillions."

"That would really be something," I said.

"Yeah. Now further suppose that there's another Terran on this planet who, uh, is seeking to make the same sort of agreement."

"Must happen all the time."

"For trillions, Dick? Trillions?"

"Hyp'thetical trillions." Bad brandy, but strong.

"Now the people who are employing you are ab-solute-ly ruthless."

"*Ma!ryso'ta,*" I said, the !tang word for "bonehungry." Close to it, anyhow.

"That's right." He was starting to blur. More wine than I'd thought. "Stop at nothing. Now how would you go about warning the other Terran?"

My fingers were icy cold and the sensation was crawling toward my elbows. My chin slipped off my hand and my head was so heavy I could hardly hold it up. I stared at the two fuzzy images across the table. "Peter." The words came out slowly, and then not at all: "You aren't drinking. . . ."

"Terrible brandy, isn't it." My vision went away, although it felt as if my eyes were still open. I heard my chin hit the table.

"Waiter?" I heard the man come over and make sympathetic noises. "My friend has had a little too much to drink. Would you help me get him to the bellbot?" I couldn't even feel them pick me up. "I'll take this brandy. He might want some in the morning." Jolly.

I finally lapsed into unconsciousness while we were waiting for the elevator, the bellbot lecturing me about temperance.

I woke up the next afternoon on the cold tile floor of my suite's bathroom. I felt like I had been taken apart by an expert surgeon and reassembled by an amateur mechanic. I looked at the tile for a long time. Then I sat for a while and studied the interesting blotches of color floating between my eyes and my brain. When I thought I could survive it, I stood up and took four Hangaways.

I sat and started counting. Hangaways hit you like a pile driver. At eighty the adrenaline shock came. Tunnel vision and millions of tiny needles being pushed out through your skin. Rivers of sweat. Cathedral bells tolling, your head the clapper. Then the dry heaves and it was over.

I staggered to the phone and ordered some clear soup and a couple of cold beers. Then I stood in the shower and contemplated suicide. By the time the soup came I was contemplating homicide.

The soup stayed down and by the second beer I was feeling almost human. Neanderthal, anyhow. I made some inquiries. Lafitte had checked out. No shuttle had left, so he was either still on the planet or he had his own ship, which was possible if he was working for the outfit I suspected he was working for. I invoked the holy name of Hartford, trying to find out to whom his expenses had been billed. Cash.

I tried to order my thoughts. If I reported Lafitte's action to the Guild he would be disbarred. Either he didn't care, because They were paying him enough to retire in luxury—for which I knew he had a taste—or he actually thought I was not going to get off the planet alive. I discarded the dramatic second notion. Last night he could have more easily killed me than warned me. Or had he actually *tried* to kill me, the talk just being insurance in case I didn't ingest a fatal dose? I had no idea what the poison could have been. That sort of knowledge isn't relevant to my line of work.

I suppose the thoroughly rational thing would have been to sit tight and let him have the deal. The fortunes of Starlodge were infinitely less important to me than my skin. He could probably offer more than I, anyhow.

The phone chimed. I thumbed the vision button and a tiny haystack materialized over the end table.

—Greetings. How is the weather?

—Indoors, it's fine. Are you Uncle?

—Not now. Inside the Council Building I am Uncle.

—I see. Can I perform some worthless service for you?

—For yourself, perhaps.

—Pray continue.

—Our Council is meeting with the Lafitte this evening, with the hope of resolving this question about the mercantile nature of land. I would be embarrassed if you did not come too. The meeting will be at *ala'ang in the Council Building.

—I would not cause you embarrassment. But could it possibly be postponed?

He exposed his arms. —We are meeting.

He disappeared and I spent a few minutes translating *ala'ang into human time. The !tang divide their day into a complicated series of varying time intervals depending on the position of the suns and state of appetite and estrous condition. Came to a little before ten o'clock, plenty of time.

I could report Lafitte, and probably should, but decided I'd be safer not doing so, retaining the threat of exposure for use as a weapon. I wrote a brief description of the situation—and felt a twinge of fear on writing the word "Syndicate"—and sealed it in an envelope. I wrote the address of the Hartford Translators' Guild across the seal and bounced up to the courier's office.

Estelle Dorring stared at me when I walked into the office. "Ricardo! You look like a corpse warmed over."

"Rough night," I said. "Touch of food poisoning."

"I never eat that Tang stuff."

"Good policy." I set the envelope in front of her. "I'm not sure whether to send this or not. If I don't come get it before the next shuttle, take it to Armpit and give it to the next Earth courier."

She nodded slowly and read the address. "Why so mysterious?"

"Just a matter of Guild ethics. I wanted to write it down while it was still fresh. Uh . . ." I'd never seen a truly penetrating stare before. "But I might have more information tonight that would invalidate it."

"If you say so, Ricardo." She slipped the envelope into a drawer. I backed out, mumbling something inane.

Down to Slim Joan's for a sandwich of stir-fried vegetables in Syrian bread. Slightly rancid and too much curry, but I didn't dare go to the Council meeting on an empty stomach; !tang sonar would scan it and they would make a symbolic offer of bread, which couldn't be refused. Estelle was partly right about "Tang" food: one bite of the bread contained enough mescaline to make you see interesting things for hours. I'd had enough of that for a while.

I toyed with the idea of taking a weapon. There was a rental service in the pharmacy, to accommodate the occasional sporting type, and I could pick up a laser or a tranquilizer there. But there would be no way to conceal it from the !tang sonar. Besides, Lafitte wasn't the kind of person who would employ direct violence.

But if it actually were the Syndicate behind Lafitte, they might well have sent more than one person here; they certainly could afford it. A hitter. But then why would Lafitte set up the elaborate poisoning scene? Why not simply arrange an accident?

My feet were taking me toward the pharmacy. Wait. Be realistic. You haven't fired a gun in twenty years. Even then, you couldn't hit the ground with a rock. If it came to a burnout, you'd be the one who got crisped. Better to leave their options open.

I decided to compromise. There was a large clasp knife in my bag; that would at least help me psychologically. I went back up to my room.

I thumbed the lock and realized that the cube I'd heard playing was my own. The door slid open and there was Lafitte, lounging on my sofa, watching an old movie.

"Dick. You're looking well."

"How the hell did you get in here?"

He held up his thumb and stripped a piece of plastic off the fleshy part. "We have our resources." He sat up straight. "I hear you're taking a flyer out to Pa'an!al. Shall we divide the cost?"

There was a bottle of wine in a bucket of ice at his feet. I got a glass out of the bathroom and helped myself. "I suppose you charged this to my room." I turned off the cube.

He shrugged. "You poked me for dinner last night, *mon frère*. Passing out like that."

I raised the glass to my lips, flinched, and set it down untouched. "Speaking of resources, what was in that brandy? And who are these resourceful friends?"

"The wine's all right. You seemed agitated; I gave you a calmative."

"A *horse* calmative! Is it the Syndicate?"

He waved that away. "The Syndicate's a myth. You—"

"Don't take me for an idiot. I've been doing this for almost as long as you have." Every ten years or so there was a fresh debunking. But the money and bodies kept piling up.

"You have indeed." He concentrated on picking at a hangnail. "How much is Starlodge willing to pay?"

I tried not to react. "How much is the Syndicate?"

"If the Syndicate existed," he said carefully, "and if it were they who had retained me, don't you think I would try to use that fact to frighten you away?"

"Maybe not directly . . . last night, you said 'desperate men.' "

"I was drunk." No, not Peter Rabbit, not on a couple of bottles of wine. I just looked at him. "All right," he said, "I was told to use any measures short of violence—"

"Poisoning isn't violence?"

"Tranquilizing, not poisoning. You couldn't have died." He poured himself some wine. "Top yours off?"

"I've become a solitary drinker."

He poured the contents of my glass into his. "I might be able to save you some trouble, if you'll only tell me what terms—"

"A case of Jack Daniels and all they can eat at Slim Joan's."

"That might do it," he said unsmilingly, "but I can offer fifteen hundred shares of Hartford."

That was $150 million, half again what I'd been authorized. "Just paper to them."

"Or a million cases of booze, if that's the way they want it." He checked his watch. "Isn't our flyer waiting?"

I supposed it would be best to have him along, to keep an eye on him. "The one who closes the deal pays for the trip?"

"All right."

On the hour-long flyer ride I considered various permutations of what I could offer. My memory had been jammed with the whole-sale prices of various kinds of machinery, booze, candy, and so forth, along with their mass and volume, so I could add in the shipping costs from Earth to Armpit to Morocho III. Lafitte surely had similar knowledge; I could only hope that his figure of 1500 shares was a bluff.

(I had good incentive to bargain well. Starlodge would give me a bonus of up to 10 percent of the difference between a thousand shares and whatever the settlement came to. If I brought it in at 900, I'd be a millionaire.)

We were turning inland; the walls of the city made a pink rectangle against the towering jungle. I tapped the pilot on the shoulder. "Can you land inside the city?"

"Not unless you want to jump from the top of a building. I can set you on the wall, though." I nodded.

"Can't take the climb, Dick? Getting old?"

"No need to waste steps." The flyer was a little wider than the wall, and it teetered as we stepped out. I tried to look just at my feet.

"Beautiful from up here," Lafitte said. "Look at that sunset." Half the large sun's disk was visible on the jungle horizon, a deeper red than Earth's sun ever shone. The bloody light stained the surf behind us purple. It was already dark in the city below; the smell of rancid fish oil burning drifted up to us.

Lafitte managed to get the inside lane of the staircase. I tried to keep my eyes on him and the wall as we negotiated the high steps.

"Believe me," he said (a phrase guaranteed to inspire trust), "it would make both our jobs easier if I could tell you who I'm representing. But I really am sworn to secrecy."

An oblique threat deserves an oblique answer. "You know I can put you in deep trouble with the Standards Committee. Poisoning a Guild brother."

"Your word against mine. And the bellbot's, the headwaiter's, the wine steward's . . . you did have quite a bit to drink."

"A couple of bottles of wine won't knock me out."

"Your capacity is well known. I don't think you want a hearing investigating it, though, not at your age. Two years till retirement?"

"Twenty months."

"I was rounding off," he said. "Yes, I did check. I wondered whether you might be in the same position as I am. My retirement's less than two months away; this is my last big-money job. So you must understand my enthusiasm."

I didn't answer. He wasn't called Rabbit for lack of "enthusiasm."

As we neared the bottom, he said, "Suppose you weren't to oppose me too vigorously. Suppose I could bring in the contract at a good deal less than—"

"Don't be insulting."

In the dim light from the torches sputtering below, I couldn't read his expression. "Ten percent of my commission wouldn't be insulting."

I stopped short; he climbed down another step. "I can't believe even *you*—"

"*Verdad*. Just joking." He laughed unconvincingly. "Everyone knows how starchy you are, Dick. I know better than most." I'd fined him several times during the years I was head of the Standards Committee.

We walked automatically through the maze of streets, our guides evidently having taken identical routes. Both of us had eidetic memories, of course, that being a minimum prerequisite for the job of interpreter. I was thinking furiously. If I couldn't out-bargain the Rabbit I'd have to somehow finesse him. Was there anything I knew about the !tang value system that he didn't? Assuming that this council would decide that land was something that could be bought and sold.

I did have a couple of interesting proposals in my portfolio, that I'd written up during the two-week trip from Earth. I wondered whether Lafitte had seen them. The lock didn't appear to have been tampered with, and it was the old-fashioned magnetic key type. You can pick it but it won't close afterward.

We turned a corner and there was the Council Building at the end of the street, impressive in the flickering light, its upper reaches lost in darkness. Lafitte put his hand on my arm, stopping. "I've got a proposition."

"Not interested."

"Hear me out, now; this is straight. I'm empowered to take you on as a limited partner."

"How generous. I don't think Starlodge would like it."

"What I *mean* is Starlodge. You hold their power of attorney, don't you?"

"Unlimited, on this planet. But don't waste your breath; we get an exclusive or nothing at all." Actually, the possibility had never been discussed. They couldn't have known I was going into a competitive bidding situation. If they had, they certainly wouldn't have sent me here slow freight. For an extra fifty shares I could have gone first class and been here a week before Peter Rabbit; could have sewn up the thing and been headed home before he got to Armpit.

Starlodge had a knack for picking places that were about to become popular—along with impressive media power, to make sure they did—and on dozens of worlds they did have literally exclusive rights to tourism. Hartford might own a spaceport hotel, but it wasn't really competition, and they were usually glad to hand it over to Starlodge anyhow. Hartford, with its ironclad lock on the tachyon drive, had no need to diversify.

There was no doubt in my mind that this was the pattern Starlodge had in mind for Morocho III. It was a perfect setup, the beach being a geologic anomaly: there wasn't another decent spot for a hotel within two thousand kilometers of the spaceport. Just bleak mountaintops sprouting occasionally out of jungles full of large and hungry animals. But maybe I could lead the Rabbit on. I leaned up against a post that supported a guttering torch. "At any rate, I certainly couldn't consider entering into an agreement without knowing who you represent."

He looked at me stone-faced for a second. "Outfit called A. W. Stoner Industries."

I laughed out loud. "Real name, I mean." I'd never heard of Stoner, and I do keep in touch.

"That's the name I know them by."

"No concern not listed in *Standard, Poor and Tueme* could come up with nine figures for extraterrestrial real-estate speculation. No legitimate concern, I mean."

"There you go again," he said mildly. "I believe they're a coalition of smaller firms."

"I don't. Let's go."

Back in my luggage I had a nasal spray that deadened the sense of smell. Before we even got inside, I knew I should have used it.

The air was gray with fish-oil smoke, and there were more than a hundred !tang sitting in neat rows. I once was treated to a "fish kill" in Texas, where a sudden ecological disaster had resulted in windrows of rotting fish piled up on the beach. This was like walking along that beach using an old sock for a muffler. By Lafitte's expression, he was also unprepared. We both walked forward with slightly greenish cheerfulness.

A !tang in the middle of the first row stood up and approached us. —Uncle? I ventured, and he waved his snout in affirmation.

—We have come to an interim decision, he said.

—Interim? Lafitte said. —Were my terms unacceptable?

—I die. My footprints are cursed. I walk around the village

not knowing that all who cross where I have been will stay in estrous zero, and bear no young. Eventually, all die. O the embarrassment. We want to hear the terms of Navarro's tribe. Then perhaps a final decision may be made.

That was frighteningly direct. I'd tried for an hour to tell him our terms before, but he'd kept changing the subject.

—May I hear the terms of Lafitte's tribe? I asked.

—Certainly. Would Lafitte care to state them, or should I?

—Proceed, Uncle, Lafitte said, and then, in Spanish, —Remember the possibility of a partnership. If we get to haggling . . .

I stopped listening to Rabbit as Uncle began a long litany of groans, creaks, pops, and whistles. I kept a running total of wholesale prices and shipping costs. Bourbon, rum, brandy, gin. Candy bars, raw sugar, honey, pastries. Nets, computers, garbage composters, water-purifying plant, hunting weapons. When he stopped, I had a total of only H620.

—Your offer, Navarro? Could it include these things as a subset?

I had to be careful. Lafitte was probably lying about the 1500, but I didn't want to push him so hard he'd be able to go over a thousand on the next round. And I didn't want to bring out my big guns until the very end.

—I can offer these things and three times the specified quantity of rum—(the largest rum distillery on Earth was a subsidiary of Starlodge) —and furthermore free you from the rigors of the winter harvest, with twenty-six fully programmed mechanical farm laborers. (The winters here were not even cool by Earth standards, but something about the season made the local animals restless enough occasionally to jump over the walls that normally protected farmland.)

—These mechanical workers would not be good to eat? For the animals?

—No, and they would be very hard for the animals even to damage.

There was a lot of whispered conversation. Uncle conferred with the !tang at the front of each row, then returned.

—I die. Before I die my body turns hair-side-in. People come from everywhere to see the insides of themselves. But the sight makes them lose the will, and all die. O the embarrassment. The rum is welcome, but we cannot accept the mechanical workers. When the beast eats someone he sleeps, and can be killed, and eaten in turn. If he does not eat he will search, and in searching destroy crops. This we know to be true.

—Then allow me to triple the quantities of gin, bourbon, and brandy. I will add two tonnes each of vermouth and hydrochloric acid, for flavoring. (That came to about H710.)

—This is gratefully accepted. Does your tribe, Lafitte, care to include these as a subset of your final offer?

—Final offer, Uncle?

—Two legs, two arms, two eyes, two mouths, two offers.

—I die, Lafitte said. —Where they bury me, the ground caves in. It swallows up the city and all die, O the embarrassment. Look, Uncle, that's the market law for material objects. You can't move land around; its ownership is an abstraction.

Uncle exposed one arm—the Council tittered—and reached down and thumped the floor twice. —The land is solid, therefore material. You can move it around with your machines; I myself saw you do this in my youth, when the spaceport was built. The market law applies.

Lafitte smiled slowly. —Then the Navarro's tribe can no longer bid. He's had two.

Uncle turned to the Council and gestured toward Rabbit, and said, —Is he standing on feet? And they cracked and snuffled at the joke. To Lafitte, he said, —The Navarro's offer was rejected, and he made a substitution. Yours was not rejected. Do you care to make his amended offer a subset of yours?

—If mine is rejected, can I amend it?

This brought an even louder reaction. —Poor one, Uncle said. —No feet, no hands. That would be a third offer. You must see that.

—All right. Lafitte began pacing. He said he would start with my amended offer and add the following things. The list was very long. It started with a hydroelectric generator and proceeded with objects of less and less value until he got down to individual bottles of exotic liqueurs. By then I realized he was giving me a message: he was coming down as closely as he could to exactly a thousand shares of Hartford. So we both had the same limit. When he finished he looked right at me and raised his eyebrows.

Victory is sweet. If the Rabbit had bothered to spend a day or two in the marketplace, watching transactions, he wouldn't have tried to defeat me by arithmetic; he wouldn't have tried by accretion to force me into partnership.

Uncle looked at me and bared his arms for a split second. —Your tribe, Navarro? Would you include this offer as a subset of your final offer?

What Rabbit apparently didn't know was that this bargaining by pairs of offers was a formalism: if I did simply add to his last offer, the haggling would start over again, with each of us allowed another pair. And so on and on. I unlocked my briefcase and took out two documents.

—No. I merely wish to add two inducements to my own previous offer (sounds of approval and expectation).

Lafitte stared, his expression unreadable.

—These contracts are in Spanish. Can you read them, Uncle?

—No, but there are two of us who can.

—I know how you like to travel. (I handed him one of the documents.) —This allows each of five hundred !tang a week's vacation on the planet of its choice, any planet where Starlodge has facilities.

"What?" Lafitte said, in English. "How the hell can you do that?"

"Deadheading," I said.

One of the Council abruptly rose. "Pardon me," he said in a weird parody of English. "We have to be dead to take this vacation? That seems of little value."

I was somewhat startled at that, in view of the other inducement I was going to offer. I told him it was an English term that had nothing to do with heads or death. —Most of the Hartford vessels that leave this planet are nearly empty. It is no great material loss to Hartford to take along nonpaying guests, so long as they do not displace regular passengers. And Hartford will ultimately benefit from an increase in tourism to !ka'al, so they were quite willing to make this agreement with my tribe.

—The market value of this could be quite high, Uncle said.

—As much as five or six hundred shares, I said, —depending on how distant each trip is.

—Very well. And what is your other inducement?

—I won't say. (I had to grin.) —It is a gift.

The Council chittered and tweeted in approval. Some even exposed their arms momentarily in a semi-obscene gesture of fellowship. "What kind of game are you playing?" Peter Rabbit said.

"They like surprises and riddles." I made a polite sound requesting attention and said, —There is one thing I will tell you about this gift: It belongs to all three mercantile classes. It is of no value, of finite value, and infinite value, all at once, and to all people.

—When considered as being of finite value, Uncle said, —how much is it worth in terms of Hartford stock?

—Exactly one hundred shares.

He rustled pleasantly at that and went to confer with the others.

"You're pretty clever, Dick," Rabbit said. "What, they don't get to find out what the last thing is unless they accept?"

"That's right. It's done all the time; I was rather surprised that you didn't do it."

He shook his head. "I've only negotiated with !tang off-planet. They've always been pretty conventional."

I didn't ask him about all the fishing he had supposedly done here. Uncle came back and stood in front of us.

—There is unanimity. The land will go to the Navarro's tribe. Now what is the secret inducement, please? How can it be every class at once, to all people?

I paused to parse out the description in !tangish. —Uncle, do you know of the Earth corporation, or tribe, Immortality Unlimited?

—No.

Lafitte made a strange noise. I went on. —This Immortality Unlimited provides a useful service to humans who are apprehensive about death. They offer the possibility of revival. A person who avails himself of this service is frozen solid as soon as possible after death. The tribe promises to keep the body frozen until such time as science discovers a way to revive it.

—The service is expensive. You pay the tribe one full share of Hartford stock. They invest it, and take for themselves one tenth of the income, which is their profit. A small amount is used to keep the body frozen. If and when revival is possible, the person is thawed, and cured of whatever was killing him, and he will be comparatively wealthy.

—This has never been done with nonhumans before, but there is nothing forbidding it. Therefore I purchased a hundred "spaces" for !tang; I leave it to you to decide which hundred will benefit.

—You see, this is of no material value to any living person, because you must die to take advantage of it. However, it is also of finite worth, since each space costs one share of Hartford. It is also of infinite worth, because it offers life beyond death.

The entire Council applauded, a sound like a horde of locusts descending. Peter Rabbit made the noise for attention, and then he made it again, impolitely loud.

—This is all very interesting, and I do congratulate the Navarro for his cleverness. However, the bidding is not over.

There was a low, nervous whirring. "Better apologize first, Rabbit," I whispered.

He bulled ahead. —Let me introduce a new mercantile class: negative value.

"Rabbit, don't—"

—This is an object or service that one does *not* want to have. I will offer not to give it to you if you accept my terms rather than the Navarro's.

—Many kilometers up the river there is a drum full of a very powerful poison. If I touch the button that opens it, all of the fish in the river, and for a great distance out into the sea, will die. You will have to move or. . . . He trailed off.

One by one, single arms snaked out, each holding a long sharp knife.

"Poison again, Rabbit? You're getting predictable in your old age."

"Dick," he said hoarsely, "they're completely nonviolent. Aren't they?"

"Except in matters of trade." Uncle was the last one to produce a knife. They moved toward us very slowly. "Unless you do something fast, I think you're about to lose your feet."

"My God! I thought that was just an expression."

"I think you better start apologizing. Tell them it was a joke."

—I die! he shouted, and they stopped advancing. —I, um . . .

—You play a joke on your friends and it backfires, I said in Greek.

Rapidly: —I play a joke on my good friends and it backfires. I, uh . . . "Christ, Dick, help me."

"Just tell the truth and embroider it a little. They know about negative value, but it's an obscenity."

—I was employed by . . . a tribe that did not understand mercantilism. They asked me, of all things, to introduce terms of negative value into a trivial transaction. My friends know I must be joking and they laugh. They laugh so much they forget to eat. All die. O the embarrassment.

Uncle made a complicated pass with his knife and it disappeared into his haybale fur. All the other knives remained in evidence, and the !tang moved into a circle around us.

—This machine in your pocket, Uncle said, —it is part of the joke?

Lafitte pulled out a small gray box. —It is. Do you want it?

—Put it on the floor. The fun would be complete if you stayed here while the Navarro took one of your marvelous floaters up the river. How far would he have to go to find the rest of the joke?

—About twelve kilometers. On an island in midstream.

Uncle turned to me and exposed his arms briefly. —Would you help us with our fun?

The air outside was sweet and pure. I decided to wait a few hours, for light.

That was some years ago, but I still remember vividly going into the Council Building the next day. Uncle had divined that Peter Rabbit was getting hungry, and they'd filled him up with !tang bread. When I came in, he was amusing them with impersonations of various Earth vegetables. The effect on his metabolism was not permanent, but when he left Morocho III he was still having mild attacks of cabbageness.

By the time I retired from Hartford, Starlodge had finished its hotel and sports facility on the beach. I was the natural choice to manage it, of course, and though I was wealthy enough not to need employment, I took the job with enthusiasm.

I even tried to hire Lafitte as an assistant—people who can handle !tangish are rare—but he had dropped out of sight. Instead, I found a young husband-and-wife team who have so much energy that I hardly have to work at all.

I'm not crazy enough to go out in the woods, hunting. But I do spend a bit of time fishing off the dock, usually with Uncle, who has also retired. Together we're doing a book that I think will help our two cultures understand one another. The human version is called *Hard Bargain*.

Almost nobody, including me, pronounces the "!" in "!tang" properly; it's a glottal click, as used in Bantu and other African languages. (If you were a folksong fan in the sixties, you might remember Miriam Makeba using the sound in her delightful performances.) In fact, the only stranger who ever did it properly was a Soviet critic who came up to me at a meeting in Moscow and said, "Ah, Mr. Haldeman—I just read 'A !Tangled Web.' Very interesting," and walked away with a mysterious smile.

This was only a couple of months after the story had appeared in *Analog*, a rather capitalistic magazine, the possession of which supposedly is illegal in the Soviet Union.

So the story of that story ends in a foreign country, and the story of the next begins in one. My wife and I were marooned in a hotel room in Tangier, Morocco: poleaxed by dysentery. The morbid thought came to me that if we should die there, the friendly concierge would probably just empty our pockets and sell our luggage and make our bodies disappear—it was a real classy hotel— and nobody would ever find out what had happened to us. Tangier is that kind of city; the guidebooks had warned us not to stop there, just get on the first train and head south.

A writer to the grisly end, though, I proceeded to make up a story out of that particular misery. I scribbled down a rough outline of it in my travel diary and that was the end of it for several years. (The story wouldn't take place in Morocco—I saved that setting for a more specifically Moroccan story, "Lindsay and the Red City Blues"—but rather in Mexico, for reasons that will become clear.)

Story notions like that sit on the back burner until some specific stimulus tells you it's time for them to be written. In this case the stimulus was a fascinating book I came across while browsing in the biography section of the local library: the diary of the wife of the American ambassador to Mexico in the years just preceding the Mexican War. It hit the period and the location of the story precisely and was a gold mine of detailed day-to-day mundania. The woman was a good writer possessed of, or by, a voracious curiosity about this exotic foreign land, and she wrote not only about the upper-crust activities that her position required her to attend but also about the middle class and *peones*. I consumed the large book in two days of delighted reading, taking a few notes as to prices of things, menus, and so forth, but mainly just getting a feel for the period.

I wanted the main character to be an uneducated but intelligent

American roughneck, which generated a problem in diction. I know how such a person would talk nowadays, but what would his speech have been like more than a hundred years ago? Dictionaries of slang don't always give date references, and to my knowledge there doesn't exist a slang dictionary that is specifically organized chronologically. (What a fascinating project that would be!) So I made my own, in a limited way, leafing through several dictionaries that did give date references for some of their slang, cant, and jargon; collecting a couple of hundred words and phrases that this character would be likely to use. (I came across dozens of expressions I couldn't use because, although they were contemporary with the story, they sounded too modern. He could call a policeman a pig, for example, or use the expression "take a back seat to.")

Then I just sat down and started writing. As happens too rarely, the story took on a life of its own, and proceeded to write itself. I hope you enjoy reading it half as much as I enjoyed writing it.

MANIFEST

DESTINY

This is the story of John Leroy Harris, but I doubt that name means much to you unless you're pretty old, especially an old lawman. He's dead anyhow, thirty years now, and nobody left around that could get hurt with this story. The fact is, I would've told it a long time ago, but when I was younger it would have bothered me, worrying about what people would think. Now I just don't care. The hell with it.

I've been on the move ever since I was a lad. At thirteen I put a knife in another boy and didn't wait around to see if he lived, just went down to the river and worked my way to St. Louis, got in some trouble there and wound up in New Orleans a few years later. That's where I came to meet John Harris.

Now you wouldn't tell from his name (he'd changed it a few times) but John was pure Spanish blood, as his folks had come from Spain before the Purchase. John was born in Natchitoches in 1815, the year of the Battle of New Orleans. That put him thirteen years older than me, so I guess he was about thirty when we met.

I was working as a greeter, what we called a "bouncer," in Mrs. Carranza's whorehouse down by the docks. Mostly I just sat around and looked big, which I was then and no fat, but sometimes I did have to calm down a customer or maybe throw him out, and I kept under my weskit a Starr pepperbox derringer in case of real trouble. It was by using this weapon that I made the acquaintance of John Harris.

Harris had been in the bar a few times, often enough for me to notice him, but to my knowledge he never put the boots to any of the women. Didn't have to pay for it, I guess; he was a handsome cuss, more than six feet tall, slender, with this kind of tragic look that women seem to like. Anyhow it was a raw rainy night in November, cold the way noplace else quite gets cold, and this customer comes downstairs complaining that the girl didn't do what he had asked her to, and he wasn't going to pay the extra. The kate came down right behind him and told me what it was, and that she had too done it, and he hadn't said nothing about it when they started, and you can take my word for it that it was something nasty.

Well, we had some words about that and he tried to walk out without paying, so I sort of brought him back in and emptied out his pockets. He didn't even have the price of a drink on him (he'd given Mrs. Carranza the two dollars but that didn't get you anything fancy). He did have a nice overcoat, though, so I took that from him and escorted him out into the rain head first.

What happened was about ten or fifteen minutes later he barges back in, looking like a drowned dog but with a Navy Colt in each hand. He got off two shots before I blew his brains out (pepperbox isn't much of a pistol but he wasn't four yards away) and a split second later another bullet takes him in the lungs. I turned around and everybody was on the floor or behind the bar but John Harris, who was still perched on a stool looking sort of interested and putting some kind of foreign revolver back into his pocket.

The cops came soon enough but there was no trouble, not with forty witnesses, except for what to do with the dead meat. He didn't have any papers and Mrs. Carranza didn't want to pay the city for the burial. I was for just taking it out back and dropping it in the water, but they said that was against the law and unsanitary. John Harris said he had a wagon and come morning he'd take care of the matter. He signed a paper and that satisfied them.

First light, Harris showed up in a fancy landau. Me and the driver, an old black, we wrestled the wrapped-up corpse into the back of the carriage. Harris asked me to come along and I did.

We just went east a little ways and rolled the damned thing into a bayou, let the gators take it. Then the driver smoked a pipe while Harris and me talked for a while.

Now he did have the damnedest way of talking. His English was like nothing you ever heard—Spanish his mother tongue and then he learned most of his English in Australia—but that's not what I really mean. I mean that if he wanted you to do something and you didn't want to do it, you had best put your fingers in your ears and start walking away. That son of a gun could sell water to a drowning man.

He started out asking me questions about myself, and eventually we got to talking about politics. Turns out we both felt about the same way towards the U.S. government, which is to say the hell with it. Harris wasn't even really a citizen, and I myself didn't exist. For good reasons there was a death certificate on me in St. Louis, and I had a couple of different sets of papers a fellow on Bourbon Street printed up for me.

Harris had noticed that I spoke some Spanish—Mrs. Carranza was Mexican and so were most of her kates—and he got around to asking whether I'd like to take a little trip to Mexico. I told him that sounded like a really bad idea.

This was late 1844, and that damned Polk had just been elected promising to annex Texas. The Mexicans had been skirmishing with Texas for years, and they said it would be war if they got statehood. The man in charge was that one-legged crazy greaser Santa Anna, who'd been such a gentleman at the Alamo some years before. I didn't fancy being a gringo stuck in that country when the shooting started.

Well, Harris said I hadn't thought it through. It was true there was going to be a war, he said, but the trick was to get in there early enough to profit from it. He asked whether I'd be interested in getting ten percent of ten thousand dollars. I told him I could feel my courage returning.

Turns out Harris had joined the army a couple of years before and got himself into the quartermaster business, the ones who shuffle supplies back and forth. He had managed to slide five hundred rifles and a big batch of ammunition into a warehouse in New Orleans. The army thought they were stored in Kentucky and the man who rented out the warehouse thought they were farming tools. Harris got himself discharged from the army and eventually got in touch with one General Parrodi, in Tampico. Parrodi agreed to buy the weapons and pay for them in gold.

The catch was that Parrodi also wanted the services of three Americans, not to fight but to serve as "interpreters"—that is to say, spies—for as long as the war lasted. We would be given Mexican citizenship if we wanted it, and a land grant, but for our own protection we'd be treated as prisoners while the war was going on. (Part of the deal was that we would eavesdrop on other prisoners.) Harris showed me a contract that spelled all of this out, but I couldn't read Spanish back then. Anyhow I was no more inclined to trust Mexicans in such matters than I was Americans, but as I say Harris could sell booze to a Baptist.

The third American was none other than the old buck who was driving, a runaway slave from Florida name of Washington. He had grown up with Spanish masters, and not as a field hand but as some kind of a butler. He had more learning than I did and could speak Spanish like a grandee. In Mexico, of course, there wasn't any slavery, and he reckoned a nigger with gold and land was just as good as anybody else with gold and land.

Looking back I can see why Washington was willing to take the risk, but I was a damned fool to do it. I was no rough neck but I'd seen some violence in my seventeen years; that citizen we'd dumped in the bayou wasn't the first man I had to kill. You'd think I'd know better than to put myself in the middle of a war. Guess I was too young to take dying seriously—and a thousand dollars was real money back then.

We went back into town and Harris took me to the warehouse. What he had was fifty long blue boxes stenciled with the name of a hardware outfit, and each one had ten Hall rifles, brand new in a mixture of grease and sawdust.

(This is why the Mexicans were right enthusiastic. The Hall was a flintlock, at least these were, but it was also a breech-loader. The old muzzle-loaders that most soldiers used, Mexican and American, took thirteen separate steps to reload. Miss one step and it can take your face off. Also, the Hall used inter-changeable parts, which meant you didn't have to find a smith when it needed repairing.)

Back at the house I told Mrs. Carranza I had to quit and would get a new boy for her. Then Harris and me had a steak and put ourselves outside of a bottle of sherry, while he filled me in on the details of the operation. He'd put considerable money into buying discretion from a dockmaster and a Brit packet captain. This packet was about the only boat that put into Tampico from New Orleans on anything like a regular basis, and Harris had the idea that smuggling guns wasn't too much of a novelty to the captain. The next Friday night we were going to load the stuff onto the packet, bound south the next morning.

The loading went smooth as cream, and the next day we boarded the boat as paying passengers, Washington supposedly belonging to Harris and coming along as his manservant. At first it was right pleasant, slipping through a hundred or so miles of bayou country. But the Gulf of Mexico ain't the Mississippi, and after a couple of hours of that I was sick from my teeth to my toenails, and stayed that way for days. Captain gave me a mixture of brandy and seawater, which like to killed me. Harris thought that was funny, but the humor wore off some when we put into Tampico and him and Washington had to off-load the cargo without much help from me.

We went on up to Parrodi's villa and found we might be out of a job. While we were on that boat there had been a revolution. Santa Anna got kicked out, having pretty much emptied the treasury, and now the *moderado* Herrera was in charge. Parrodi and Harris argued for a long time. The Mexican was willing to pay for the rifles, but he figured that half the money was for our service as spies.

They finally settled on eight thousand, but only if we would stay in Tampico for the next eighteen months, in case a war did start. Washington and I would get fifty dollars a month for walking-around money.

The next year was the most boring year of my life. After New Orleans, there's just not much you could say about Tampico. It's an old city but also brand new. Pirates burnt it to the ground a couple of hundred years ago. Santa Anna had it rebuilt in the twenties, and it was still not much more than a garrison town when we were there. Most of the houses were wood, imported in pieces from the States and nailed together. Couple of whorehouses and cantinas downtown, and you can bet I spent a lot of time and fifty bucks a month down there.

Elsewhere, things started to happen in the spring. The U.S. Congress went along with Polk and voted to annex Texas, and Mexico broke off diplomatic relations and declared war, but Washington didn't seem to take notice. Herrera must have had his hands full with the Carmelite Revolution, though things were quiet in Tampico for the rest of the year.

I got to know Harris pretty well. He spent a lot of time teaching me to read and write Spanish—though I never could talk it without sounding like a gringo—and I can tell you he was hellfire as a teacher. The schoolmaster used to whip me when I was a kid, but that was easier to take than Harris's tongue. He could make you feel about six inches tall. Then a few minutes later you get a verb right and you're a hero.

We'd also go into the woods outside of town and practice with the pistol and rifle. He could do some awesome things with a Colt. He taught me how to throw a knife and I taught him how to use a lasso.

We got into a kind of routine. I had a room with the Galvez family downtown. I'd get up pretty late mornings and peg away at my Spanish books. About midday Harris would come down (he was staying up at the General's place) and give me my daily dose of sarcasm. Then we'd go down to a cantina and have lunch, usually with Washington. Afternoons, when most of the town napped, we might go riding or shooting in the woods south of town. We kept the Galvez family in meat that way, getting a boar or a deer every now and then. Since I was once a farm boy I knew how to dress out animals and how to smoke or salt meat to keep it. Sra. Galvez always deducted the value of the meat from my rent.

Harris spent most evenings up at the villa with the officers, but sometimes he'd come down to the cantinas with me and drink pulque with the off-duty soldiers, or sometimes just sit around the kitchen table with the Galvez family. They took a shine to him.

He was really taken with old Doña Dolores, who claimed to be over a hundred years old and from Spain. She wasn't a relative but had been a friend of Sra. Galvez's grandmother. Anyhow she also claimed to be a witch, a white witch who could heal and predict things and so forth.

If Harris had a weakness it was superstition. He always wore a lucky gold piece on a thong around his neck and carried an Indian finger bone in his pocket. And though he could swear the bark off a tree he never used the names of God or Jesus, and when somebody else did he always crossed the fingers of his left hand. Even though he laughed at religion and I never saw him go in a church. So he was always asking Dolores about this or that, and always ready to listen to her stories. She only had a couple dozen but they kept changing.

Now I never thought that Dolores wasn't straight. If she wasn't a witch she sure as hell *thought* she was. And she did heal, with her hands and with herbs she picked in the woods. She healed me of the grippe and a rash I picked up from one of the girls. But I didn't believe in spells or fortune-telling, not then. When anybody's eighteen he's a smart Alec and knows just how the world works. I'm not so sure anymore, especially with what happened to Harris.

Every week or so we got a newspaper from Monterrey. By January I could read it pretty well, and looking back I guess you could say it was that month the war really started, though it would be spring before any shots were fired. What happened was that Polk sent some four thousand troops into what he claimed was part of Texas. The general was Zach Taylor, who was going to be such a crackajack president a few years later. Herrera seemed about to make a deal with the States, so he got booted out and they put Paredes in office. The Mexicans started building up an army in Monterrey, and it looked like we were going to earn our money after all.

I was starting to get a little nervous. You didn't have to look too hard at the map to see that Tampico was going to get trouble. If the U.S. wanted to take Mexico City they had the choice of marching over a couple thousand miles of mountains and desert, or taking a Gulf port and only marching a couple hundred miles. Tampico and Vera Cruz were about the same distance from Mexico City, but Vera Cruz had a fort protecting it. All we had was us.

Since the Civil War, nobody remembers much about the Mexican one. Well, the Mexicans were in such bad shape even Taylor could beat them. The country was flat broke. Their regular army had more officers than men. They drafted illiterate Indians and *mestizos* and herded them by the thousands into certain death from American artillery and cavalry—some of them had never even fired a shot before they got into battle. That was Santa Anna economizing. He could've lost that war even if Mexico had all the armies of Europe combined.

Now we thought we'd heard the last of that one-legged son of a bitch. When we got to Tampico he'd just barely got out of Mexico with his skin, exiled to Cuba. But he got back, and he damn near killed me and Harris with his stupidity. And he did kill Washington, just as sure as if he pulled the trigger.

In May of that year Taylor had a show-down up by Mata-
moros, and Polk got around to declaring war. We started seeing
American boats all the time, going back and forth out of cannon
range, blockading the port. It was nervous-making. The soldiers
were fit to be tied—but old Dolores said there was nothing to
worry about. Said she'd be able to "see" if there was going to be
fighting, and she didn't see anything. This gave Harris considerable more comfort than it gave me.

What we didn't find out until after the war was that Santa
Anna got in touch with the United States and said he could get
Mexico to end the war, give up Texas and California and for all
I know the moon. Polk, who must have been one fine judge of
character, gave Santa Anna safe passage through the American
blockade.

Well, in the meantime the people in Mexico City had gotten
a belly full of Paredes, who had a way of getting people he dis-
agreed with shot, and they kicked him out. Santa Anna limped
in and they made him president. He doublecrossed Polk, got together another twenty thousand soldiers, and got ready to head
north and kick the stuffing out of the gringos.

Now you figure this one out. The Mexicans intercepted a
message to the American naval commander, telling him to take
Tampico. What did Santa Anna do? He ordered Parrodi to desert
the place.

I was all for the idea myself, and so were a lot of the soldiers,
but the General was considerable upset. It was bad enough that
he couldn't stand and fight, but on top of that he didn't have near
enough mules and horses to move out all the supplies they had
stockpiled there.

Well, we sure as hell were going to take care of *our* supplies.
Harris had a buckboard and we'd put a false bottom under the
seat. Put our money in there and the papers that identified us
as loyal Americans. In another place we put our Mexican citizenship papers and the deeds to our land grant, up in the Mesilla
Valley. Then we drew weapons from the armory and got ready
to go up to San Luis Potosí with a detachment that was leaving
in the morning.

I was glad we wouldn't be in Tampico when the American
fleet rolled in, but then San Luis Potosí didn't sound like any
picnic either. Santa Anna was going to be getting his army to-

gether there, and it was only a few hundred miles from Taylor's army. One or the other of them would probably want to do something with all those soldiers.

Harris was jumpy. He kept putting his hand in his pocket to rub that Indian bone. That night, before he went up to the villa, he came to the hacienda with me, and told Dolores he'd had a bad premonition about going to San Luis Potosí. He asked her to tell his fortune and tell him flat out if he was going to die. She said she couldn't tell a man when he was going to die, even when she saw it. If she did her powers would go away. But she would tell his fortune.

She studied his hands for a long time, without saying anything. Then she took out a shabby old deck of cards and dealt some out in front of him, face up. (They weren't regular cards. They had faded pictures of devils and skeletons and so forth.)

Finally she told him not to worry. He was not going to die in San Luis. In fact, he would not die in Mexico at all. That was plain.

Now I wish I had Harris's talent for shucking off worries. He laughed and gave her a gold real, and then he dragged me down to the cantina, where we proceeded to get more than half corned on that damned pulque, on his money. We carried out four big jars of the stuff, which was a good thing. I had to drink half one in the morning before I could see through the agony. That stuff is not good for white men. Ten cents a jug, though.

The trek from Tampico to San Luis took more than a week, with Washington riding in the back of the buckboard and Harris and me taking turns riding and walking. There was about two hundred soldiers in our group, no more used to walking than us, and sometimes they eyed that buckboard. It was hilly country and mostly dry. General Parrodi went on ahead, and we never saw him again. Later on we learned that Santa Anna court-martialed him for desertion, for letting the gringos take Tampico. Fits.

San Luis Potosí looked like a nice little town, but we didn't see too damned much of it. We went to the big camp outside of town. Couldn't find Parrodi, so Harris sniffed around and got us attached to General Pacheco's division. General looked at the contract and more or less told us to pitch a tent and stay out of the way.

You never seen so many greasers in your life. Four thousand

who Taylor'd kicked out of Monterrey, and about twenty thousand more who might or might not have known which end the bullet comes out of.

We got a good taste of what they call *santanismo* now. Santa Anna had all these raw boys, and what did he do to get them in shape for a fight? He had them dress up and do parades, while he rode back and forth on his God damned horse. Week after week. A lot of the boys ran away, and I can't say I blame them. They didn't have a thousand dollars and a ranch to hang around for.

We weren't the only Americans there. A whole bunch of Taylor's men, more than 200, had absquatulated before he took Monterrey. The Mexicans gave them land grants too. They were called the "San Pats," the San Patricio battalion. We were told not to go near them, so that none of them would know we weren't actually prisoners.

After a couple of months of this, we found out what the deal was going to be. Taylor'd had most of his men taken away from him, sent down to Tampico to join up with another bunch that was headed for Mexico City. What Santa Anna said we were going to do was go north and wipe out Taylor, then come back and defend the city. The first part did look possible, since we had four or five men for every one of Taylor's. Me and Harris and Washington decided we'd wait and see how the first battle went. We might want to keep going north.

It took three days to get all those men on the road. Not just men, either; a lot of them had their wives and children along, carrying food and water and firewood. It was going to be three hundred miles, most of it barren. We saw Santa Anna go by, in a carriage drawn by eight white mules, followed by a couple carriages of whores. If I'd had the second sight Dolores claimed to have, I might've spent a pill on that son of a bitch. I still wonder why nobody ever did.

It wasn't easy going even for us, with plenty of water and food. Then the twelfth day a norther came in, the temperature dropped way below freezing and a God damned blizzard came up. We started passing dead people by the side of the road. Then Washington lost his voice, coughed blood for a while, and died. We carried him till night and then buried him. Had to get a pick from the engineers to get through the frozen ground. I never cried over a nigger before or since. Nor a white man, now I think of it. Could be it was the wind. Harris and me split his share of the gold and burnt his papers.

It warmed up just enough for the snow to turn to cold drizzle, and it rained for two days straight. Then it stopped and the desert sucked up the water, and we marched the rest of the way through dust and heat. Probably a fourth of Santa Anna's men died or deserted before we got to where Zach Taylor was waiting, outside of Saltillo in a gulch called Buena Vista. Still, we had them so outnumbered we should've run them into the ground. Instead, Santa Anna spent the first whole day fiddling, shuffling troops around. He didn't even do that right. Any shavetail would've outflanked and surrounded Taylor's men. He left all their right flank open, as well as the road to Saltillo. I heard a little shooting, but nothing much happened.

It turned cold and windy that night. Seemed like I just got to sleep when drums woke me up—American drums, sounding reveille; that's how close we were. Then a God damned band, playing "Hail Columbia." Both Taylor and Santa Anna belonged on a God damned parade ground.

A private came around with chains and leg irons, said he was supposed to lock us to the buckboard. For twenty dollars he accidentally dropped the key. I wonder if he ever lived to spend it. It was going to be a bad bloody day for the Mexicans.

We settled in behind the buckboard and watched about a thousand cavalrymen charge by, lances and machetes and blood in their eye, going around behind the hills to our right. Then the shooting started, and it didn't let up for a long time.

To our left, they ordered General Blanco's division to march into the gulch column-style, where the Americans were set up with field artillery. Canister and grapeshot cut them to bloody rags. Then Santa Anna rode over and ordered Pacheco's division to go for the gulch. I was just as glad to be chained to a buckboard. They walked right into it, balls but no brains, and I guess maybe half of them eventually made it back. Said they'd killed a lot of gringos, but I didn't notice it getting any quieter.

I watched all this from well behind the buckboard. Every now and then a stray bullet would spray up dirt or plow into the wood. Harris just stood out in the open, as far from cover as the chain would let him, standing there with his hands in his pockets. A bullet or a piece of grape knocked off his hat. He dusted it off and wiggled his finger at me through the hole, put it back on his head, and put his hands back in his pockets. I reminded him that if he got killed I'd take all the gold. He just smiled. He was absolutely not going to die in Mexico. I told him even if I *believed* in that bunkum I'd want to give it a little help. A God damned cannonball whooshed by and he didn't blink, just kept smiling. It exploded some ways behind us and I got a little piece in the part that goes over the fence last, which isn't as funny as it might sound, since it was going to be a month before I could sit proper.

Harris did leave off being a target long enough to do some doctoring on me. While he was doing that a whole bunch of troops went by behind us, following the way the cavalry went earlier, and they had some nice comments for me. I even got to show my bare butt to Santa Anna, which I guess not too many people do and live.

We heard a lot of noise from their direction but couldn't see anything because of the hills. We also stopped getting shot at, which was all right by me, though Harris seemed bored.

Since then I've read everything I could get my hands on about that battle. The Mexicans had 1,500 to 2,000 men killed and wounded at Buena Vista, thanks to Santa Anna's generaling. The Americans were unprepared and outnumbered, and some of them actually broke and ran—where even the American accounts admit that the greasers were all-fired brave. If we'd had a real general, a real battle plan, we would've walked right over the gringos.

And you can't help but wonder what would've happened. What if Zach Taylor'd been killed, or even just lost the battle? Who would the Whigs have run for president; who would have been elected? Maybe somebody who didn't want a war between the states.

Anyhow the noise died down and the soldiers straggled back. It's a funny thing about soldiering. After all that bloody fighting, once it was clear who had won the Americans came out on the battlefield and shared their food and water with us, and gave some medical help. But that night was terrible with the sounds of the dying, and the retreat was pure hell. I was for heading north, forget the land grant, but of course Harris knew that he was going to make it through no matter what.

Well, we were lucky. When we got to San Luis an aide to Pacheco decided we weren't being too useful as spies, so we got assigned to a hospital detail, and stayed there while others went on south with Santa Anna to get blown apart at Cerro Gordo and Chapultepec. A few months later the war was over and Santa Anna was back in exile—which was temporary, as usual. That son of a bitch was president eleven times.

Now this is where the story gets strange, and if somebody else was telling it I might call him a liar. You're welcome to that opinion, but anyhow it's true.

We had more than a thousand acres up in Mesilla, too much to farm by ourselves, so we passed out some handbills and got a couple dozen ex-soldiers to come along with their families, to be sort of tenant farmers. It was to be a fifty-fifty split, which looked pretty good on the surface, because although it wasn't exactly Kansas the soil was supposedly good enough for maize and agave, the plant that pulque was made from. What they didn't tell us about was the Apaches. But that comes later.

Now the Mesilla Valley looked really good on the map. It had a good river and it was close to the new American border. I still had my American citizenship papers and sort of liked the idea of being only a couple of days away in case trouble started. Anyhow we got outfitted in San Luis and headed our little wagon train north by northwest. More than a thousand miles, through Durango and Chihuahua. It was rough going, just as dry as hell, but we knew that ahead of time and at least there was nobody shooting at us. All we lost was a few mules and one wagon, no people.

Our grants were outside of the little town of Tubac, near the silver mines at Cerro Colorado. There was some irrigation but not nearly enough, so we planted a small crop and worked like beavers digging ditches so the next crop could be big enough for profit.

Or I should say the greasers and me worked like beavers. Harris turned out not to have too much appetite for that kind of thing. Well, if I had eight thousand in gold I'd probably take a couple years' vacation myself. He didn't even stay on the grant, though. Rented a little house in town and proceeded to make himself a reputation.

Of course Harris had always been handy with a pistol and a knife, but he also used to have a healthy respect for what they could do to you. Now he took to picking fights—or actually, getting people so riled that they picked fights with him. With his tongue that was easy.

And it did look like he was charmed. I don't know how many people he shot and stabbed, without himself getting a scratch. I don't know because I stopped keeping regular company with him after I got myself a nasty stab wound in the thigh, because of his big mouth. We didn't seek each other out after that, but it wasn't such a big town and I did see him every now and then. And I was with him the night he died.

There was this cantina in the south part of town where I liked to go, because a couple of Americans, engineers at the mine, did their drinking there. I walked down to it one night and almost went right back out when I heard Harris's voice. He was talking at the bar, fairly quiet but in that sarcastic way of his, in English. Suddenly the big engineer next to him stands up and kicks his stool halfway across the room, and at the top of his voice calls Harris something I wouldn't say to the devil himself. By this time anybody with horse sense was grabbing a piece of the floor, and I got behind the doorjamb myself, but I did see everything that happened.

The big guy reaches into his coat and suddenly Harris has his Navy Colt in his hand. He has that little smile I saw too often. I hear the Colt's hammer snap down and this little "puff" sound. Harris's jaw drops because he knows as well as I do what's happened: bad round, and now there's a bullet jammed in the barrel. He couldn't shoot again even if he had time.

Then the big guy laughs, almost good natured, and takes careful aim with this little ladies' gun, a .32 I think. He shoots Harris in the arm, evidently to teach him a lesson. Just a graze, doesn't even break a bone. But Harris takes one look at it and his face goes blank and he drops to the floor. Even if you'd never seen a man die, you'd know he was dead by the way he fell.

Now I've told this story to men who were in the Civil War, beside which the Mexican War looks like a Sunday outing, and some of them say that's not hard to believe. You see enough men die and you see everything. One fellow'll get both legs blown off and sit and joke while they sew him up; the next'll get a little scratch and die of the shock. But that one just doesn't sound like Harris, not before or after Doña Dolores's prediction made him reckless. What signifies to me is the date that Harris died: December 30th, 1853.

Earlier that year, Santa Anna had managed to get back into office, for the last time. He did his usual trick of spending all the money he could find. Railroad fellow named James Gadsden showed up and offered to buy a little chunk of northern Mexico, to get the right-of-way for a transcontinental railroad. It was the Mesilla Valley, and Santa Anna signed it over on the thirtieth of December. We didn't know it for a couple of weeks, and the haggling went on till June—but when Harris picked a fight that night, he wasn't on Mexican soil. And you can make of that what you want.

As for me, I only kept farming for a few more years. Around about '57 the Apaches started to get rambunctious, Cochise's gang of murderers. Even if I'd wanted to stay I couldn't've kept any help. Went to California but didn't pan out. Been on the move since, and it suits me. Reckon I'll go almost anyplace except Mexico.

Because old Dolores liked me and she told my fortune many times. I never paid too much attention, but I know if she'd seen the sign that said I wasn't going to die in Mexico, she would've told me, and I would've remembered. Maybe it's all silliness. But I ain't going to be the one to test it.

As I say, that story more or less wrote itself, once I'd absorbed all the background information. If writing were always that much fun, it would be more popular than television.

But it's not always fun. Sometimes it's excruciating drudgery. A few years back I contracted to write a novel that seemed like an interesting project at the time. A couple of chapters in, though, I could see that it just wasn't going to work. It was too trivial a project, and I disliked myself for wasting time on it. I wrote the publisher, saying I just couldn't do it, offering to return the advance. They answered no—we don't want your money; we want *our book*.

In the fullness of time, as they say, I did finish the damned thing. An adventure novel, I had expected to write it in three months; instead, it took most of a year—grinding teeth, growling around the house, cold-bloodedly trying to inject life and intelligence into the dead dumb thing. Strangely enough, it turned out to be not too bad a book. But the single thing I enjoyed most about it was taking the manuscript up to New York, dropping it on the editor's desk, and saying goodbye.

From New York we drove down to my mother-in-law's horse farm in Maryland, a lovely quiet place where I have a back room to myself in the mornings and usually write well.

After the drudgery of this novel, I wanted to write something that was fun. I'd never written a story about a private eye (forgiving a dreadful Mickey Spillane parody that you can be glad didn't make it into this collection), and I'd just read an article in *Esquire* about the ways modern private investigators actually conduct business. Pretty drab stuff, actually; they don't even carry guns. Mostly they seem to study and take advantage of bureaucratic and jurisprudential loopholes, quite legally enabling their clients to stick it to their ex-husbands or deadbeat creditors or whomever. Raymond Chandler would have had an awful time with these bozos, sitting underneath their twenty-dollar haircuts, offices full of lawbooks and nary gat nor bottle in their desk drawers.

Well, things would have to be more interesting in the future. I groped around in the science fiction bag of tricks and came up with some clones and computers and enough weaponry to take over a small Central American nation. For a setting, I closed my eyes and tried to recapture two heavenly days of sailing and skin-diving in the placid turquoise waters around St. Thomas.

Then added a spatter of blood.

B L O O D

S I S T E R S

So I used to carry two different business cards: J. Michael Loomis, Data Concentration, and Jack Loomis, Private Investigator. They mean the same thing, nine cases out of ten. You have to size up a potential customer, decide whether he'd feel better hiring a shamus or a clerk.

Some people still have these romantic notions about private detectives and get into a happy sweat at the thought of using one. But it *is* the twenty-first century and, endless Bogart reruns notwithstanding, most of my work consisted in sitting at my office console and using it to subvert the privacy laws of various states and countries—finding out embarrassing things about people, so other people can divorce them or fire them or get a piece of the slickery.

Not to say I didn't go out on the street sometimes; not to say I didn't have a gun and a ticket for it. There are Forces of Evil out there, friends, although most of them would probably rather be thought of as businessmen who use the law rather than fear it. Same as me. I was always happy, though, to stay on this side of murder, treason, kidnapping—any lobo offense. This brain may not be much, but it's all I have.

I should have used it when the woman walked into my office. She had a funny way of saying hello:

"Are you licensed to carry a gun?"

Various retorts came to mind, most of them having to do with her expulsion, but after a period of silence I said yes and asked who had referred her to me. Asked politely, too, to make up for staring. She was a little more beautiful than anyone I'd ever seen before.

"My lawyer," she said. "Don't ask who he is."

With that, I was pretty sure that this was some sort of elaborate joke. Story detectives always have beautiful mysterious customers. My female customers tend to be dowdy and too talkative, and much more interested in alimony than romance.

"What's your name, then? Or am I not supposed to ask that either?"

She hesitated. "Ghentlee Arden."

I turned the console on and typed in her name, then a seven-digit code. "Your legal firm is Lee, Chu, and Rosenstein. And your real name is Maribelle Four Ghentlee: fourth clone of Maribelle Ghentlee."

"Arden is my professional name. I dance." She had a nice blush.

I typed in another string of digits. Sometimes this sort of thing would lose a customer. "Says here you're a registered hooker."

"Call girl," she said frostily. "Class One courtesan. I was getting to that."

I'm a liberal-minded man; I don't have anything against hookers *or* clones. But I like my customers to be frank with me. Again, I should have shown her the door—then followed her through it.

Instead: "So. You have a problem?"

"Some men are bothering me, one man in particular. I need some protection."

That gave me pause. "Your union has a Pinkerton contract for that sort of thing."

"*My* union." Her face trembled a little. "They don't let clones in the union. I'm an associate, for classification. No protection, no medical, no *anything*."

"Sorry, I didn't know that. Pretty old-fashioned." I could see the reasoning, though. Dump a thousand Maribelle Ghentlees on the market, and a merely ravishing girl wouldn't have a chance.

"Sit down." She was on the verge of tears. "Let me explain to you what I can't do.

"I can't hurt anyone physically. I can't trace this cod down and wave a gun in his face, tell him to back off."

"I know," she sobbed. I took a box of Kleenex out of my drawer, passed it over.

"Listen, there are laws about harassment. If he's really bothering you, the cops'll be glad to freeze him."

"I can't go to the police." She blew her nose. "I'm not a citizen."

I turned off the console. "Let me see if I can fill in some blanks without using the machine. You're an unauthorized clone."

She nodded.

"With bought papers."

"Of course I have papers. I wouldn't be in your *machine* if I didn't."

Well, she wasn't dumb, either. "This cod. He isn't just a disgruntled customer."

"No." She didn't elaborate.

"One more guess," I said, "and then you do the talking for a while. He knows you're not legal."

"He should. He's the one who pulled me."

"Your own daddy. Any other surprises?"

She looked at the floor. "Mafia."

"Not the legal one, I assume."

"Both."

The desk drawer was still open; the sight of my own gun gave me a bad chill. "There are two reasonable courses open to me. I could handcuff you to the doorknob and call the police. Or I could knock you over the head and call the Mafia. That would probably be safer."

She reached into her purse; my hand was halfway to the gun when she took out a credit flash, thumbed it, and passed it over the desk. She easily had five times as much money as I make in a good year, and I'm in a comfortable seventy percent bracket.

"You must have one hell of a case of bedsores."

"Don't be stupid," she said, suddenly hard. "You can't make that kind of money on your back. If you take me on as a client, I'll explain."

I erased the flash and gave it back to her. "Miz Ghentlee. You've already told me a great deal more than I want to know. I don't want the police to put me in jail, I don't want the courts to scramble my brains with a spoon. I don't want the Mafia to take bolt cutters to my appendages."

"I could make it worth your while."

"I've got all the money I can use. I'm only in this profession because I'm a snoopy bastard." It suddenly occurred to me that that was more or less true.

"That wasn't completely what I meant."

"I assumed that. And you tempt me, as much as any woman's beauty has ever tempted me."

She turned on the waterworks again.

"Christ. Go ahead and tell your story. But I don't think you can convince me to do anything for you."

"My real clone-mother wasn't named Maribelle Ghentlee."

"I could have guessed that."

"She was Maxine Kraus." She paused. "Maxine . . . Kraus."

"Is that supposed to mean something to me?"

"Maybe not. What about *Werner* Kraus?"

"Yeah." Swiss industrialist, probably the richest man in Europe. "Some relation?"

"She's his daughter and only heir."

I whistled. "Why would she want to be cloned, then?"

"She didn't know she was being cloned. She thought she was having a Pap test." She smiled a little. "Ironic posture."

"And they pulled you from the scraping."

She nodded. "The Mafia bought her physician. Then killed him."

"You mean the real Mafia?" I said.

"That depends on what you call real. Mafia Incorporated comes into it too, in a more or less legitimate way. I was supposedly one of six Maribelle Ghentlee clones that they had purchased to set up as courtesans in New Orleans, to provoke a test case. They claimed that the Sisterhood's prohibition against clone prostitutes constituted unfair restraint of trade."

"Never heard of the case. I guess they lost."

"Of course. They wouldn't have done it in the South if they'd wanted to win."

"Wait a minute. Jumping ahead. Obviously, they plan ultimately to use you as a substitute for the real Maxine Kraus."

"When the old man dies, which will be soon."

"Then why would they parade you around in public?"

"Just to give me an interim identity. They chose Ghentlee as a clone-mother because she was the closest one available to Maxine Kraus's physical appearance. I had good makeup; none of the real Ghentlee clones suspected I wasn't one of them."

"Still . . . what happens if you run into someone who knows

what the real Kraus looks like? With your face and figure, she must be all over the gossip sheets in Europe."

"You're sweet." Her smile could make me do almost anything. Short of taking on the Mafia. "She's a total recluse, though, for fear of kidnappers. She probably hasn't seen twenty people in her entire life.

"And she isn't beautiful, though she has the raw materials for it. Her mother died when she was still a baby—killed by kidnappers."

"I remember that."

"So she's never had a woman around to model herself after. No one ever taught her how to do her hair properly, or use makeup. A man buys all her clothes. She doesn't have anyone to be beautiful *for*."

"You feel sorry for her."

"More than that." She looked at me with an expression that somehow held both defiance and hopelessness. "Can you understand? She's my mother. I was force-grown so we're the same apparent age, but she's still my only parent. I love her. I won't be part of a plan to kill her."

"You'd rather die?" I said softly. She was going to.

"Yes. But that wouldn't accomplish anything, not if the Mafia does it. They'd take a few cells and make another clone. Or a dozen, or a hundred, until one came along with a personality to go along with matricide."

"Once they know you feel this way—"

"They do know. I'm running."

That galvanized me. "They know who your lawyer is?"

"My lawyer?" She gasped when I took the gun out of the drawer. People who only see guns on the cube are usually surprised at how solid and heavy they actually look.

"Could they trace you here, is what I mean." I crossed the room and slid open the door. No one in the corridor. I twisted a knob and twelve heavy magnetic bolts slammed home.

"I don't think so. The lawyers gave me a list of names, and I just picked one I liked."

I wondered whether it was Jack or J. Michael. I pushed a button on the wall and steel shutters rolled down over the view of Central Park. "Did you take a cab here?"

"No, subway. And I went up to One hundred and twenty-fifth and back."

"Smart." She was staring at the gun. "It's a .48 Magnum Recoilless. Biggest handgun a civilian can buy."

"You need one so big?"

"Yes." I used to carry a .25 Beretta, small enough to conceal in a bathing suit. I used to have a partner, too. It was a long story, and I didn't like to tell it. "Look," I said. "I have a deal with the Mafia. They don't do divorce work and I don't drop bodies into the East River. Understand?" I put the gun back in the drawer and slammed it shut.

"I don't blame you for being afraid—"

"Afraid? Miz Four Ghentlee, I'm not afraid. I'm *terrified!* How old do you think I am?"

"Call me Belle. You're thirty-five, maybe forty. Why?"

"You're kind—and I'm rich. Rich enough to buy youth: I've been in this *business* almost forty years. I take lots of vitamins and try not to fuck with the Mafia."

She smiled and then was suddenly somber. Like a baby. "Try to understand me. You've lived sixty years?"

I nodded. "Next year."

"Well, I've been alive barely sixty *days*. After four years in a tank, growing and learning.

"Learning isn't *being,* though. Everything is new to me. When I walk down a street, the sights and sounds and smells, it's . . . it's like a great flower opening to the sun. Just to sit alone in the dark—"

Her voice broke.

"You can't even *know* how much I want to live—and that's not condescending; it's a statement of fact. Yet I want you to kill me."

I could only shake my head.

"If you can't hide me you have to kill me." She was crying now, and wiped the tears savagely from her cheeks. "Kill me and make sure every cell in my body is destroyed."

She took out her credit card flash and set it on the desk.

"You can have all my money, whether you save me or kill me."

She started walking around the desk. Along the way she did something with a clasp and her dress slithered to the floor. The sudden naked beauty was like an electric shock.

"If you save me, you can have me. Friend, lover, wife . . . slave. Forever." She held a posture of supplication for a moment, then eased toward me. Watching the muscles of her body work made my mouth go dry. She reached down and started unbuttoning my shirt.

I cleared my throat. "I didn't know clones had navels."

"Only special ones. I have other special qualities."

Idiot, something reminded me, every woman you've ever loved has sucked you dry and left you for dead. I clasped her hips with my big hands and drew her warmth to me. Close up, the navel wasn't very convincing; nobody's perfect.

I'd done drycleaning jobs before, but never so cautiously or thoroughly. That she was a clone made the business a little more delicate than usual, since clones' lives are more rigidly supervised by the government than ours are. But the fact that her identity was false to begin with made it easier; I could second-guess the people who had originally drycleaned her.

I hated to meddle with her beauty, and that beauty made plastic surgery out of the question. Any legitimate doctor would be suspicious, and going to an underworld doctor would be suicidal. So we dyed her hair black and bobbed it. She stopped wearing makeup and bought some truly froppy clothes. She kept a length of tape stuck across her buttocks to give her a virgin-schoolgirl kind of walk. For everyone but me.

The Mafia had given her a small fortune—birdseed to them—both to ensure her loyalty and to accustom her to having money, for impersonating Kraus. We used about half of it for the drycleaning.

A month or so later there was a terrible accident on a city bus. Most of the bodies were burned beyond recognition; I did some routine bribery, and two of them were identified as the clone Maribelle Four Ghentlee and John Michael Loomis, private eye. When we learned the supposed clone's body had disappeared from the morgue, we packed up our money—long since converted into currency—and a couple of toothbrushes and pulled out.

I had a funny twinge when I closed the door on that console. There couldn't be more than a half-dozen people in the world who were my equals at using that instrument to fish information out of the System. But I had to either give it up or send Belle off on her own.

We flew to the West Indies and looked around. Decided to settle on the island of St. Thomas. I'd been sailing all my life, so we bought a fifty-foot boat and set up a charter service for tourists. Some days we took parties out to skindive or fish. Other days we anchored in a quiet cove and made love like happy animals.

After about a year, we read in the little St. Thomas paper that Werner Kraus had died. They mentioned Maxine but didn't print a picture of her. Neither did the San Juan paper. We watched all the news programs for a couple of days (had to check into a hotel to get access to a video cube) and collected magazines for a month. No pictures, to our relief, and the news stories remarked that Fraulein Kraus went to great pains to stay out of the public eye.

Sooner or later, we figured, some *paparazzo* would find her, and there would be pictures. But by then it shouldn't make any difference. Belle had let her hair grow out to its natural chestnut, but we kept it cropped boyishly short. The sun and wind had darkened her skin and roughened it, and a year of fighting the big boat's rigging had put visible muscle under her sleekness.

The marina office was about two broom closets wide. It was a beautiful spring morning, and I'd come in to put my name on the list of boats available for charter. I was reading the weather printout when Belle sidled through the door and squeezed in next to me at the counter. I patted her on the fanny. "With you in a second, honey."

A vise grabbed my shoulder and spun me around.

He was over two meters tall and so wide at the shoulders that he literally couldn't get through the door without turning sideways. Long white hair and pale blue eyes. White sport coat with a familiar cut: tailored to deemphasize the bulge of a shoulder holster.

"You don't do that, friend," he said with a German accent.

I looked at the woman, who was regarding me with aristocratic amusement. I felt the blood drain from my face and damned near said her name out loud.

She frowned. "Helmuth," she said to the guard, *"Sie sind ihm erschrocken.* I'm sorry," she said to me, "but my friend has quite a temper." She had a perfect North Atlantic accent, and her voice sent a shiver of recognition down my back.

"I am sorry," he said heavily. Sorry he hadn't had a chance to throw me into the water, he was.

"I must look like someone you know," she said. "Someone you know rather well."

"My wife. The similarity is . . . quite remarkable."

"Really? I should like to meet her." She turned to the woman behind the counter. "We'd like to charter a sailing boat for theday."

The clerk pointed at me. "He has a nice fifty-foot one."

"That's fine! Will your wife be aboard?"

"Yes . . . yes, she helps me. But you'll have to pay the full rate," I said rapidly. "The boat normally takes six passengers."

"No matter. Besides, we have two others."

"And you'll have to help me with the rigging."

"I should hope so. We love to sail." That was pretty obvious. We had been wrong about the wind and sun, thinking that Maxine would have led a sheltered life; she was almost as weathered as Belle. Her hair was probably long, but she had it rolled up in a bun and tied back with a handkerchief.

We exchanged false names: Jack Jackson and Lisa von Hollerin. The bodyguard's name was Helmuth Zwei Kastor. She paid the clerk and called her friends at the marina hotel, telling them to meet her at the *Abora,* slip 39.

I didn't have any chance to warn Belle. She came up from the galley as we were swinging aboard. She stared open-mouthed and staggered, almost fainting. I took her by the arm and made introductions, everybody staring.

After a few moments of strange silence, Helmuth Two whispered, *"Du bist ein Klon."*

"She can't be a clone, silly man," Lisa said. "When did you ever see a clone with a navel?" Belle was wearing shorts and a halter. "But we could be twin sisters. That *is* remarkable."

Helmuth Two shook his head solemnly. Belle had told me that a clone can always recognize a fellow clone, by the eyes. Never be fooled by a man-made navel.

The other two came aboard. Helmuth One was, of course, a Xerox of Helmuth Two. Lisa introduced Maria Salamanca as her lover: a small olive-skinned Basque woman, no stunning beauty, but having an attractive air of friendly mystery about her.

Before we cast off, Lisa came to me and apologized. "We are a passing strange group of people. You deserve something extra for putting up with us." She pressed a gold Krugerrand into my palm—worth at least triple the charter fare—and I tried to act suitably impressed. We had over a thousand of them in the keel, for ballast.

The *Abora* didn't have an engine; getting it in and out of the crowded marina was something of an accomplishment. Belle and Lisa handled the sails expertly, while I manned the wheel. They kept looking at each other, then touching. When we were in the harbor, they sat together at the prow, holding hands. Once we were in open water, they went below together. Maria went into a sulk, but the two clones jollied her out of it.

I couldn't be jealous of her. An angel can't sin. But I did wonder what you would call what they were doing. Was it a weird kind of incest? Transcendental masturbation? I only hoped Belle would keep her mouth shut, at least figuratively.

After about an hour, Lisa came up and sat beside me at the wheel. Her hair was long and full, and flowed like dark liquid in the wind, and she was naked. I tentatively rested my hand on her thigh. She had been crying.

"She told me. She had to tell me." Lisa shook her head in wonder. "Maxine One Kraus. She had to stay below for a while. Said she couldn't trust her legs." She squeezed my hand and moved it back to the wheel.

"Later, maybe," she said. "And don't worry; your secret is safe with us." She went forward and put an arm around Maria, speaking rapid German to her and the two Helmuths. One of the guards laughed and they took off their incongruous jackets, then carefully wrapped up their weapons and holsters. The sight of a .48 Magnum Recoilless didn't arouse any nostalgia in me. Maria slipped out of her clothes and stretched happily. The guards did the same. They didn't have navels but were otherwise adequately punctuated.

Belle came up then, clothed and flushed, and sat quietly next to me. She stroked my bicep and I ruffled her hair. Then I heard Lisa's throaty laugh and suddenly turned cold.

"Hold on a second," I whispered. "We haven't been using our heads."

"Speak for yourself." She giggled.

"Oh, be serious. This stinks of coincidence. That she should turn up here, that she should wander into the office just as—"

"Don't worry about it."

"Listen. She's no more Maxine Kraus than you are. They've found us. She's another clone, one that's going to—"

"She's Maxine. If she were a clone, I could tell immediately."

"Spare me the mystical claptrap and take the wheel. I'm going below." In the otherwise empty engine compartment, I'd stored an interesting assortment of weapons and ammunition.

She grabbed my arm and pulled me back down to the seat. "You spare *me* the private eye claptrap and listen—you're right, it's no coincidence. Remember that old foreigner who came by last week?"

"No."

"You were up on the stern, folding sail. He was just at the slip for a second, to ask directions. He seemed flustered—"

"I remember. Frenchman."

"I thought so too. He was Swiss, though."

"And that was no coincidence, either."

"No, it wasn't. He's on the board of directors of one of the banks we used to liquify our credit. When the annual audit came up, they'd managed to put together all our separate transactions —"

"Bullshit. That's impossible."

She shook her head and laughed. "You're good, but they're good, too. They were curious about what we were trying to hide, using their money, and traced us here. Found we'd started a business with only one percent of our capital.

"Nothing wrong with that, but they were curious. This director was headed for a Caribbean vacation anyhow; he said he'd come by and poke around."

I didn't know how much of this to believe. I gauged the distance between where the Helmuths were sunning and the prow, where they had carefully stowed their guns against the boat's heeling.

"He'd been a lifelong friend of Werner Kraus. That's why he was so rattled. One look at me and he had to rush to the phone."

"And we're supposed to believe," I said, "that the wealthiest woman in the world would come down to see what sort of innocent game we were playing. With only two bodyguards."

"Five. There are two other Helmuths, and Maria is . . . versatile."

"Still can't believe it. After a lifetime of being protected from her own shadow—"

"That's just it. She's tired of it. She turned twenty-five last month, and came into full control of the fortune. Now she wants to take control of her own life."

"Damned foolish. If it were me, I would've sent my giants down alone." I had to admit that I essentially did believe the tale. We'd been alone in open water for more than an hour, and would've long been shark bait if that had been their intent. Getting sloppy in your old age, Loomis.

"I probably would have too," Belle said. "Maxine and I are the same woman in some ways, but you and the Mafia taught me caution. She's been in a cage all her life, and just wanted out. Wanted to sail someplace besides her own lake, too."

"It was still a crazy chance to take."

"So she's a little crazy. Romantic, too, in case you haven't noticed."

"Really? When I peeked in you were playing checkers."

"Bastard." She knew the one place I was ticklish. Trying to get away, I jerked the wheel and nearly tipped us all into the drink.

We anchored in a small cove where I knew there was a good reef. Helmuth One stayed aboard to guard while the rest of us went diving.

The fish and coral were beautiful as ever, but I could only watch Maxine and Belle. They swam slowly hand-in-hand, kicking with unconscious synchrony, totally absorbed. Though the breathers kept their hair wrapped up identically, it was easy to tell them apart, since Maxine had an all-over tan. Still, it was an eerie kind of ballet, like a mirror that didn't quite work. Maria and Helmuth Two were also hypnotized by the sight.

I went aboard early, to start lunch. I'd just finished slicing ham when I heard the drone of a boat, rather far away. Large siphon-jet, by the rushing sound of it.

The guard shouted, "Zwei—komm' herauf!"

Hoisted myself up out of the galley. The boat was about two kilometers away, and coming roughly in our direction, fast.

"Trouble coming?" I asked him.

"Cannot tell yet, sir. I suggest you remain below." He had a gun in each hand, behind his back.

Below, good idea. I slid the hatch off the engine compartment and tipped over the cases of beer that hid the weaponry. Fished out two heavy plastic bags, left the others in place for the time being. It was all up-to-date American Coast Guard issue, and had cost more than the boat.

I had rehearsed this a thousand times in my mind, but I hadn't realized the bags would be slippery with condensation and oil and be impossible to tear with your hands. I stood up to get a knife from the galley, and it was almost the last thing I ever did.

I looked up at a loud succession of splintering sounds and saw a line of holes marching toward me from the bow, letting in blue light and lead. I dropped and heard bullets hissing over my head; heard the regular cough-cough-cough of Helmuth One's return fire. At the stern there was a cry of pain and then a splash; they must have caught the other guard coming up the ladder.

Also not in the rehearsals was the effect of absolute death-panic on bladder control; some formal corner of my mind was glad I hadn't yet dressed. I controlled my trembling well enough to cut open the bag that held the small-caliber spitter, and it only took three tries to get the cassette of ammunition fastened to the receiver. I jerked back the arming lever and hurried back to the galley hatch, carrying an armload of cassettes.

The spitter was made for sinking boats, quickly. It fired small flechettes, the size of old-fashioned metal stereo needles, fifty rounds per second. The flechettes moved at supersonic speed and each carried a small explosive charge. In ten seconds, they could do more damage to a boat than a man with a chainsaw could, with determination and leisure.

I resisted the urge to blast away and get back under cover (not that the hull afforded much real protection). We had clamped traversing mounts for the gun on three sides of the galley hatch—nautically inclined customers usually asked what they were; I always shrugged and said they'd come with the boat—because the spitter is most effective if you can hold the point of aim precisely on the waterline.

They were concentrating fire on the bow, most of it going high. Helmuth One was evidently shooting from a prone position, difficult target. I slid the spitter onto its mount and cranked up its scope to maximum power.

When I looked through the scope, a lifetime of target-shooting reflexes took over: deep breath, half let out, do the Zen thing. Their boat moved toward the center of the scope's field, and I waited. It was a Whaler Unsinkable. One man crouched at the bow, firing what looked like a .20-mm. recoilless, clamped on the rail above a piece of steel plate. They were less than a hundred meters away.

The Whaler executed a sharp starboard turn, evidently to give the gunner a better angle on our bow. Good boatmanship, good tactics, but bad luck. Their prow touched the junction of my crosshairs right at the waterline, and I didn't even have to track. I just pressed the trigger and watched a cloud of black smoke and steam zip from prow to stern. Not even an Unsinkable can stay upright with its keel sliced off. The boat slewed sideways into the water, spilling people, and turned turtle. Didn't sink, though.

I snapped a fresh cassette into place and tried to remember where the hydrogen tank was on that model. Second burst found it, and the boat dutifully exploded. The force of the blast was enough to ram the scope's eyepiece back into my eye, painfully.

Helmuth One peered down at me. "What is that?"

"Coast Guard weapon, a spitter."

"May I try it?"

"Sure." I traded places with him, glad to be up in the breeze. My boat was a mess. The mainmast had been shattered by a direct hit, waist high. The starboard rail was splinters, forward, and near misses had gouged up my nice teak foredeck. My eye throbbed, and for some reason my ears were ringing.

I remembered why the next second, as Helmuth fired. The spitter makes a sound like a cat dying, but louder. I had been too preoccupied to hear it.

I unshipped a pair of binoculars to check his marksmanship. He was shooting at the floating bodies. What a spitter did to one was terrible to see.

"Jesus, Helmuth . . ."

"Some of them may yet live," he said apologetically.

At least one did. Wearing a life jacket, she had been floating face down but suddenly began treading water. She was holding an automatic pistol in both hands. She looked exactly like Belle and Maxine.

I couldn't say anything; couldn't take my eyes off her. She fired two rounds, and I felt them slap into the hull beneath me. I heard Helmuth curse, and suddenly her shoulders dissolved in a spray of meat and bone and her head fell into the water.

My gorge rose and I didn't quite make it to the railing. Deck was a mess anyhow.

Helmuth Two, it turned out, had been hit in the side of the neck, but it was a big neck and he survived. Maxine called a helicopter, which came out piloted by Helmuth Three.

After an hour or so, Helmuth Four joined us in a large speed-boat loaded down with gasoline, thermite, and shark chum. By that time, we had transferred the gold and a few more important things from my boat onto the helicopter. We chummed the area thoroughly and, as sharks began to gather, towed both hulks out to deep water, where they burned brightly and sank.

The Helmuths spent the next day sprinkling the island with money and threats, while Maxine got to know Belle and me better, behind the heavily guarded door of the honeymoon suite of the quaint old Sheraton that overlooked the marina. She made us a job offer—a life offer, actually—and we accepted without hesitation. That was six years ago.

Sometimes I do miss our old life—the sea, the freedom, the friendly island, the lazy idylls with Belle. Sometimes I even miss New York's hustle and excitement, and the fierce independence of my life there.

We do travel on occasion, but with extreme caution. The clone that Helmuth killed in that lovely cove might have been Belle's sister, pulled from Maxine, or Belle's own daughter, since the Mafia had had plenty of opportunities to collect cells from her body. It's immaterial. What's important is that if they could make one, they could make an army of them.

Like our private army of Helmuths and Lamberts and Delias. I'm chief of security, and the work is interesting, most of it at a console as good as the one I had in Manhattan. No violence since that one afternoon six years ago, not yet. I did have to learn German, though, which was an outrage to a brain as old as mine.

We haven't made any secret of the fact that Belle is Maxine's clone. The official story is that Fraulein Kraus had a clone made of herself, for "companionship." This started a fad among the wealthy, being the first new sexual wrinkle since the invention of the vibrator.

Belle and Maxine take pains to dress alike and speak alike and have even unconsciously assimilated one another's mannerisms. Most of the non-clone employees can't tell which is which, and even I sometimes confuse them, at a distance.

Close up, which happens with gratifying frequency, there's no problem. Belle has a way of looking at me that Maxine could never duplicate. And Maxine is literally a trifle prettier: you can't beat a real navel.

I don't "slant" stories for a given market; I just let the characters go ahead and do whatever seems right for them. After the thing is finished, of course, I squint at it and decide which magazine would be the most likely victim. When I tore the last page of "Blood Sisters" out of the typewriter I ran into the living room chortling, and said, "By God, I've written a *Playboy* story!" My wife read it and agreed, so we bundled it off to the Big Bunny in Chicago.

It came back with unseemly haste, with a note saying that it hadn't been read; *Playboy* was no longer looking at unsolicited manuscripts.

That's a euphemism that may need clarifying. "No unsolicited manuscripts" doesn't mean that when the editor needs a story she picks up the phone and says "Hello, Norman? How 'bout a long story about sex in ancient Egypt?" No, a "solicited" manuscript is any story that comes from someone who has previously published in the magazine, or who is represented by an approved agent.

My agent doesn't normally handle short stories for me, since ten percent of what a science fiction magazine pays would hardly cover the postage expenses. The Big Bunny has big money, though, so I called him up. And that's where it gets weird.

Before I could get around to the topic, he said that *Playboy* had called last week and asked whether I might do a story for them. That was probably while "Blood Sisters" was being railroaded through the mailroom. So I sent it through my agent and they bought it. For one glorious month, there I was, 1/64th of an inch away from a naked Playmate. Alas, probably as close as I'll ever get. They never asked me to any of those wild parties at the Mansion.

The story that follows has nothing in common with "Blood Sisters" other than the similarity in titles and light intent—and the volumes of Type O sloshed about. It's a "sword and sorcery" tale, which is a genre I thought I would never invade. Conan and his relatives put me to sleep.

It all started at a science fiction convention, a locale where many of us lose our bearings temporarily. Robert Asprin collared me and said he wanted to do a collection called *Thieves' World*, where a dozen or so writers would make up stories with a common background and setting. We would all be in on the synthesis of this imaginary world—we would have each other's characters doing walk-ons and so forth—and the thing would be of high literary quality, as well as being a great gripping page-turner.

I was somewhere between dubious and lukewarm about the project. But I do like to tackle new things, and some of the names Bob dropped were names to conjure with, like Carolyn Cherryh and John Brunner—good company. So I agreed to look at it, and even went so far as to type up a sketch of One-Thumb, the tavernkeeper who would be my main character.

It was One-Thumb's personality that finally hooked me. Most of the villains in my stories, when the stories have villains, are not truly evil. They are misunderstood, or they misunderstand the situation, or they are caught in a System that forces them to do harm—the usual moral furniture of secular determinism. Here I had a chance to write about someone who was simply evil. He knows what he's doing is wrong and enjoys doing it *because* it's wrong. Wealthy from his misdeeds, he'd still cross the street to steal a penny from a blind man's cup.

It would be nice to be able to say that I learned something significant about the nature of good and evil by writing this tale. I didn't. I cackled audibly all the way through it.

BLOOD
BROTHERS

Smiling, bowing as the guests leave. A good luncheon, much re-assuring talk from the gentry assembled: the economy of Sanctuary is basically sound. Thank you, my new cook . . . he's from Twand, isn't he a marvel? *The host appears to be rather more in need of a new diet than a new cook, though the heavy brocades he affects may make him look stouter than he actually is.* Good leave . . . certainly, tomorrow. Tell your aunt I'm thinking of her.

You will stay, of course, Amar. *One departing guest raises an eyebrow slightly, our host a boylover?* We do have business.

Enoir, you may release the servants until dawn. Give yourself a free evening as well. We will be dining in the city.

And thank you for the excellent service. Here.

He laughs. Don't thank me. Just don't spend it all on one woman. *As the servantmaster leaves, our host's bluff expression fades to one of absolute neutrality. He listens to the servantmaster's progress down the stone steps, overhears him dismissing the servants. Turns and gestures to the pile of cushions by the huge fireplace. The smell of winter's ashes masked by incense fumes.*

I have a good wine, Amar. Be seated while I fetch it.

Were you comfortable with our guests?

Merchants, indeed. But one does learn from other classes, don't you agree?

He returns with two goblets of wine so purple it is almost black. He sets both goblets in front of Amar: choose. Even closest friends follow this ritual in Sanctuary, where poisoning is art, sport, profession. Yes, it was the color that intrigued me. Good fortune.

No, it's from a grove in the mountains, east of Syr. Kalos or something; I could never get my tongue around their barbaric . . . yes. A good dessert wine. Would you care for a pipe?

Enoir returns, jingling his bell as he walks up the steps.

That will be all for today, thank you. . . .

No, I don't want the hounds fed. Better sport Ilsday if they're famished. We can live with their whimpering.

The heavy front door creaks shut behind the servantmaster. You don't? You would not be the only noble in attendance. Let your beard grow a day or two, borrow some rag from a servant. . . .

Well, there are two schools of thinking. Hungry dogs are weaker but fight with desperation. And if your dogs aren't fed for a week, there's a week they can't be poisoned by the other teams.

Oh, it does happen—I think it happened to me once. Not a killing poison, just one that makes them listless, uncompetitive. Perhaps a spell. Poison's cheaper.

He drinks deeply, then sets the goblet carefully on the floor. He crosses the room and mounts a step and peers through a slot window cut in the deep wall.

I'm sure we're alone now. Drink up; I'll fetch the krrf. *He is gone for less than a minute and returns with a heavy brick wrapped in soft leather.*

Caronne's finest, pure black, unadulterated. *He unfolds the package: ebony block embossed all over its surface with a foreign seal.* Try some?

He nods. "A wise vintner who avoids his wares." You have the gold?

He weighs the bag in his hand. This is not enough. Not by half.

He listens and hands back the gold. Be reasonable. If you feel you can't trust my assay, take a small amount back to Ranke; have anyone test it. Then bring me the price we established.

The other man suddenly stands and claws at his falchion, but it barely clears its sheath, then clatters on the marble floor. He falls to his hands and knees, trembling, stutters a few words, and collapses.

No, not a spell, though nearly as swift, don't you think? That's the virtue of coadjuvant poisons. The first ingredient you had along with everyone else, in the sauce for the sweetmeats. Everyone but me. The second part was in the wine, part of its sweetness.

He runs his thumbnail along the block, collecting a pinch of krrf, which he rubs between thumb and forefinger and then sniffs. You really should try it. Makes you feel young and brave. But then you are young and brave, aren't you.

He carefully wraps the krrf up and retrieves the gold. Excuse me. I have to go change. *At the door he hesitates.* The poison is not fatal; it only leaves you paralyzed for a while. Surgeons use it.

The man stares at the floor for a long time. He is conscious of drooling and other loss of control.

When the host returns, he is barely recognizable. Instead of the gaudy robe, he wears a patched and stained houppelande with a rope for a belt. The pomaded white mane is gone; his bald scalp is creased with a webbed old scar from a swordstroke. His left thumb is missing from the second joint. He smiles and shows almost as much gap as tooth.

I am going to treat you kindly. There are some who would pay well to use your helpless body, and they would kill you afterwards.

He undresses the limp man, clucking, and again compliments himself for his charity and the man for his well-kept youth. He lifts the grate in the fireplace and drops the garment down the shaft that serves for disposal of ashes.

In another part of town, I'm known as One-Thumb; here, I cover the stump with a taxidermist's imitation. Convincing, isn't it? *He lifts the man easily and carries him through the main door.* No fault of yours, of course, but you're distantly related to the magistrate who had my thumb off. *The barking of the dogs grows louder as they descend the stairs.*

Here we are. *He pushes open the door to the kennels. The barking quiets to pleading whines. Ten fighting hounds, each in an individual run, up against its feeding trough, slavering politely, yawning gray sharp fangs.*

We have to feed them separately, of course. So they don't hurt each other.

At the far end of the room is a wooden slab at waist-level, with channels cut in its surface leading to hanging buckets. On the wall above it, a rack with knives, cleavers, and a saw.

He deposits the mute staring man on the slab and selects a heavy cleaver.

I'm sorry, Amar. I have to start with the feet. Otherwise it's a terrible mess.

There are philosophers who argue that there is no such thing as evil *qua* evil; that, discounting spells (which of course relieve an individual of responsibility), when a man commits an evil deed he is the victim himself, the slave of his progeniture and nurturing. Such philosophers might profit by studying Sanctuary.

Sanctuary is a seaport, and its name goes back to a time when it provided the only armed haven along an important caravan route. But the long war ended, the caravans abandoned that route for a shorter one, and Sanctuary declined in status— but not in population, because for every honest person who left to pursue a normal life elsewhere, a rogue drifted in to pursue *his* normal life.

Now, Sanctuary is still appropriately named, but as a haven for the lawless. Most of them, and the worst of them, are concentrated in that section of town known as the Maze, a labyrinth of streets and nameless alleys and no churches. There is communion, though, of a rough kind, and much of it goes on in a tavern named the Vulgar Unicorn, which features a sign in the shape of that animal improbably engaging itself, and is owned by the man who usually tends bar on the late shift, an ugly sort of fellow by the name of One-Thumb.

One-Thumb finished feeding the dogs, hosed the place down, and left his estate by way of a long tunnel that led from his private rooms to the basement of the Lily Garden, a respectable whorehouse a few blocks from the Maze.

He climbed the long steps up from the basement and was greeted by a huge eunuch with a heavy glaive balanced insolently over his shoulder.

"Early today, One-Thumb."

"Sometimes I like to check on the help at the Unicorn."

"Surprise inspection?"

"Something like that. Is your mistress in?"

"Sleeping. You want a wench?"

"No, just business."

The eunuch inclined his head. "That's business."

"Tell her I have what she asked for, and more, if she can afford it. When she's free. If I'm not at the Unicorn, I'll leave word as to where we can meet."

"I know what it is," the eunuch said in a singsong voice.

"Instant maidenhead." One-Thumb hefted the leather-wrapped brick. "One pinch, properly inserted, turns you into a girl again."

The eunuch rolled his eyes. "An improvement over the old method."

One-Thumb laughed along with him. "I could spare a pinch or so, if you'd care for it."

"Oh . . . not on duty." He leaned the sword against the wall and found a square of parchment in his money belt. "I could save it for my off time, though." One-Thumb gave him a pinch. He stared at it before folding it up. "Black . . . Caronne?"

"The best."

"You have that much of it." He didn't reach toward his weapon.

One-Thumb's free hand rested on the pommel of his rapier. "For sale, twenty *grimales*."

"A man with no scruples would kill you for it."

Gap-toothed smile. "I'm doubly safe with you, then."

The eunuch nodded and tucked away the krrf, then retrieved the broadsword. "Safe with anyone not a stranger." Everyone in the Maze knew of the curse that One-Thumb expensively maintained to protect his life: if he were killed, his murderer would never die, but live forever in helpless agony:

Burn as the stars burn;
Burn on after they die.
Never to the peace of ashes,
Out of sight and succor
From men or gods or ghost:
To the ends of time, burn.

One-Thumb himself suspected that the spell would be effective only for as long as the sorcerer who cast it lived, but that was immaterial. The reputation of th sorcerer, Mizraith, as well as the severity of the spell, kept blades in sheaths and poison out of his food.

"I'll pass the message on. Many thanks."

"Better mix it with snuff, you know. Very strong." One-Thumb parted a velvet curtain and passed through the foyer, exchanging greetings with some of the women who lounged there in soft veils (the cut and color of the veils advertised price and, in some cases, curious specialties), and stepped out into the waning light of end of day.

The afternoon had been an interesting array of sensations for a man whose nose was as refined as it was large. First the banquet, with all its aromatic Twand delicacies, then the good rare wine with a delicate tang of half-poison, then the astringent krrf sting, the rich charnel smell of butchery, the musty sweat of the tunnel's rock walls, perfume and incense in the foyer, and now the familiar stink of the street. As he walked through the gate into the city proper, he could tell the wind was westering; the earthy smell from the animal pens had a slight advantage over the tanners' vats of rotting urine. He even sorted out the delicate cucumber fragrance of freshly butchered fish, like a whisper in a jabbering crowd; not many snouts had such powers of discrimination. As ever, he enjoyed the first few minutes within the city walls, before the reek stunned even his nose to dullness.

Most of the stalls in the Farmers' Market were shuttered now, but he was able to trade two coppers for a fresh melon, which he peeled as he walked into the bazaar, the krrf inconspicuous under his arm.

He haggled for a while with a coppersmith, new to the bazaar, for a brace of lamps to replace the ones that had been stolen from the Unicorn last night. He would send one of his urchins around to pick them up. He watched the acrobats for a while, then went to the various wine merchants for bids on the next week's ordinaries. He ordered a hundredweight of salt meat, sliced into snacks, to be delivered that night, and checked the guild hall of the mercenaries to find a hall guard more sober than the one who had allowed the lamps to be stolen. Then he went down to the Wideway and had an early dinner of raw fish and crab fritters. Fortified, he entered the Maze.

As the eunuch had said, One-Thumb had nothing to fear from the regular denizens of the Maze. Desperadoes who would disembowel children for sport (a sport sadly declining since the introduction of a foolproof herbal abortifacient) tipped their hats respectfully or stayed out of his way. Still, he was careful. There were always strangers, often hot to prove themselves or desperate for the price of bread or wine; and although One-Thumb was a formidable opponent with or without his rapier, he knew he looked rather like an overweight merchant whose ugliness interfered with his trade.

He also knew evil well, from the inside, which is why he dressed shabbily and displayed no outward sign of wealth. Not to prevent violence, since he knew the poor were more often victims than the rich, but to restrict the class of his possible opponents to those who would kill for coppers. They generally lacked skill.

On the way to the Unicorn, on Serpentine, a man with the conspicuously casual air of a beginner pickpocket fell in behind him. One-Thumb knew that the alley was coming up and would be in deep shadow, and it had a hiding-niche a few paces inside. He turned into the alley and, drawing the dagger from his boot, slipped into the niche and set the krrf between his feet.

The man did follow, proof enough, and when his steps faltered at the darkness, One-Thumb spun out of the niche behind him, clamped a strong hand over his mouth and nose, and methodically slammed the stiletto into his back, time and again, aiming for kidneys. When the man's knees buckled, One-Thumb let him down slowly, slitting his throat for silence. He took the money belt and a bag of coin from the still-twitching body, cleaned and replaced his dagger, picked up the krrf, and resumed his stroll down the Serpentine. There were a few bright spatters of blood on his houppelande, but no one on that street would be troubled by it. Sometimes guardsmen came through, but not to harass the good citizens or criticize their quaint customs.

Two in one day, he thought; it had been a year or more since the last time that happened. He felt vaguely good about it, though neither man had been much of a challenge. The cutpurse was a clumsy amateur and the young noble from Ranke a trusting fool (whose assassination had been commissioned by one of his father's ministers).

He came up the street south of the Vulgar Unicorn's entrance and let himself in the back door. He glanced at the inventory in the storeroom, noted that it must have been a slow day, and went through to his office. He locked up the krrf in a strongbox and then poured himself a small glass of lemony aperitif and sat down at the one-way mirror that allowed him to watch the bar unseen.

For an hour he watched money and drink change hands. The bartender, who had been the cook aboard a pirate vessel until he'd lost a leg, seemed good with the customers and reasonably

honest, though he gave short measures to some of the more in-
toxicated patrons—probably not out of concern for their welfare.
He started to pour a third glass of the liqueur and saw Amoli,
the Lily Garden's mistress, come into the place, along with the
eunuch and another bodyguard. He went out to meet them.

"Wine over here," he said to a serving wench, and escorted
the three to a curtained-off table.

Amoli was almost beautiful, though she was scarcely younger
than One-Thumb, in a trade that normally aged one rapidly. She
came to the point at once. "Kalem tells me you have twenty
grimales of Caronne for sale."

"Prime and pure."

"That's a rare amount." One-Thumb nodded. "Where, may I
ask, did it come from?"

"I'd rather not say."

"You'd better say. I had a twenty-*grimale* block in my bedroom safe. Yesterday it was stolen."

One-Thumb didn't move or change expression. "That's an
interesting coincidence."

She snorted. They sat without speaking while a pitcher of
wine and four glasses were slipped through the curtain.

"Of course I'm not accusing you of theft," she said. "But you
can understand why I'm interested in the person you bought it
from."

"In the first place, I didn't buy it. In the second, it didn't come
from Sanctuary."

"I can't afford riddles, One-Thumb. Who was it?"

"That has to remain secret. It involves a murder."

"You might be involved in another," she said tightly.

One-Thumb slowly reached down and brought out his dagger.
The bodyguards tensed. He smiled and pushed it across the table
to Amoli. "Go ahead, kill me. What happens to you will be rather
worse than going without krrf."

"Oh—" She knocked the knife back to him. "My temper is
short nowadays. I'm sorry. But the krrf's not just for me; most
of my women use it, and take part of their pay in it, which is
why I like to buy in large amounts." One-Thumb was pouring
the wine; he nodded. "Do you have any idea how much of my
capital was tied up in that block?"

He replaced the half-full glasses on the round serving tray
and gave it a spin. "Half?"

"And half again of that. I *will* get it back, One-Thumb!" She selected a glass and drank.

"I hope you do. But it can't be the same block."

"Let me judge that—have you had it for more than two days?"

"No, but it must have left Ranke more than a week ago. It came on the Anenday caravan. Hidden inside a cheese."

"You can't know for sure that it was on the caravan all the time. It could have been waiting here until the caravan came."

"I can hear your logic straining, Amoli."

"But not without reason. How often have you seen a block as large as twenty *grimales?*"

"Only this time," he admitted.

"And is a pressed design stamped all over it uniformly, an eagle within a circle?"

"It is. But that only means a common supplier, his mark."

"Still, I think you owe me information."

One-Thumb sipped his wine. "All right. I know I can trust the eunuch. What about the other?"

"I had a vassal spell laid on him when I bought him. Besides . . . show him your tongue, Gage." The slave opened his mouth and showed pink scar tissue nested in bad teeth. "He can neither speak nor write."

"We make an interesting table," he said. "Missing thumb, tongue, and tamale. What are you missing, Amoli?"

"Heart. And a block of krrf."

"All right." He drank off the rest of his small glass and refilled it. "There is a man high in the court of Ranke, old and soon to die. His son, who would inherit his title, is slothful, incompetent, dishonest. The old man's counselors would rather the daughter succeed; she is not only more able but easier for them to control."

"I think I know the family you speak of," Amoli said.

"When I was in Ranke on other business, one of the counselors got in touch with me and commissioned me to dispose of this young pigeon, but to do it in Sanctuary. The twenty *grimales* was my pay, and also the goad, the bait. The boy is no addict, but he is greedy, and the price of krrf is three times higher in the court of Ranke than it is in the Maze. It was arranged for me to befriend him and, eventually, offer to be his wholesaler.

"The counselor procured the krrf from Caronne and sent word to me. I sent back a tempting offer to the boy. He contrived to make the journey to Sanctuary, supposedly to be introduced to the emperor's brother. He'll miss the appointment."

"That's his blood on your sleeve?" the eunuch asked.

"Nothing so direct; that was another matter. When he's supposed to be at the palace tomorrow, he'll be floating in the harbor, disguised as the shit of dogs."

"So you got the krrf and the boy's money as well," Amoli said.

"Half the money. He tried to croy me." He refilled the woman's glass. "But you see. There can be no connection."

"I believe there may be. Anenday was when mine disappeared."

"Did you keep it wrapped in a cheese?"

She ignored that. "Who delivered yours?"

"Marype, the youngest son of my sorcerer Mizraith. He does all of my caravan deliveries."

The eunuch and Amoli exchanged glances. "That's it! It was from Marype I bought the block. Not two hours after the caravan came in." Her face was growing red with fury.

One-Thumb drummed his fingers on the table. "I didn't get mine till evening," he admitted.

"Sorcery?"

"Or some more worldly form of trickery," One-Thumb said slowly. "Marype is studying his father's trade, but I don't think he's adept enough to transport material objects . . . could your krrf have been an illusion?"

"It was no illusion. I tried a pinch."

"Do you recall from what part of the block you took it?"

"The bottom edge, near one corner."

"Well, we can settle one thing," he said, standing. "Let's check mine in that spot."

She bade the bodyguards stay and followed One-Thumb. At the door to his office, while he was trying to make the key work, she took his arm and moved softly up against him. "You never tarry at my place any more. Are you keeping your own woman, out at the estate? Did we do something—"

"You can't have all my secrets, woman." In fact, for more than a year he had not taken a woman normally, but needed the starch of rape. This was the only part of his evil life that shamed him, and certainly not because of the women he had hurt and twice killed. He dreaded weakness more than death, and wondered which part would fail him next.

Amoli idly looked through the one-way mirror while One-Thumb attended to the strongbox. She turned when she heard him gasp.

"Gods!" The leather wrapping lay limp and empty on the floor of the box.

They both stared for a moment. "Does Marype have his father's protection?" Amoli asked.

One-Thumb shook his head. "It was the father that did this."

Sorcerers are not omnipotent. They can be bargained with. They can even be killed, with stealth and surprise. And spells cannot normally be maintained without effort; a good sorcerer might hold six or a dozen at once. It was Mizraith's fame that he maintained past a hundred, although it was well known that he did this by casting secondary spells on lesser sorcerers, tapping their power unbeknownst. Still, gathering all these strings and holding them, as well as the direct spells that protected his life and fortune, used most of his concentration, giving him a distracted air. The unwary might interpret this as senility—a half-century without sleep had left its mark—and might try to take his purse or life, as their last act.

But Mizraith was rarely seen on the streets, and certainly never near the noise and smell of the Maze. He normally kept to his opulent apartments in the easternmost part of town, flanked by the inns of Wideway, overlooking the sea.

One-Thumb warned the pirate cook that he might have to take a double shift, and took a bottle of finest brandy to give to Mizraith, and a skin of the ordinary kind to keep up their courage as they went to face the man who guarded his life. The emptied skin joined the harbor's flotsam before they'd gone half of Wideway, and they continued in grim silence.

Mizraith's eldest son let them in, not seeming surprised at their visit. "The bodyguards stay here," he said, and made a pass with one hand. "You'll want to leave all your iron here, as well."

One-Thumb felt the dagger next to his ankle grow warm; he tossed it away and also dropped his rapier and the dagger sheathed to his forearm. There was a similar scattering of weapons from the other three. Amoli turned to the wall and reached inside her skirts, inside herself, to retrieve the ultimate birth-control device, a sort of diaphragm with a spring-loaded razor attached (no one would have her without paying in some coin). The hardware glowed dull red briefly, then cooled.

"Is Marype at home?" One-Thumb asked.

"He was, briefly," the older brother said. "You came to see Father, though." He turned to lead them up a winding flight of stairs.

Velvet and silk embroidered in arcane patterns. A golden samovar bubbling softly in the corner: flower-scented tea. A naked girl, barely of childbearing age, sitting cross-legged by the samovar, staring. A bodyguard much larger than the ones downstairs, but slightly transparent. In the middle of this sat Mizraith, on a pile of pillows, or maybe of gold, bright eyes in dark hollows, smiling openmouthed at something unseeable.

The brother left them there. Magician, guardian, and girl all ignored them. "Mizraith?" One-Thumb said.

The sorcerer slowly brought his eyes to bear on him and Amoli. "I've been waiting for you, Lastel, or what is your name in the Maze, One-Thumb. . . . I could grow that back for you, you know."

"I get along well enough—"

"And you brought me presents! A bottle and a bauble—more my age than this sweetmeat." He made a grotesque face at the naked girl and winked.

"No, Mizraith, this woman and I, we both believe we've been wronged by you. Cheated and stolen from," he said boldly, but his voice shook. "The bottle is a gift."

The bodyguard moved toward them, its steps making no noise. "Hold, spirit." It stopped, glaring. "Bring that bottle here."

As One-Thumb and Amoli walked toward Mizraith, a low table materialized in front of him, then three glasses. "You may serve, Lastel." Nothing had moved but his head.

One-Thumb poured each glass full; one of them rose a handspan above the table and drained itself, then disappeared. "Very good. Thank you. Cheated, now? My, oh my. Stolen? Hee. What could you have that I need?"

"It's only we who need it, Mizraith, and I don't know why you would want to cheat us out of it—especially me. You can't have many commissions more lucrative than mine."

"You might be surprised, Lastel. You might be surprised. *Tea!*" The girl decanted a cup of tea and brought it over, as if in a trance. Mizraith took it and the girl sat at his side, playing with her hair. "Stolen, eh? What? You haven't told me. What?"

"Krrf," he said.

Mizraith gestured negligently with his free hand, and a small snowstorm of gray powder drifted to the rug and disappeared.

"No." One-Thumb rubbed his eyes. When he looked at the pillows, they were pillows; when he looked away, they turned to blocks of gold. "Not conjured krrf." It had the same gross effect but no depth, no nuance.

"Twenty *grimales* of black krrf from Caronne," Amoli said.

"Stolen from both of us," One-Thumb said. "It was sent to me by a man in Ranke, payment for services rendered. Your son Marype picked it up at the caravan depot, hidden inside a cheese. He extracted it somehow and sold it to this woman, Amoli—"

"Amoli? You're the mistress of a . . . of the Slippery Lily?"

"No, the Lily *Garden*. The other place is in the Maze, a good place for pox and slatterns."

One-Thumb continued. "After he sold it to her, it disappeared. He brought it to me last night. This evening, it disappeared from my own strongbox."

"Marype couldn't do that," Mizraith said.

"The conjuring part, I know he couldn't—which is why I say that you must have been behind it. Why? A joke?"

Mizraith sipped. "Would you like tea?"

"No. Why?"

He handed the half-empty cup to the girl. "More tea." He watched her go to the samovar. "I bought her for the walk. Isn't that fine? From behind, she could be a boy."

"Please, Mizraith. This is financial ruin for Amoli and a gross insult to me."

"A joke, eh? You think I make stupid jokes?"

"I know that you do things for reasons I cannot comprehend," he said tactfully. "But this is serious—"

"*I* know that!" He took the tea and fished a flower petal from it, rubbed it away. "More serious than you think, if my son is involved. Did it all disappear? Is there any tiny bit of it left?"

"The pinch you gave to my eunuch," Amoli said. "He may still have it."

"Fetch it," Mizraith said. He stared slack-jawed into his tea for a minute. "I didn't do it, Lastel. Some other did."

"With Marype's help."

"Perhaps unwilling. We shall see. . . . Marype is adept enough to have sensed the worth of the cheese, and I think he is worldly enough to recognize a block of rare krrf and know where to sell it. By himself, he would not be able to charm it away."

"You fear he's betrayed you?"

Mizraith caressed the girl's long hair. "We have had some argument lately. About his progress . . . he thinks I am teaching him too slowly, withholding . . . mysteries. The truth is, spells are complicated. Being able to generate one is not the same as being able to control it; that takes practice and maturity. He sees what his brothers can do and is jealous, I think."

"You can't know his mind directly?"

"No. That's a powerful spell against strangers, but the closer you are to a person, the harder it is. Against your own blood . . . no. His mind is closed to me."

Amoli returned with the square of parchment. She held it out apologetically. "He shared it with the other bodyguard and your son. Is this enough?" There was a dark patch in the center of the square.

He took it between thumb and forefinger and grimaced. "Markmor!" The second most powerful magician in Sanctuary— an upstart not even a century old.

"He's in league with your strongest competitor?" One-Thumb said.

"In league or in thrall." Mizraith stood up and crossed his arms. The bodyguard disappeared; the cushions became a stack of gold bricks. He mumbled some gibberish and opened his arms wide.

Marype appeared in front of him. He was a handsome lad: flowing silver hair, striking features. He was also furious, naked, and rampant.

"*Father!* I am *busy!*" He made a flinging gesture and disappeared.

Mizraith made the same gesture and the boy came back. "We can do this all night. Or you can talk to me."

Noticeably less rampant. "This is unforgivable." He raised his arm to make the pass again; then checked it as Mizraith did the same. "Clothe me." A brick disappeared, and Marype was wearing a tunic of woven gold.

"Tell me you are not in the thrall of Markmor."

The boy's fists were clenched. "I am not."

"Are you quite certain?"

"We are friends, partners. He is teaching me things."

"You know I will teach you everything, eventually. But—"

Marype made a pass and the stack of gold turned to a heap of stinking dung. "Cheap," Mizraith said, wrinkling his nose. He held his elbow a certain way and the gold came back. "Don't you see he wants to take advantage of you?"

"I can see that he wants access to you. He was quite open about that."

"Stefab," Mizraith whispered. "Nesteph."

"You need the help of my brothers?"

The two older brothers appeared, flanking Mizraith. "What I need is some sense out of you." To the others: "Stay him!"

Heavy golden chains bound his wrists and ankles to sudden rings in the floor. He strained and one broke; a block of blue ice encased him. The ice began to melt.

Mizraith turned to One-Thumb and Amoli. "You weaken us with your presence." A bar of gold floated over to the woman. "That will compensate you. Lastel, you will have the krrf, once I take care of this. Be careful for the next few hours. Go."

As they backed out, other figures began to gather in the room. One-Thumb recognized the outline of Markmor flickering.

In the foyer, Amoli handed the gold to her eunuch. "Let's get back to the Maze," she said. "This place is dangerous."

One-Thumb sent the pirate cook home and spent the rest of the night in the familiar business of dispensing drink and krrf and haggling over rates of exchange. He took a judicious amount of krrf himself—the domestic kind—to keep alert. But nothing supernatural happened, and nothing more exciting than a routine eye-gouging over a dice dispute. He did have to step over a deceased ex-patron when he went to lock up at dawn. At least he'd had the decency to die outside, so no report had to be made.

One reason he liked to take the death shift was the interesting ambience of Sanctuary in the early morning. The sunlight was hard, revealing rather than cleansing. Litter and excrement in the gutters. A few exhausted revelers, staggering in small groups or sitting half-awake, blade out, waiting for a bunk to clear at first bell. Dogs nosing the evening's remains. Decadent, stale, worn, mortal. He took dark pleasure in it. Double pleasure this morning, a light krrf overdose singing deathsong in his brain.

He almost went east, to check on Mizraith. "Be careful for the next few hours"—that must have meant his bond to Mizraith made him somehow vulnerable in the weird struggle with Markmor over Marype. But he had to go back to the estate and dispose of the bones in the dogs' troughs and then be Lastel for a noon meeting.

There was one drab whore in the waiting room of the Lily Garden, who gave him a thick smile and then recognized him and slumped back to doze. He went through the velvet curtain to where the eunuch sat with his back against the wall, glaive across his lap.

He didn't stand. "Any trouble, One-Thumb?"

"No trouble. No krrf, either." He heaved aside the bolt on the massive door to the tunnel. "For all I know, it's still going on. If Mizraith had lost, I'd know by now, I think."

"Or if he'd won," the eunuch said.

"Possibly. I'll be in touch with your mistress if I have anything for her." One-Thumb lit the waiting lamp and swung the door closed behind him.

Before he'd reached the bottom of the stairs, he knew something was wrong. Too much light. He turned the wick all the way down; the air was slightly glowing. At the foot of the stairs, he set down the lamp, drew his rapier, and waited.

The glow coalesced into a fuzzy image of Mizraith. It whispered, "You are finally in dark, Lastel. One-Thumb. Listen: I may die soon. Your charm, I've transferred to Stefab, and it holds. Pay him as you've paid me. . . ." He wavered, disappeared, came back. "Your krrf is in this tunnel. It cost more than you can know." Darkness again.

One-Thumb waited a few minutes more in the darkness and silence (fifty steps from the light above) before relighting the lamp. The block of krrf was at his feet. He tucked it under his left arm and proceeded down the tunnel, rapier in hand. Not that steel would be much use against sorcery, if that was to be the end of this. But an empty hand was less.

The tunnel kinked every fifty steps or so, to restrict line-of-sight. One-Thumb went through three corners and thought he saw light at the fourth. He stopped, doused the lamp again, and listened. No footfalls. He set down the krrf and lamp and filled his left hand with a dagger, then headed for the light. It didn't have to be magic; three times he had surprised interlopers in the tunnel. Their husks were secreted here and there, adding to the musty odor.

But no stranger this time. He peered around the corner and saw Lastel, himself, waiting with sword out.

"Don't hold back there," his alter ego said. "Only one of us leaves this tunnel."

One-Thumb raised his rapier slowly. "Wait . . . if you kill me, you die forever. If I kill you, the same. This is a sorcerer's trap."

"No, Mizraith's dead."

"His son is holding the spell."

Lastel advanced, crabwise dueler's gait. "Then how am I here?"

One-Thumb struggled with his limited knowledge of the logic of sorcery. Instinct moved him forward, point in line, left-hand weapon ready for side parry or high block. He kept his eye on Lastel's point, krrf-steady as his own. The krrf sang doom and lifted his spirit.

It was like fencing with a mirror. Every attack drew instant parry, reprise, parry, reprise, parry, re-reprise, break to counter. For several minutes, a swift yet careful ballet, large twins mincing, the tunnel echoing clash.

One-Thumb knew he had to do something random, unpredictable; he lunged with a cutover, impressing to the right.

Lastel knew he had to do something random, unpredictable; he lunged with a double-disengage, impressing to the right.

They missed each other's blades.

Slammed home.

One-Thumb saw his red blade emerge from the rich brocade over Lastel's back, tried to shout, and coughed blood over his killer's shoulder. Lastel's rapier had cracked breastbone and heart and slit a lung as well.

They clung to each other. One-Thumb watched bright blood spurt from the other's back and heard his own blood falling, as the pain grew. The dagger still in his left hand, he stabbed, almost idly. Again he stabbed. It seemed to take a long time. The pain grew. The other man was doing the same. A third stab, he watched the blade rise and slowly fall, and inching slide back out of the flesh. With every second, the pain seemed to double; with every second, the flow of time slowed by half. Even the splash of blood was slowed, like a viscous oil falling through water as it sprayed away. And now it stopped completely, a thick scarlet web frozen there between his dagger and Lastel's back—his own back—and as the pain spread and grew, marrow itself on fire, he knew he would look at that forever. For a flickering moment he saw the image of two sorcerers, smiling.

I thought that was real clever, killing off One-Thumb like that. The best places to be in an anthology supposedly are the first story or the last story. If other people were going to be using One-Thumb, I reasoned, then by disposing of him I would force the editor to put my story last. Another consideration was that I knew there was going to be a sequel to the book, and I thought one sword-and-sorcery story was my limit. With my main character dead, I was safe from being asked to do another.

Wrong, wrong. A person killed by sorcery, they told me, can also be revived by sorcery. Not only did I not win the final position in the book, but when I refused to do a story for the sequel, they handed my character to another writer! A dirty trick, by Crom.

(Actually, I have no right to complain—the story was fun to write and it's made more money than most of the stories in this volume. Asprin turned *Thieves' World* into a board game and I get a percent or two of the profits, which are unseemly.)

From the commercial and fun to the serious and rather painful. The novella that follows was originally the middle section of my novel *The Forever War.* I like it better than the version that got into print.

The Forever War wound up being my most successful novel, sweeping the science fiction awards for 1976, and still going strong in its umpteenth printing. But it wasn't an immediate success; it was turned down by eighteen publishers before St. Martin's Press took a chance on it. Most of the publishers felt it was an okay story, but nobody wanted to buy a book that was so transparently a metaphor about Vietnam.

While the outline-plus-sample-chapters package was being rejected by all those publishers, I of course continued writing the book. It's an episodic story, so I was able to sell the individual sections as more or less independent novellas. *Analog* magazine picked them up, and the editor, Ben Bova, was of immeasurable help, for moral support as well as canny storytelling advice. (In fact, it was Ben who convinced St. Martin's, who did not at that time publish adult science fiction, to take a look at it.)

He sent this novella back, though, with grave misgivings. Most of *The Forever War* is set in outer space—where the war is—but most of this story takes place back on Earth. He felt that including it in the novel would slow it to a halt. Besides, the dystopian view of future America was too depressing.

Maybe he was right. After some thought I did set it aside, and wrote the shorter novelette "We Are Very Happy Here," of which less than five pages takes place in the United States, and that's what wound up in the book. It does move faster than it would have with this story, which is certainly a virtue in a novel of adventure. But I still like this one better as a story.

YOU
CAN NEVER
GO BACK

1

I was scared enough.

Sub-major Stott was pacing back and forth behind the small podium in the assembly room/chop hall/gymnasium of the *Anniversary*. We had just made our final collapsar jump, from Tet-38 to Yod-4. We were decelerating at 1½ gravities and our velocity relative to that collapsar was a respectable .90c. We were being chased.

"I wish you people would relax for a while and just trust the ship's computer. The Tauran vessel at any rate will not be within strike range for another two weeks. Mandella!"

He was always very careful to call me "Sergeant" Mandella in front of the company. But everybody at this particular briefing was either a sergeant or a corporal: squad leaders. "Yes, sir."

"You're responsible for the psychological as well as the physical well-being of the men and women in your squad. Assuming that you are aware that there is a morale problem aboard this vessel, what have you done about it?"

"As far as my squad is concerned, sir?"

"Of course."

"We talk it out, sir."

"And have you arrived at any cogent conclusion?"

"Meaning no disrespect, sir, I think the major problem is obvious. My people have been cooped up in this ship for four-teen—"

"Ridiculous! Every one of us has been adequately conditioned against the pressures of living in close quarters *and* the enlisted people have the privilege of confraternity." That was a delicate way of putting it. "Officers must remain celibate, and yet *we* have no morale problem."

If he thought his officers were celibate, he should sit down and have a long talk with Lieutenant Harmony. Maybe he just meant line officers, though. That would be just him and Cortez. Probably 50 percent right. Cortez was awfully friendly with Corporal Kamehameha.

"Sir, perhaps it was the detoxification back at Stargate; maybe—"

"No. The therapists only worked to erase the hate conditioning—everybody knows how *I* feel about that—and they may be misguided but they are skilled.

"Corporal Potter." He always called her by her rank to remind her why she hadn't been promoted as high as the rest of us. Too soft. "Have you 'talked it out' with your people, too?"

"We've discussed it, sir."

The sub-major could "glare mildly" at people. He glared mildly at Marygay until she elaborated.

"I don't believe it's the fault of the conditioning. My people are impatient, just tired of doing the same thing day after day."

"They're anxious for combat, then?" No sarcasm in his voice.

"They want to get off the ship, sir."

"They *will* get off the ship," he said, allowing himself a microscopic smile. "And then they'll probably be just as impatient to get back on."

It went back and forth like that for a long while. Nobody wanted to come right out and say that their squad was scared: scared of the Tauran cruiser closing on us, scared of the landing on the portal planet. Sub-major Stott had a bad record of dealing with people who admitted fear.

I fingered the fresh T/O they had given us. It looked like this:

TABLE OF ORGANIZATION
Strike Force Alpha
Yod-4 Campaign

First Platoon

COMMANDING: SM Stott...............CMD Martinez...........

2ECHN: 1LT Cortez

3ECHN: FFSGT (vac)

                                                FIELD MEDIC
                                                2LT Wilson M.D.

4ECHN: 2LT (vac)

5ECHN: PSGT Rogers

6ECHN: Sgt. Mandella   Sgt. Ching   Cpl. Potter

Sgt. Mandella	Sgt. Ching	Cpl. Potter
Cpl Tate	Cpl Petrov	Cpl Struve
Cpl Yukawa	Pvt Luthuli	Pvt Alexandrov
Pvt Hofstadter	Pvt Herz	Pvt Kurosawa
Pvt Mulroy	Pvt Heyrovsky	Pvt Bergman
Pvt Shockley	Pvt Pauling	Pvt Renault
Pvt Rabi	Pvt Katawba	Pvt Stiller

SPECIALISTS: 1LTs Bok [CK] , Levine [CPR] , Pastori [PSY] ,
Winebrenner [MED] ; 2LTs Harmony [MED] , Princewell [DAT]
3LTs Stonewell [ARM] , Theodopolis [RAD] ; ESG Singe [NAV] ;
PSGTs Dalton [MAIN] , Namgyal [SUP] .

Issued STARGATE TACBD/1003-9674-1300/20 Mar 2007 SG:

BY AUTH STFCOM Commander

DIST: PRM: All personnel 1PLT/STFALPHA
       SEC: All personnel STFALPHA 6ECHN and above
       TRT: Personnel STFCOM 5ECHN and above NTK basis.

By and for 4GEN Mubutu Ngako COMM

Arlathea Lincoln.

FOR THE COMMANDER:
Arlathea Lincoln BGEN STFCOM
20 Mar 2007 SG

TACBD/1003/9674/1300/100 cop

I knew most of the people from the raid on Aleph, the first face-to-face contact between humans and Taurans. The only new people in my platoon were Luthuli and Heyrovsky. In the company as a whole (excuse me, the "strike force"), we had twenty replacements for the nineteen people we lost from the Aleph raid: one amputation, four deaders, fourteen psychotics.

I couldn't get over the "20 Mar 2007" at the bottom of the T/O. I'd been in the army ten years, though it felt like less than two. Time dilation, of course; even with the collapsar jumps, traveling from star to star eats up the calendar.

After this raid, I would probably be eligible for retirement, with full pay. If I lived through the raid, and if they didn't change the rules on us. Me a twenty-year man, and only twenty-five years old.

Stott was summing up when there was a knock on the door, a single loud rap. "Enter," he said.

An ensign I knew vaguely walked in casually and handed Stott a slip of paper, without saying a word. He stood there while Stott read it, slumping with just the right degree of insolence. Technically, Stott was out of his chain of command; everybody in the navy disliked him anyhow.

Stott handed the paper back to the ensign and looked through him.

"You will alert your squads that preliminary evasive maneuvers will commence at 2010, fifty-eight minutes from now." He hadn't looked at his watch. "All personnel will be in acceleration shells by 2000. Tench . . . hut!"

We rose and, without enthusiasm, chorused, "Fuck you, sir." Idiotic custom.

Stott strode out of the room and the ensign followed, smirking.

I turned my ring to my assistant squad leader's position and talked into it: "Tate, this is Mandella." Everyone else in the room was doing the same.

A tinny voice came out of the ring. "Tate here. What's up?"

"Get ahold of the men and tell them we have to be in the shells by 2000. Evasive maneuvers."

"Crap. They told us it would be days."

"I guess something new came up. Or maybe the Commodore has a bright idea."

"The Commodore can stuff it. You up in the lounge?"

"Yeah."

"Bring me back a cup when you come, okay? Little sugar?"

"Roger. Be down in about half an hour."

"Thanks. I'll get on it."

There was a general movement toward the coffee machine. I got in line behind Corporal Potter.

"What do you think, Marygay?"

"Maybe the Commodore just wants us to try out the shells once more."

"Before the real thing."

"Maybe." She picked up a cup and blew into it. She looked worried. "Or maybe the Taurans had a ship way out, waiting for us. I've wondered why they don't do it. We do, at Stargate."

"Stargate's a different thing. It takes seven cruisers, moving all the time, to cover all the possible exit angles. We can't afford to do it for more than one collapsar, and neither could they."

She didn't say anything while she filled her cup. "Maybe we've stumbled on their version of Stargate. Or maybe they have more ships than we do by now."

I filled and sugared two cups, sealed one. "No way to tell." We walked back to a table, careful with the cups in the high gravity.

"Maybe Singhe knows something," she said.

"Maybe he does. But I'd have to get him through Rogers and Cortez. Cortez would jump down my throat if I tried to bother him now."

"Oh, I can get him directly. We . . ." She dimpled a little bit. "We've been friends."

I sipped some scalding coffee and tried to sound nonchalant. "So that's where you've been disappearing to."

"You disapprove?" she said, looking innocent.

"Well . . . damn it, no, of course not. But—but he's an officer! A *navy* officer!"

"He's attached to us and that makes him part army." She twisted her ring and said, "Directory." To me: "What about you and Little Miss Harmony?"

"That's not the same thing." She was whispering a directory code into the ring.

"Yes, it is. You just wanted to do it with an officer. Pervert." The ring bleated twice. Busy. "How was she?"

"Adequate." I was recovering.

"Besides, Ensign Singhe is a perfect gentleman. And not the least bit jealous."

"Neither am I," I said. "If he ever hurts you, tell me and I'll break his ass."

She looked at me across her cup. "If Lieutenant Harmony ever hurts you, tell me and I'll break *her* ass."

"It's a deal." We shook on it solemnly.

2

The acceleration shells were something new, installed while we rested and resupplied at Stargate. They enabled us to use the ship at closer to its theoretical efficiency, the tachyon drive boosting it to as much as 25 gravities.

Tate was waiting for me in the shell area. The rest of the squad was milling around, talking. I gave him his coffee.

"Thanks. Find out anything?"

"Afraid not. Except the swabbies don't seem to be scared, and it's their show. Probably just another practice run."

He slurped some coffee. "What the hell. It's all the same to us, anyhow. Just sit there and get squeezed half to death. God, I hate those things."

"Maybe they'll eventually make us obsolete, and we can go home."

"Sure thing." The medic came by and gave me my shot.

I waited until 1950 and hollered to the squad, "Let's go. Strip down and zip up."

The shell is like a flexible spacesuit; at least the fittings on the inside are pretty similar. But instead of a life support package, there's a hose going into the top of the helmet and two coming out of the heels, as well as two relief tubes per suit. They're crammed in shoulder-to-shoulder on light acceleration couches; getting to your shell is like picking your way through a giant plate of olive drab spaghetti.

When the lights in my helmet showed that everybody was suited up, I pushed the button that flooded the room. No way to see, of course, but I could imagine the pale blue solution—ethylene glycol and something else—foaming up around and over us. The suit material, cool and dry, collapsed in to touch my skin at every point. I knew that my internal body pressure was increasing rapidly to match the increasing fluid pressure outside. That's what the shot was for; keep your cells from getting squished between the devil and the pale blue sea. You could still feel it, though. By the time my meter said "2" (external pressure equivalent to a column of water two nautical miles deep), I felt that I was at the same time being crushed and bloated. By 2005 it was at 2.7 and holding steady. When the maneuvers began at 2010, you couldn't feel the difference. I thought I saw the needle fluctuate a tiny bit, though.

The major drawback to the system is that, of course, anybody caught outside of his shell when the *Anniversary* hit 25 G's would be just so much strawberry jam. So the guiding and the fighting have to be done by the ship's tactical computer—which does most of it anyway, but it's nice to have a human overseer.

Another small problem is that if the ship gets damaged and the pressure drops, you'll explode like a dropped melon. If it's the internal pressure, you get crushed to death in a microsecond.

And it takes ten minutes, more or less, to get depressurized and another two or three to get untangled and dressed. So it's not exactly something you can hop out of and come up fighting.

The accelerating was over at 2038. A green light went on and I chinned the button to depressurize.

Marygay and I were getting dressed outside.

"How'd that happen?" I pointed to an angry purple welt that ran from the bottom of her right breast to her hipbone.

"That's the second time," she said, mad. "The first one was on my back—I think that shell doesn't fit right, gets creases."

"Maybe you've lost weight."

"Wise guy." Our caloric intake had been rigorously monitored ever since we left Stargate the first time. You can't use a fighting suit unless it fits you like a second skin.

A wall speaker drowned out the rest of her comment. "Attention all personnel. Attention. All army personnel echelon six and above and all navy personnel echelon four and above will report to the briefing room at 2130."

It repeated the message twice. I went off to lie down for a few minutes while Marygay showed her bruise to the medic and the armorer. I didn't feel a bit jealous.

The Commodore began the briefing. "There's not much to tell, and what there is is not good news.

"Six days ago, the Tauran vessel that is pursuing us released a drone missile. Its initial acceleration was on the order of 80 gravities.

"After blasting for approximately a day, its acceleration suddenly jumped to 148 gravities." Collective gasp.

"Yesterday, it jumped to 203 gravities. I shouldn't need to remind anyone here that this is twice the accelerative capability of the enemy's drones in our last encounter.

"We launched a salvo of drones, four of them, intersecting what the computer predicted to be the four most probable future trajectories of the enemy drone. One of them paid off, while we were doing evasive maneuvers. We contacted and destroyed the Tauran weapon about ten million kilometers from here."

That was practically next door. "The only encouraging thing we learned from the encounter was from spectral analysis of the blast. It was no more powerful an explosion than ones we have observed in the past, so at least their progress in propulsion hasn't been matched by progress in explosives.

"This is the first manifestation of a very important effect that has heretofore been of interest only to theorists. Tell me, soldier." He pointed at Negulesco. "How long has it been since we first fought the Taurans, at Aleph?"

"That depends on your frame of reference, Commodore," she answered dutifully. "To me, it's been about eight months."

"Exactly. You've lost about nine years, though, to time dilation, while we maneuvered between collapsar jumps. In an engineering sense, as we haven't done any important research and development aboard ship . . . that enemy vessel comes from our future!" He paused to let that sink in.

"As the war progresses, this can only become more and more pronounced. The Taurans don't have any cure for relativity, of course, so it will be to our benefit as often as to theirs.

"For the present, though, it is *we* who are operating with a handicap. As the Tauran pursuit vessel draws closer, this handicap will become more severe. They can simply outshoot us.

"We're going to have to do some fancy dodging. When we get within five hundred million kilometers of the enemy ship, everybody gets in his shell and we just have to trust the logistic computer. It will put us through a rapid series of random changes in direction and velocity.

"I'll be blunt. As long as they have one more drone than we, they can finish us off. They haven't launched any more since that first one. Perhaps they are holding their fire . . . or maybe they only had one. In that case, it's we who have them.

"At any rate, all personnel will be required to be in their shells with no more than ten minutes' notice. When we get within a thousand million kilometers of the enemy, you are to stand *by* your shells. By the time we are within five hundred million kilometers, you will be in them, and all shell compounds flooded and pressurized. We cannot wait for anyone.

"That's all I have to say. Sub-major?"

"I'll speak to my people later, Commodore. Thank you."

"Dismissed." And none of this "fuck you, sir" nonsense. The navy thought that was just a little beneath their dignity. We stood at attention—all except Stott—until he had left the room. Then some other swabbie said "dismissed" again, and we left.

My squad had clean-up detail, so I told everybody who was to do what, put Tate in charge, and left. Went up to the NCO room for some company and maybe some information.

There wasn't much happening but idle speculation, so I took Rogers and went off to bed. Marygay had disappeared again, hopefully trying to wheedle something out of Singhe.

3

We had a get-together with the sub-major the next morning, where he more or less repeated what the Commodore had said, in infantry terms and in his staccato monotone. He emphasized the fact that all we knew about the Tauran ground forces was that if their naval capability was improved, it was likely that they would be able to handle us better than last time.

But that brings up an interesting point. In our only previous ground contact with the Taurans, we had a tremendous advantage: they seemed not to be able to understand exactly what was going on. As belligerent as they had been in space, we had expected them to be real Huns on the ground . . . but instead they just lined up and allowed themselves to be slaughtered. One escaped and presumably described the idea of old-fashioned infighting to his fellows.

But that didn't mean the word had necessarily gotten out to this particular bunch. The only way we know of to communicate faster than the speed of light is to physically carry a message through collapsar jumps. And there was no telling how many jumps there were between Yod-4 and the Taurans' home base—

so they could be just as passive as the last bunch, or they might have been practicing infantry techniques for nearly a decade. We would find out when we got there.

The armorer and I were helping my squad pull maintenance on their fighting suits when we passed the thousand-million-kilometer mark and had to go up to the shells.

We had about five hours to kill before we had to get in our cocoons. I played a game of chess with Rabi and lost. Then Rogers led the platoon in some vigorous calisthenics, perhaps for no other reason than to get their minds off the prospect of having to lie half crushed in the shells for at least four hours. The longest we'd gone before was half that.

Ten minutes before the five-hundred-million-kilometer mark, we squad leaders took over and supervised buttoning everybody up. By the time my pressure dial read 2.7, we were at the mercy of—or safe in the arms of—the logistic computer.

While I was lying there being squeezed, a silly thought took hold of me and went round and round like a charge in a super-conductor: according to military formalism, the conduct of war divides neatly into two categories, tactics and logistics. Logistics has to do with just about everything but the actual fighting, which is (are?) tactics. And now we're fighting, but we don't have a tactical computer to guide us through attack and defense. Just a huge, superefficient cybernetic grocery clerk of a logistic computer.

And the other side of my brain, which was not quite as pinched, would argue that it doesn't matter what name you give to a computer, it's just a bunch of memory crystals, logic banks, nuts and bolts . . . if you program it to be Ghengis Khan, it is a tactical computer, even if its usual function is to monitor the stock market or control sewage conversion.

But the other side was obdurate and said that by that kind of reasoning, a man is only a hank of hair and a piece of bone and some stringy meat; and if you teach him well you can take a Zen monk and turn him into a warrior.

Then what the hell are you/we, am I? answered the other side. A peace-loving vacuum-welding-specialist physics teacher snatched up by the Elite Conscription Act and reprogrammed to be a killing machine. You/I have killed and liked it.

But that was hypnotism, motivational conditioning, I argued back at myself. They don't do it anymore.

And the only reason they don't do it is because they think you'll kill better without it. That's logic.

Speaking of logic, the original question was, Why do they send a logistic computer to do a man's job? or something like that. . . .

The light blinked green and I chinned the switch automatically. We were down to 1.3 before I realized that it meant we were alive, we had won the first skirmish.

I was only partly right.

We were standing in the hall, stretching and groaning, when Bohrs came staggering down the corridor. His face was gray. I took his shoulder.

"What's wrong, Bohrs?"

"Negulesco's squad. They're all dead."

"What?" He didn't nod or anything, just stared at the wall.

"And the whole fourth platoon: Keating, Thomas, Chu, Fruenhauf . . . twenty-four in all, crushed to death."

I didn't know what to say. "At least they . . ." I let it trail off. I was going to say, At least they didn't feel anything, but who knows what you would feel?

"Attention, all personnel. Attention. All infantry personnel echelon six and above will assemble in five minutes in the assembly room." The speaker crackled for a few seconds and a new voice came on, a weary voice:

"This is the Commodore. We met and destroyed the enemy vessel at 0254. At 0252, the enemy launched a missile at us, and we expended seven drones intercepting it. It was destroyed . . . less than five hundred kilometers from the *Anniversary,* and many of the ship's electronic systems have sustained . . . considerable radiation damage. The life support units for squad bays Five, Six, Seven, and Eight went out while the bays were fully pressurized, and all of the occupants perished." He paused a long time. "There will be a memorial service at 0800 tomorrow. That is all."

The other voice came back on. "All medical personnel report immediately to sick bay. All maintenance personnel report immediately to your prime stations. Lieutenant Pastori report to sick bay."

Marygay and Ching and Rogers and I got dressed and went up to the assembly area in silence.

At the meeting they explained what had happened, very little that we didn't already know, and assigned a burial detail. All squad leaders were on it, and we had to choose a person from each of our squads. I did it by casting dice, and Shockley went along with me. It wasn't too bad except for the ones whose suits had split.

4

We were in a synchronous orbit above the uninhabited side of the one planet-sized chunk in the ring of detritus that circled the cold black pit of Yod-4. From the other side of the frozen cinder, the Tauran base acknowledged our presence by periodically tossing bubble missiles at the *Anniversary*. We knew how to handle those from the last time. Just touch them with a laser.

Since our attack plans, for what they were worth, were set up requiring four platoons, they took Ching's squad from my platoon and Al-Sadat's from the second platoon. They promoted Ching to prime-sergeant and put him in charge. Gave us four platoons of about thirteen people each.

We were all packed into the assembly area. Cortez came through the door and picked his way to the podium.

"All right, if you all want to shut up . . . quiet!" Cortez had been phenomenally ugly when we first met him, a year ago—or ten!—back on Charon. He didn't improve with age: grotesquely scarred, bald, little white beard, skin the texture of old leather; strong and tough and fast and always in control; hard and intelligent and very cruel in a calculating way. He had fought in the two last wars on Earth, before the United Nations broke down and re-formed. He had been a soldier for almost forty years.

"Now the computer's going to show you a graphical picture of our path, the way we're going to approach the enemy base." He gestured, and we turned to watch the holograph screen at the opposite end of the room. It showed a conventional picture of a sphere with lines of latitude and longitude, slowly rotating. The *Anniversary* was a tiny model up in one corner.

"We've stepped up the time rate by a factor of a hundred. Now watch." A bunch of little lights popped out of the *Anniversary* and dropped slowly to the planet, weaving around in a complex random pattern. "The four red lights are the scoutships, one for each platoon. The rest"—about twenty white lights—"are programmed decoys, like last time."

The attack plan was pretty simple. We'd drop almost to the surface, on the side of the planet opposite the enemy base. Then we'd fan out and approach the base from all different directions, maneuvering erratically but in a coordinated way, so we'd all hit the base at the same time. The ships would be pre-programmed; no manual control at all (that didn't sit too well).

"Now here's the best recon picture we have." The globe disappeared and an aerial holograph took its place. "Many of these features should look familiar to you, from last time. Of course, we know a little more about their functions now."

A moving arrow pointed to the structures as Cortez talked about them. "The Flower. This is the first target; you remember, it's where the bubbles come from. We better get this out before the ground attack.

"Almost as important, here, these lines of white silo things, the ships. No Taurans are getting away alive this time, except as prisoners.

"These are the targets your scoutships—and the decoys—are programmed to knock out, before you land. Every ship has twenty missiles, Class Three tachs. The attack is coordinated so that every ship will release half its missiles at once, timed for all two hundred and fifty to converge on the base simultaneously.

"If this destroys the Flower and the ships, you'll land immediately and attack. If not, the decoys will continue to seek targets of opportunity while your scoutships concentrate on staying in one piece.

"Each ship also has a gigawatt laser, but we don't know whether we'll be able to maintain one bearing for long enough to burn anything. We'll see."

He rubbed his beard and smiled that funny little smile of his. "If the aerial attack isn't successful, and I have a hunch it won't be, we have to get in there with our launchers and lasers and do the job on foot. Same priority: first knock out the ships and the Flower.

"It's going to be a fast and furious attack. We won't have more than thirty seconds from the time we let loose our bombs to the time we roll out on the ground. Be only two or three seconds if the initial salvo gets its targets."

He gripped the podium and said, almost in a whisper, "I will have to have *ab*solute, *un*conditional blind obedience. I swear to

God I'll burn anybody who doesn't follow my orders just like a robot.

"We still have to take a prisoner. Once we have one of the Taurans to interrogate and examine, maybe we'll be able to stop going in on foot. Maybe. The Commodore is sure that he could destroy that base completely, with the *Anniversary*'s armament . . . but that remains to be seen.

"All right. We knock out the Flower and the ships and then, ladies and gentlemen, we go hunting. Once we get a live Tauran, I can whistle up the ships, we withdraw, and the Commodore will see whether he can knock out the base. Assuming the Taurans will sit there and let us leave."

He pulled down the drawing sheet behind him, shook it to randomize the charge, then smoothed it against its backing. He drew a lopsided circle. "This is the base," he said, and drew in symbols showing where the various installations were. It looked like this:

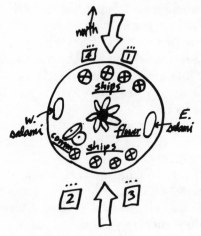

"Now, this dead rock doesn't have a magnetic field, so your inertial compasses will be set pointing toward the geometric 'north' of the planet. From the orientation of the base, it's obvious that the Taurans use the same system.

"First and fourth platoons will roll out about five hundred meters east-northeast of this line of ships at the top. Private Herz!"

"Sir?"

"You will be issued the heavy rocket launcher that belonged to the old fourth platoon. The instant you roll out of that scout-ship, check whether any of the enemy ships are still standing. If they are, knock them out.

"After Herz has taken care of that, odd-numbered squads in both platoons advance about a hundred meters while the even-numbered squads lay down covering fire. Then evens come up and pass them while odds cover. Herz, when you get within range of the Flower, kill it."

He pointed to the two Salamis. "We know from Aleph that these structures are living quarters. Don't fire on them unless you have to. Not until I say to.

"Second and third platoons, you'll be doing about the same thing. Who's got the heavy launcher in third?"

"Right here." Corporal Conte.

"While you're taking care of the ships on your side, knock out their communications dome. They may have forces elsewhere on the planet, though it seems unlikely. Still, we don't want them to be able to call for reinforcements.

"Once we knock out the Flower, first and fourth assemble near the east Salami; second and third take the west. Don't bunch up; everybody just get within good striking range and try to find cover and wait for my orders.

"Questions?"

"Lieutenant," I asked, "all this seems to assume that their defensive setup is the same here as it was on Aleph, but Aleph was a jungle world—"

"—and this one is hard-frozen stone. Sergeant, you know there's no answer to that. Aleph is all we have to go on. The structures look similar, and we have to assume they serve similar functions. It's all guesswork until we attack.

"It's possible that our biggest danger won't be from the Tau-rans but from the planet itself. Charon and Stargate are similar worlds, of course, and we've done hundreds of maneuvers on them . . . but never against a live, unpredictable enemy. You all know what happens if you stumble into a pool of helium two or touch a cold rock with the fins of your heat exchanger. Nobody's suspending the laws of physics just to help you concentrate on the enemy."

Somehow I'd managed not to think about that too much. When we left Stargate the second time, the total number of people killed in training exercises—all three strike forces—was forty-one. That's under controlled conditions, where a hundred people are ready to drop everything and help you. Most of them were heat-exchanger detonations, though; nothing you can do to help in those cases.

"You platoon leaders and squad leaders get together with your people and make sure they know exactly what they have to do. We'll have full gear inspection tonight at 1900, after chop. Unless there are any gross deficiencies, we'll be on ready status from then on."

"Sir," Kamehameha asked, "do you have any idea when the attack is going to be?"

Anybody else, he would have chewed out. "If I knew, I'd have told you," he said mildly. "Within a couple of days, I suspect. Depends on the logistic computer. Anybody else?" No response. "Dismissed."

Then the litany.

5

I was up in the NCO lounge, trying to concentrate on a game of O'wari with Al-Sadat, when we got the word. Everybody had been on edge for the past three days.

The speaker crackled and Al-Sadat looked up at it, letting his handful of pebbles trickle to the floor. We both knew the game was over.

"Attention all personnel. Planetside operations will commence in exactly one hour. All infantry and active support units report at once to your scoutship bays. Attention all personnel. Planetside operations will . . ."

My stomach flipped twice and, getting out of the chair, I had to swallow back nervous bile. I'd felt about the same, every time the speaker had crackled in the two days since the first muster. It wasn't simply fear of going into combat—that was bad enough— but also the terrifying uncertainty of the whole thing. This could be a milk run or a suicide mission or anything in between. Al-Sadat and I ran down the corridor and jumped into the lift, hoping to beat our squads to the scoutships.

Marygay was already there and getting into her suit when I slipped through the lock. I had one glimpse of Marygay's white flesh before she closed the front plate and dogged it. I stripped and backed into my own suit, and while I was making the attachments it occurred to me that that one flash might have been the last time I'd see her alive. She meant more to me than anybody else on this ship, probably more than anybody on Earth, but all I felt was a dulling, empty *better you than me, dear*. I hated myself for thinking it, but it was true.

The relief tubes went on all right, but the biometrical monitors wouldn't stay put on my sweat-drenched skin. I could just reach my tunic without getting out of the suit; managed to dry the spots sufficiently for the silver chloride electrodes to stick. The first platoon was coming through the lock by twos and threes by the time I got everything hitched up and put my arms in the suit's arms and closed up the front. The babble of conversation stopped and then continued, muted, sound conduction through the metal floor. I chinned Marygay's frequency.

"Ready, dear?"

"William? I guess, I—no, I'm not. Why couldn't they have given us more warning? I was so nervous anyhow, to have it come all of a sudden like that . . ."

"I know. Maybe it's better, though, rather than worry about it for days."

"All right get a move on let's go goddammit!" Cortez on the general frequency. Must have been on external monitor, too; all the people getting into their suits turned to look at him. "Let me have Sergeants Rogers and Mandella and Corporal Potter on my freak."

Cortez began a second after I chinned his frequency: "I'll be riding down with your platoon but, Rogers, remember that you're in charge, don't look my way for any kind of help. I've got three other platoons to worry about, and yours is supposed to be the best. And you others, listen up. If Ching gets it, one of you has to take over the fourth platoon. Mandella first, Potter if Mandella gets it. Understood?" We roger'd, but why the hell hadn't he told us sooner?

He clicked back to the general frequency. "Platoon leaders sound off." One at a time: Rogers, Akwasi, Bohrs, Ching. "All right, I'll give it to you and you can pass it on to your platoons after they're all dressed. We attack at 1131—that is, at 1131 we rip over the horizon and let loose all those good bombs. That means we've got to drop out of orbit in . . . exactly nine minutes, twenty seconds. So make your people move."

I couldn't control my shakes, so before I cut in the waldo circuits I swallowed a trank. Otherwise, trembling, I might have broken something. After the trank calmed me down, I took a stimtab to fire the old carcass back up to fighting order, activated my arms and legs, and began walking down the scoutship.

It seemed so big. The *Anniversary* itself was two kilometers long, but you could only visualize it in an abstract way. A scoutship was nearly a hundred meters of gleaming black metal, and inside the bay you never got far enough away that perspective didn't deform the streamlined shape and make it seem even longer.

Rogers waited back at the assembly area to make sure everybody got their suits and weapons in order. Marygay and Cortez and I entered the ship and strapped in and, speaking for myself, tried to relax a little.

After a few minutes, everybody was strapped down and waiting. Through the skin of the ship you could hear a high-pitched, fading whistle as they evacuated air from the bay. Then a slight bump and, through the porthole by my shoulder, I could see the struts and catwalks slide away and we were in space. It was 1027.

The descent to the surface, which had looked so smooth and graceful on Cortez's simulation, was a bone-wrenching ordeal as the ship twisted and swooped in the predetermined evasive pattern. There was a swabbie pilot up front, but he never touched the controls.

Skimming along the surface was a little easier to take. But the enemy must have been keeping pretty close tabs on our position, because six or seven times the laser flared out at a bubble. You couldn't see it happen, of course; just a green flicker on the tortured landscape rushing below and static electricity making your hair rustle.

1130: "Filters down. Prepare to disembark." Cortez's voice was flat with just a trace of controlled eagerness. He actually liked this crap.

Then a series of quick shudders as the bombs took off toward the enemy. I saw one streak to the horizon and explode in a glare so bright it hurt the eyes, even with the filter. It must have run into a bubble; the bombs didn't have the capabilities for defense and evasion that a scoutship had.

I turned on the pink light on the back of my suit that would identify me as a squad leader and tried to prepare myself mentally for the ejection. The trank was still holding pretty well; the fear was there, but it seemed detached, a memory. I wanted a smoke in the worst way.

Suddenly the base rolled over the horizon and I could see rubble strewn all over the plain; our ships, no way to tell whether they were drones—the Flower was still intact, spewing out bubbles. Ten or twelve ships flared by in different directions. Only two enemy ships were standing.

We decelerated to zero abruptly and my buckles unsnapped themselves, the side of the ship slid away, and I was falling free, less than ten meters from the ground. I was still falling when the ship flared and jumped away.

I landed kind of sloppily on hands and knees and chinned the squad frequency. "First squad sound off!"

"One." Tate.

"Two." Yukawa.

"Three." Shockley.

"Four." Hofstadter.

"Five." Rabi.

"Six." Mulroy.

Rogers: "Mandella, get your people on line; your squad goes up first."

"First squad line up on me." They were almost in position already. "Shockley, you're too close to Yukawa. Move this way about ten meters."

In the few seconds we had before advancing, I tried to figure out who was winning. Hard to tell. One of the standing enemy ships exploded as I watched, but the Flower was still bubbling away.

Something looked different about the bubbles—at first I thought it was just a trick of perspective, but then I saw that some of them were actually rolling along the ground! They'd been enough trouble on Aleph, where you just had to keep your head down to avoid them. Cortez shouted over the general frequency for everybody to watch out for the goddam bubbles, they were coming in low.

I supposed there was a chance that they had thought that up independently, but most likely it meant that they had been in contact with the one Aleph survivor. By inference, that meant they'd probably be capable of infighting, if it came to that.

Herz and the other heavy launcher fired round after round

at the Flower, without success. The bubbles were too thick and maneuverable that near their source.

Bubbles kept rolling toward us, but—the same as on Aleph—one brush with a laser would pop them.

Somebody managed to destroy the last ship. At least none of them would be getting away. Would any of us?

Cortez came on the general frequency in the middle of a sentence. "—the casualty report for later, I don't have time—listen once, everybody! We can't reach the Flower with the heavies. Have to move in, move in fast to grenade range, and saturate the area. Second platoon, can you salvage the gigawatt ship?" So at least one scoutship was down.

"All right, forget it. Odd-numbered squads, move out!"

I got up and started to jog, the rest of my squad spread out in a shallow V-formation behind me. Covering laser fire lanced around us, stopping bubbles—good thing; it's almost impossible to use a laser finger while you're moving. You're liable to hit almost anything except what you're aiming at.

After thirty or forty meters, we went to ground. The second squad advanced and slipped through us while we did target practice on the bubbles.

Then Bergman got it. He topped a small rise and there was a bubble, so close that his body shielded it from our fire. He fired one wild burst and then the lower half of his body dissolved into crimson spray and Marygay screamed. Even with explosive decompression, he didn't die right away but hopped a dozen meters, his death tremors magnified by the suit's waldo circuits. The bubble rolled on, glowing more brightly with its grisly fuel, until Tate recovered and popped it. I was dazed but kept covering my sector automatically.

Second squad went down and we advanced again, trying to ignore the splash of dark-red crystal where Bergman had died. We were within about four hundred meters of the Flower and Cortez cut in:

"All right, everybody hold your positions; grenadiers, open fire on the Flower. Everybody else cover."

Pretty soon we didn't have any bubbles to shoot at, up close. With eight grenadiers firing at once, it was all the Flower could do to protect itself. We walked forward without any resistance and started using our lasers on the building. They were attenuated considerably by the distance, but we managed to pop a few bubbles even that far away. That may have been what made the difference—four microton grenades hit the Flower simultaneously, each one a bright flash and a spray of debris. The bubbles stopped coming out.

"Hold your fire—hold it!" One last grenade sailed in and hit the building right at the ground line, causing one petal to collapse.

"Maybe we'll get our prisoner here . . . first squads out of the first and second platoons, move in fast and take a look."

Goddam, why us? On Aleph, all the Taurans were holed up in the Flower when we attacked, though we later discovered that the Salamis were their living quarters. That had been a surprise attack, too; they'd had plenty of warning this time. I chinned Tate.

"Tate, what the hell is the combination for first squad, second platoon?"

"Two left, one right." Of course. Getting addle-brained.

I chinned it as we advanced toward the nearest petal. "Al-Sadat, this is Mandella. Which of us goes first?"

"You're senior, Mandella. Besides, I was ahead at O'wari."

"Yeah. Crap. Okay. Hell, I don't even know how to get into the goddam thing. Burn it down, I guess."

"Mandella, this is Cortez. Don't you burn that door down if you can get in without depressurizing the petal. Once we get our prisoner, you can rape and pillage all you want. Kid gloves until then, understand?"

"Roger, Lieutenant." Maybe they'd open the door *for* me. That'd be jolly.

I decided a simple plan would be best. Hard to think: scared and suddenly tired. Swallowed another stimtab, knowing I'd pay for it in a couple of hours. But I figured that in a couple of hours I'd either be back in the ship or dead. "Al-Sadat, hold your people back for cover until we get inside, then follow us."

"Roger."

Chinned my squad frequency. "Tate, Yukawa, Shockley come with me—no, Tate, you stay behind, in case—rest of the squad give me a half perimeter about ten meters from the entrance. And for chrissake don't get trigger-happy."

While they were assembling, I took Yukawa and Shockley to the entrance. It was obviously a door, wide and squat with a small red circle painted in the exact center, windowless and with no hardware. Didn't look much like our complicated airlocks.

"Why don't you push on the circle, Sergeant?" That was Shockley, who was technically the most expendable. Smart, though; I'd look pretty silly now, ordering him to do it.

I checked to see that everybody was in position and pressed the circle. The door slid open.

No airlock. Just a long, well-lit corridor full of vacuum and cold. Lots of similar doors lining the corridor. With the uneasy feeling that it was some kind of a trap, I stepped inside.

"Okay, squad, follow me." Change frequency. "Al-Sadat?"

"I'm coming."

"Leave your second-in-command with Tate at the door."

"I've got a better idea—why don't I send my second up with you and—"

"Knock it off, Al. It's lovely in here. Soothing. Tauran dancing girls."

Cortez: "Will you all cut the crap and get me a prisoner?"

When all thirteen of us had crowded into the corridor, I touched the first door and it slid open. It revealed a softly lit cubicle, empty except for a strung wire hammock and what looked like a piece of abstract sculpture in one corner. I described it to Cortez.

"All right. Leave it alone and go on to the next."

The next cubicle was exactly the same, and so were all the rest, along both sides of the corridor. I would have guessed that they were living quarters, except that they didn't look at all like the dormitory affairs we found on Aleph, inside the Salamis. The inside of the Flower on Aleph had been filled with arcane machinery.

We approached the end of the corridor with caution. Corridors from all the other petals converged there in a large circular hall. In the center was a vertical metallic tube, two meters thick, that was connected with the bubble generator. The hall was littered with rubble and the tube seemed to be standing at a slight angle.

"Al, get your people on the left side of the corridor. I'll take the right. We'll move out along the walls and see what happens."

We spread ourselves evenly around the edge of the circular hall and waited for something to happen. Nothing did. I decided to maybe precipitate some action by having a grenadier launch one down one of the halls. Rabi was well-positioned.

"Rabi—" I didn't finish because suddenly we were all floating a meter off the ground and slowly rising.

"What the hell, Mandella—"

"Shut up, Al. Everybody! Get ready to open fire—we'll burn this thing to the ground if we—"

"What's going on in there, goddammit?" Cortez.

"We're going up." That sounded inadequate. "Floating up. Under their control."

Cortez was silent for a second. "Ah . . . all right. Do what you have to do to protect yourself. But remember I need a prisoner. We get one and we're home free."

We floated to a second level and stopped. Everybody jumped onto the rail-less balcony. Only one corridor on this level. I walked around to it.

"Hofstadter, Rabi, come along with me." We walked down about ten meters to a door at the end of the corridor, just like the ones downstairs.

It also slid open at a touch, but instead of the hammock and sculpture, there were rows of what looked like library-style book-cases, covered with overlapping metal shingles. Each row was a different shade of blue. At the end of one row was a Tauran, looking at us.

The only movement was in his too-many-fingered hands, which undulated nervously. I felt a mixture of revulsion and pity at seeing his bloated/scrawny hourglass-shaped orange body, all huge swellings and ridiculously flimsy limbs—I'd seen so many of those bodies laser-slashed and smoldering in the slaughter at Aleph—but still, they weren't human even though they were upright bipeds. You could feel more kinship with an egret.

"Keep an eye on him, Tate." I walked up and down the rows to see whether there were any others. The room was a large doughnut-shaped affair. I hadn't been in its counterpart on Aleph, but Fruenhauf had described it to me as being similar. It was evidently their computer. At last report—I had to keep reminding myself that it had been nearly a decade ago—they hadn't yet figured out what made it work.

The rest of the place was deserted. I made a report to Cortez.

"Good. You and three others stay and guard him. Send the rest back down and we'll go ahead with the battle plan, take the Salamis. They must be in there."

"If they haven't already left, sir."

"That's right. What do you think they would have left in, Sergeant? A matter transmitter? We got all the ships."

Possibly, I thought. They might have a matter transmitter out in the back yard, just didn't think to use it before.

"Let me have Tate, Mulroy, Hofstadter. We're going to stand guard on this . . . prisoner. Sergeant Al-Sadat—" That sounded too military. "Al, you're in charge of everybody else. Take them down and join up with your platoons."

"Sure, Mandella. How the hell do we get down?"

"I've got a rope, Sergeant." That was Wiley, demolition "man." Somehow, it wouldn't sound right to call her a "demolition woman."

They filed out and we surrounded the Tauran. His clustered eyes didn't follow Tate and Mulroy as they went behind him; he just kept staring straight ahead, either unconcerned or paralyzed. The soap bubble that held his personal environment shimmered slightly in the light that seemed to come evenly from ceiling, floor, and walls.

There was a meter-high ribbon of window running all around the outside wall. I could see Cortez and the two platoons taking up positions around the east Salami. It occurred to me that perhaps that was what the Tauran was staring at, not us. I switched to the general frequency and positioned myself so that I could watch the Tauran and the Salami at the same time.

Al-Sadat and his men had just left the Flower and were moving toward Cortez when everything started to happen at once.

The far end of the Salami opened and Taurans, seemingly hundreds of them, came boiling out. And they came out shooting.

Each one of them had a box that looked incongruously like a suitcase, handle, clasps, and all, and held a flexible tube that led into the box. They handled it like a laser, fanning it back and forth.

Our laser beams danced through their ranks. If they had stayed bunched up, they would have all been dead in a couple of seconds. But they spread out quickly and took what cover the terrain and buildings allowed.

One touch with a laser would pop their life-support bubble, but to my horror I saw that their weapon was no less effective. All over the plain men and women were whirling and jerking in waldo-amplified agony, dying too slowly. Cortez was screaming.

"Pick a target and *hit it!* Stay with it till you hit it! Grenadiers, use your fingers—second platoon, third platoon, who the
hell's in charge over there? Akwasi! Bohrs! Report!"

I turned to look at the west Salami, farther away, and it was
obvious the same thing was happening there.

"Busia! Maxwell! Who the hell's in charge?"

"Busia here, Lieutenant—I don't know, maybe I'm in charge.
I can't raise Akwasi or Bohrs. I—ai!" A short yelp and no more
transmission.

"Second platoon, third platoon, listen up. You've got weapons
superiority, so use it. Everybody-just-pick-a-target. And stay with
it until you kill it! We're winning over here and you should be
winning too—heavies! Herz! Conte! Knock down those fuckin'
Salamis, there might be more inside."

Two quick rockets reduced the west Salami to rubble. The
east stood.

"Lieutenant, this is Ching. Herz is dead."

"Well then pick up the launcher yourself. God . . . damn!"

"Luthuli here, I've got it." The first rocket went in low and
scooped out a big crater in front of the building. The second
knocked off a rounded corner and the third hit it dead center and
collapsed it.

I chinned Marygay's frequency. "Marygay, this is William.
Are you all right?"

Nothing.

"Are you all right?"

Cortez's voice cracked over the general freak. "Goddammit,
cut the private jawin', we haven't won yet. That includes you
spectators up there. Luthuli to your right watch out! Good!"

The Tauran was still staring impassively.

My count showed only six Taurans alive to the east, and one
of them got caulked while I was counting. I cranked my image
amplifier up to twenty log two and looked west, but from this
angle it was hard to tell what the score was. Plenty of activity
going on.

"All right, that's it," Cortez yelled. "Follow me, let's help the
second and third."

What was left of the first and fourth platoons sprinted across
the plain after Cortez. They left ten inert figures behind. One of
them was Marygay.

Numb, I raised my finger and pointed it at the Tauran. But

I couldn't get up any hate for him. I tried to hate Cortez, but that didn't work either. It was as if we were all just caught up in some impersonal catastrophe, and you couldn't blame some individual person or creature for the wrath of the elements.

The battle to the west was over by the time Cortez and his men got there. They had lost twelve. Cortez called for the ships.

I had expected that if we were going to have any trouble with the Tauran, it would be now, trying to get him outside and into a ship. But he seemed to understand our gestures and went along quietly. Whatever it was that had lifted us to the second floor worked both ways; following him, we just stepped over the edge and drifted gently down.

He walked to the ship without any protest and seemed to know what an acceleration couch was. We tried to strap him in, but the belt only encircled his bubble. The swabbie said that was all right; he was going to take it easy anyhow, not knowing how much tolerance a Tauran had for acceleration.

You couldn't help wondering why the Tauran was so docile. It occurred to me that perhaps he was a boobytrap; a bomb that could walk into the middle of the *Anniversary* and explode. Somebody else had thought of that too, for there was a portable fluoroscope waiting for us when we docked. It didn't show anything unusual.

All things considered, the *Anniversary* was pretty well equipped for taking a Tauran prisoner. We had a special "brig" which duplicated the atmosphere we had found in the Salamis on Aleph, and a case of food containers from the same source. We turned the Tauran over to the xenobiologists and retired to lick our wounds.

We had come to Yod-4 with seventy-three people and were leaving with twenty-seven, by my count. They hadn't released the casualty figures yet. But there were a lot of familiar faces missing. I had to find out sooner or later, so I went to Cortez. I rapped on the door of his cabin.

"Who is it?" he said gruffly.

"Sergeant Mandella, sir."

"All right. Enter."

He was sitting on his spartan bunk cradling a coffee cup in both hands. There was a bottle at his feet that I recognized as being some of Lieutenant Bok's homemade booze. "Well?"

"Sir, I wanted to—I had to know . . . know how Marygay died."

He looked at me for a long moment, without expression. Then he took a drink and snorted. "Corporal Potter is not dead."

"Not dead! She was . . . wounded?"

"No. Nobody was wounded. Nobody was wounded and lived."

"Then . . . sir? What happened?"

"Catatonic." He poured a slosh of liquor into the cup and twirled it around, stared at it, sniffed it. "I don't know exactly what happened. I don't really care. She's in sick bay. You may check with Lieutenant Pastori."

She was alive! "Thank you, sir." I turned to leave.

"Sergeant."

"Sir?"

"Don't get your hopes up. Depending on Lieutenant Pastori's evaluation, she may still face a court-martial. There is only one penalty for cowardice under fire."

"Yes sir." Even that couldn't blunt my relief, my happiness.

"You may go."

Halfway down the corridor I met Kamehameha. She had on a fresh tunic and even some cosmetics, God knows where she got them. I threw her a salute and a wink and whispered, "Carry on, Corporal."

6

The only other person in the sick bay waiting room was Ensign Singhe.

"Good afternoon, Ensign."

"In a way, Sergeant. Have a seat."

I sat down. "Heard anything?"

"About Corporal Potter? No."

I crossed to the bulletin board and read a dozen different things that had nothing to do with me. Then Pastori came out. Singhe jumped up but I got him first.

"Doctor—how is Corporal Potter?"

"Who are you, that I should give you a progress report?"

"Uh . . . sir, I'm Sergeant Mandella, from her platoon."

"You'll be reporting to Lieutenant Cortez?" he said with just a faint hint of sarcasm. He knew who I was.

"No, uh, sir, my interest is personal. I'll be glad to report if you—"

"No." He waggled his head loosely. "I'll take care of the red tape. My aide needs something to keep him busy. Sit down. Who are you, Ensign?"

"Personal interest too."

"My, my. Such charms my patient must have had. Still has," he added quickly. "Neither of you ought to worry about this too much. It's a common enough malady among soldiers; I've treated a couple of dozen cases like it since Aleph. Responds very well to hypnotherapy."

"Battle fatigue?" Singhe asked.

"That's a polite term for it. Another is 'neurasthenia.' I think the sub-major calls it cowardice."

I remembered what Cortez had said, and a ripple of fear ran up my back and crawled over my scalp.

"In Corporal Potter's case," he continued, "it's quite understandable. I got the details from her under light hypnosis.

"When the Taurans attacked, she was one of the first to see them coming out of the building. She went to ground immediately, but a couple of other people in her squad didn't. They were cut down in the first instant of the attack. They died horribly and she just couldn't handle it; she felt she was in some way responsible, both because she was their squad leader and because she hadn't said anything by way of warning. Actually, I doubt that there was any time to warn them.

"I suppose she also feels some guilt simply because she lived and they died. At any rate, she went into a state of shock right there and just withdrew completely. In civilian life, and in layman's terms, you would say she'd had a profound nervous breakdown."

That didn't sound so good. "Then, doctor . . . what will your recommendation be?"

"Recommendation?"

"To the court-martial board. Sir."

"What, are they really talking about trying her? For cowardice?" I nodded. "Ridiculous. A normal reaction to an insupportable situation. This is a medical condition, not a moral one."

I guess my relief was obvious.

"Now don't you go telling tales. Sub-major Stott is a good soldier, but I know he thinks discipline is getting poor and he's probably looking for a sacrificial lamb. Nothing you say is going to help her. Just wait for my report. That goes for you too, Ensign. The word is, you didn't get to see her; you don't know anything except that she's resting comfortably."

"When will I"—he looked at me—"we get to see her?"

"Not for at least a week, maybe two. I'm going to . . ." He shook his head. "It's impossible to explain without using technical terms. In a way, it's just making her look at the incident rationally, with a full knowledge of . . . what part of her psychological makeup made her react the way she did. To do this I have to make her regress to infancy and grow up again, pointing out stops along the way that have bearing on the situation. It's a standard technique, ninety-nine percent successful."

We exchanged politenesses and left.

I could have slept the clock around, reaction from the stimtabs, but we had an announcement saying that all infantry personnel would assemble after chop. I skipped chop and asked Tate to wake me up in time.

When I got to the chop hall, everybody was sitting in one corner, the empty seats crowding in on them like tombstones. It hit me with new force: we had left the training center in Missouri with one hundred people, and had picked up twenty more along the way. And now this little cluster of survivors.

I sat and listened to the talk without joining in. Most of it concerned going home: how much the world would have changed in the nearly twenty years we'd been gone, whether we'd have to retrain to get into the job market. . . . Alenandrov pointed out that we had twenty years' pay waiting for us, and it had been drawing compound interest. Plus a retirement pension. We might never have to work again. Nobody mentioned reenlisting. Nobody mentioned the fact that they might not let us go. It costs a lot to haul twenty-seven people from Stargate to Earth.

Stott walked in and, as we were rising, said, "Sit down."

He looked at the little group, and I could tell by his dark expression that he was thinking the same thing I had. He walked around in front of us.

"I'm not a religious man," he rasped. "If there is anyone here who would like to offer a prayer or a eulogy of some kind, let him do so now." There was a long silence.

"Very well." He reached into his tunic and pulled out a small plastic box. "Normally of course smoking is forbidden on the *Anniversary*. However, I have made a special arrangement with the maintenance people." He opened the box and inside there was a stack of factory joints. He set them carefully on the table. I wondered how long he'd had them.

He walked back to the door, very stiffly and without his usual briskness, and stopped. Facing out, he said, almost to himself, "You fought well." Then he left.

After a year of abstinence, and as tired as I was, the marijuana hit me hard. I smoked half a joint and fell asleep in the chair. I didn't dream.

After a week, waiting for the analysts to finish up planetside, we dropped through Yod-4 and popped out of Tet-38. We had to make a quarter-light-year circle around Tet-38 to position ourselves for the jump to Sade-20 and thence to Stargate.

It was during this long loop that we were first allowed to see Marygay.

She was in bed, the only person in sick bay. She looked very drawn and appeared to have lost considerable weight. *Won't be able to wear her fighting suit,* I thought inanely.

I sat by her bed for half an hour, watching her sleep. Ensign Singhe came in and nodded at me and left again.

After a while she opened her eyes. She looked at me for a long moment without expression, then smiled.

"Does this mean I'm well, William?"

"Better, anyhow."

"I thought so. The therapy . . . he took me back to where I was a little baby, made me grow up again. Yesterday we finally got back to the present. I think it's the present—William, how old am I?"

"Ship time, I think you're twenty-two."

She nodded without raising her head from the pillow. "I wonder what the year is on Earth."

"Last I heard it, it'll be 2017 when we reach Stargate."

She giggled. "I'll be a middle-aged lady."

"You'll never be a lady to me, dear." I patted her bare arm.

"That reminds me," she said, dropping to a conspiratorial whisper. "I'm horny."

"You mean that wasn't included in the therapy?"

"Nuh-uh."

"What do you expect me to do about it?"

"The obvious. Or maybe call up Ensign Singhe."

"Here? What if Pastori comes in?"

"He'd just take notes. You can't shock a psychiatrist."

The one good thing about these floppy tunics is that you can get out of one in half a second.

7

Pastori's report saved Marygay from a court-martial. The next seven months were uneventful, going from Tet-38 to Sade-20 to Stargate. We still had the regular rounds of calisthenics and inspections, though even Stott must have known that none of us intended to stay in the Force; none of us would ever fight again. It worried me a little, this insistence on maintaining the military life. I thought it might mean they weren't going to let us out.

The more likely explanation was that it was the easiest way to keep order aboard the ship.

The Tauran prisoner had died two days after he was captured. As far as anyone could tell, it wasn't suicide; he seemed to be cooperating with the xenobiologists—maybe he was one himself—but they learned very little, watching him waste away. An autopsy revealed that he had become totally dehydrated, although we had kept him well supplied with water. For some reason he just didn't assimilate it.

And, of course, with the Tauran dead, there went the only reason for our going planetside rather than sitting in a safe orbit and dropping missiles.

Things had shifted around a little bit, so it was 2019 when we arrived at Stargate.

Stargate had grown astonishingly in the past twelve years. The base was one building the size of Tycho City, housing about ten thousand people. There were seventy-eight ships the size of the *Anniversary* or larger, involved in raids on Tauran-held portal planets. Another ten guarded Stargate itself, and two were in orbit waiting for their infantry to be out-processed. One other ship, the *Earth's Hope II,* had returned from fighting while we were gone. They also had failed to bring home a live Tauran.

We went planetside in two scoutships.

General Botsford (who had only been a full major the first time we met him, when Stargate was two huts and twenty-four graves) received us in an elegantly appointed seminar room. He was pacing back and forth at the end of the room, in front of a huge holographic operations chart.

"You know," he said, too loud, and then, more conversationally, "you know that we could disperse you into other strike forces and send you right out again. The Elite Conscription Act has been changed now, five years' subjective in service instead of two.

"And I don't see why some of you don't *want* to stay in! Another couple of years and compound interest would make you independently wealthy for life. Sure, you took heavy losses—but that was inevitable, you were the first. Things are going to be easier now. The fighting suits have been improved, we know more about the Taurans' tactics, our weapons are more effective . . . there's no need to be afraid."

He sat down at the head of the table and looked at nobody in particular.

"My own memories of combat are over a half-century old. To me it was exhilarating, strengthening. I must be a different kind of person than all of you."

Or have a very selective memory, I thought.

"But that's neither here nor there. I have one alternative to offer you, one that doesn't involve direct combat.

"We're very short of qualified instructors. The Force will offer any one of you a lieutenancy if you will accept a training position. It can be on Earth; on the Moon at double pay; on Charon at triple pay; or here at Stargate for quadruple pay. Furthermore, you don't have to make up your mind now. You're all getting a free trip back to Earth—I envy you, I haven't been back in fifteen years, will probably never go back—and you can get the feel of being a civilian again. If you don't like it, just walk into any UNEF installation and you'll walk out an officer. Your choice of assignment.

"Some of you are smiling. I think you ought to reserve judgment. Earth is not the same place you left."

He pulled a little card out of his tunic and looked at it, smiling. "Most of you have something on the order of four hundred thousand dollars coming to you, accumulated pay and interest. But Earth is on a war footing and, of course, it is the citizens of Earth who are supporting the war. Your income puts you in a ninety-two-percent income-tax bracket: thirty-two thousand might last you about three years if you're careful.

"Eventually you're going to have to get a job, and this is one job for which you are uniquely trained. There are not that many jobs available. The population of Earth is nearly nine billion, with five or six billion unemployed.

"Also keep in mind that your friends and sweethearts of two years ago are now going to be twenty-one years older than you. Many of your relatives will have passed away. I think you'll find it a very lonely world.

"But to tell you something about this world, I'm going to turn you over to Captain Siri, who just arrived from Earth. Captain?"

"Thank you, General." It looked as if there was something wrong with his skin, his face; and then I realized he was wearing powder and lipstick. His nails were smooth white almonds.

"I don't know where to begin." He sucked in his upper lip and looked at us, frowning. "Things have changed so very much since I was a boy.

"I'm twenty-three, so I was still in diapers when you people left for Aleph . . . to begin with, how many of you are homosexual?" Nobody. "That doesn't really surprise me. I am, of course. I guess about a third of everybody in Europe and America is.

"Most governments encourage homosexuality—the United Nations is neutral, leaves it up to the individual countries—they encourage homolife mainly because it's the one sure method of birth control."

That seemed specious to me. Our method of birth control in the army is pretty foolproof: all men making a deposit in the sperm bank, and then vasectomy.

"As the General said, the population of the world is nine billion. It's more than doubled since you were drafted. And nearly two-thirds of those people get out of school only to go on relief.

"Speaking of school, how many years of public schooling did the government give you?"

He was looking at me, so I answered. "Fourteen."

He nodded. "It's eighteen now. More, if you don't pass your examinations. And you're required by law to pass your exams before you're eligible for any job or Class One relief. And brother-boy, anything besides Class One is hard to live on. Yes?" Hofstadter had his hand up.

"Sir, is it eighteen years public school in every country? Where do they find enough schools?"

"Oh, most people take the last five or six years at home or in a community center, via holoscreen. The UN has forty or fifty information channels, giving instruction twenty-four hours a day.

"But most of you won't have to concern yourselves with that. If you're in the Force, you're already too smart by half."

He brushed hair from his eyes in a thoroughly feminine gesture, pouting a little. "Let me do some history to you. I guess the first really important thing that happened after you left was the Ration War.

"That was 2007. A lot of things happened at once. Locust plague in North America, rice blight from Burma to the South China Sea, red tides all along the west coast of South America: suddenly there just wasn't enough food to go around. The UN stepped in and took over food distribution. Every man, woman, and child got a ration booklet, allowing thim to consume so many calories per month. If tha went over ther monthly allotment, tha just went hungry until the first of the next month."

Some of the new people we'd picked up after Aleph used "tha, ther, thim" instead of "he, his, him," for the collective pronoun. I wondered whether it had become universal.

"Of course, an illegal market developed, and soon there was great inequality in the amount of food people in various strata of society consumed. A vengeance group in Ecuador, the Imparciales, systematically began to assassinate people who appeared to be well-fed. The idea caught on pretty quickly, and in a few months there was a full-scale, undeclared class war going on all over the world. The United Nations managed to get things back under control in a year or so, by which time the population was down to four billion, crops were more or less recovered, and the food crisis was over. They kept the rationing, but it's never been really severe again.

"Incidentally, the General translated the money coming to you into dollars just for your own convenience. The world has only one currency now, calories. Your thirty-two thousand dollars comes to about three thousand million calories. Or three million κ's, kilocalories.

"Ever since the Ration War, the UN has encouraged subsistence farming wherever it's practical. Food you grow yourself, of course, isn't rationed. . . . It got people out of the cities, onto UN farming reservations, which helped alleviate some urban problems. But subsistence farming seems to encourage large families, so the population of the world has more than doubled since the Ration War.

"Also, we no longer have the abundance of electrical power I remember from boyhood . . . probably a good deal less than you remember. There are only a few places in the world where you can have power all day and night. They keep saying it's a temporary situation, but it's been going on for over a decade."

He went on like that for a long time. Well, hell, it wasn't really surprising, much of it. We'd probably spent more time in the past two years talking about what home was going to be like than about anything else. Unfortunately, most of the bad things we'd prognosticated seemed to have come true, and not many of the good things.

The worst thing for me, I guess, was that they'd taken over most of the good parkland and subdivided it into little farms. If you wanted to find some wilderness, you had to go someplace where they couldn't possibly make a plant grow.

He said that the relations between people who chose homolife and the ones he called "breeders" were quite smooth, but I wondered. I never had much trouble accepting homosexuals myself, but then I'd never had to cope with such an abundance of them.

He also said, in answer to an impolite question, that his powder and paint had nothing to do with his sexual orientation. It was just stylish. I decided I'd be an anachronism and just wear my face.

I don't guess it should have surprised me that language had changed considerably in twenty years. My parents were always saying things were "cool," joints were "grass," and so on.

We had to wait several weeks before we could get a ride back to Earth. We'd be going back on the *Anniversary,* but first she had to be taken apart and put back together again.

Meanwhile, we were put in cosy little two-man billets and released from all military responsibilities. Most of us spent our days down at the library, trying to catch up on twenty-two years of current events. Evenings, we'd get together at the Flowing Bowl, an NCO club. The privates, of course, weren't supposed to be there, but we found that nobody argues with a person who has two of the fluorescent battle ribbons.

I was surprised that they served heroin fixes at the bar. The waiter said that you get a compensating shot to keep you from getting addicted to it. I got really stoned and tried one. Never again.

Sub-major Stott stayed at Stargate, where they were assembling a new Strike Force Alpha. The rest of us boarded the *Anniversary* and had a fairly pleasant six-month journey. Cortez didn't insist on everything being capital-M military, so it was a lot better than the trip from Yod-4.

8

I hadn't given it too much thought, but of course we were celebrities on Earth: the first vets home from the war. The Secretary General greeted us at Kennedy and we had a week-long whirl of banquets, receptions, interviews, and all that. It was enjoyable enough, and profitable—I made a million κ's from Time-Life/Fax—but we really saw little of Earth until after the novelty wore off and we were more or less allowed to go our own way.

I picked up the Washington monorail at Grand Central Station and headed home. My mother had met me at Kennedy, suddenly and sadly old, and told me my father was dead. Flyer accident. I was going to stay with her until I could get a job.

She was living in Columbia, a satellite of Washington. She had moved back into the city after the Ration War—having moved out in 1980—and then failing services and rising crime had forced her out again.

She was waiting for me at the monorail station. Beside her stood a blond giant in a heavy black vinyl uniform, with a big gunpowder pistol on his hip and spiked brass knuckles on his right hand.

"William, this is Carl, my bodyguard and very dear friend." Carl slipped off the knuckles long enough to shake hands with surprising gentleness. "Pleasameecha Misser Mandella."

We got into a groundcar that had "Jefferson" written on it in bright orange letters. I thought that was an odd thing to name a car, but then found out that it was the name of the high-rise Mother and Carl lived in. The groundcar was one of several that belonged to the community, and she paid 100κ per kilometer for the use of it.

I had to admit that Columbia was rather pretty: formal gardens and lots of trees and grass. Even the high-rises, roughly conical jumbles of granite with trees growing out at odd places, looked more like mountains than buildings. We drove into the base of one of these mountains, down a well-lit corridor to where a number of other cars were parked. Carl carried my solitary bag to the elevator and set it down.

"Miz Mandella, if is awright witcha, I gots to go pick up Miz Freeman in like five. She over West Branch."

"Sure, Carl, William can take care of me. He's a soldier, you know." That's right, I remember learning eight silent ways to kill a man. Maybe if things got really tight, I could get a job like Carl's.

"Righty-oh, yeah, you tol' me. Whassit like, man?"

"Mostly boring," I said automatically. "When you aren't bored, you're scared."

He nodded wisely. "Thass what I heard. Miz Mandella, I be 'vailable anytime affer six. Righty-oh?"

"That's fine, Carl."

The elevator came and a tall skinny boy stepped out, an unlit joint dangling from his lips. Carl ran his fingers over the spikes on his knuckles, and the boy walked rapidly away.

"Gots ta watch out fer them riders. T'care a yerself, Miz Mandella."

We got on the elevator and Mother punched 47. "What's a rider?"

"Oh, they're just young toughs who ride up and down the elevators looking for defenseless people without bodyguards. They aren't too much of a problem here."

The forty-seventh floor was a huge mall filled with shops and offices. We went to a food store.

"Have you gotten your ration book yet, William?" I told her I hadn't, but the Force had given me travel tickets worth a hundred thousand "calories" and I'd used up only half of them.

It was a little confusing, but they'd explained it to us. When the world went on a single currency, they'd tried to coordinate it with the food rationing in some way, hoping to eventually eliminate the ration books, so they'd made the new currency ĸ's, kilocalories, because that's the unit for measuring the energy equivalent of food. But a person who eats 2,000 kilocalories of steak a day obviously has to pay more than a person eating the same amount of bread. So they instituted a sliding "ration factor," so complicated that nobody could understand it. After a few weeks they were using the books again, but calling food kilocalories "calories" in an attempt to make things less confusing. Seemed to me they'd save a lot of trouble all around if they'd just call money dollars again, or rubles or sisterces or whatever . . . anything but kilocalories.

Food prices were astonishing, except for grains and legumes. I insisted on splurging on some good red meat: 1500 calories worth of ground beef, costing 1730κ. The same amount of fake-steak, made from soy beans, would have cost 80κ.

I also got a head of lettuce for 140κ and a little bottle of olive oil for 175κ. Mother said she had some vinegar. Started to buy some mushrooms but she said she had a neighbor who grew them and could trade something from her balcony garden.

At her apartment on the ninety-second floor, she apologized for the smallness of the place. It didn't seem so little to me, but then she'd never lived on a spaceship.

Even this high up, there were bars on the windows. The door had four separate locks, one of which didn't work because some-body had used a crowbar on it.

Mother went off to turn the ground beef into a meatloaf and I settled down with the evening 'fax. She pulled some carrots from her little garden and called the mushroom lady, whose son came over to make the trade. He had a riot gun slung under his arm.

"Mother, where's the rest of the *Star?*" I called into the kitchen.

"As far as I know, it's all there. What were you looking for?"

"Well . . . I found the classified section, but no 'Help Wanted.' "

She laughed. "Son, there hasn't been a 'Help Wanted' ad in ten years. The government takes care of jobs . . . well, most of them."

"Everybody works for the government?"

"No, that's not it." She came in, wiping her hands on a frayed towel. "The government, they tell us, handles the distribution of all natural resources. And there aren't many resources more valuable than empty jobs."

"Well, I'll go talk to them tomorrow."

"Don't bother, son. How much retirement pay you say you're getting from the Force?"

"Twenty thousand κ a month. Doesn't look like it'll go far."

"No, it won't. But your father's pension gave me less than

half that, and they wouldn't give me a job. Jobs are assigned on a basis of need. And you've got to be living on rice and water before the Employment Board considers you needy."

"Well, hell, it's a bureaucracy—there must be somebody I can pay off, slip me into a good—"

"No. Sorry, that's one part of the UN that's absolutely incorruptible. The whole shebang is cybernetic, untouched by human souls. You can't—"

"But you said you *had* a job!"

"I was getting to that. If you want a job badly enough, you can go to a dealer and sometimes get a hand-me-down."

"Hand-me-down? Dealer?"

"Take my job as an example, son. A woman named Hailey Williams has a job in a hospital, running a machine that analyzes blood, a chromatography machine. She works six nights a week, for 12,000k a week. She gets tired of working, so she contacts a dealer and lets him know that her job is available.

"Some time before this, I'd given the dealer his initial fee of 50,000k to get on his list. He comes by and describes the job to me and I say fine, I'll take it. He knew I would and already has fake identification and a uniform. He distributes small bribes to the various supervisors who might know Miss Williams by sight.

"Miss Williams shows me how to run the machine and quits. She still gets the weekly 12,000k credited to her account, but she pays me half. I pay the dealer ten percent and wind up with 5400k per week. This, added to the nine grand I get monthly from your father's pension, makes me quite comfortable.

"Then it gets complicated. Finding myself with plenty of money and too little time, I contact the dealer again, offering to sublet half my job. The next day a girl shows up who also has 'Hailey Williams' identification. I show her how to run the machine, and she takes over Monday-Wednesday-Friday. Half of my real salary is 2700k, so she gets half that, 1350k, and pays the dealer 135."

She got a pad and a stylus and did some figuring. "So the real Hailey Williams gets 6000k weekly for doing nothing. I work three days a week for 4050k. My assistant works three days for 1115k. The dealer gets 100,000k in fees and 735k per week. Lopsided, isn't it?"

"Hmm . . . I'll say. Quite illegal, too, I suppose."

"For the dealer. Everybody else might lose their job and have to start over, if the Employment Board finds out. But the dealer gets brainwiped."

"Guess I better find a dealer, while I can still afford the fifty-grand bite." Actually, I still had over three million, but planned to run through most of it in a short time. Hell, I'd earned it.

I was getting ready to go the next morning when Mother came in with a shoebox. Inside, there was a small pistol in a clip-on holster.

"This belonged to your father," she explained. "Better wear it if you're planning to go downtown without a bodyguard."

It was a gunpowder pistol with ridiculously thin bullets. I hefted it in my hand. "Did Dad ever use it?"

"Several times . . . just to scare away riders and hitters, though. He never actually shot anybody."

"You're probably right that I need a gun," I said, putting it back. "But I'd have to have something with more heft to it. Can I buy one legally?"

"Sure, there's a gun store down in the Mall. As long as you don't have a police record, you can buy anything that suits you." Good; I'd get a little pocket laser. I could hardly hit the wall with a gunpowder pistol.

"But . . . William, I'd feel a lot better if you'd hire a bodyguard, at least until you know your way around." We'd gone all around that last night. Being an official Trained Killer, I thought I was tougher than any clown I might hire for the job.

"I'll check into it, Mother. Don't worry—I'm not even going downtown today, just into Hyattsville."

"That's just as bad."

When the elevator came, it was already occupied. He looked at me blandly as I got in, a man a little older than me, clean-shaven and well dressed. He stepped back to let me at the row of buttons. I punched 47 and then, realizing his motive might not have been politeness, turned to see him struggling to get at a metal pipe stuck in his waistband. It had been hidden by his cape.

"Come on, fella," I said, reaching for a nonexistent weapon. "You wanna get caulked?"

He had the pipe free but let it hang loosely at his side. "Caulked?"

"Killed. Army term." I took one step toward him, trying to remember. Kick just under the knee, then either groin or kidney. I decided on the groin.

"No." He put the pipe back in his waistband. "I don't want to get 'caulked.'" The door opened at 47 and I backed out.

The gun shop was all bright white plastic and gleamy black metal. A little bald man bobbed over to wait on me. He had a pistol in a shoulder rig.

"And a fine morning to you, sir," he said and giggled. "What will it be today?"

"Lightweight pocket laser," I said. "Carbon dioxide."

He looked at me quizzically and then brightened. "Coming right up, sir." Giggle. "Special today, I throw in a handful of tachyon grenades."

"Fine." They'd be handy.

He looked at me expectantly. "So? What's the popper?"

"Huh?"

"The punch, man; you set me up, now knock me down. Laser." He giggled.

I was beginning to understand. "You mean I can't buy a laser."

"Of *course* not, sweetie," he said and sobered. "You didn't know that?"

"I've been out of the country for a long time."

"The world, you mean. You've been out of the world a long time." He put his left hand on a chubby hip in a gesture that incidentally made his gun easier to get. He scratched the center of his chest.

I stood very still. "That's right. I just got out of the Force."

His jaw dropped. "Hey, no bully-bull? You been out shootin' 'em up, out in space?"

"That's right."

"Hey, all that crap about you not gettin' older, there's nothin' to that, is there?"

"Oh, it's true. I was born in 1975."

"Well, god . . . damn. You're almost as old as I am." He giggled. "I thought that was just something the gover'ment made up."

"Anyhow . . . you say I can't buy a laser—"

"Oh, no. No no no. I run a legal shop here."

"What can I buy?"

"Oh, pistol, rifle, shotgun, knife, body armor . . . just no lasers or explosives or fully automatic weapons."

"Let me see a pistol. The biggest you have."

"Ah, I've got just the thing." He motioned me over to a display case and opened the back, taking out a huge revolver.

"Four-ten-gauge six-shooter." He cradled it in both hands. "Dinosaur-stopper. Authentic Old West styling. Slugs or flechettes."

"Flechettes?"

"Sure—uh, they're like a bunch of tiny darts. You shoot and they spread out in a pattern. Hard to miss that way."

Sounded like my speed. "Anyplace I can try it out?"

" 'Course, of course, we have a range in back. Let me get my assistant." He rang a bell and a boy came out to watch the store while we went in back. He picked up a red-and-green box of shotgun shells on the way.

The range was in two sections, a little anteroom with a plastic transparent door and a long corridor on the other side of the door with a table at one end and targets at the other. Behind the targets was a sheet of metal that evidently deflected the bullets down into a pool of water.

He loaded the pistol and set it on the table. "Please don't pick it up until the door's closed." He went into the anteroom, closed the door, and picked up a microphone. "Okay. First time, you better hold on to it with both hands." I did so, raising it up in line with the center target, a square of paper looking about the size of your thumbnail at arm's length. Doubted I'd even come near it. I pulled the trigger and it went back easily enough, but nothing happened.

"No, no," he said over the microphone with a tinny giggle. "Authentic Old West styling. You've got to pull the hammer back."

Sure, just like in the flicks. I hauled the hammer back, lined it up again, and squeezed the trigger.

The noise was so loud it made my face sting. The gun bucked up and almost hit me on the forehead. But the three center targets were gone: just tiny tatters of paper drifting in the air.

"I'll take it."

He sold me a hip holster, twenty shells, a chest-and-back

shield, and a dagger in a boot sheath. I felt more heavily armed than I had in a fighting suit. But no waldos to help me cart it around.

The monorail had two guards for each car. I was beginning to feel that all my heavy artillery was superfluous, until I got off at the Hyattsville station.

Everyone who got off at Hyattsville was either heavily armed or had a bodyguard. The people loitering around the station were all armed. The police carried lasers.

I pushed a "cab call" button, and the readout told me mine would be No. 3856. I asked a policeman and he told me to wait for it down on the street; it would cruise around the block twice.

During the five minutes I waited, I twice heard staccato arguments of gunfire, both of them rather far away. I was glad I'd bought the shield.

Eventually the cab came. It swerved to the curb when I waved at it, the door sliding open as it stopped. Looked as if it worked the same way as the autocabs I remembered. The door stayed open while it checked the thumbprint to verify that I was the one who had called, then slammed shut. It was thick steel. The view through the windows was dim and distorted; probably thick bulletproof plastic. Not quite the same as I remembered.

I had to leaf through a grimy book to find the code for the address of the bar in Hyattsville where I was supposed to meet the dealer. I punched it out and sat back to watch the city go by.

This part of town was mostly residential: grayed-brick warrens built around the middle of the last century competing for space with more modern modular setups and, occasionally, individual houses behind tall brick or concrete walls with jagged broken glass and barbed wire at the top. A few people seemed to be going somewhere, walking very quickly down the sidewalks, hands on weapons. Most of the people I saw were either sitting in doorways, smoking, or loitering around shopfronts in groups of no fewer than six. Everything was dirty and cluttered. The gutters were clotted with garbage, and shoals of waste paper drifted with the wind of the light traffic.

It was understandable, though; street-sweeping was probably a very high-risk profession.

The cab pulled up in front of Tom & Jerry's Bar and Grill

and let me out after I paid 430ᴋ. I stepped to the sidewalk with my hand on the shotgun-pistol, but there was nobody around. I hustled into the bar.

It was surprisingly clean on the inside, dimly lit and furnished in fake leather and fake pine. I went to the bar and got some fake bourbon and, presumably, real water for 120ᴋ. The water cost 20ᴋ. A waitress came over with a tray.

"Pop one, brother-boy?" The tray had a rack of old-fashioned hypodermic needles.

"Not today, thanks." If I was going to "pop one," I'd use an aerosol. The needles looked unsanitary and painful.

She set the dope down on the bar and eased onto the stool next to me. She sat with her chin cupped in her palm and stared at her reflection in the mirror behind the bar. "God. Tuesdays."

I mumbled something.

"You wanna go in back fer a quickie?"

I looked at her with what I hoped was a neutral expression. She was wearing only a short skirt of some gossamer material, and it plunged in a shallow V in the front, exposing her hipbones and a few bleached pubic hairs. I wondered what could possibly keep it up. She wasn't bad looking, could have been anywhere from her late twenties to her early forties. No telling what they could do with cosmetic surgery and makeup nowadays, though. Maybe she was older than my mother.

"Thanks anyhow."

"Not today?"

"That's right."

"I can get you a nice boy, if—"

"No. No thanks." What a world.

She pouted into the mirror, an expression that was probably older than *Homo sapiens*. "You don't like me."

"I like you fine. That's just not what I came here for."

"Well . . . different funs for different ones." She shrugged. "Hey, Jerry. Get me a short beer."

He brought it.

"Oh, damn, my purse is locked up. Mister, can you spare forty calories?" I had enough ration tickets to take care of a whole banquet. Tore off a fifty and gave it to the bartender.

"Jesus." She stared. "How'd you get a full book at the end of the month?"

I told her in as few words as possible who I was and how I managed to have so many calories. There had been two months' worth of books waiting in my mail, and I hadn't even used up the ones the Force had given me. She offered to buy a book from me for ten grand, but I didn't want to get involved in more than one illegal enterprise at a time.

Two men came in, one unarmed and the other with both a pistol and a riot gun. The bodyguard sat by the door and the other came over to me.

"Mr. Mandella?"

"That's right."

"Shall we take a booth?" He didn't offer his name.

He had a cup of coffee, and I sipped a mug of beer. "I don't keep any written records, but I have an excellent memory. Tell me what sort of a job you're interested in, what your qualifications are, what salary you'll accept, and so on."

I told him I'd prefer to wait for a job where I could use my physics—teaching or research, even engineering. I wouldn't need a job for two or three months, since I planned to travel and spend money for a while. Wanted at least 20,000k monthly, but how much I'd accept would depend on the nature of the job.

He didn't say a word until I'd finished. "Righty-oh. Now, I'm afraid . . . you'd have a hard time, getting a job in physics. Teaching is out; I can't supply jobs where the person is constantly exposed to the public. Research, well, your degree is almost a quarter of a century old. You'd have to go back to school, maybe five or six years."

"Might do that," I said.

"The one really marketable feature you have is your combat experience. I could probably place you in a supervisory job at a bodyguard agency for even more than twenty grand. You could make almost that much, being a bodyguard yourself."

"Thanks, but I wouldn't want to take chances for somebody else's hide."

"Righty-oh. Can't say I blame you." He finished his coffee in a long slurp. "Well, I've got to run, got a thousand things to do. I'll keep you in mind and talk to some people."

"Good. I'll see you in a few months."

"Righty-oh. Don't need to make an appointment. I come in here every day at eleven for coffee. Just show up."

I finished my beer and called a cab to take me home. I wanted to walk around the city, but Mother was right. I'd get a bodyguard first.

9

I came home and the phone was blinking pale blue. Didn't know what to do so I punched "Operator."

A pretty young girl's head materialized in the cube. "Jefferson operator," she said. "May I help you?"

"Yes . . . what does it mean when the cube is blinking blue?"

"Huh?"

"What does it mean when the phone—"

"Are you serious?" I was getting a little tired of this kind of thing.

"It's a long story. Honest, I don't know."

"When it blinks blue you're supposed to call the operator."

"Okay, here I am."

"No, not me, the *real* operator. Punch nine. Then punch zero."

I did that and an old harridan appeared. "Ob-a-ray-duh."

"This is William Mandella at 301-52-574-3975. I was supposed to call you."

"Juzza segun." She reached outside the field of view and typed something. "You godda call from 605-19-556-2027."

I scribbled it down on the pad by the phone. "Where's that?"

"Juzza segun. South Dakota."

"Thanks." I didn't know anybody in South Dakota.

A pleasant-looking old woman answered the phone. "Yes?"

"I had a call from this number . . . uh . . . I'm—"

"Oh. Sergeant Mandella! Just a second."

I watched the diagonal bar of the holding pattern for a second, then fifty or so more. Then a head came into focus.

Marygay. "William. I had a heck of a time finding you."

"Darling, me too. What are you doing in South Dakota?"

"My parents live here, in a little commune. That's why it took me so long to get to the phone." She held up two grimy hands. "Digging potatoes."

"But when I checked . . . the records said—the records in Tucson said your parents were both dead."

"No, they're just dropouts—you know about dropouts?—new name, new life. I got the word through a cousin."

"Well—well, how've you been? Like the country life?"

"That's one reason I've been wanting to get you. Willy, I'm bored. It's all very healthy and nice, but I want to do something dissipated and wicked. Naturally I thought of you."

"I'm flattered. Pick you up at eight?"

She checked a clock above the phone. "No, look, let's get a good night's sleep. Besides, I've got to get in the rest of the potatoes. Meet me at . . . the Ellis Island jetport at ten tomorrow morning. Mmm . . . Trans-World information desk."

"Okay. Make reservations for where?"

She shrugged. "Pick a place."

"London used to be pretty wicked."

"Sounds good. First class?"

"What else? I'll get us a suite on one of the dirigibles."

"Good. Decadent. How long shall I pack for?"

"We'll buy clothes along the way. Travel light. Just one stuffed wallet apiece."

She giggled. "Wonderful. Tomorrow at ten."

"Fine—uh . . . Marygay, do you have a gun?"

"It's that bad?"

"Here around Washington it is."

"Well, I'll get one. Dad has a couple over the fireplace. Guess they're left over from Tucson."

"We'll hope we won't need them."

"Willy, you know it'll just be for decoration. I couldn't even kill a Tauran."

"Of course." We just looked at each other for a second. "Tomorrow at ten, then."

"Right. Love you."

"Uh . . ."

She giggled again and hung up.

That was just too many things to think about all at once.

I got us two round-the-world dirigible tickets; unlimited stops as long as you kept going east. It took me a little over two hours to get to Ellis by autocab and monorail. I was early, but so was Marygay.

She was talking to the girl at the desk and didn't see me

coming. Her outfit was really arresting, a tight coverall of plastic in a pattern of interlocking hands; as your angle of sight changed, various strategic hands became transparent. She had a ruddy sun-glow all over her body. I don't know whether the feeling that rushed over me was simple honest lust or something more complicated. I hurried up behind her.

Whispering: "What are we going to do for three hours?"

She turned and gave me a quick hug and thanked the girl at the desk, then grabbed my hand and pulled me along to a slide-walk.

"Um . . . where are we headed?"

"Don't ask questions, Sergeant. Just follow me."

We stepped onto a roundabout and transferred to an eastbound slidewalk.

"Do you want something to eat or drink?" she asked innocently.

I tried to leer. "Any alternatives?"

She laughed gaily. Several people stared. "Just a second . . . here!" We jumped off. It was a corridor marked "Roomettes." She handed me a key.

That damned plastic coverall was held on by static electricity. Since the roomette was nothing but a big waterbed, I almost broke my neck the first time it shocked me.

I recovered.

We were lying on our stomachs, looking through the one-way glass wall at the people rushing around down on the concourse. Marygay passed me a joint.

"William, have you used that thing yet?"

"What thing?"

"That hawg-leg. The pistol."

"Only shot it once, in the store where I bought it."

"Do you really think you could point it at someone and blow him apart?"

I took a shallow puff and passed it back. "Hadn't given it much thought, really. Until we talked last night."

"Well?"

"I . . . I don't really know. The only time I've killed was on Aleph, under hypnotic compulsion. But I don't think it would . . . bother me, not that much, not if the person was trying to kill me in the first place. Why should it?"

"Life," she said plaintively, "life is . . ."

"Life is a bunch of cells walking around with a common purpose. If that common purpose is to get my ass—"

"Oh, William. You sound like old Cortez."

"Cortez kept us alive."

"Not many of us," she snapped.

I rolled over and studied the ceiling tiles. She traced little designs on my chest, pushing the sweat around with her fingertip. "I'm sorry, William. I guess we're both just trying to adjust."

"That's okay. You're right, anyhow."

We talked for a long time. The only urban center Marygay had been to since our publicity rounds (which were very sheltered) was Sioux Falls. She had gone with her parents and the commune bodyguard. It sounded like a scaled-down version of Washington: the same problems, but not as acute.

We ticked off the things that bothered us: violence, high cost of living, too many people everywhere. I'd have added homolife, but Marygay said I just didn't appreciate the social dynamic that had led to it; it had been inevitable. The only thing she said she had against it was that it took so many of the prettiest men out of circulation.

And the main thing that was wrong was that everything seemed to have gotten just a little worse, or at best remained the same. You would have predicted that at least a few facets of everyday life would improve markedly in twenty-two years. Her father contended the War was behind it all: any person who showed a shred of talent was sucked up by UNEF; the very best fell to the Elite Conscription Act and wound up being cannon fodder.

It was hard not to agree with him. Wars in the past often accelerated social reform, provided technological benefits, even sparked artistic activity. This one, however, seemed tailor-made to provide none of these positive by-products. Such improvements as had been made on late-twentieth-century technology were— like tachyon bombs and warships two kilometers long—at best, interesting developments of things that only required the synergy of money and existing engineering techniques. Social reform? The world was technically under martial law. As for art, I'm not sure I know good from bad. But artists to some extent have to reflect the temper of the times. Paintings and sculpture were full of torture and dark brooding; movies seemed static and plotless; music was dominated by nostalgic revivals of earlier forms; architecture was mainly concerned with finding someplace to put everybody; literature was damn near incomprehensible. Most people seemed to spend most of their time trying to find ways to outwit the government, trying to scrounge a few extra K's or ration tickets without putting their lives in too much danger.

And in the past, people whose country was at war were constantly in contact with the war. The newspapers would be full of reports, veterans would return from the front; sometimes the front would move right into town, invaders marching down Main Street or bombs whistling through the night air—but always the sense of either working toward victory or at least delaying defeat. The enemy was a tangible thing, a propagandist's monster whom you could understand, whom you could hate.

But this war . . . the enemy was a curious organism only vaguely understood, more often the subject of cartoons than nightmares. The main effect of the war on the home front was economic, unemotional—more taxes but more jobs as well. After twenty-two years, only twenty-seven returned veterans; not enough to make a decent parade. The most important fact about the war to most people was that if it ended suddenly, Earth's economy would collapse.

You approached the dirigible by means of a small propeller-driven aircraft that drifted up to match trajectories and docked alongside. A clerk took our baggage and we checked our weapons with the purser, then went outside.

Just about everybody on the flight was standing out on the promenade deck, watching Manhattan creep toward the horizon. It was an eerie sight. The day was very still, so the bottom thirty or forty stories of the buildings were buried in smog. It looked like a city built on a cloud, a thunderhead floating. We watched it for a while and then went inside to eat.

The meal was elegantly served and simple: filet of beef, two vegetables, wine. Cheese and fruit and more wine for dessert. No fiddling with ration tickets; a loophole in the rationing laws implied that they were not required for meals consumed en route, on intercontinental transport.

We spent a lazy, comfortable three days crossing the Atlantic. The dirigibles had been a new thing when we first left Earth, and now they had turned out to be one of the few successful new financial ventures of the late twentieth century . . . the company that built them had bought up a few obsolete nuclear weapons; one bomb-sized hunk of plutonium would keep the whole fleet in the air for years. And, once launched, they never did come down. Floating hotels, supplied and maintained by regular shuttles, they were one last vestige of luxury in a world where nine billion people had something to eat, and almost nobody had enough.

London was not as dismal from the air as New York City had been; the air was clean even if the Thames was poison. We packed our handbags, claimed our weapons, and landed on a VTO pad atop the London Hilton. We rented a couple of tricycles at the hotel and, maps in hand, set off for Regent Street, planning on dinner at the venerable Cafe Royal.

The tricycles were little armored vehicles, stabilized gyroscopically so they couldn't be tipped over. Seemed overly cautious for the part of London we traveled through, but I supposed there were probably sections as rough as Washington.

I got a dish of marinated venison and Marygay got salmon; both very good but astoundingly expensive. At first I was a bit overawed by the huge room, filled with plush and mirrors and faded gilding, very quiet even with a dozen tables occupied, and we talked in whispers until we realized that was foolish.

Over coffee I asked Marygay what the deal was with her parents.

"Oh, it happens often enough," she said. "Dad got mixed up in some ration ticket thing. He'd gotten some black market tickets that turned out to be counterfeit. Cost him his job and he probably would have gone to jail, but while he was waiting for trial a bodysnatcher got him."

"Bodysnatcher?"

"That's right. All the commune organizations have them. They've got to get reliable farm labor, people who aren't eligible for relief . . . people who can't just lay down their tools and walk off when it gets rough. Almost everybody can get enough assistance to stay alive, though; everyone who isn't on the government's fecal roster."

"So he skipped out before his trial came up?"

She nodded. "It was a case of choosing between commune life, which he knew wasn't easy, and going on the dole after a few years' working on a prison farm; ex-convicts can't get legitimate jobs. They had to forfeit their condominium, which they'd put up for bail, but the government would've gotten that anyhow, once he was in jail.

"So the bodysnatcher offered him and Mother new identities, transportation to the commune, a cottage, and a plot of land. They took it."

"And what did the bodysnatcher get?"

"He himself probably didn't get anything. The commune got their ration tickets; they were allowed to keep their money, although they didn't have very much—"

"What happens if they get caught?"

"Not a chance." She laughed. "The communes provide over half the country's produce—they're really just an unofficial arm of the government. I'm sure the CBI knows exactly where they are. . . . Dad grumbles that it's just a fancy way of being in jail anyhow."

"What a weird setup."

"Well, it keeps the land farmed." She pushed her empty dessert plate a symbolic centimeter away from her. "And they're eating better than most people, better than they ever had in the city. Mom knows a hundred ways to fix chicken and potatoes."

After dinner we went to a musical show. The hotel had gotten us tickets to a "cultural translation" of the old rock opera *Hair*. The program explained that they had taken some liberties with the original choreography, because back in those days they didn't allow actual coition on stage. The music was pleasantly old-fashioned, but neither of us was quite old enough to work up any blurry-eyed nostalgia over it. Still, it was much more enjoyable than the movies I'd seen, and some of the physical feats performed were quite inspiring. We slept late the next morning.

We dutifully watched the changing of the guard at Buckingham Palace, walked through the British Museum, ate fish and chips, ran up to Stratford-on-Avon and caught the Old Vic doing an incomprehensible play about a mad king, and didn't get into any trouble until the day before we were to leave for Lisbon.

It was about 2 A.M. and we were tooling our tricycles down a nearly deserted thoroughfare. Turned a corner and there was a gang of boys beating the hell out of someone. I screeched to the curb and leaped out of my vehicle, firing the shotgun-pistol over their heads.

It was a girl they were attacking; it was rape. Most of them scattered, but one pulled a pistol out of his coat and I shot him. I remember trying to aim for his arm. The blast hit his shoulder and ripped off his arm and what seemed to be half of his chest; it flung him two meters to the side of a building and he must have been dead before he hit the ground.

The others ran, one of them shooting at me with a little pistol as he went. I watched him trying to kill me for the longest time before it occurred to me to shoot back. I sent one blast way high and he dove into an alley and disappeared.

The girl looked dazedly around, saw the mutilated body of her attacker, and staggered to her feet and ran off screaming, naked from the waist down. I knew I should have tried to stop her, but I couldn't find my voice and my feet seemed nailed to the sidewalk. A tricycle door slammed and Marygay was beside me.

"What hap—" She gasped, seeing the dead man. "Wh-what was he doing?"

I just stood there stupefied. I'd certainly seen enough death these past two years, but this was a different thing . . . there was nothing noble in being crushed to death by the failure of some electronic component, or in having your suit fail and freeze you solid; or even dying in a shoot-out with the incomprehensible enemy . . . but death seemed natural in that setting. Not on a quaint little street in old-fashioned London, not for trying to steal what most people would give freely.

Marygay was pulling my arm. "We've got to get out of here. They'll *brainwipe* you!"

She was right. I turned and took one step and fell to the concrete. I looked down at the leg that had betrayed me and bright red blood was pulsing out of a small hole in my calf. Marygay tore a strip of cloth from her blouse and started to bind it. I remember thinking it wasn't a big enough wound to go into shock over, but my ears started to ring and I got lightheaded and everything went red and fuzzy. Before I went under, I heard a siren wailing in the distance.

Fortunately, the police also picked up the girl, who was wandering down the street a few blocks away. They compared her version of the thing with mine, both of us under hypnosis. They let me go with a stern admonition to leave law enforcement up to professional law enforcers.

I wanted to get out of the cities: just put a pack on my back and wander through the woods for a while, get my mind straightened out. So did Marygay. But we tried to make arrangements and found that the country was worse than the cities. Farms were practically armed camps, the areas between ruled by nomad gangs who survived by making lightning raids into villages and farms, murdering and plundering for a few minutes, and then fading back into the forest, before help could arrive.

Still, Britishers called their island "the most civilized country in Europe." From what we'd heard about France and Spain and Germany, especially Germany, they were probably right.

I talked it over with Marygay, and we decided to cut short our tour and go back to the States. We could finish the tour after we'd become acclimated to the twenty-first century. It was just too much foreignness to take in one dose.

The dirigible line refunded most of our money and we took a conventional suborbital flight back home. The high altitude made my leg throb, though it was nearly healed. They'd made great strides in the treatment of gunshot wounds, in the past twenty years. Lots of practice.

We split up at Ellis. Her description of commune life appealed to me more than the city; I made arrangements to join her after a week or so, and went back to Washington.

10

I rang the bell and a strange woman answered the door, opening it a couple of centimeters and peering through.

"Pardon me," I said, "isn't this Mrs. Mandella's residence?"

"Oh, you must be William!" She closed the door and unfastened the chains and opened it wide. "Beth, look who's here!"

My mother came into the living room from the kitchen, drying her hands on a towel. "Willy . . . what are you doing back so soon?"

"Well, it's—it's a long story."

"Sit down, sit down," the other woman said. "Let me get you a drink, don't start till I get back."

"Wait," my mother said. "I haven't even introduced you two. William, this is Rhonda Wilder. Rhonda, William."

"I've been so looking forward to meeting you," she said. "Beth has told me all about you—one cold beer, right?"

"Right." She was likable enough, a trim middle-aged woman. I wondered why I hadn't met her before. I asked my mother whether she was a neighbor.

"Uh . . . really more than that, William. She's been my room-mate for a couple of years. That's why I had an extra room when you came home—a single person isn't allowed two bedrooms."

"But why—"

"I didn't tell you because I didn't want you to feel that you were putting her out of her room while you stayed here. And you weren't, actually; she has—"

"That's right." Rhonda came in with the beer. "I've got relatives in Pennsylvania, out in the country. I can stay with them any time."

"Thanks." I took the beer. "Actually, I won't be here long. I'm kind of en route to South Dakota. I could find another place to flop."

"Oh, no," Rhonda said. "I can take the couch." I was too old-fashioned male-chauv to allow that; we discussed it for a minute and I wound up with the couch.

I filled Rhonda in on who Marygay was and told them about our disturbing experiences in England, how we came back to get our bearings. I had expected my mother to be horrified that I had killed a man, but she accepted it without comment. Rhonda clucked a little bit about our being out in a city after midnight, especially without a bodyguard.

We talked on these and other topics until late at night, when Mother called her bodyguard and went off to work.

Something had been nagging at me all night, the way Mother and Rhonda acted toward each other. I decided to bring it out into the open, once Mother was gone.

"Rhonda—" I settled down in the chair across from her. I didn't know exactly how to put it. "What, uh, what exactly is your relationship with my mother?"

She took a long drink. "Good friends." She stared at me with a mixture of defiance and resignation. "Very good friends. Some-times lovers."

I felt very hollow and lost. My mother?

"Listen," she continued. "You had better stop trying to live in the nineties. This may not be the best of all possible worlds, but you're stuck with it."

She crossed and took my hand, almost kneeling in front of

me. Her voice was softer. "William . . . look, I'm only two years older than you are—that is, I was born two years before—what I mean is, I can understand how you feel. B—your mother understands too. It, our . . . relationship, wouldn't be a secret to anybody else. It's perfectly normal. A lot has changed, these twenty years. You've got to change too."

I didn't say anything.

She stood up and said firmly, "You think, because your mother is sixty, she's outgrown her need for love? She needs it more than you do. Even now. Especially now."

Accusation in her eyes. "Especially now with you coming back from the dead past. Reminding her of how old she is. How—old I am, twenty years younger." Her voice quavered and cracked, and she ran to her room.

I wrote Mother a note saying that Marygay had called; an emergency had come up and I had to go immediately to South Dakota. I called a bodyguard and left.

A whining, ozone-leaking, battered old bus let me out at the intersection of a bad road and a worse one. It had taken me an hour to go the 2000 kilometers to Sioux Falls, two hours to get a chopper to Geddes, 150 kilometers away, and three hours waiting and jouncing on the dilapidated bus to go the last 12 kilometers to Freehold, an organization of communes where the Potters had their acreage. I wondered if the progression was going to continue and I would be four hours walking down this dirt road to the farm.

It was a half-hour before I even came to a building. My bag was getting intolerably heavy and the bulky pistol was chafing my hip. I walked up a stone path to the door of a simple plastic dome and pulled a string that caused a bell to tinkle inside. A peephole darkened.

"Who is it?" Voice muffled by thick wood.

"Stranger asking directions."

"Ask." I couldn't tell whether it was a woman or a child.

"I'm looking for the Potters' farm."

"Just a second." Footsteps went away and came back. "Down the road one point nine clicks. Lots of potatoes and green beans on your right. You'll probably smell the chickens."

"Thanks."

"If you want a drink we got a pump out back. Can't let you in without my husband's at home."

"I understand. Thank you." The water was metallic-tasting but wonderfully cool.

I wouldn't know a potato or green bean plant if it stood up and took a bite out of my ankle, but I knew how to walk a half-meter step. So I resolved to count to 3800 and take a deep breath. I supposed I could tell the difference between the smell of chicken manure and the absence thereof.

At 3650 there was a rutted path leading to a complex of plastic domes and rectangular buildings apparently made of sod. There was a pen enclosing a small population explosion of chickens. They had a smell but it wasn't strong.

Halfway down the path, a door opened and Marygay came running out, wearing one tiny wisp of cloth. After a slippery but gratifying greeting, she asked what I was doing here so early.

"Oh, my mother had friends staying with her. I didn't want to put them out. Suppose I should have called."

"Indeed you should have . . . save you a long dusty walk—but we've got plenty of room, don't worry about that."

She took me inside to meet her parents, who greeted me warmly and made me feel definitely overdressed. Their faces showed their age but their bodies had no sag and few wrinkles.

Since dinner was an occasion, they let the chickens live and instead opened a can of beef, steaming it along with a cabbage and some potatoes. To my plain tastes it was equal to most of the gourmet fare we'd had on the dirigible and in London.

Over coffee and goat cheese (they apologized for not having wine; the commune would have a new vintage out in a couple of weeks), I asked what kind of work I could do.

"Will," Mr. Potter said, "I don't mind telling you that your coming here is a godsend. We've got five acres that are just sitting out there, fallow, because we don't have enough hands to work them. You can take the plow tomorrow and start breaking up an acre at a time."

"More potatoes, Daddy?" Marygay asked.

"No, no . . . not this season. Soybeans—cash crop and good for the soil. And Will, at night we all take turns standing guard. With four of us, we ought to be able to do a lot more sleeping." He took a big slurp of coffee. "Now, what else . . ."

"Richard," Mrs. Potter said, "tell him about the greenhouse."

"That's right, yes, the greenhouse. The commune has a two-acre greenhouse down about a click from here, by the recreation center. Mostly grapes and tomatoes. Everybody spends one morning or one afternoon a week there.

"Why don't you children go down there tonight . . . show Will the night life in fabulous Freehold? Sometimes you can get a real exciting game of checkers going."

"Oh, Daddy. It's not that bad."

"Actually, it isn't. They've got a fair library and a coin-op terminal to the Library of Congress. Marygay tells me you're a reader. That's good."

"Sounds fascinating." It did. "But what about guard?"

"No problem. Mrs. Potter—April—and I'll take the first four hours—oh," he said, standing, "let me show you the setup."

We went out back to "the tower," a sandbag hut on stilts. Climbed up a rope ladder through a hole in the middle of the hut.

"A little crowded in here, with two," Richard said. "Have a seat." There was an old piano stool beside the hole in the floor. I sat on it. "It's handy to be able to see all the field without getting a crick in your neck. Just don't keep turning in the same direction all the time."

He opened a wooden crate and uncovered a sleek rifle, wrapped in oily rags. "Recognize this?"

"Sure." I'd had to sleep with one in basic training. "Army standard issue T-sixteen. Semi-automatic, twelve-caliber tumblers—where the hell did you get it?"

"Commune went to a government auction. It's an antique now, son." He handed it to me and I snapped it apart. Clean, too clean.

"Has it ever been used?"

"Not in almost a year. Ammo costs too much for target practice. Take a couple of practice shots, though, convince yourself that it works."

I turned on the scope and just got a washed-out bright green. Set for nighttime. Clicked it back to log zero, set the magnification at ten, reassembled it.

"Marygay didn't want to try it out. Said she'd had her fill of that. I didn't press her, but a person's got to have confidence in ther tools."

I clicked off the safety and found a clod of dirt that the rangefinder said was between 100 and 120 meters away. Set it at 110, rested the barrel of the rifle on the sandbags, centered the clod in the crosshairs, and squeezed. The round hissed out and kicked up dirt about five centimeters low.

"Fine." I reset it for night use and safetied it and handed it back. "What happened a year ago?"

He wrapped it up carefully, keeping the rags away from the eyepiece. "Had some jumpers come in. Fired a few rounds and scared 'em away."

"All right, what's a jumper?"

"Yeah, you wouldn't know." He shook out a tobacco cigarette and passed me the box. "I don't know why they don't just call 'em thieves, that's what they are. Murderers, too, sometimes.

"They know that a lot of the commune members are pretty well off. If you raise cash crops you get to keep half the cash; besides, a lot of our members were prosperous when they joined.

"Anyhow, the jumpers take advantage of our relative isolation. They come out from the city and try to sneak in, usually hit one place, and run. Most of the time, they don't get this far in, but the farms closer to the road . . . we hear gunfire every couple of weeks. Usually just scaring off kids. If it keeps up, a siren goes off and the commune goes on alert."

"Doesn't sound fair to the people living close to the road."

"There're compensations. They only have to donate half as much of their crop as the rest of us do. And they're issued heavier weapons."

Marygay and I took the family's two bicycles and pedaled down to the recreation center. I only fell off twice, negotiating the bumpy road in the dark.

It was a little livelier than Richard had described it. A young nude girl was dancing sensuously to an assortment of homemade drums near the far side of the dome. Turned out she was still in school; it was a project for a "cultural relativity" class.

Most of the people there, in fact, were young and therefore still in school. They considered it a joke, though. After you had learned to read and write and could pass the Class I literacy test, you only had to take one course per year, and some of those you could pass just by signing up. So much for the "eighteen years' compulsory education" they had startled us with at Stargate.

Other people were playing board games, reading, watching the girl gyrate, or just talking. There was a bar that served soya, coffee, or thin homemade beer. Not a ration ticket to be seen; all made by the commune or purchased outside with commune tickets.

We got into a discussion about the war, with a bunch of people who knew Marygay and I were veterans. It's hard to describe their attitude, which was pretty uniform. They were angry in an abstract way that it took so much tax money to support; they were convinced that the Taurans would never be any danger to Earth; but they all knew that nearly half the jobs in the world were associated with the war, and if it stopped, everything would fall apart.

I thought everything was in shambles already, but then I hadn't grown up in this world. And they had never known "peacetime."

We went home about midnight and Marygay and I each stood two hours' guard. By the middle of the next morning, I was wishing I had gotten a little more sleep.

The plow was a big blade on wheels with two handles for steering, atomic powered. Not very much power, though; enough to move it forward at a slow crawl if the blade was in soft earth. Needless to say, there was little soft earth in the unused five acres. The plow would go a few centimeters, get stuck, freewheel until I put some back into it, then move a few more centimeters. I finished a tenth of an acre the first day and eventually got it up to a fifth of an acre a day.

It was hard, hardening work, but pleasant. I had an earclip that piped music to me, old tapes from Richard's collection, and the sun browned me all over. I was beginning to think I could live that way forever, when suddenly it was finished.

Marygay and I were reading up at the recreation center one evening when we heard faint gunfire down by the road. We decided it'd be smart to get back to the house. We were less than halfway there when firing broke out all along our left, on a line that seemed to extend from the road to far past the recreation center: a coordinated attack. We had to abandon the bikes and crawl on hands and knees in the drainage ditch by the side of the road, bullets hissing over our heads. A heavy vehicle rumbled by, shooting left and right. It took a good twenty minutes to crawl home. We passed two farmhouses that were burning brightly. I was glad ours didn't have any wood.

I noticed there was no return fire coming from our tower, but didn't say anything. There were two dead strangers in front of the house as we rushed inside.

April was lying on the floor, still alive but bleeding from a hundred tiny fragment wounds. The living room was rubble and dust; someone must have thrown a bomb through a door or window. I left Marygay with her mother and ran out back to the tower. The ladder was pulled up, so I had to shinny up one of the stilts.

Richard was sitting slumped over the rifle. In the pale green glow from the scope I could see a perfectly round hole above his left eye. A little blood had trickled down the bridge of his nose and dried.

I laid his body on the floor and covered his head with my shirt. I filled my pockets with clips and took the rifle back to the house.

Marygay had tried to make her mother comfortable. They were talking quietly. She was holding my shotgun-pistol and had another gun on the floor beside her. When I came in she looked up and nodded soberly, not crying.

April whispered something and Marygay asked, "Mother wants to know whether . . . Daddy had a hard time of it. She knows he's dead."

"No. I'm sure he didn't feel anything."

"That's good."

"It's something." I should keep my mouth shut. "It is good, yes."

I checked the doors and windows for an effective vantage point. I couldn't find anyplace that wouldn't allow a whole platoon to sneak up behind me.

"I'm going to go outside and get on top of the house." Couldn't go back to the tower. "Don't you shoot unless somebody gets inside . . . maybe they'll think the place is deserted."

By the time I had clambered up to the sod roof, the heavy truck was coming back down the road. Through the scope I could see that there were five men on it, four in the cab and one who was on the open bed, cradling a machine gun, surrounded by loot.

He was crouched between two refrigerators, but I had a clear shot at him. Held my fire, not wanting to draw attention. The truck stopped in front of the house, sat for a minute, and turned in. The window was probably bulletproof, but I sighted on the driver's face and squeezed off a round. He jumped as it ricocheted, whining, leaving an opaque star on the plastic, and the man in back opened up. A steady stream of bullets hummed over my head; I could hear them thumping into the sandbags of the tower. He didn't see me.

The truck wasn't ten meters away when the shooting stopped. He was evidently reloading, hidden behind the refrigerator. I took careful aim and when he popped up to fire I shot him in the throat. The bullet being a tumbler, it exited through the top of his skull.

The driver pulled the truck around in a long arc so that, when it stopped, the door to the cab was flush with the door of the house. This protected them from the tower and also from me, though I doubted they yet knew where I was; a T-16 makes no flash and very little noise. I kicked off my shoes and stepped cautiously onto the top of the cab, hoping the driver would get out on his side. Once the door opened I could fill the cab with ricocheting bullets.

No good. The far door, hidden from me by the roof's overhang, opened first. I waited for the driver and hoped that Marygay was well hidden. I shouldn't have worried.

There was a deafening roar, then another and another. The heavy truck rocked with the impact of thousands of tiny flechettes. One short scream that the second shot ended.

I jumped from the truck and ran around to the back door. Marygay had her mother's head on her lap, and someone was crying softly. I went to them and Marygay's cheeks were dry under my palms.

"Good work, dear."

She didn't say anything. There was a steady heavy dripping sound from the door and the air was acrid with smoke and the smell of fresh meat. We huddled together until dawn.

I had thought April was sleeping, but in the dim light her eyes were wide open and filmed. Her breath came in shallow rasps. Her skin was gray parchment and dried blood. She didn't answer when we talked to her.

A vehicle was coming up the road, so I took the rifle and went outside. It was a dump truck with a white sheet draped over one side and a man standing in the back with a megaphone repeating, "Wounded . . . wounded." I waved and the truck came in. They took April out on a makeshift litter and told us which hospital they were going to. We wanted to go along but there was simply no room; the bed of the truck was covered with people in various stages of disrepair.

Marygay didn't want to go back inside because it was getting light enough to see the men she had killed so completely. I went back in to get some cigarettes and forced myself to look. It was messy enough, but just didn't disturb me that much. *That* bothered me, to be confronted with a pile of human hamburger and mainly notice the flies and ants and smell. Death is so much neater in space.

We buried her father behind the house, and when the truck came back with April's small body wrapped in a shroud, we buried her beside him. The commune's sanitation truck came by a little later, and gas-masked men took care of the jumpers' bodies.

We sat in the baking sun, and finally Marygay wept, for a long time, silently.

11

We spent that night in a hotel room in Sioux Falls, talking more than sleeping. It went like this:

Earth was not a fit place to live, and by all signs it was getting worse rather than better. And there was nothing to hold us here.

But the only people allowed in space were members of UNEF.

Therefore we had to either join up again or try to learn to live with the crime and crowding and filth and so on.

We had been promised training positions if we reenlisted. We could be assigned to the moon if we asked, and would have commissions. All these things would make army life a lot more tolerable than it had been.

And except for the combat, we had been happier in the army than during most of our stay on Earth.

We took the morning flight to Miami and monorailed to the Cape.

"In case you're interested, you aren't the first combat veterans to come back." The recruiting officer was a muscular lieutenant of indeterminate sex. I flipped a coin mentally and it came up tails.

"Last I heard, there had been nine others," she said in her husky tenor. "All of them opted for the moon . . . maybe you'll find some of your friends there." She slid two simple forms across the desk. "Sign these and you're in again. Second lieutenants."

The form was a simple request to be assigned to active duty; we had never really gotten out of the Force, since they extended the draft law, but had just been on inactive status. I scrutinized the paper.

"There's nothing on this about the guarantees we were given at Stargate."

"That won't be necessary. The Force will—"

"I think it is necessary, Lieutenant." I handed back the form. So did Marygay.

"Let me check." She left the desk and disappeared into an office. After a while we heard a printer rattle.

She brought back the same two sheets, with an addition typed under our names: GUARANTEED LOCATION OF CHOICE [LUNA] AND ASSIGNMENT OF CHOICE [COMBAT TRAINING SPECIALIST].

We got a thorough physical checkup and were fitted for new fighting suits, made our financial arrangements, and caught the next morning's shuttle. We laid over at Earthport, enjoying zero gravity for a few hours, and then caught a ride to Luna, setting down at the Grimaldi base.

On the door to the Transient Officers' Billet, some wag had scraped "abandon hope all ye who enter." We found our two-man cubicle and began changing for chow.

Two raps on the door. "Mail call, sirs."

I opened the door and the sergeant standing there saluted. I just looked at him for a second and then remembered I was an officer and returned the salute. He handed me two identical 'faxes. I gave one to Marygay and we both gasped at the same time:

* * O R D E R S * * O R D E R S * * O R D E R S

THE FOLLOWING NAMED PERSONNEL:
Mandella, William 2LT [11 575 278] COCOMM D CO GRITRABN
AND
Potter, Marygay 2LT [17 386 907] COCOMM B CO GRITRABN
ARE HEREBY REASSIGNED TO:

Lt Mandella: PLCOMM 2 PL STFTHETA STARGATE
Lt Potter: PLCOMM 3 PL STFTHETA STARGATE.
DESCRIPTION OF DUTIES:
Command infantry platoon in Tet-2 Campaign.
THE ABOVE NAMED PERSONNEL WILL REPORT IMMEDIATELY TO
GRIMALDI TRANSPORTATION BATTALION TO BE MANIFESTED TO
STARGATE.
ISSUED STARGATE TACBD/1298–8684–1450/20 Aug 2019 SG:
BY AUTHO STFCOM Commander.

* * O R D E R S * * O R D E R S * * O R D E R S

"They didn't waste any time, did they?" Marygay said bit-terly.

"Must be a standing order. Strike Force Command's light-weeks away; they can't even know we've re-upped yet."

"What about our . . ." She let it trail off.

"The guarantee. Well, we were given our assignment of choice. Nobody guaranteed we'd have the assignment for more than an hour."

"It's so dirty."

I shrugged. "It's so army."

But I couldn't shake the feeling that we were going home.

As may be too obvious, that was a story I felt I had to write, trying to deal with the hangover of pain and confusion that haunted most of us when we came back from Vietnam. I've met writers who can only write about themes that come from these dark levels, and they have my admiration and pity in about equal parts. I am not one of them. Give me a stack of paper and something that will make marks on it, and I'll come up with a story. Most of the people I know who write for a living share this small talent, this consid-erable obsession.

Yet the question we're asked most frequently is "where do you get your (crazy) ideas?" To me this question sounds like the old story about the person who asks the salesman in a showroom how much the yacht costs: If you have to ask, the salesman says, you can't afford it. If you have to ask the "ideas" question, you likely won't understand the answer. Or you won't believe it. They come out of thin air. The ideas are just there. The only trick is to make yourself receptive to them.

This is the basis for the first assignment I made to my science fiction writing students at MIT. When I took roll the first day, I asked each student to pick a number between 8 and 188. These corresponded to page numbers in the excellent source book *The Science in Science Fiction* (by Peter Nicholls and David Langford, Knopf, 1983). I told them to take the topic that's discussed on that page and begin a story about it. Then I further restricted them by asking that they look through the *Science Fiction Hall of Fame* collection (Robert Silverberg and Ben Bova, editors; Avon, 1971 and 1974), reading the first page of every story, and find a beginning that seemed attractive—then write a pastiche of that beginning, applying its structure to the random topic.

Part of the lesson taught by this seemingly capricious assignment is that art thrives on restrictions. A larger part is to generate in the students the sudden *Ah-ha!* feeling: A minute ago there was nothing. Now there's a story. Where the hell did it come from?

The *where* it came from (he says, dusting the chalk from his vest) is named by different cultures and eras according to whatever symbology is comfortable to them: the Muses, the collective unconscious, the tension between left- and right-brain activity. Naming it isn't important. It's the same place whether you're a blind poet mumbling immortal lines on the Aegean shore or a chain-smoking hack writer facing a deadline and the baleful screen of a word processor. Before, there was nothing. Now there's a story.

Out of curiosity and a sense of fairness, I made myself do all the assignments I gave to the students. My random number was 142, which came up "cyborg," and the beginning I chose to emulate was from Daniel Keyes's marvelous tale *Flowers for Algernon*. This is what happened.

MORE THAN

THE SUM OF

HIS PARTS

21 August 2058

They say I am to keep a detailed record of my feelings, my perceptions, as I grow accustomed to the new parts. To that end, they gave me an apparatus that blind people use for writing, like a tablet with guide wires. It is somewhat awkward. But a recorder would be useless, since I will not have a mouth for some time, and I can't type blind with only one hand.

Woke up free from pain. Interesting. Surprising to find that it has only been five days since the accident. For the record, I am, or was, Dr. Wilson Cheetham, Senior Engineer (Quality Control) for U.S. Steel's Skyfac station, a high-orbit facility that produces foamsteel and vapor deposition materials for use in the cislunar community. But if you are reading this, you must know all that.

Five days ago I was inspecting the aluminum deposition facility and had a bad accident. There was a glitch in my jetseat controls, and I flew suddenly straight into the wide beam of charged aluminum vapor. Very hot. They turned it off in a second, but there was still plenty of time for the beam to breach the suit and thoroughly roast three quarters of my body.

Apparently there was a rescue bubble right there. I was unconscious, of course. They tell me that my heart stopped with the shock, but they managed to save me. My left leg and arm are gone, as is my face. I have no lower jaw, nose, or external ears. I can hear after a fashion, though, and will have eyes in a week or so. They claim they will craft for me testicles and a penis.

I must be pumped full of mood drugs. I feel too calm. If I were myself, whatever fraction of myself is left, perhaps I would resist the insult of being turned into a sexless half-machine.

Ah well. This will be a machine that can turn itself off.

22 August 2058

For many days there was only sleep or pain. This was in the weightless ward at Mercy. They stripped the dead skin off me bit by bit. There are limits to anesthesia, unfortunately. I tried to scream but found I had no vocal cords. They finally decided not to try to salvage the arm and leg, which saved some pain.

When I was able to listen, they explained that U.S. Steel valued my services so much that they were willing to underwrite a state-of-the-art cyborg transformation. Half the cost will be absorbed by Interface Biotech on the Moon. Everybody will deduct me from their taxes.

This, then, is the catalog. First, new arm and leg. That's fairly standard. (I once worked with a woman who had two cyborg arms. It took weeks before I could look at her without feeling pity and revulsion.) Then they will attempt to build me a working jaw and mouth, which has been done only rarely and imperfectly, and rebuild the trachea, vocal cords, esophagus. I will be able to speak and drink, though except for certain soft foods, I won't eat in a normal way; salivary glands are beyond their art. No mucous membranes of any kind. A drastic cure for my chronic sinusitis.

Surprisingly, to me at least, the reconstruction of a penis is a fairly straightforward procedure, for which they've had lots of practice. Men are forever sticking them into places where they don't belong. They are particularly excited about my case because of the challenge in restoring sensation as well as function. The prostate is intact, and they seem confident that they can hook up the complicated plumbing involved in ejaculation. Restoring the ability to urinate is trivially easy, they say.

(The biotechnician in charge of the urogenital phase of the project talked at me for more than an hour, going into unnecessarily grisly detail. It seems that this replacement was done occasionally even before they had any kind of mechanical substitute, by sawing off a short rib and transplanting it, covering it with a skin graft from elsewhere on the body. The recipient thus was blessed with a permanent erection, unfortunately rather strange-looking and short on sensation. My own prosthesis will look very much like the real, shall we say, thing, and new developments in tractor-field mechanics and bionic interfacing should give it realistic response patterns.)

I don't know how to feel about all this. I wish they would leave my blood chemistry alone, so I could have some honest grief or horror, whatever. Instead of this placid waiting.

4 September 2058

Out cold for thirteen days and I wake up with eyes. The arm and leg are in place but not powered up yet. I wonder what the eyes look like. (They won't give me a mirror until I have a face.) They feel like wet glass.

Very fancy eyes. I have a box with two dials that I can use to override the "default mode"—that is, the ability to see only normally. One of them gives me conscious control over pupil dilation, so I can see in almost total darkness or, if for some reason I wanted to, look directly at the sun without discomfort. The other changes the frequency response, so I can see either in the infrared or the ultraviolet. This hospital room looks pretty much the same in ultraviolet, but in infrared it takes on a whole new aspect. Most of the room's illumination then comes from bright bars on the walls, radiant heating. My real arm shows a pulsing tracery of arteries and veins. The other is of course not visible except by reflection and is dark blue.

(Later) Strange I didn't realize I was on the Moon. I thought it was a low-gravity ward in Mercy. While I was sleeping they sent me down to Biotech. Should have figured that out.

5 September 2058

They turned on the "social" arm and leg and began patterning exercises. I am told to think of a certain movement and do its mirror image with my right arm or leg while attempting to execute it with my left. The trainer helps the cyborg unit along, which generates something like pain, though actually it doesn't resemble any real muscular ache. Maybe it's the way circuits feel when they're overloaded.

By the end of the session I was able to make a fist without help, though there is hardly enough grip to hold a pencil. I can't raise the leg yet, but can make the toes move.

They removed some of the bandages today, from shoulder to hip, and the test-tube skin looks much more real than I had prepared myself for. Hairless and somewhat glossy, but the color match is perfect. In infrared it looks quite different, more uniform in color than the "real" side. I suppose that's because it hasn't aged forty years.

While putting me through my paces, the technician waxed rhapsodic about how good this arm is going to be—this set of arms, actually. I'm exercising with the "social" one, which looks much more convincing than the ones my coworker displayed ten years ago. (No doubt more a matter of money than of advancing technology.) The "working" arm, which I haven't seen yet, will be all metal, capable of being worn on the outside of a spacesuit. Besides having the two arms, I'll be able to interface with various waldos, tailored to specific functions.

I am fortunately more ambidextrous than the average person. I broke my right wrist in the second grade and kept re-breaking it through the third, and so learned to write with both hands. All my life I have been able to print more clearly with the left.

They claim to be cutting down on my medication. If that's the truth, I seem to be adjusting fairly well. Then again, I have nothing in my past experience to use as a basis for comparison. Perhaps this calmness is only a mask for hysteria.

6 September 2058

Today I was able to tie a simple knot. I can lightly sketch out the letters of the alphabet. A large and childish scrawl but recognizably my own.

I've begun walking after a fashion, supporting myself between parallel bars. (The lack of hand strength is a neural problem, not a muscular one; when rigid, the arm and leg are as strong as metal crutches.) As I practice, it's amusing to watch the reactions of people who walk into the room, people who aren't paid to mask their horror at being studied by two cold lenses embedded in a swath of bandages formed over a shape that is not a head.

Tomorrow they start building my face. I will be essentially unconscious for more than a week. The limb patterning will continue as I sleep, they say.

14 September 2058

When I was a child my mother, always careful to have me do "normal" things, dressed me in costume each Halloween and escorted me around the high-rise, so I could beg for candy I did not want and money I did not need. On one occasion I had to wear the mask of a child star then popular on the cube, a tightly fitting plastic affair that covered the entire head, squeezing my pudgy features into something more in line with some Platonic ideal of childish beauty. That was my last Halloween. I embarrassed her.

This face is like that. It is undeniably my face, but the skin is taut and unresponsive. Any attempt at expression produces a grimace.

I have almost normal grip in the hand now, though it is still clumsy. As they hoped, the sensory feedback from the fingertips and palms seems to be more finely tuned than in my "good" hand. Tracing my new forefinger across my right wrist, I can sense the individual pores, and there is a marked temperature gradient as I pass over tendon or vein. And yet the hand and arm will eventually be capable of superhuman strength.

Touching my new face I do not feel pores. They have improved on nature in the business of heat exchange.

22 September 2058

Another week of sleep while they installed the new plumbing. When the anesthetic wore off I felt a definite *something,* not pain, but neither was it the normal somatic heft of genitalia. Everything was bedded in gauze and bandage, though, and catheterized, so it would feel strange even to a normal person.

(Later) An aide came in and gingerly snipped away the bandages. He blushed; I don't think fondling was in his job description. When the catheter came out there was a small sting of pain and relief.

It's not much of a copy. To reconstruct the face, they could consult hundreds of pictures and cubes, but it had never occurred to me that one day it might be useful to have a gallery of pictures of my private parts in various stages of repose. The technicians had approached the problem by bringing me a stack of photos culled from urological texts and pornography, and having me sort through them as to "closeness of fit."

It was not a task for which I was well trained, by experience or disposition. Strange as it may seem in this age of unfettered hedonism, I haven't seen another man naked, let alone rampant, since leaving high school, twenty-five years ago. (I was stationed on Farside for eighteen months and never went near a sex bar, preferring an audience of one. Even if I had to hire her, as was usually the case.)

So this one is rather longer and thicker than its predecessor— would all men unconsciously exaggerate?—and has only approximately the same aspect when erect. A young man's rakish angle.

Distasteful but necessary to write about the matter of masturbation. At first it didn't work. With my right hand, it felt like holding another man, which I have never had any desire to do. With the new hand, though, the process proceeded in the normal way, though I must admit to a voyeuristic aspect. The sensations were extremely acute. Ejaculation more forceful than I can remember from youth.

It makes me wonder. In a book I recently read, about brain chemistry, the author made a major point of the notion that it's a mistake to completely equate "mind" with "brain." The brain, he said, is in a way only the thickest and most complex segment of the nervous system; it coordinates our consciousness, but the actual mind suffuses through the body in a network of ganglia. In fact, he used sexuality as an example. When a man ruefully observes that his penis has a mind of its own, he is stating part of a larger truth.

But I in fact do have actual brains imbedded in my new parts: the biochips that process sensory data coming in and action commands going back. Are these brains part of my consciousness the way the rest of my nervous system is? The masturbation experience indicates they might be in business for themselves.

This is premature speculation, so to speak. We'll see how it feels when I move into a more complex environment, where I'm not so self-absorbed.

23 September 2058

During the night something evidently clicked. I woke up this morning with full strength in my cyborg limbs. One rail of the bed was twisted out of shape where I must have unconsciously gripped it. I bent it back quite easily.

Some obscure impulse makes me want to keep this talent secret for the time being. The technicians thought I would be able to exert three or four times the normal person's grip; this is obviously much more than that.

But why keep it a secret? I don't know. Eventually they will read this diary and I will stand exposed. There's no harm in that, though; this is supposed to be a record of my psychological adjustment or maladjustment. Let *them* tell *me* why I've done it.

(Later) The techs were astonished, ecstatic. I demonstrated a pull of 90 kilograms. I know if I'd actually given it a good yank, I could have pulled the stress machine out of the wall. I'll give them 110 tomorrow and inch my way up to 125.

Obviously I must be careful with force vectors. If I put too much stress on the normal parts of my body I could do permanent injury. With my metal fist I could certainly punch a hole through an airlock door, but it would probably tear the prosthesis out of its socket. Newton's laws still apply.

Other laws will have to be rewritten.

24 September 2058

I got to work out with three waldos today. A fantastic experience!

The first one was a disembodied hand and arm attached to a stand, the setup they use to train normal people in the use of waldos. The difference is that I don't need a waldo sleeve to imperfectly transmit my wishes to the mechanical double. I can plug into it directly.

I've been using waldos in my work ever since graduate school, but it was never anything like this. Inside the waldo sleeve you get a clumsy kind of feedback from striated pressor field generators embedded in the plastic. With my setup the feedback is exactly the kind a normal person feels when he touches an object, but much more sensitive. The first time they asked me to pick up an egg, I tossed it up and caught it (no great feat of coordination in lunar gravity, admittedly, but I could have done it as easily in Earth-normal).

The next waldo was a large earthmover that Western Mining uses over at Grimaldi Station. That was interesting, not only because of its size but because of the slight communications lag. Grimaldi is only a few dozens of kilometers away, but there aren't enough unused data channels between here and there for me to use the land-line to communicate with the earthmover hand. I had to relay via comsat, so there was about a tenth-second delay between the thought and the action. It was a fine feeling of power, but a little confusing: I would cup my hand and scoop downward, and then a split-second too late would feel the resistance of the regolith. And then casually hold in my palm several tonnes of rock and dirt. People standing around watching; with a flick of my wrist I could have buried them. Instead I dutifully dumped it on the belt to the converter.

But the waldo that most fascinated me was the micro. It had been in use for only a few months; I had heard of it, but hadn't had a chance to see it in action. It is a fully articulated hand barely a tenth of a millimeter long. I used it in conjunction with a low-power scanning electron microscope, moving around on the surface of a microcircuit. At that magnification it looked like a hand on a long stick wandering through the corridors of a building, whose walls varied from rough stucco to brushed metal to blistered gray paint, all laced over with thick cables of gold. When necessary, I could bring in another hand, manipulated by my right from inside a waldo sleeve, to help with simple carpenter and machinist tasks that, in the real world, translated into fundamental changes in the quantum-electrodynamic properties of the circuit.

This was the real power: not crushing metal tubes or lifting tonnes of rock, but pushing electrons around to do my bidding. My first doctorate was in electrical engineering; in a sudden epiphany I realize that I am the first *actual* electrical engineer in history.

After two hours they made me stop; said I was showing signs

of strain. They put me in a wheelchair, and I did fall asleep on the way back to my room. Dreaming dreams of microcosmic and infinite power.

25 September 2058

The metal arm. I expected it to feel fundamentally different from the "social" one, but of course it doesn't, most of the time. Circuits are circuits. The difference comes under conditions of extreme exertion: the soft hand gives me signals like pain if I come close to the level of stress that would harm the fleshlike material. With the metal hand I can rip off a chunk of steel plate a centimeter thick and feel nothing beyond "muscular" strain. If I had two of them I could work marvels.

The mechanical leg is not so gifted. It has governors to restrict its strength and range of motion to that of a normal leg, which is reasonable. Even a normal person finds himself brushing the ceiling occasionally in lunar gravity. I could stand up sharply and find myself with a concussion, or worse.

I like the metal arm, though. When I'm stronger (hah!) they say they'll let me go outside and try it with a spacesuit. Throw something over the horizon.

Starting today, I'm easing back into a semblance of normal life. I'll be staying at Biotech for another six or eight weeks, but I'm patched into my Skyfac office and have started clearing out the backlog of paperwork. Two hours in the morning and two in the afternoon. It's diverting, but I have to admit my heart isn't really in it. Rather be playing with the micro. (Have booked three hours on it tomorrow.)

26 September 2058

They threaded an optical fiber through the micro's little finger, so I can watch its progress on a screen without being limited to the field of an electron microscope. The picture is fuzzy while the waldo is in motion, but if I hold it still for a few seconds, the computer assist builds up quite a sharp image. I used it to roam all over my right arm and hand, which was fascinating. Hairs a tangle of stiff black stalks, the pores small damp craters. And everywhere the evidence of the skin's slow death; translucent sheafs of desquamated cells.

I've taken to wearing the metal arm rather than the social one. People's stares don't bother me. The metal one will be more useful in my actual work, and I want to get as much practice as possible. There is also an undeniable feeling of power.

27 September 2058

Today I went outside. It was clumsy getting around at first. For the past eleven years I've used a suit only in zerogee, so all my reflexes are wrong. Still, not much serious can go wrong at a sixth of a gee.

It was exhilarating but at the same time frustrating, since I couldn't reveal all my strength. I did almost overdo it once, starting to tip over a large boulder. Before it tipped, I realized that my left boot had crunched through about ten centimeters of regolith, in reaction to the amount of force I was applying. So I backed off and discreetly shuffled my foot to fill the telltale hole.

I could indeed throw a rock over the horizon. With a sling, I might be able to put a small one into orbit. Rent myself out as a lunar launching facility.

(Later) Most interesting. A pretty nurse who has been on this project since the beginning came into my room after dinner and proposed the obvious experiment. It was wildly successful.

Although my new body starts out with the normal pattern of excitation-plateau-orgasm, the resemblance stops there. I have no refractory period; the process of erection is completely under conscious control. This could make me the most popular man on the Moon.

The artificial skin of the penis is as sensitive to tactile differentiation as that of the cyborg fingers: suddenly I know more about a woman's internal topography than any man who ever lived—more than any *woman!*

I think tomorrow I'll take a trip to Farside.

28 September 2058

Farside has nine sex bars. I read the guidebook descriptions, and then asked a few locals for their recommendations, and wound up going to a place cleverly called the Juice Bar.

In fact, the name was not just an expression of coy eroticism. They served nothing but fruit and juices there, most of them fantastically expensive Earth imports. I spent a day's pay on a glass of pear nectar and sought out the most attractive woman in the room.

That in itself was a mistake. I was not physically attractive even before the accident, and the mechanics have faithfully restored my coarse features and slight paunch. I was rebuffed.

So I went to the opposite extreme and looked for the plainest woman. That would be a better test, anyway: before the accident I always demanded, and paid for, physical perfection. If I could duplicate the performance of last night with a woman to whom I was not sexually attracted—and do it in public, with no pressure from having gone without—then my independence from the autonomic nervous system would be proven beyond doubt.

Second mistake. I was never good at small talk, and when I located my paragon of plainness I began talking about the accident and the singular talent that had resulted from it. She suddenly remembered an appointment elsewhere.

I was not so open with the next woman, also plain. She asked whether there was something wrong with my face, and I told her half of the truth. She was sweetly sympathetic, motherly, which did not endear her to me. It did make her a good subject for the experiment. We left the socializing section of the bar and went back to the so-called "love room."

There was an acrid quality to the air that I suppose was compounded of incense and sweat, but of course my dry nose was not capable of identifying actual smells. For the first time, I was grateful for that disability; the place probably had the aroma of a well-used locker room. Plus pheromones.

Under the muted lights, red and blue as well as white, more than a dozen couples were engaged more or less actively in various aspects of amorous behavior. A few were frankly staring at others, but most were either absorbed with their own affairs or furtive in their voyeurism. Most of them were on the floor, which was a warm soft mat, but some were using tables and chairs in fairly ingenious ways. Several of the permutations would no doubt have been impossible or dangerous in Earth's gravity.

We undressed and she complimented me on my evident spryness. A nearby spectator made a jealous observation. Her own body was rather flaccid, doughy, and under previous circumstances I doubt that I would have been able to maintain enthusiasm. There was no problem, however; in fact, I rather enjoyed it. She required very little foreplay, and I was soon repeating the odd sensation of hypersensitized exploration. Gynecological spelunking.

She was quite voluble in her pleasure, and although she lasted less than an hour, we did attract a certain amount of attention. When she, panting, regretfully declined further exercise, a woman who had been watching, a rather attractive young blonde, offered to share her various openings. I obliged her for a while; although the well was dry the pump handle was unaffected.

During that performance I became aware that the pleasure involved was not a sexual one in any normal sense. Sensual, yes, in the way that a fine meal is a sensual experience, but with a remote subtlety that I find difficult to describe. Perhaps there is a relation to epicurism that is more than metaphorical. Since I can no longer taste food, a large area of my brain is available for the evaluation of other experience. It may be that the brain is reorganizing itself in order to take fullest advantage of my new abilities.

By the time the blonde's energy began to flag, several other women had taken an interest in my satyriasis. I resisted the temptation to find what this organ's limit was, if indeed a limit exists. My back ached and the right knee was protesting. So I threw the mental switch and deflated. I left with a minimum of socializing. (The first woman insisted on buying me something at the bar. I opted for a banana.)

29 September 2058

Now that I have eyes and both hands, there's no reason to scratch this diary out with a pen. So I'm entering it into the computer. But I'm keeping two versions.

I recopied everything up to this point and then went back and edited the version that I will show to Biotech. It's very polite, and will remain so. For instance, it does not contain the following:

After writing last night's entry, I found myself still full of energy, and so I decided to put into action a plan that has been forming in my mind.

About two in the morning I went downstairs and broke into the waldo lab. The entrance is protected by a five-digit combination lock, but of course that was no obstacle. My hypersensitive fingers could feel the tumblers rattling into place.

I got the micro-waldo set up and then detached my leg. I guided the waldo through the leg's circuitry and easily disabled the governors. The whole operation took less than twenty minutes.

I did have to use a certain amount of care walking, at first. There was a tendency to rise into the air or to limpingly overcompensate. It was under control by the time I got back to my room. So once more they proved to have been mistaken as to the limits of my abilities. Testing the strength of the leg, with a halfhearted kick I put a deep dent in the metal wall at the rear of my closet. I'll have to wait until I can be outside, alone, to see what full force can do.

A comparison kick with my flesh leg left no dent, but did hurt my great toe.

30 September 2058

It occurs to me that I feel better about my body than I have in the past twenty years. Who wouldn't? Literally eternal youth in these new limbs and organs; if a part shows signs of wear, it can simply be replaced.

I was angry at the Biotech evaluation board this morning. When I simply inquired as to the practicality of replacing the right arm and leg as well, all but one were horrified. One was amused. I will remember him.

I think the fools are going to order me to leave Nearside in a day or two and go back to Mercy for psychiatric "help." I will leave when I want to, on my own terms.

1 October 2058

This is being voice-recorded in the Environmental Control Center at Nearside. It is 10:32; they have less than ninety minutes to accede to my demands. Let me backtrack.

After writing last night's entry I felt a sudden access of sexual desire. I took the shuttle to Farside and went back to the Juice Bar.

The plain woman from the previous night was waiting, hoping that I would show up. She was delighted when I suggested that we save money (and whatever residue of modesty we had left) by keeping ourselves to one another, back at my room.

I didn't mean to murder her. That was not in my mind at all. But I suppose in my passion, or abandon, I carelessly propped my strong leg against the wall and then thrust with too much strength. At any rate there was a snap and a tearing sound. She gave a small cry and the lower half of my body was suddenly awash in blood. I had snapped her spine and evidently at the same time caused considerable internal damage. She must have lost consciousness very quickly, though her heart did not stop beating for nearly a minute.

Disposing of the body was no great problem, conceptually. In the laundry room I found a bag large enough to hold her comfortably. Then I went back to the room and put her and the sheet she had besmirched into the bag.

Getting her to the recycler would have been a problem if it had been a normal hour. She looked like nothing so much as a body in a laundry bag. Fortunately, the corridor was deserted.

The lock on the recycler room was child's play. The furnace door was a problem, though; it was easy to unlock but its effective diameter was only 25 centimeters.

So I had to disassemble her. To save cleaning up, I did the job inside the laundry bag, which was clumsy, and made it difficult to see the fascinating process.

I was so absorbed in watching that I didn't hear the door slide open. But the man who walked in made a slight gurgling sound, which somehow I did hear over the cracking of bones. I stepped over to him and killed him with one kick.

At this point I have to admit to a lapse in judgment. I relocked the door and went back to the chore at hand. After the woman was completely recycled, I repeated the process with the man— which was, incidentally, much easier. The female's layer of subcutaneous fat made disassembly of the torso a more slippery business.

It really was wasted time (though I did spend part of the time thinking out the final touches of the plan I am now engaged upon). I might as well have left both bodies there on the floor. I had kicked the man with great force—enough to throw me to the ground in reaction and badly bruise my right hip—and had split him open from crotch to heart. This made a bad enough mess, even if he hadn't compounded the problem by striking the ceiling. I would never be able to clean that up, and it's not the sort of thing that would escape notice for long.

At any rate, it was only twenty minutes wasted, and I gained more time than that by disabling the recycler room lock. I cleaned up, changed clothes, stopped by the waldo lab for a few minutes, and then took the slidewalk to the Environmental Control Center.

There was only one young man on duty at the ECC at that hour. I exchanged a few pleasantries with him and then punched him in the heart, softly enough not to make a mess. I put his body where it wouldn't distract me and then attended to the problem of the "door."

There's no actual door on the ECC, but there is an emergency wall that slides into place if there's a drop in pressure. I typed up a test program simulating an emergency, and the wall obeyed. Then I walked over and twisted a few flanges around. Nobody would be able to get into the Center with anything short of a cutting torch.

Sitting was uncomfortable with the bruised hip, but I managed to ease into the console and spend an hour or so studying logic and wiring diagrams. Then I popped off an access plate and moved the micro-waldo down the corridors of electronic thought. The intercom began buzzing incessantly, but I didn't let it interfere with my concentration.

Nearside is protected from meteorite strike or (far more likely) structural failure by a series of 128 bulkheads that, like the emergency wall here, can slide into place and isolate any area where there's a pressure drop. It's done automatically, of course, but can also be controlled from here.

What I did, in essence, was to tell each bulkhead that it was under repair, and should not close under any circumstance. Then I moved the waldo over to the circuits that controlled the city's eight airlocks. With some rather elegant microsurgery, I transferred control of all eight solely to the pressure switch I now hold in my left hand.

It is a negative-pressure button, a dead-man switch taken from a power saw. So long as I hold it down, the inner doors of the airlocks will remain locked. If I let go, they will all iris open. The outer doors are already open, as are the ones that connect the airlock chambers to the suiting-up rooms. No one will be able to make it to a spacesuit in time. Within thirty seconds, every corridor will be full of vacuum. People behind airtight doors may choose between slow asphyxiation and explosive decompression.

My initial plan had been to wire the dead-man switch to my pulse, which would free my good hand and allow me to sleep. That will have to wait. The wiring completed, I turned on the intercom and announced that I would speak to the Coordinator, and no one else.

When I finally got to talk to him, I told him what I had done and invited him to verify it. That didn't take long. Then I presented my demands:

Surgery to replace the rest of my limbs, of course. The surgery would have to be done while I was conscious (a heartbeat dead-man switch could be subverted by a heart machine) and it would have to be done here, so that I could be assured that nobody fooled with my circuit changes.

The doctors were called in, and they objected that such profound surgery couldn't be done under local anesthetic. I knew they were lying, of course; amputation was a fairly routine procedure even before anesthetics were invented. Yes, but I would faint, they said. I told them that I would not, and at any rate I was willing to take the chance, and no one else had any choice in the matter.

(I have not yet mentioned that the ultimate totality of my plan involves replacing all my internal organs as well as all of the limbs—or at least those organs whose failure could cause untimely death. I will be a true cyborg then, a human brain in an "artificial" body, with the prospect of thousands of years of life. With a few decades—or centuries!—of research, I could even do something about the brain's shortcomings. I would wind up interfaced to EarthNet, with all of human knowledge at my disposal, and with my faculties for logic and memory no longer fettered by the slow pace of electrochemical synapse.)

A psychiatrist, talking from Earth, tried to convince me of the error of my ways. He said that the dreadful trauma had "obviously" unhinged me, and the cyborg augmentation, far from effecting a cure, had made my mental derangement worse. He demonstrated, at least to his own satisfaction, that my behavior followed some classical pattern of madness. All this had been taken into consideration, he said, and if I were to give myself up, I would be forgiven my crimes and manumitted into the loving arms of the psychiatric establishment.

I did take time to explain the fundamental errors in his way of thinking. He felt that I had quite literally lost my identity by losing my face and genitalia, and that I was at bottom a "good" person whose essential humanity had been perverted by physical and existential estrangement. Totally wrong. By his terms, what I actually *am* is an "evil" person whose true nature was revealed to himself by the lucky accident that released him from existential propinquity with the common herd.

And "evil" is the accurate word, not maladjusted or amoral or even criminal. I am as evil by human standards as a human is evil by the standards of an animal raised for food, and the analogy is accurate. I will sacrifice humans not only for my survival but for comfort, curiosity, or entertainment. I will allow to live anyone who doesn't bother me, and reward generously those who help.

Now they have only forty minutes. They know I am
—end of recording—

25 September 2058

Excerpt from Summary Report

I am Dr. Henry Janovski, head of the surgical team that worked on the ill-fated cyborg augmentation of Dr. Wilson Cheetham.

We were fortunate that Dr. Cheetham's insanity did interfere with his normally painstaking, precise nature. If he had spent more time in preparation, I have no doubt that he would have put us in a very difficult fix.

He should have realized that the protecting wall that shut him off from the rest of Nearside was made of steel, an excellent conductor of electricity. If he had insulated himself behind a good dielectric, he could have escaped his fate.

Cheetham's waldo was a marvelous instrument, but basically it was only a pseudo-intelligent servomechanism that obeyed well-defined radio-frequency commands. All we had to do was override the signals that were coming from his own nervous system.

We hooked a powerful amplifier up to the steel wall, making it in effect a huge radio transmitter. To generate the signal we wanted amplified, I had a technician put on a waldo sleeve that was holding a box similar to Cheetham's dead-man switch. We wired the hand closed, turned up the power, and had the technician strike himself on the chin as hard as he could.

The technician struck himself so hard he blacked out for a few seconds. Cheetham's resonant action, perhaps a hundred times more powerful, drove the bones of his chin up through the top of his skull.

Fortunately, the expensive arm itself was not damaged. It is not evil or insane by itself, of course. Which I shall prove.

The experiments will continue, though of course we will be more selective as to subjects. It seems obvious in retrospect that we should not use as subjects people who have gone through the kind of trauma that Cheetham suffered. We must use willing volunteers. Such as myself.

I am not young, and weakness and an occasional tremor in my hands limit the amount of surgery I can do—much less than my knowledge would allow, or my nature desire. My failing left arm I shall have replaced with Cheetham's mechanical marvel, and I will go through training similar to his—but for the good of humanity, not for ill.

What miracles I will perform with the knife!

───

I don't often see direct influences of the literary sort in my work, but that story's an exception. I was going through a Poe phase, having read Julian Symons's fascinating biography *The Tell-Tale Heart* (Harper & Row, 1978) and then rereading the short stories. For the love of God, Montressor.

When the last page came out of the typewriter, I was afraid I had written an absolutely unpublishable (or at least unsalable) story. Too much graphic sex and violence for the science fiction magazines; too much hard science for the slicks. Indeed, I sent it off to a science fiction magazine and got back a more-in-sorrow-than-in-anger rejection letter. My wife talked me into sending it to *Playboy*, though, and they accepted it by return mail. (Her services as a literary consultant are available for a very high fee.)

Playboy didn't care for the title. I suggested "Tom Swift and His Electric Penis," but for some reason they decided the original one was okay after all.

This next story also resulted from an arbitrarily chosen topic. I was stranded in St. Louis for five days in midsummer, the temperature hitting three digits before noon each day. I had a room with an air conditioner and a typewriter, though, and was facing a science fiction convention where I would have to do a reading. Decided to write a funny story for it.

"Write what you know" is a solemn and totally false adage you find in bad books about writing. It occurred to me, though, that I'd never written a story about what I know best: being a science fiction writer. That seemed like fertile ground for a silly tale.

SEVEN AND

THE STARS

Sometimes it's best to settle for part of the truth. When you're at a cocktail party and some stranger asks what you do for a living, you don't come right out and say "I'm a science fiction writer." Sometimes it's better to say "I'm a novelist," or "I'm a freelance writer," or even "I'm between jobs right now." Because you can get the damnedest responses.

Now, I'm not bothered by the philistines who mumble something about "that Buck Rogers stuff" and wander vaguely away. Nor even the people who have a terrific story idea and will split fifty-fifty, if you'll do the writing. (I always tell them I'm deadlined and give them my ex-agent's phone number.) What bothers me is some of the nuts you meet, if they're unpleasant ones, and the people who think that you yourself must be a nut.

People find out you write science fiction and they automatically think you share their belief in flying saucers, yetis, the Loch Ness monster, the Tooth Fairy, anything. Most of the sf writers I know don't even believe in NASA.

Still, you can't stay away from cocktail parties. If a writer refuses a free drink, they find out about it and take away his Guild membership.

So I was at this West Village cocktail party, having canapés for dinner, when an elegant woman in fifty-dollar jeans came up and asked me the Question. You can't lie to fifty-dollar jeans. There's something sincere about that kind of excess.

"Oh," she said, "you must be interested in UFOs."

Here I have to admit to some incipient sexism, or at least an optimistic mating instinct. If she'd been a man, I would've rolled my eyes ceilingward and said something disparaging. And life would be simpler now. As it was, I put on a serious expression and said only that I didn't think there was enough evidence to come to a conclusion.

She dimpled gloriously and said she thought she had evidence. My instincts should have told me that screwballs come in all shapes and sizes. But I was attracted to her, and she didn't seem too loony, and in the back of my mind was the idea that there might be a story here—not science fiction, but the cheap kind of breathless exploitation that fuels the weekly tabloids. I'd never stooped that low before. But the rent was due and I actually was at that party for the canapés.

"What sort of evidence?" I asked. "I've never seen a photograph, or anything, that I thought was very convincing."

"It's . . . hard to describe. You might think I was crazy or something."

"Not at all. That's not an accusation a science fiction writer would make lightly. Six impossible things before breakfast, you know."

"If you really are interested, I'd rather show you. Come to my place after the party?"

No, I'd rather be poked in the eye with something sharp. I told her I'd be ready to leave whenever she was. She circulated for a while and I finished my dinner.

I should have smelled a rat. One minute of conversation and she wants me to come spend the evening. It was not for my lean and hairy personage.

We walked to an underground lot and picked up her car, a well-restored old Jaguar sedan. On the drive out to Westchester I learned that she was an analyst for a municipal-fund outfit. So I was able to check her out—a couple of years ago I had some Hollywood money and put it into municipals—and found that she was very sharp. About her "evidence," though, she offered nothing. I didn't ask, of course.

Her name was Lydia Martell. She lived in North Tarrytown, in an upper-middle-class stucco house overlooking the Hudson and the train. I expressed surprise that she had such a large place; she said she'd been married once.

The first thing I noticed, inside, was a strong citrus odor, like those sachets little old ladies bring back from Florida. Other than that, the house was severely modern, unrelentingly tasteful. When Lydia went off to make coffee, I did some discreet snooping. Most of the wall hangings were numbered-and-signed contemporary prints, though pride of place went to a spare drawing by Picasso, an original nude. If she was a nut, she was the richest one I'd ever met.

She returned with a tray, two cups of coffee, and a metal tube.

"Exhibit A," she said.

The tube was very peculiar-looking. It was the kind of silvery blue you might associate with outdoors equipment: pack frames and ski poles of anodized aluminum. But it seemed to glow, and it was too heavy to be aluminum. Much too heavy. I hefted it in the palm of my hand.

"Right," she said. "If that were made of solid gold it would weigh less."

"It's impressive." I peered through it; it was just an empty tube of thin metal. "What's the story?"

"Exhibit B." She took the tube from me and stood it on its end, on the coffee table. "Come on out, Seven."

A voice came from the tube. "You found one." Behind me, I heard a door click open. I turned—and saw one of those six impossible things you're supposed to believe before breakfast.

He, or she, or it was about eight feet tall and scrawny. It had the right number of legs and arms and eyes. No mouth to speak of, or with. Another blue tube swung on a chain around its neck, and it walked slowly, with the aid of two staffs. It was scaly blue and smelled like an orange grove in heat.

"Uh," I said.

"He is a scientist?" the tube said.

"Not exactly," Lydia said. "A science fiction writer."

"Please explain."

"They're people who tell stories about the future, usually in terms of science."

"We have those on my world," it said. "We keep them in a special place. Away from the young."

"Well, there weren't any scientists at the party. The biologist didn't show up. If you'd let me go to the university—"

"No, not yet. One at a time. Do you, science fiction writer, know much about science?"

"I—I read the magazines," I said. "You're . . . from another planet? Another dimension?"

"Yes, both. Perhaps he will do."

My brain was sitting there with the clutch in. The only mundane explanation I could come up with was that this was some elaborate joke involving psychedelics. I'd been turning down LSD for twenty years; now I wished I'd tried it once, for a data base. Everything else seemed so real.

"Lydia, this isn't some kind of a hoax? Like a Muppet, or—"

"Seven, shake hands with him."

The creature clumped over, transferred both staffs to its left hand, and offered its right. It was rough and dry and hotter than a fevered child's skin. "I am real," it said. "At least as real as you are."

Then it sat down, a painfully slow operation accompanied by alarming noises. Sitting on the floor, it was almost at eye level. And too close.

"Please explain in a way he can understand, Lydia."

"Seven is marooned here. He's . . . well, something like a tourist. His ship's drive broke down, and Earth was the nearest place where he could survive and maybe get help. He orbited for a few weeks, monitoring our broadcasts, and then landed here."

"Reluctantly," Seven said. "I'm not really sure you can help me. From your programs it seems likely you will harm me."

"But those are just entertainments," I started to protest. "Nobody—"

"Exactly. Fiction is truth is fiction."

I took a sip of coffee and was surprised that the cup didn't rattle; I didn't spill any of it. That would happen in fiction. "How did you wind up here? Why did you choose Lydia?"

"My garage door was open," she said.

"That seems like an awful chance. If we're so dangerous."

"As individuals, you aren't dangerous to me. Examine your own feelings. Aren't you surprised not to be a little afraid?" I thought that was due to my science-fictional objectivity. "No, I don't have control over your mind, and I can't 'read' it. You trust me because you can sense my intentions directly. It's not a well-developed talent in humans, though, and I doubt that it would work in a crowd, or over television. It's in groups that you are dangerous."

I'd noticed that myself. "You flew a flying saucer through Westchester and parked it in her garage?"

"No lights," Seven said. "Four in the morning."

"It's not a flying saucer," Lydia added. "It's a big black sphere, like a huge bowling ball."

"And it's broken down," I said. "You can orbit Earth, slip down, and tuck it into someone's garage, but you can't go from star to star. Is that it?"

"He could go to other stars," Lydia said, "but it would take a long time."

"I could reach the star nearest here in about twelve years. But it would take nearly a hundred centuries for me to get home that way. Most of my friends would be dead."

"It's like if you drove to California," Lydia said, "and your car broke down there and you only had first gear. You could drive back to New York, but it makes more sense to look for a mechanic."

"But there are not mechanics in this part of California," Seven said. "I have to find some intelligent—what was that word?"

"Blacksmith."

"—blacksmith, and see whether he can fix it under my guidance. But I'm not a mechanic either. I know a little about the basic principles involved, but that's all." He rested his chin on one bony knee. "I'm not even sure how to take it apart safely."

"What's its power source?"

"Simple fusion of hydrogen atoms."

"That could be dangerous, all right."

"No, that's not what bothers me. It's the part that makes distances smaller. You're not supposed to use that near a planet."

"Makes distances smaller?"

"Yes. If you used it near a planet, it would make part of the planet very small. I think the rest of it would come apart, stretching."

"How does it work?"

"It makes distances smaller, so you don't have to travel as long."

I rubbed my eyes. When I opened them he was still there. "I understand that part. What I mean is, do you know how it makes distances smaller?"

"The process?"

"That's right."

"This is why I need a scientist." He daintily took a sugar cube from the bowl on the tray and rubbed it between his palms. It disappeared. "All I know is that you tell the ship where you want to go, and it tells you how long it will take. You can stay awake or sleep. When you are ready, it goes."

"You must know some scientists," Lydia said.

"Yeah. A magician, too."

"I don't want many people to know I'm here. Not until I can leave quickly."

I had to admit that made sense. "Why don't you do this," Lydia said. "Pretend it's for a story. . . . Ask some scientists whether there's some rationale for a drive like this thing you made up. You must do that sort of thing all the time."

"Yeah." Like the physicist who told me my antigravity device violated the laws of conservation of energy, momentum, and natural resources. Sort of condescending. "Worth a try, I guess."

"I could show you the vehicle," Seven said. Now that did sound interesting. I helped him to his feet, and Lydia took us around to the back door of the garage.

It really wasn't too helpful. The spaceship looked like a prop for a low-budget TV movie. A featureless flat black sphere about eight feet in diameter. Seven said something to it and it clamshelled open. It looked pretty low-rent inside, too. Just a comfy-looking settee in a small round room wallpapered with shabby red satin. There were three gray boxes under the settee that he identified as the fusion drive, the "shrinker," and a life-support center. He didn't know how to get the boxes open.

I couldn't really fault him for that. I've been riding the subway all my life, but if one stopped dead I wouldn't have the faintest idea of how to get it started again.

That analogy stuck in my mind as I rattled home in the last train back to the city. Suppose the subway broke down and when I got out there was no one around but a bunch of Stone Age savages. Or even colonial Americans, say. *Well, it's run by an electrical motor. You know—electricity? Ben Franklin?*

Maybe somewhere in the city there was someone fiddling with the equivalent of Leyden jars and kites and keys. Even if I could find him, could we turn him into a metaphorical subway repairman?

The next morning I called Lydia and she confirmed that it hadn't been a dream, hallucination, or joke. So I took a jigger's worth out of my own private life-support center and splashed my way through the freezing rain to the public library.

There's a section there that has all the publications of the New York Academy of Sciences. I scanned titles and skimmed a few articles, looking for people who had an interest in exotic propulsion systems. I discarded a few names as being too prominent, figuring they'd have had too much experience with screwballs. By afternoon I had three names to call. One turned out to be on sabbatical, one was openly contemptuous, and one was Lazlo Crane.

Dr. Crane is an assistant professor in the aerospace engineering department of NYU. He had written a paper with a new angle on using black holes for interstellar flight. I couldn't even understand the one-paragraph summary, but the title was clear enough. His office wasn't too far, and I was out of phone change, so I slogged on over.

He looked sort of like a Lazlo. Tall and skinny, with a wisp of beard; prematurely bald, squinting through thick glasses. He was working on a crossword puzzle, standing up with the newspaper folded on top of a filing cabinet. Like Thomas Wolfe used to do, writing, though Wolfe was beefier and not quite Lazlo's seven feet.

"What's a five-letter word meaning 'sanctuary'?" he asked without looking up. "The middle letter's a *k,* I'm sure of it."

"Sekos," I said, and spelled it.

"Fits." He scribbled it in, using a pencil. Amateur. "Do I know you?" He peered at me over his glasses.

I introduced myself and he gave the rare response: "The science fiction writer?"

I replied modestly in the affirmative. He shook hands and said, "Used to read your stuff," without elaborating. Too busy, I supposed, what with all the space drives and crossword puzzles.

He sat down and nodded in the direction of the only other chair. "Can I do something for you?"

"I read your paper in the last Academy Proceedings. I thought maybe you could help me with a problem."

"A science problem? I thought you stayed away from that. Sort of made it up as you went along."

Pleasant fellow. "Trying to clean up my act," I said, and outlined what I knew of Seven's drive. It didn't take long, of course.

He pulled on his lower lip a couple of times and rubbed his beard out of shape. "Why do you need an explanation? Why not just say there's this black box that makes distances shorter?"

Gray box. "That would be kind of absurd, wouldn't it?"

"Not really." He shrugged, a quick spasm. "Like the way you handled time travel in *Time and the Chinaman*—"

"*Time and/or the Chinaman.*"

"Whatever. You just presented it as an established fact. If they actually had this distance-shrinker, they wouldn't stand around talking about it. They'd just use it, wouldn't they?"

"Well, that's one way to handle it. A good way, usually, if you do it convincingly. But even if I don't actually describe it in detail, I'd like to know how it works, what it looks like."

"A black box, probably." He leaned back and thought for a minute. "There is an angle. You know how to make artificial gravity?"

"Sure, you spin the thing around—"

"No, that's not gravity. It's just imposing a rotating frame of reference. If you drop something it doesn't fall in a straight line. It doesn't even drop, really. It only seems to."

"Okay." I think.

"The only way we know how to make artificial gravity is to put a mass under the thing. You put a scale on a table and put something on it that weighs a pound. Roll a ten-ton lead weight under the table, and it weighs a tiny fraction of an ounce more."

"That's not really artificial gravity, though," I said. "That's natural, organic gravity."

"Semantics. Don't think of that block of lead in Newtonian terms—more mass, therefore a greater attractive force. Don't think in terms of force at all. Think of it as a device that changes the shape of space." He stood up quickly. "Let's go to the undergraduate lab."

I followed him through the door and down the hall. "You know about the rubber sheet model?"

"I've seen pictures."

"We have one here. Here." He pushed open a door and we went into a large room full of long tables cluttered with electronic gear. In one corner was a round table a couple of yards in diameter, a taut rubber sheet nailed to a wooden frame with a wooden lip around it. Lazlo reached into a jar and took out a marble-sized ball bearing and rolled it across the sheet.

"Straight lines, see?" The ball bearing bounced from the opposite side and came back. Lazlo picked it up. "Now we put a planet in there, or a sun." He filled his hand with a metal sphere about half the size of a bowling ball and set it in the center of the sheet, turning it into a kind of elastic bowl.

"We use this thing to demonstrate different kinds of orbits." He rolled the ball bearing out and it dipped down in a graceful curve, came out banking to the left, rolled back in, and began looping around in a series of ellipses. He scooped up a handful of the ball bearings and rolled them in at various angles and speeds. "See there, there, that one's almost a circle, like the earth's orbit."

"Kind of a miniature solar system," I said.

"Except that it runs down. Friction with the air and the rubber surface."

It was a hypnotic sight. We watched them whispering around for a minute.

"Now the important thing is that these things are still moving in a kind of straight line, though it doesn't look like it from our point of view."

"Path of least resistance?" I said.

"Something like that. The path they follow is called a geodesic. How much it deviates from a simple straight line, obviously, depends on how massive the central object is and how far it is from the orbiting object."

"The closer they get, the faster they roll," I said. "Then they go out again and slow down."

"Right. Now what we're actually talking about, at any given moment, is the angle the rubber sheet makes, from the horizontal, at the spot right under the ball bearing. The greater the angle is, the more the ball's influenced."

"Sure." Pretty sure, anyhow.

"That angle corresponds to what in four-dimensional space-time we call the gravitational gradient."

"If you say so."

"Come on, now, it's not that hard. You read the black hole paper, didn't you?"

Moment of truth. "Look. Dr. Crane, twenty years ago I flunked calculus and switched to English. The part of your paper that was in English, I read."

He twisted his beard. "Not much, eh?"

"Enough to see that you might have what I want. Go ahead. The gravitational gradient."

"Well, what's interesting in terms of your space drive is what happens to the gravitational gradient very close to a tremendously massive, very small object. Like a black hole."

He pulled the weight out of the middle of the sheet and the ball bearings sort of relaxed, rolling off and clicking against the sides of the table and each other.

"Now look." He pushed his finger down into the sheet and one ball bearing, the closest, rolled into the dimple he made. None of the others was affected. "If you think about the push being the same, here, but the scale much reduced—the ball is smaller than a BB and my finger is narrower than a hypodermic needle—you can see you're approaching a condition where the sides of the gravity well, the rubber sheet, are almost vertical. As it approaches the point of the needle, the BB falls faster and faster."

"But not for long."

"That's the point. It's like rolling the lead weight under the scale. I think I have a way to fool space-time. Make it seem as if there were a small black hole just a tiny distance away, constantly retreating in the direction you want to go. It's only the *gradient* that makes a difference, not the overall situation." He poked the rubber sheet again. "See? The other ball bearings don't even know I'm here. The gradient becomes infinitesimal, out where they are."

"Suppose it were a spaceship-sized thing. Wouldn't the gee forces get intolerable?"

"Not a bit. You're in free fall, just like orbiting a planet. Zero gravity, to the people aboard the spaceship."

"You couldn't go any faster than the speed of light, though," I said. "It doesn't get by relativity."

He picked up a ball bearing and stared at it, frowning. "I'd have to say no." He tossed it onto the sheet and it bounced over the lip to rattle across the floor. "Certainly within the context of my paper, I didn't say anything about exceeding the speed of light. I did want to get it published."

"You saw a catch to it?"

"There's a paradox . . . having to do with the allowable range of initial conditions. I'm waiting to see whether anybody notices it." He gestured at the rubber sheet. "If you were to interpret the paradox in terms of this model, well, it would be like changing the elasticity of the rubber, at the point where the BB is. Or being able to reach up from the other side of the sheet and twist it out of shape.

"The net result, looking at it one way, *is* that it goes faster than the speed of light. Another way to look at it, which is no more comfortable, is that . . . well, it shrinks space. Like your black box, it makes distances shorter. You accelerate for a certain period—falling, so to speak—and then reverse the process, decelerating, and you wind up having gone much farther than you seem to have gone. Much farther than you should be able to go, on the energy expended."

That was enough for me. "Would you be willing to explain this to some friends of mine—other people who are helping me with this thing?"

He shook his head. "I don't want any publicity."

"Nothing like that. They aren't even writers. We'd just get together for dinner and chat."

The word "dinner" provoked some interest. Science fiction writers and junior professors have something in common. "They aren't a bunch of nuts, now?"

"One of them is pretty weird—but levelheaded." Flat on top, actually. "You might get a kick out of him. He's even taller than you are."

"That would be novel. Okay, go ahead and set it up. I'm free most nights."

I called Lydia from his phone and set it up for that evening, then went off to my local check-bouncing service to get enough for our train fares.

I don't recall now what I actually expected in the way of a reaction, when Lazlo Crane confronted Seven. He was remarkably subdued.

Lydia had charmed him with herself and with a magnificent dinner of duck à *l'orange,* the cooking of which masked Seven's citric effluvium. After dessert she took out the blue tube and for the first time mentioned the reason for Crane's presence.

"Lazlo, there's someone we'd like you to talk to. About the paper you wrote."

To Seven's credit, he went around the long way, so as not to sneak up from behind. As he walked across the great room to where we were sitting, I watched Lazlo carefully. He didn't freak or faint or even go bug-eyed or stammer. Both eyebrows went up a bit, true, and he blinked. Then he looked at the blue tube and at me. "It's not really a story, then," he said.

"No. It's all true."

He nodded. "I didn't think you wrote that sort of thing."

They talked for a couple of hours, Lazlo questioning Seven closely about the range of his machine, duration of voyages, the sensations he felt, and so forth. Seven showed some fantastic pictures of the places he'd been, like home movies but with three dimensions and smell.

Then Lydia and I opened the garage door and checked to make sure the coast was clear, and the two of them took off for a joyride in the black machine, which was silent and nearly invisible. They came back ninety minutes later, having been around the moon.

When we asked whether he could fix it, Lazlo said he wasn't sure. "It's not so much like a blacksmith trying to fix a car. More like an auto mechanic trying to repair an atom bomb, having read a couple of popular science articles. We need sort of a back-yard Manhattan Project: people, secrecy, money, influence . . ."

"You get the people," Lydia said. "Leave the rest to me."

"Wait," I said. "What about safety? I thought Seven said that thing could pull a planet apart."

"Maybe it could," Lazlo admitted. "That's why we'll be doing the blacksmith part on the moon."

Lydia had quite a bit of money, but not enough to swing a project of this magnitude. That's how *Seven and the Stars* was born.

Seven had home movies of 115 alien worlds. If we set up his projector inside a room with white walls and a white floor, it was just like absolute reality. All I had to do was go into the room with a gas mask and a good half-inch color tape machine, and we had instant documentary. Seven rambled on about the places into a tape recorder, and I rewrote his monologue into a sort of cross between National Geographic specials and the venerable *Mork & Mindy*—tongue-in-cheek science fiction, with special effects that no one in the industry could match.

We paid union dues for a platoon of nonexistent animators and special-effects people, made a package of thirteen shows, and showed them to all five networks. The bidding was furious. CBS won, and they ran *Seven and the Stars* right after *Ninety Minutes* Sunday evening—and within four weeks we were outdrawing our lead-in, our commercials getting the highest prices in the industry.

We were a real mystery. Our corporation owned an ex-dude ranch in Nevada, with security to match the sophistication of our supposed special effects. That was where Lazlo and his gang were, of course, when they weren't riding Seven's bowling ball to the moon.

Seven himself was a slight problem. He had a great natural delivery for my lines, but he got sophisticated, started mugging for laughs. I had to tone him down. There's nothing very funny about a cross between Jack Benny and a gila monster.

In a way, it's a race against time. We've done not quite half of Seven's worlds: when we run out, the series is over. But it looks as if we are going to make it. Lazlo's people have gotten to the point where they can open the gray box and poke around with the whatzis inside. I keep looking up into the sky to see if the moon's still there.

I'll hate to see it end. Right now I have the reputation of having produced the most imaginative science fiction ever—from the Thought-Eaters of Prrn to the Sensuous Siblings of Sirius VI—and sooner or later the whole world will know that it wasn't fiction at all.

So I'll have to return all the Hugos and Nebulas and stumble back into obscurity, with nothing to comfort me but a brilliant and beautiful wife—and the largest residuals in the history of television. Nobody ever said a writer's life was easy.

From the totally frivolous, now, to the rather gritty.

Among the various countries I've visited, Morocco stands out in my memory as having been the most unfriendly. I've never been anyplace where the people were so openly and immediately hostile toward you for the crime of being a foreigner—not even in Vietnam, where we were actively engaged in turning their country into a dioxin-tainted ash heap. I'm sure there are many good and gracious Moroccans, and in fact I've met some in America and Spain and England. Maybe in Morocco there's a law requiring that sort of person to stay indoors when foreigners are around.

At any rate, it's a natural setting for a story, since the essence of "story" is trouble. They give you plenty of that, from the first body search on entering the country to the last bribe you have to pay to get out.

I started to write this as a horror story, but partway through decided that wasn't necessary; there was plenty of weirdness and trouble without invoking the supernatural. Besides, I was going to the Iowa Writers' Workshop at the time, and craved legitimacy. If I could place a story in the *Atlantic* or *Harper's* they would have to admit I was a real author, not just a token invader from the outer space of commercial writing.

After about a year of collecting rejection letters from all the finest places, my agent suggested I pursue the original plan and put the horror back in. He even offered to buy the story for his anthology *Dark Forces* (Viking, 1980). Suitably chastised by the mainstream microcosm, I slunk back to my typewriter and expanded the story to include a dark force indeed.

LINDSAY AND

THE RED

CITY BLUES

"The ancient red city of Marrakesh," his guidebook said, "is the last large oasis for travelers moving south into the Sahara. It is the most exotic of Moroccan cities, where Arab Africa and Black Africa meet in a setting that has changed but little in the past thousand years."

In midafternoon, the book did not mention, it becomes so hot that even the flies stop moving.

The air conditioner in his window hummed impressively but neither moved nor cooled the air. He had complained three times, and the desk clerk responded with two shrugs and a blank stare. By two o'clock his little warren was unbearable. He fled to the street, where it was hotter.

Scott Lindsay was a salesman who demonstrated chemical glassware for a large scientific-supply house in the suburbs of Washington, D.C. Like all Washingtonians, Lindsay thought that a person who could survive summer on the banks of the Potomac could survive it anywhere. He saved up six weeks of vacation time and flew to Europe in late July. Paris was pleasant enough, and the Pyrenees were even cool, but nobody had told him that on August first all of Europe goes on vacation; every good hotel room has been sewed up for six months, restaurants are jammed or closed, and you spend all your time making bad travel connections to cities where only the most expensive hotels have accommodations.

In Nice a Canadian said he had just come from Morocco, where it was hotter than hell but there were practically no tourists this time of year. Scott looked wistfully over the poisoned but still blue Mediterranean, felt the pressure of twenty million fellow travelers at his back, remembered Bogie, and booked the next flight to Casablanca.

Casablanca combined the charm of Pittsburgh with the climate of Dallas. The still air was thick with dust from high-rise construction. He picked up a guidebook and riffled through it and, on the basis of a few paragraphs, took the predawn train to Marrakesh.

"The Red City," it went on, "takes its name from the color of the local sandstone from which the city and its ramparts were built." It would be more accurate, Scott reflected, though less alluring, to call it the Pink City. The Dirty Pink City. He stumbled along the sidewalk on the shady side of the street. The twelve-inch strip of shade at the edge of the sidewalk was crowded with sleeping beggars. The heat was so dry he couldn't even sweat.

He passed two bars that were closed and stepped gratefully into a third. It was a Moslem bar, a milk bar, no booze, but at least it was shade. Two young men slumped at the bar, arguing in guttural whispers, and a pair of ancients in burnooses sat at a table playing a static game of checkers. An oscillating fan pushed the hot air and dust around. He raised a finger at the bartender, who regarded him with stolid hostility, and ordered in schoolboy French a small bottle of Vichy water, carbonated, without ice, and, out of deference to the guidebook, a glass of hot mint tea. The bartender brought the mint tea and a liter bottle of Sidi Harazim water, not carbonated, with a glass of ice. Scott tried to argue with the man but he only stared and kept repeating the price. He finally paid and dumped the ice (which the guidebook had warned him about) into the ashtray. The young men at the bar watched the transaction with sleepy indifference.

The mint tea was an aromatic infusion of mint leaves in hot sugar water. He sipped and was surprised, and perversely annoyed, to find it quite pleasant. He took a paperback novel out of his pocket and read the same two paragraphs over and over, feeling his eyes track, unable to concentrate in the heat.

He put the book down and looked around with slow deliberation, trying to be impressed by the alienness of the place. Through the open front of the bar he could see across the street, where a small park shaded the outskirts of the Djemaa El Fna, the largest open-air market in Morocco and, according to the guidebook, the most exciting and colorful; which itself was the gateway to the mysterious labyrinthine medina, where even this moment someone was being murdered for his pocket change, goats were being used in ways of which Allah did not approve, men were smoking a mixture of camel dung and opium, children were merchandised like groceries; where dark men and women would do anything for a price, and the price would not be high. Scott touched his pocket unconsciously, and the hard bulge of the condom was still there.

The best condoms in the world are packaged in a blue plastic cylinder, squared off along the prolate axis, about the size of a small matchbox. The package is a marvel of technology, held fast by a combination of geometry and sticky tape, and a cool-headed man, under good lighting conditions, can open it in less than a minute. Scott had bought six of them in the drugstore in Dulles International, and had opened only one. He hadn't opened it for the Parisian woman who had looked like a prostitute but had returned his polite proposition with a storm of outrage. He opened it for the fat customs inspector at the Casablanca airport, who had to have its function explained to him, who held it between two dainty fingers like a dead sea thing and called his compatriots over for a look.

The Djemaa El Fna was closed against the heat, pale-orange dusty tents slack and pallid in the stillness. And the trees through which he stared at the open-air market, the souk, were also covered with pale dust; the sky was so pale as to be almost white, and the street and sidewalk were the color of dirty chalk. It was like a faded watercolor displayed under too strong a light.

"Hey, mister." A slim Arab boy, evidently in his early teens, had slipped into the place and was standing beside Lindsay. He was well scrubbed and wore Western-style clothing, discreetly patched.

"Hey, mister," he repeated. "You American?"

"Nu. Eeg bin Jugoslav."

The boy nodded. "You from New York? I got four friends New York."

"Jugoslav."

"You from Chicago? I got four friends Chicago. No, five. Five friends Chicago."

"Jugoslav," he said.

"Where in U.S. you from?" He took a melting ice cube from the ashtray, buffed it on his sleeve, popped it into his mouth, crunched.

"New Caledonia," Scott said.

"Don't like ice? Ice is good this time day." He repeated the process with another cube. "New what?" he mumbled.

"New Caledonia. Little place in the Rockies, between Georgia and Wisconsin. I don't like polluted ice."

"No, mister, this ice okay. Bottle-water ice." He rattled off a stream of Arabic at the bartender, who answered with a single harsh syllable. "Come on, I guide you through medina."

"No."

"I guide you free. Student, English student. I take you free, take you my father's factory."

"You'll take me, all right."

"Okay, we go now. No touris' shit, make good deal."

Well, Lindsay, you wanted experiences. How about being knocked over the head and raped by a goat? "All right, I'll go. But no pay."

"Sure, no pay." He took Scott by the hand and dragged him out of the bar, into the park.

"Is there any place in the medina where you can buy cold beer?"

"Sure, lots of place. Ice beer. You got cigarette?"

"Don't smoke."

"That's okay, you buy pack up here." He pointed at a gazebo-shaped concession on the edge of the park.

"Hell, no. You find me a beer and I might buy you some cigarettes." They came out of the shady park and crossed the packed-earth plaza of the Djemaa El Fna. Dust stung his throat and nostrils, but it wasn't quite as hot as it had been earlier; a slight breeze had come up. One industrious merchant was rolling up the front flap of his tent, exposing racks of leather goods. He called out, "Hey, you buy!" but Scott ignored him, and the boy made a fist gesture, thumb erect between the two first fingers.

Scott had missed one section of the guidebook: "Never visit the medina without a guide; the streets are laid out in crazy, unpredictable angles and someone who doesn't live there will be hopelessly lost in minutes. The best guides are the older men or young Americans who live there for the cheap narcotics; with them you can arrange the price ahead of time, usually about 5 dirham ($1.10). *Under no circumstances* hire one of the street urchins who pose as students and offer to guide you for free; you will be cheated or even beaten up and robbed."

They passed behind the long double row of tents and entered the medina through the Bab Agnou gateway. The main street of the place was a dirt alley some eight feet wide, flanked on both sides by small shops and stalls, most of which were closed, either with curtains or steel shutters or with the proprietor dozing on the stoop. None of the shops had a wall on the side fronting the alley, but the ones that served food usually had chest-high counters. If they passed an open shop the merchant would block their way and importune them in urgent simple French or English, plucking at Scott's sleeve as they passed.

It was surprisingly cool in the medina, the sun's rays partially blocked by wooden lattices suspended over the alleyway. There was a roast-chestnut smell of semolina being parched, with accents of garlic and strange herbs smoldering. Slight tang of exhaust fumes and sickly-sweet hint of garbage and sewage hidden from the sun. The boy led him down a side street, and then another. Scott couldn't tell the position of the sun and was quickly disoriented.

"Where the hell are we going?"

"Cold beer. You see." He plunged down an even smaller alley, dark and sinister, and Lindsay followed, feeling unarmed.

They huddled against a damp wall while a white-haired man on an antique one-cylinder motor scooter hammered by. "How much farther is this place? I'm not going to—"

"Here, one corner." The boy dragged him around the corner and into a musty-smelling dark shop. The shopkeeper, small and round, smiled gold teeth and greeted the boy by name, Abdul. "The word for beer is 'bera,' " he said. Scott repeated the word to the fat little man and Abdul added something. The man opened two beers and set them down on the counter, along with a pack of cigarettes.

It's a new little Arab, Lindsay, but I think you'll be amused by its presumption. He paid and gave Abdul his cigarettes and beer. "Aren't you Moslem? I thought Moslems didn't drink."

"Hell yes, man." He stuck his finger down the neck of the bottle and flicked away a drop of beer, then tilted the bottle up and drained half of it in one gulp. Lindsay sipped at his. It was warm and sour.

"What you do in the States, man?" He lit a cigarette and held it awkwardly.

Chemical glassware salesman? "I drive a truck." The acrid Turkish tobacco smoke stung his eyes.

"Make lots of money."

"No, I don't." He felt foolish saying it. World traveler, Lindsay, you spent more on your ticket than this boy will see in his life.

"Let's go my father's factory."

"What does your father make?"

"All kinds of things. Rugs."

"I wouldn't know what to do with a rug."

"We wrap it, mail to New Caledonia."

"No. Let's go back to—"

"I take you my uncle's factory. Brass, very pretty."

"No. Back to the plaza, you got your cig—"

"Sure, let's go." He gulped down the rest of his beer and stepped back into the alley, Scott following. After a couple of twists and turns they passed an antique-weapons shop that Scott knew he would have noticed, if they'd come by it before. He stopped.

"Where are you taking me now?"

He looked hurt. "Back to Djemaa El Fna. Like you say."

"The hell you are. Get lost, Abdul. I'll find my own way back." He turned and started retracing their path. The boy followed about ten paces behind him, smoking.

He walked for twenty minutes or so, trying to find the relatively broad alleyway that would lead back to the gate. The character of the medina changed: there were fewer and fewer places selling souvenirs, and then none; only residences and little general-merchandise stores, and some small-craft factories, where one or two men, working at a feverish pace, cranked out the items that were sold in the shops. No one tried to sell him anything, and when a little girl held out her hand to beg, an old woman shuffled over and slapped her. Everybody stared when he passed.

Finally he stopped and let Abdul catch up with him. "All right, you win. How much to lead me out?"

"Ten dirham."

"Stuff it. I'll give you two."

Abdul looked at him for a long time, hands in pockets. "Nine dirham." They haggled for a while and finally settled on seven dirham, about $1.50, half now and half at the gate.

They walked through yet another part of the medina, single file through narrow streets, Abdul smoking silently in the lead. Suddenly he stopped.

Scott almost ran into him. "Say, you want girl?"

"Uh . . . I'm not sure," Scott said, startled into honesty.

He laughed, surprisingly deep and lewd. "A boy, then?"

"No, no." Composure, Lindsay. "Your sister, no doubt."

"*What?*" Wrong thing to say.

"American joke. She a friend of yours?"

"Good friend, good fuck. Fifty dirham."

Scott sighed. "Ten." Eventually they settled on thirty-two, Abdul to wait outside until Scott needed his services as a guide again.

Abdul took him to a caftan shop, where he spoke in whispers with the fat owner and gave him part of the money. They led Lindsay to the rear of the place, behind a curtain. A woman sat on her heels beside the bed, patiently crocheting. She stood up gracelessly. She was short and slight, the top of her head barely reaching Scott's shoulders, and was dressed in traditional costume: lower part of the face veiled, dark blue caftan reaching her ankles. At a command from the owner, she hiked the caftan up around her hips and sat down on the bed with her legs spread apart.

"You see, very clean," Abdul said. She was the skinniest woman Scott had ever seen naked, partially naked, her pelvic girdle prominent under smooth brown skin. She had very little pubic hair and the lips of her vulva were dry and gray. But she was only in her early teens, Scott estimated; that, and the bizarre prospect of screwing a fully clothed masked stranger, stimulated him instantly, urgently.

"All right," he said, hoarse. "I'll meet you outside."

She watched with alert curiosity as he fumbled with the condom package, and the only sound she made throughout their encounter was to giggle when he fitted the device over his penis. It was manufactured to accommodate the complete range of possible sizes, and on Scott it had a couple of inches to spare.

This wonder condom, first-class special-delivery French letter is coated with a fluid so similar to natural female secretions, so perfectly intermiscible and isotonic, that it could fool the inside of a vagina. But Scott's ran out of juice in seconds, and the aloof lady's physiology didn't supply any replacement, so he had to fall back on saliva and an old familiar fantasy. It was a long dry haul, the bedding straw crunching monotonously under them, she constantly shifting to more comfortable positions as he angrily pressed his weight into her, finally a draining that was more hydrostatics than passion, which left him jumpy rather than satisfied. When he rolled off her the condom stayed put, there being more lubrication inside it than out. The woman extracted it and, out of some obscure motive, twisted a knot in the end and dropped it behind the bed.

When he'd finished dressing, she held out her hand for a tip. He laughed and told her in English that he was the one who ought to be paid, he'd done all the work, but gave her five dirham anyhow, for the first rush of excitement and her vulnerable eyes.

Abdul was not waiting for him. He tried to interrogate the caftan dealer in French, but got only an interesting spectrum of shrugs. He stepped out onto the street, saw no trace of the little scoundrel, went back inside, and gave the dealer a five while asking the way to Djemaa El Fna. He nodded once and wrote it down on a slip of paper in clear, copybook English.

"You speak English?"

"No," he said with an Oxford vowel.

Scott threaded his way through the maze of narrow streets, carefully memorizing the appearance of each corner in case he had to backtrack. No street was identified by name. The sun was down far enough for the medina to be completely in shadow, and it was getting cooler. He stopped at a counter to drink a bottle of beer, and a pleasant lassitude fell over him, the first time he had not felt keyed up since the Casablanca airport. He strolled on, taking a left at the corner of dye shop and motor scooter.

Halfway down the street, Abdul stood with seven or eight other boys, chattering away, laughing.

Scott half ran toward the group and Abdul looked up, startled, when he roared "You little bastard!"—but Abdul only smiled and muttered something to his companions, and all of them rushed him.

Not a violent man by any means, Scott had nevertheless suffered enough at the hands of this boy, and he planted his feet, balled his fists, bared his teeth, and listened with his whole body to the sweet singing adrenaline. He'd had twelve hours of hand-to-hand combat instruction in basic training, the first rule of which (If you're outnumbered, run) he ignored; the second rule of which (Kick, don't punch) he forgot, and swung a satisfying roundhouse into the first face that came within reach, breaking lips and teeth and one knuckle (he would realize later); then assayed a side-kick to the groin, which only hit a hip but did put the victim out of the fray; touched the ground for balance and bounced up, shaking a child off his right arm while swinging his left at Abdul's neck, and missing; another side-kick, this time straight to a kidney, producing a good loud shriek; Abdul hanging out of reach, boys all over him, kicking, punching, finally dragging him to his knees; Abdul stepping forward and kicking him in the chest, then the solar plexus; the taste of dust as someone keeps kicking his head; losing it, losing it, fading out as someone takes his wallet, then from the other pocket, his traveler's checks, Lindsay, tell them to leave the checks, they can't, nobody will, just doing it to annoy me, fuck them.

It was raining and singing. He opened one eye and saw dark brown. His tongue was flat on the dirt, interesting crunchy dirt-taste in his mouth. Lindsay, reel in your tongue, this is stupid, people piss in this street. Raining and singing. I have died and gone to Marrakesh. He slid forearm and elbow under his chest and pushed up a few inches. An irregular stain of blood caked the dust in front of him, and blood was why he couldn't open the other eye. He wiped the mud off his tongue with his sleeve, then used the other sleeve to unstick his eyelid.

The rain was a wrinkled old woman without a veil, patiently sprinkling water on his head, from a pitcher, looking very old and sad. When he sat up, she offered him two white tablets with the letter "A" impressed on them, and a glass of the same water. He took them gratefully, gagged on them, used another glass of water to wash them farther down. Thanked the impassive woman in three languages, hoped it was bottled water, stood up shakily, sledgehammer headache. The slip of paper with directions lay crumpled in the dust, scuffed but still legible. He continued on his way.

The singing was a muezzin, calling the faithful to prayer. He could hear others singing, in more distant parts of the city. Should he take off his hat? No hat. Some natives were simply walking around, going about their business. An old man was prostrate on a prayer rug in the middle of the street; Scott tiptoed around him.

He came out of the medina through a different gate, and the Djemaa El Fna was spread out in front of him in all its early-evening frenzy. A troupe of black dancers did amazing things to machine-gun drum rhythms: acrobats formed high shaky pyramids, dropped, re-formed; people sang, shouted, laughed.

He watched a snake handler for a long time, going through a creepy repertoire of cobras, vipers, scorpions, tarantulas. He dropped a half-dirham in the man's cup and went on. A large loud group was crowded around a bedsheet-sized game board where roosters strutted from one chalked area to another, pecking at a vase of plastic flowers here, a broken doll there, a painted tin can or torn deck of playing cards elsewhere; men laying down incomprehensible bets, collecting money, shouting at the roosters, baby needs a new pair of sandals.

Then a quiet, patient line, men and women squatting, waiting for the services of a healer. The woman being treated had her dress tucked modestly between her thighs, back bared from shoulders to buttocks, while the healer burned angry welts in a symmetrical pattern with the smoldering end of a length of clothesline, and Scott walked on, charmed in the old sense of the word: hypnotized.

People shrank from his bloody face and he laughed at them, feeling like part of the show, then feeling like something apart, a visitation. Drifting down the rows of merchants: leather, brass, ceramics, carvings, textiles, books, junk, blankets, weapons, hardware, jewelry, food. Stopping to buy a bag of green pistachio nuts, the vendor gives him the bag and then waves him away, flapping; no pay, just leave.

Gathering darkness and most of the merchants closed their tents, but the thousands of people didn't leave the square. They moved in around men, perhaps a dozen of them, who sat on blankets scattered around the square, in the flickering light of kerosene lanterns, droning the same singsong words over and over. Scott moved to the closest and shouldered his way to the edge of the blanket and squatted there, an American gargoyle, staring. Most of the people gave him room but light fingers tested his hip pocket; he swatted the hand away without looking back. The man in the center of the blanket fixed on his bloody stare and smiled back a tight smile, eyes bright with excitement. He raised both arms and the crowd fell silent, switched off.

A hundred people breathed in at once when he whispered the first words, barely audible words that must have been the Arabic equivalent of "Once upon a time." And then the storyteller shouted and began to pace back and forth, playing out his tale in a dramatic staccato voice, waving his arms, hugging himself, whispering, moaning—and Lindsay followed it perfectly, laughing on cue, crying when the storyteller cried, understanding nothing and everything. When it was over, the man held out his cap first to the big American with the bloody face, and Scott emptied his left pocket into the cap: dirham and half-dirham pieces and leftover francs and one rogue dime.

And he stood up and turned around and watched his long broad shadow dance over the crowd as the storyteller with his lantern moved on around the blanket, and he spotted his hotel and pushed toward it through the mob.

It was worth it. The magic was worth the pain and humiliation.

He forced himself to think of practical things, as he approached the hotel. He had no money, no credit cards, no traveler's checks, no identification. Should he go to the police? Probably it would be best to go to American Express first. Collect phone call to the office. Have some money wired. Identity established, so he could have the checks replaced. Police here unlikely to help unless "tipped."

Ah, simplicity. He did have identification: his passport, that he'd left at the hotel desk. That had been annoying, now a lifesaver. Numbers of traveler's checks in his suitcase.

There was a woman in the dusty dim lobby of the hotel. He walked right by her and she whispered "Lin—say."

He remembered the eyes and stopped. "What do you want?"

"I have something of yours." Absurdly, he thought of the knotted condom. But what she held up was a fifty-dollar traveler's check. He snatched it from her; she didn't attempt to stop him.

"You sign that to me," she said. "I bring you everything else the boys took."

"Even the money?" He had had over five hundred dirhams in cash.

"What they gave me, I bring you."

"Well, you bring it here, and we'll see."

She shook her head angrily. "No, I bring *you*. I bring you . . . *to* it. Right now. You sign that to me."

He was tempted. "At the caftan shop?"

"That's right. Wallet and 'merican 'spress check. You come."

The medina at night. A little sense emerged. "Not now. I'll come with you in the morning."

"Come now."

"I'll see you here in the morning." He turned and walked up the stairs.

Well, he had fifty out of the twelve hundred dollars. He checked the suitcase, and the list of numbers was where he'd remembered. If she wasn't there in the morning, he would be able to survive the loss. He caressed the dry leather sheath of the antique dagger he'd bought in the Paris flea market. If she was waiting, he would go into the medina armed. It would simplify things to have the credit cards. He fell asleep and had violent dreams.

He woke at dawn. Washed up and shaved. The apparition that peered back from the mirror looked worse than he felt; he was still more exhilarated than otherwise. He took a healing drink of brandy and stuck the dagger in his belt, in the back so he wouldn't have to button his sport coat. The muezzin's morning wail stopped.

She was sitting in the lobby's only chair, and stood when he came down the stairs.

"No tricks," he said. "If you have what you say, you get the fifty dollars."

They went out of the hotel and the air was almost cool, damp smell of garbage. "Why did the boys give this to you?"

"Not *give*. Business deal, I get half."

There was no magic in the Djemaa El Fna in the morning, just dozens of people walking through the dust. They entered the medina, and it was likewise bereft of mystery and danger. Sleepy collection of closed-off shopfronts, everything beaded with dew, quiet and stinking. She led him back the way he had come yesterday afternoon. Passing the alley where he had encountered the boys, he noticed there was no sign of blood. Had the old woman neatly cleaned up, or was it simply scuffed away on the sandals of negligent passersby? Thinking about the fight, he touched the dagger, loosening it in its sheath. Not for the first time, he wondered whether he was walking into a trap. He almost hoped so. But all he had left of value was his signature.

Lindsay had gotten combat pay in Vietnam, but the closest he'd come to fighting was to sit in a bunker while mortars and rockets slammed around in the night. He'd never fired a shot in anger, never seen a dead man, never this, never that, and he vaguely felt unproven. The press of the knife both comforted and frightened him.

They entered the caftan shop, Lindsay careful to leave the door open behind them. The fat caftan dealer was seated behind a table. On the table were Lindsay's wallet and a china plate with a small pile of dried mud.

The dealer watched impassively while Lindsay snatched up his wallet. "The checks."

The dealer nodded. "I have a proposition for you."

"You've learned English."

"I believe I have something you would like to buy with those checks."

Lindsay jerked out the dagger and pointed it at the man's neck. His hand and voice shook with rage. "I'll cut your throat first. Honest to God, I will."

There was a childish giggle and the curtain to the "bedroom" parted, revealing Abdul with a pistol. The pistol was so large he had to hold it with both hands, but he held it steadily, aimed at Lindsay's chest.

"Drop the knife," the dealer said.

Lindsay didn't. "This won't work. Not even here."

"A merchant has a right to protect himself."

"That's not what I mean. You can kill me, I know, but you can't force me to sign those checks at gunpoint. *I will not do it!*"

He chuckled. "That is not what I had in mind, not at all. I truly do have something to sell you, something beyond worth. The gun is only for my protection; I assumed you were wise enough to come armed. Relinquish the knife and Abdul will leave."

Lindsay hesitated, weighing obscure odds, balancing the will to live against his newly born passion. He dropped the dagger.

The merchant said something in Arabic while the prostitute picked up the knife and set it on the table. Abdul emerged from the room with no gun and two straight wooden chairs. He set one next to the table and one behind Lindsay, and left, slamming the door.

"Please sign the check you have and give it to the woman. You promised."

He signed it and asked in a shaking voice, "What do you have that you think I'll pay twelve hundred dollars for?"

The woman reached into her skirts and pulled out the tied-up condom. She dropped it on the plate.

"This," he said, "your blood and seed." With the point of the dagger he opened the condom and its contents spilled into the dirt. He stirred them into mud.

"You are a modern man—"

"What kind of mumbo-jumbo—"

"—a modern man who certainly doesn't believe in magic. Are you Christian?"

"Yes. No." He was born Baptist but hadn't gone inside a church since he was eighteen.

He nodded. "I was confident the boys could bring back some of your blood last night. More than I needed, really." He dipped his thumb in the vile mud and smeared a rough cross on the woman's forehead.

"I can't believe this."

"But you can." He held out a small piece of string. "This is a symbolic restraint." He laid it over the glob of mud and pressed down on it.

Lindsay felt himself being pushed back into the chair. Cold sweat peppered his back and palms.

"Try to get up."

"Why should I?" Lindsay said, trying to control his voice. "I find this fascinating." Insane, Lindsay, voodoo only works on people who believe in it. Psychosomatic.

"It gets even better." He reached into a drawer and pulled out Lindsay's checkbook, opened it, and set it in front of Lindsay with a pen. "Sign."

Get up get up. "No."

He took four long sharp needles out of the drawer and began talking in a low monotone, mostly Arabic but some nonsense

English. The woman's eyes drooped half shut and she slumped in the chair.

"Now," he said in a normal voice, "I can do anything to this woman, and she won't feel it. You will." He pulled up her left sleeve and pinched her arm. "Do you feel like writing your name?"

Lindsay tried to ignore the feeling. You can't hypnotize an unwilling subject. Get up get up get up.

The man ran a needle into the woman's left triceps. Lindsay flinched and cried out. Deny him, get up.

He murmured something and the woman lifted her veil and stuck out her tongue, which was long and stained blue. He drove a needle through it and Lindsay's chin jerked back onto his chest, tongue on fire, bile foaming up in his throat. His right hand scrabbled for the pen, and the man withdrew the needles.

He scrawled his name on the fifties and hundreds. The merchant took them wordlessly and went to the door. He came back with Abdul, armed again.

"I am going to the bank. When I return, you will be free to go." He lifted the piece of string out of the mud. "In the meantime, you may do as you wish with this woman; she is being paid well. I advise you not to hurt her, of course."

Lindsay pushed her into the back room. It wasn't proper rape, since she didn't resist, but whatever it was he did it twice, and was sore for a week. He left her there and sat at the merchant's table, glaring at Abdul. When he came back, the merchant told Lindsay to gather up the mud and hold it in his hand for at least a half-hour. And get out of Marrakesh.

Out in the bright sun he felt silly with the handful of crud, and ineffably angry with himself, and he flung it away and rubbed the offended hand in the dirt. He got a couple of hundred dollars on his credit cards, at an outrageous rate of exchange, and got the first train back to Casablanca and the first plane back to the United States.

Where he found himself to be infected with gonorrhea.

And over the next few months paid a psychotherapist and a hypnotist over two thousand dollars, and nevertheless felt rotten for no organic reason.

And nine months later lay on an examining table in the emergency room of Suburban Hospital, with terrible abdominal pains of apparently psychogenic origin, not responding to muscle relaxants or tranquilizers, while a doctor and two aides watched in helpless horror as his own muscles cracked his pelvic girdle into sharp knives of bone, and his child was born without pain four thousand miles away.

━━━━━━━━━━━━━

That story oozed up from a dark well of alienation and xenophobia. This next one sprang from John Leggett's beard.

John Leggett is a fine writer and courtly gentleman who for several years has been the director of the Iowa Writers' Workshop. I came back to Iowa one September and found that he was growing a beard.

No problem with that, but it never seemed to get past the "starting to grow" stage—always about an eighth of an inch long, Yasir Arafat style. Obviously it took some care to maintain at that length, more trouble than simply shaving, and eventually I had to ask John what the devil he was up to.

He told me, and I was charmed by the practicality of it. So a few years later, when I sat down to write a story that had to have a writer as the viewpoint character, I gave the man John Leggett's tonsorial idiosyncrasy.

NO FUTURE

IN IT

It's not easy to keep exactly one-eighth inch of beard on your face. For a writer, though, it's good protective coloration. With a suit and tie, you look like a gentleman who's decided to grow a beard. With rumpled old Salvation Army clothes, you look like a down-and-out rummy. It depends on the class of people you want to listen to, study.

I was in the rummy outfit when I met Bill Caddis and heard his incredible story. At first I thought Bill was on the same scam I was; he talked too well to be in the dreg business. He was for real, though.

There's this wonderful sleaze bar in downtown Tampa. No name, just a bunch of beer signs in the window. The one for Pearl has a busted laser that flutters stroboscopically. You don't want to sit too near the window. It's a good bar for private conversations because it's right under the twelve-laner that sweeps out over the bay, and there's a constant moan of traffic, all day and all night. There's a fine gritty layer of plaster dust everywhere, and not too much light. The bartender is missing an eye and ten front teeth, and smiles frequently. The booze is cheap; they make most of their money upstairs, and like to have lots of customers in the bar, for camouflage.

I sat down at the bar and the bartender polished glasses while one of the whores, a pretty boy-girl, sidled in for the kill. When I said no she pleaded mechanically, saying she was saving for a real pair of tits and the Operation. I hesitated—I string for the Bad News wire service sometimes, and they like sexy bathos—but turned her down more finally. Bad News doesn't pay that well.

When she left the bartender came over and I ordered a Myers's with a beer chaser, suitable hard-core combination. I'd taken two Flame-outs before I came, though, so I could drink a dozen or so without too ill effect. Until morning.

"Little early in the day for that, isn't it?" The man next to me chuckled hoarsely. "Not to criticize." He was nursing a double bourbon or scotch, neat.

"Dusty," I said. The man was dressed a little more neatly than I, in faded work clothes. He looked too old to be a laborer, shock of white hair with a yellowish cast. But he did have the deep tan and permanent squint of one who's spent decades in the Florida sun. I tossed back the jigger of rum and sipped the beer. "Come here often?"

"Pretty often," he said. "When my check comes in I put a few bucks on a number. Otherwise . . ." He shrugged. "Cheap whiskey and pretty women. To look at."

"How many of them do you think are women?"

"Just looking, who cares?" He squinted even more, examining me. "Could I see your palms?"

Oh, boy, I thought, a fortuneteller. Might be a story if he actually believes in it. I held out my hands.

He glanced at them and stared at my face. "Yeah, I could tell by the eyes," he said softly. "You're no alcoholic. You're not as old as you look, either. Cop?"

"No. Used to be a teacher." Which was true. "Every now and then I go on these binges."

He nodded slowly. "Used to be a teacher, too. Until '83. Then I worked the sponge boats twenty years." When he picked up his glass, his hand had the regular slow shake of a confirmed alky. "It was good work."

I reached in my pocket and turned on the tape recorder. "Why was it you stopped teaching? Booze?"

"No . . . who drank in the eighties?" I didn't, but I wasn't old enough. "It's an interesting sort of pancake. You want to hear a story?"

"Sure." I signaled the bartender for two drinks.

"Now, you don't have to buy me anything. You won't believe the story, anyhow."

"Try me."

"You a social worker? Undercover social worker?" He smiled wryly.

"Is there such a thing?"

"Should be. I know. You're a writer."

"When I get work, yeah. How could you tell, Sherlock?"

"You've got two pens in your pocket and you want to hear a story." He smiled. "Steal a story, maybe. But you'll never get it published. It's too fantastic."

"But true."

"It's true, all right. Thank you kindly." He touched his new drink to see whether it was real, then drained off the old one in one gulp and sighed.

"My name's Bill Caddis. Doctor William Caddis, it used to be."

"Medical doctor?"

"I detect a note of reproof. As if no medico ever—well. No, I was an academic, newly tenured at Florida State. History department. Modern American history."

"Hard to get a job then as it is now?"

"Just about. I was a real whiz."

"But you got fired in '83."

"That's right. And it's not easy to fire a tenured professor."

"What, boffing the little girls?"

That was the only time he laughed that day, a kind of wheeze. "Undergraduates were made for boffing. No, I was dismissed on grounds of mental instability; with my wife's help, my then wife, they almost had me institutionalized."

"Strong stuff."

"Strong." He stared into his drink and swirled it around. "I never know how to start this. I've told dozens of people and they all think I'm crazy before I get halfway into it. You'll think I'm crazy too."

"Just jump in feet first. Like you say, I'm a writer. I can believe in six impossible things before my first drink in the morning."

"All right. I'm not from . . . here."

A loony, I thought; there goes the price of a double. "Another planet," I said seriously.

"See? Now you want me to say something about UFOs and how I'm bringing the secret of eternal peace to mankind." He raised the glass to me. "Thanks for the drink."

I caught his arm before he could slug it down. "Wait. I'm sorry. Go on."

"Am I wrong?"

"You're right, but go on. You don't *act* crazy."

He set the drink down. "Layman's error. Some of the most reasonable people you meet are strictly Almond Joy."

"If you're not from 'here,' where are you from?"

"Miami." He smiled and took a sip. "I'm a time traveler. I'm from a future."

I just nodded.

"That usually takes some explaining. There's no 'the' future. There's a myriad of futures radiating from every instant. If I were to drop this glass on the floor, and it broke, we would shift into a future where this bar owned one less glass."

"And the futures where the glass wasn't broken . . ."

"They would be. And we would be in them; we are now."

"Doesn't it get sort of crowded up there? Billions of new futures every second?"

"You can't crowd infinity."

I was trying to think of an angle, a goofball feature. "How does this time travel work?"

"How the hell should I know? I'm just a tourist. It has something to do with chronons. Temporal Uncertainty Principle. Conservation of coincidence. I'm no engineer."

"Are there lots of these tourists?"

"Probably not, here and now. You get quite a crowd clustered around historically important events. You can't see them, of course."

"I can see you."

He shrugged. "Something went wrong. Power failure or something; someone tripped over a cable. Happens."

"They didn't try to come back and rescue you?"

"How could they? There are lots of futures but only one past. Once I materialized *here,* I wasn't in my own past anymore. See?"

"So you can kill your own grandfather," I said.

"Why would I want to do that? He's a nice old bird."

"No, I mean, there's no paradox involved? If you killed him before you were born, you wouldn't cease to exist?"

"Of course not. I'd have to be there to kill him." He sipped. "For that matter, I could go back and kill myself, as a boy. If I could afford it. Travel gets more expensive, the closer you get to the present. Like compressing an infinitely tough spring."

"Hold it." I had him. "I'll buy another round if you can talk your way out of this one. The Earth is moving all the time, spinning around, going around the Sun; the Sun's moving through space. How the hell do you *aim* this time machine?"

He bleared at me. "Don't they teach you anything about relativity? Look, if you get up from the bar, go to the john, and come back in a couple of minutes—the bar's moved thousands of miles. But it's still here. You're on the same track, that's all."

"But I'm talking about time and you're talking about *space!*"

"There's a difference?" He drained his glass and slid it toward me with one finger.

I decided I'd stay long enough to find out what his con was. Maybe do a one-pager for a crime magazine. I ordered him another double. "You folks from the future can sure hold your liquor."

"Couple of centuries of medicine," he said. "I'm ninety-two years old." He looked about seventy.

Looked like I was going to have to push him for the gaff. "Seems to me you could be a millionaire. Knowing where to invest . . ."

"It's not that easy. I tried. I should have left well enough alone." His drink came and he stuck his fingertip in it; flicked a drop away. "I'm sort of a Moslem," he said. "Not supposed to drink a drop of liquor.

"People try it all the time; there's no law against it. But put yourself in this position: you're going to deliberately strand yourself two hundred years in the past. What do you do for capital? Buy old money from collectors?"

"You could take gold and diamonds."

"Sure. But if you can afford that—and time travel isn't cheap either—why not invest it in your own present? Remember, once you materialize, you aren't in your own past anymore. You can never tell what might have changed. People do try it, though. Usually they take gadgets."

"Does it work?"

"Who knows? They can't come back to tell about it."

"Couldn't they build their own time machine, go back to the future?"

"Aren't you hearing me? There's no such thing as *the* future. Even if you could travel forward, there's no way you could find the right one."

Somebody came into the bar; I waited until the door eased shut, muting the traffic noise. "So what happened to you? You made some bad investments?"

"In spades. Seemed like a sure thing.

"Let me explain. Where I come from, almost nobody lives on Earth, just caretakers and the time travel people. It's like a big park, a big museum. Most of us live in orbital settlements, some on other planets.

"I really was a history professor, specializing in the history of technology. I saved up my money to go back and see the first flight to the Moon."

"That was in '70?"

"No, '69. It was during the launch when the accident happened. Nobody noticed me materializing; I didn't even notice until I tried to walk through someone afterward.

"Fortunately, that was a time when everybody dressed as they damn well pleased, so my clothes didn't look especially outrageous. I bummed my way down to Homestead and picked up some work sorting tomatoes, that kind of thing. Saved up enough to get fake IDs made up, eventually went back to school and wound up teaching again. Married along the way."

"The one who tried to put you in the peanut jar."

"That's right. Here's what happened. If there was one sure thing to invest in, it was space. My wife didn't agree, but there was no way I could tell her why I was so sure.

"I went ahead and invested heavily in space industries— really heavily, buying on margin, wheeling, dealing—but my wife thought it was all going into a conservative portfolio of municipals. I even snitched some stationery from our accountant and wrote up annual reports to show her."

"I think I see what's coming." Not a bad story.

"Yeah. The Soviet-American Orbital Nonproliferation Treaty, the goddamned Proxmire Bill."

"Well, killer satellites . . ."

"That's the kicker. That's really the kicker. In *my* future's past, it was the killer satellites that ended the possibility of

nuclear war forever! They finally scrapped the missiles and settled down to shouting across tables."

"Well, you can't think we're in any danger of nuclear war
now. Not realistically."

"Yeah. I liked our way better. Anyway, the bottom dropped
out. I had to tell my wife that we were broke and in debt; I had
to tell her everything. I thought I knew her. I thought she would
believe. The rest is pretty obvious."

"Sponge boats."

"Right." He took a long drink and stared moodily into the
cloudy mirror behind the bar.

"That's it?" No scam?

"That's it. Write it up. You'll never sell it."

I checked my watch. Could just make the 1:35 to Atlanta, get
in a half day at the typewriter. "Well, I gotta run. Thanks for
the story, Bill."

I stood up and put my hand on his shoulder. "Take it easy
on the sauce, okay? You're no spring chicken anymore."

"Sure." He never looked at me.

On the way to the subway terminal it occurred to me that I
shouldn't try to sell the thing as a human-interest feature. Just
write it up as fiction and I could hawk it to *Planet Stories* or one
of those rags.

The ticket machine gave me an argument about changing a
hundred-ruble note and I had to go find a conductor. Then there
were repairs going on and it took us twenty minutes to get to
Atlanta; I had to sprint to make my Seattle connection.

Space settlements. Time travel. Nobody would swallow that
kind of bull, not in 1924.

■■■■■■■■■■

After that story appeared in *Omni* I got some inevitable mail. Is
the year a misprint? No. Can you explain what it means? I could,
but won't. Life is too short.

Maybe fifteen years of this business has eroded my patience:
worn down the ability to suffer fools gladly. Though actually, the
people who write letters are rarely fools—at least they like to read
and write, and sometimes feel and think. The truly insufferable

ones are the ones you meet under the vitreous gaze of the television camera: interviewers.

Not all are bad. The first person who interviewed me on television was the late Charles Haslam (founder of the huge Haslam's book emporium in St. Petersburg, Florida), who did a weekly local show called *Book Beat.* His questions revealed that he had read the book carefully—had read many books carefully—and had invested a lot of time and effort in structuring the show.

That was not the last good interview I've had, but I could probably count the good ones on the fingers of one hand. Generally the best you can expect is that someone on the staff has read the promotional material and perhaps scanned the book, so as to cobble together a few questions that the "personality" will see for the first time when you both sit down in front of the prompter. Sometimes the questions come from a cursory glance at the flap copy. Often the interviewer doesn't even know the name of the book.

The inevitable first question is, what is this book about? That's easy to answer if the book's about pickling geraniums or shining your cat. It's not that easy with a novel; the honest answer—"It's about whatever went through my head during the two and a half years I sweated over it"—isn't exactly what they're looking for. So you come prepared with a plot synopsis and theme statement that you hope will not sound too dumb or pretentious and won't give away the ending. (When John Cheever was asked this question he gave the deadpan perfect answer: "Love and death.")

It's at this point that the worst, or least prepared, interviewers discover that they have a science fiction writer, as opposed to a real writer, on their hands. So the next question is liable to be about UFOs or life on Mars, and the interview goes downhill from there.

This next story came from one such experience. Perhaps fortunately, the interviewer didn't quite get my name right, and for some minutes she proceeded not to improve on that auspicious beginning, while I tried not to squirm visibly. Afterward I went down to the studio's Green Room to watch an instant replay of my electronic canonization.

It was even worse watching it from the consumer's side of the tube. While reliving my still-fresh agonies, though, I came to a sudden realization: Hey! Here I am watching that guy on television and I know exactly what's going through his mind! Not a profound epiphany, I suppose, but it got me to thinking, and this was the result.

THE PILOT

The set is out of adjustment: a green streak slashes diagonally through the viewing cube, impales the smiling host.

She tries to adjust it by softly licking a molar, remembers, curses economically, turns a knob until the streak disappears, another knob to sharpen the image. Host smiling goodbye to someone. Feel of cold metal sticks to her thumb and finger until she rubs it away on her thigh, disgusted, nose wrinkling. How many filthy traveling salesmen and conventioneers and hotel maids have touched these knobs since they were last sterilized? Have they ever been sterilized?

"Our next guest is a woman with a marvelously rare occupation." *Occupation!* He smiles offcube and the picture scale diminishes to include her as well, not smiling, trying not to fidget on the filthy leather chair. "She is a spaceship pilot"—*I am a spaceship*—"but no ordinary rocket jock. She pilots a slowboat between the Earth and the outer solar system—the asteroids, even as far as Saturn. Her name is Lydia Meinenger and she's a fellow New Yorker." *New Yorker.* "Lydia, would you tell us something about slowboats: how they—"

"In the first place," she interrupts, "they aren't slow. They go much faster than anything you use in the Earth-Moon system. The name is a hangover from the old robot tugs that crawled along on Hohmann transfer orbits, to minimize fuel use. A Hohmann tug took six years to get to Saturn; I can make it in thirteen months. Nine months, with a Jupiter flyby. But I can't do that with passengers."

"Because of the radiation?"

"That's right." *Warm like summer sunshine.* "They can't wrap everyone up in lead, the way I am."

"That's probably the most fascinating aspect of your job, Lydia. The way you're wired up to the ship, you're actually part of it." *I am the ship, you actual fool.*

" 'Wired up' is a little extreme. They don't use surgical implants anymore, just induction plates pasted over various organs. There are a few small wires associated with the somatic feedback system"—*O slow ecstasy*—"but they enter through natural body openings and you hardly feel them once they're in place."

"This feedback thing, this is how you control the ship?"

"That's right. There's an initial calibration that, well, as long as I feel good"—*Good!*—"then every system in the ship is working properly. If any system varies from its expected performance, I feel it as an illness or slight pain. The nature and intensity of the wrongness tells me which system is involved and gives me an idea as to the severity of the malfunction. For instance, a hydrogen ullage problem, where the fuel flow is momentarily uneven, I feel as a hot spasm of"—screen goes white, low chime—"tum."

Host smirking behind filthy hand. "Afraid the censor won't let *that* slip by, Lydia." *They live in shit so can't talk about it?* Chuckles. "It doesn't seem very precise."

"The important thing is sensitivity, not precision. Instantly knowing which system is hurting. Then I call up the appropriate system parameters and compare them to the ideal mission profile. I can usually fix the trouble with the help of the ship's diagnostic library. If not, I call Company Control on the Moon."

"So your main job is troubleshooting."

"Yes." *Like you troubleshoot your body? Filthy fool couldn't find your liver with both hands.* "I make decisions regarding the maintenance of the ship."

"It doesn't sound very exciting. . . ."

"It is."

Looking at her expectantly: she doesn't continue. "You must have quite a technical background." *For a woman, say it fool.*

"No. I majored in classical Latin and Greek. The technical part is easy. Any reasonably intelligent woman could do it."

"I, uh, see . . . you—"

"There are no male slowboat pilots. I don't suppose your censor wants me to discuss that. You'll just have to go ask a twelve-year-old." She flashes him a bright metal smile. "Much nicer than—" Chime.

Weak try at an urbane chuckle. "There's an interesting side benefit to your job. I'll bet viewers would be surprised to know how old you are."

She lets him wait just long enough; as he opens his mouth to save himself: "Sixty-five."

"Now, isn't that marvelous? You could pass for twenty."

"As could anybody who didn't have to contend with gravity and sun and wind and this"—chime—"that passes for your food and drink and air. I've spent most of my life immersed in oxygenated fluorocarbon, weightless, fed a perfect diet, exercised by machines."

"But your job is dangerous."

"Not very. Perhaps one in thirty is lost."

"More dangerous than holovision." His image turns a little fuzzy; she touches the filthy knob to sharpen him. "The atomic drive itself must be hazardous." Carries her contaminated hand into the bathroom, listening. "Not to mention meteors and—" *Fool.*

"No, actual catastrophes are very rare." She washes the offended fingers carefully. "The dangerous time is turnaround, when the ship is going with maximum velocity. It's supposed to flip and slow down for the last half of the journey." Leaves the soap on warm clean fingers. "Sometimes they don't flip, though; just keep going, faster and faster. Too fast for the Company's rescue ship."

"How terrible." Standing in front of the set, dry hand tugs elastic, urgent. *Clothes!* "They just keep going . . ."

"Forever." *Ecstasy, O!* "The pilot may live for centuries."

"Well . . . if ever a cliché was true . . . that does sound like a fate worse than death." *Fool.*

She nods soberly. "Indeed it does." *Fool, fool, O damn, doesn't last this way.* She sinks back onto the bed and starts to cry. *Fry them dead.*

He puts a filthy finger to his lips. "Well. Are you, um, going to be on Earth long?"

"Only another two days." Hurting herself, she stops, wipes eyes, soap sting brings new tears. "I like being back in New York, but the gravity is tiring. The air makes me cough. I look forward to going out again." *Last time, fry the bastards.*

"Saturn this time?"

"No, for a change I'm going to the inner system. Taking five hundred colonists to the new Venus settlement." *Taking them to burn.*

"Is that more dangerous? I mean, I don't know much about space, but isn't there a danger that you could fall into the Sun?"

She smiles politely. "No, none." Sharp metal teeth; she runs her tongue along behind her teeth but the switches aren't connected. "It would take as much energy to 'fall' into the Sun as it takes to escape from the solar system." *Less to skim it, though, fry.* "All that gravity. I suppose it might be possible; I've never made the calculation." *Characteristic velocity 17.038 emos, exit inclination 0.117 rad, goodbye solar system, goodbye filth.*

Blank stare. "Yes . . . oh, Jimmy's giving me the signal." *Right at perihelion, goose it all the way up, emergency override, nineteen gees, crush their dry baked bodies into dust.* "I'm afraid we've run out of time."

Cargo shit baked to sterile dust. "We certainly have enjoyed having you here, Lydia." He holds out his hand and she looks at it.

Bound for the stars, forever young, the dear ship inside of my ecstasy. "Thank you."

That's one of only two prose stories I've written in one sitting. If it happened more often, I'd probably write a lot of them. Instant gratification. Normally, though, my short stories accrete at the same slow rate as the novels, five or six hundred words on a good day.

Like most people who write fiction for a living, I spend most of my time on novels. Not only are they more remunerative than short stories, but they feel more "serious," more worthwhile. That's a fallacy, of course; one good short story is worth more than a closet full of mediocre novels. But the feeling is real, and the practical side of it can't be disputed: a person who writes as slowly as I do would have to hit *Playboy* or *The New Yorker* every month to make a living from short stories.

(I don't want to appear to be making a virtue out of slow writing.

Balzac, Stendhal, Dostoevski, Stevenson, Dickens—the list goes on and on—were all good careful writers who managed to turn out thousands of words a day, most of them with dip pens. Stendhal even kept a pocket watch on his writing desk, requiring himself to write one page, 250 words, every fifteen minutes. Stevenson famously wrote the 40,000-word *Dr. Jekyll and Mr. Hyde* in one long rather drug-crazed sitting. If these guys had had word processors, a degree in literature would take eight years.)

Anyhow, novels are the meat, and the gravy, but short stories are the succulent dessert. Their irresistible attraction is that the end is always in sight. There's a special satisfaction to finishing something, anything, and we slowpokes have to wait a couple of years to get that satisfaction from a novel.

I think this desire to actually get things *finished* is the main reason I returned to poetry, after more than a decade of deliberately not writing any. I started out writing only poetry—my first poem was published when I was nine years old—and it must have been good training, since when I did finally sit down to try fiction I sold the first two stories I wrote. But when I decided to become a full-time writer, I made the cold-blooded decision that the poetry had to go. I couldn't afford to spend time on work that would eventually be paid for with two copies of an obscure journal. (I did allow myself to write a song every now and then, usually as a reward for finishing a book.)

I always felt a little churlish about this, as if I had abandoned a dear relative who had helped me get started in the business. But business *is* business, I told myself, and one thing a freelance writer does not do is ply his lance for free.

My resolve started to weaken a few summers back, when my wife and I were BritRailing around England. Eventually we came to Elsmere, a quaint little tourist town in the Lake District.

Elsmere is where Wordsworth lived his strangely romantic life with Dorothy, his sister, and their cottage there is open to tourists. Wordsworth was one of my favorites when I was young, so I looked forward to seeing where he had lived and worked. But I wasn't prepared for the intensity of the experience.

I don't believe in ghosts but I do know that some people leave a "presence" behind in the place where they lived, a palpable stamp that their personality embedded there. Hemingway's house in Key West has it, as does the room where Samuel Johnson rode herd over his minions, assembling the great Dictionary. The mansion where Toulouse-Lautrec's brooding crippled genius developed; the laboratory where Edison slaved; the small square of stones that's the remains of the cabin on Walden Pond. Wordsworth's cottage had it in every board—and the spirit suffused out to include the hills and heaths, the lakes and streams, where he and Dorothy would stride along on their daily ten- or twenty-mile hikes, stopping every now and then to jot down a few lines or a stanza.* I knew I would have to come back to Elsmere some day for an extended stay, to write, and not to write prose.

I haven't made it back yet, but the idea was planted firmly and grew into a mild obsession: What are you missing by not writing poetry? It's true that the pay is negligible and the audience is small— but why did you start writing in the first place? And isn't your primary audience yourself? So I started spending a couple of days a month writing poetry and verse.

The following three pieces are story poems—two rather serious and one just plain goofy—and their stories are science fiction, so I feel justified in including them here.

---

*Dorothy was quite a good writer herself, and her brother was not above filching from her. The lines "My heart leaps up when I behold a rainbow in the sky" and "The child is father to the man" evidently originated in her diary.

THE BIG

BANG THEORY

EXPLAINED

(IN LIGHT VERSE)

Premise the First: Immortality—or even greatly prolonged life—would be no blessing. You were born with all the brain cells you'll ever have, and you lose a certain number of them every year, because of background radiation. Live long enough and you'll have the intelligence of a bright cabbage.

Premise the Second: If you have enough money it will take care of itself.

"Wake me when the Dow-Jones hits a million," he said,
And took a few grams of Sweet Dreams Hydrochloride,
Closed his eyes, lay back, rested his head,
And while diverted by raunchy fantasy, died.

The friendly machines, they opened his veins:
Sucked out the blood from flesh and from bone;
Replaced it with stable polymer chains,
Then froze his wealthy ass into stone.

He owned a salt mine, miles deep but cool.
His gold coffin rested there, blissly serene,
Facing millenniums, immersed in a pool
Of nitrogen, tended by friendly machines.

To backtrack:
This wasn't a thing that our hero did lightly,
Nor fearing death: he'd died twice before
These past two centuries, and found it just slightly
Boring, lying in wait for his cash to restore
Some old failed organ—beef up his muscles—brighten his blood . . .
Come out of his coffin a centuries-old stud.

But there was a limit. Because the brain
Cannot be replaced—yet it slowly decays
Assaulted in silence by treacherous rays
Of the alpha, beta, and gamma persuasion,
Destroying your brain by ablation.

You can lock yourself up in a box made of lead,
And be safe from the fallout and all cosmic ray—
But no such protection will save your poor head,
For the elements comprising your body betray
You with unstable isotopes that leak radiation,
Subjecting your neurons to steady predation.

Our hero knew this, and it made him quite mad
To know that by quantum-mechanical fiat
His ultimate fate was both sordid and sad:
The world's first immortal blithering idiot.

But over the centuries our hero'd evolved
A method for dealing with logical goblins:
"Deluge it with money until it gets solved!"
It had cracked the world's most intractable problems.

It worked: they invented a magical box
Where he sat all day long, for dozens of years,
Cleansing his body of isotope pox
By exchanging atoms with poor volunteers.

He finally was clean! No Geiger could count
The tiniest click from his corpus pristine.
His eye on the future, he gleefully mount-
Ed his coffin-cum-time-space-and-money machine.

To backtrack again:
By creating a fortune so diverse and broad,
He'd created something resembling life:
It would feed and excrete; be active and nod,
And when confronted with problems or strife
Could act on its own, without consultation
Of the genius financial who'd sparked its creation.

Which suited him fine. He wanted to know
Whether this creature of dollars and francs,
Without him, would simply continue to grow
Sucking up offices, factories, and banks,
Expanding its own ecological niche—
Quietly making him rich.

And it did—beyond his most fabulous dreams!
Not being omniscient, though, he couldn't know
He'd own the whole planet with his little scheme
And still have a hundred centuries to go.

It followed humanity out into space;
Annexing whole planets, and systems, and more,
Till it finally ran into a greedier race—
And plunged the whole Galaxy into a war.

It won, though it took it some eight thousand years,
In which time humanity changed for the worse.
They stopped using money, stopped having careers—
They thought owning things was *perverse!*

The friendly machines that our hero'd entrusted
With all of his wealth had long ago rusted.
But their n-times-great-grandchildren covered the planet,
Waiting to wake up the man who once ran it.

But they spent a few centuries converting those dollars
To things of real worth, according to scholars:
A Galaxy's worth of compassion and pain;
Quintillions of lives to maintain.

And so in a salt mine in Texas, in autumn,
They opened his casket, injected, and thawed 'im.
He looked in the eyes of metallic envoys
And asked, "What the hell is that noise?"

Sparrows falling.
What?
They drop like flies. You have to keep track of every one.
Hey. I'm just a banker.
So was I. Now you've got one nanosecond to count each hair on everybody's head.
Everybody?
I didn't make up the rules.
(sighs) I can count pretty fast, it seems. But they grow faster.
It's your baby now.
What's going on here? What went wrong?
Nothing. It all went according to plan. I've been in charge of this circus for four and a half billion years. It's all yours now.
What? All *mine?*
Somebody has to do it.
But I'm just a *banker!*
Tell it to the Judge. Look. I evolved you from a fish. Gave you opposable thumbs and supply-side economics. Set you up, I admit it. You'll excuse me? I'm going to get some sleep now.
Hold it! What about these goddamned sparrows?
They do make a racket. Do whatever you want.
What do you mean?
Hey! Come back!
Aw hell. Might as well start over.

THE GIFT

Feel behind the ear, the small hole
(left for women, right for men). Now
insert the wire until a cold
sensation comes beneath the eye. See how

twirling the wire makes you smile?
When it feels like sunshine on your face,
raise your hand. In a little while
a friend will come to calibrate. Solace

will be yours another year. Just
turn the wire until it feels like sun;
that's good. Another year of trust.
No fear. Loving peace for everyone.

> *I take the wire and bend it till it breaks!*
> *They can't do this! Can't you see it makes*
> *us into simple blobs of happy clay?*
> *Most of us can think back to a day*
> *when living wasn't easy. There was pain*
> *and trouble in the world—but then again,*
> *at least it all was real. What they destroy*
> *is not just pain, but love, and awe, and joy.*

One unit fails to comprehend
this can't be done unless it's done for all.
His childish need for pain could end
this heaven that we've made for you. You called

for us in desperate need. You prayed
that somehow we could save you from your fate.
An so we came in answer. But we said
you'd have to change your nature. It's too late
to turn you into angels. Now
the best that we can do is try to make
you harmless. Don't ask how.
Trust in us. We do it for your sake.

> *So long as one man lives who won't submit,*
> *then all your words and wires won't work. That's it.*
> *Right? For all your talk, you just want slaves.*
> *I can't believe that no one else is brave*
> *enough to break the wire and take the world*
> *as it was given us—a clashing whirl*
> *of good and bad in nearly equal parts.*
> *Not turned to harmless pap by your black arts.*

We will not argue. But we care
how this experiment turns out. Let's try
a kind of vote. If there
is only on in ten who'll take your side

then we will go. And take along
these wires and words you think will make you slaves.
Ready? Counting. Sorry. Wrong.
We counted every one and found that they've

decided we were right. You're wrong.
So you must go. Take your broken wire
and twisted heart. Your pagan song:
Your empty merely human angry fire.

> *Done. Now you are at peace. Not slaves.*
> *We ask for nothing. If you just don't pull*
> *the wires, your world's forever saved.*
> *Forever happy. If a little dull.*

SAUL'S

DEATH

1.

I used to be a monk, but gave it over
Before books and prayer and studies cooled my blood,
And joined with Richard as a mercenary soldier.
(No Richard that you've heard of, just
A man who'd bought a title for his name.)
And it was in his service I met Saul.

The first day of my service I liked Saul;
His easy humor quickly won me over.
He confided Saul was not his name;
He'd taken up another name for blood.
(So had I—my fighting name was just
A word we use at home for private soldier.)

I felt at home as mercenary soldier
I liked the company of men like Saul.
(Though most of Richard's men were just
Fighting for the bounty when it's over.)
I loved the clash of weapons, splashing blood—
I lived the meager promise of my name.

Saul promised that he'd tell me his real name
When he was through with playing as a soldier.
(I said the same; we took an oath in blood.)
But I would never know him but as Saul;

He'd die before the long campaign was over,
Dying for a cause that was not just.

Only fools require a cause that's just.
Tools, and children out to make a name.
Now I've had sixty years to think it over
(Sixty years of being no one's soldier).
Sixty years since broadsword opened Saul
And splashed my body with his precious blood.

But damn! we lived for bodies and for blood.
The reek of dead men rotting, it was just
A sweet perfume for those like me and Saul.
(My peaceful language doesn't have a name
For lewd delight in going off to soldier.)
It hurts my heart sometimes to know it's over.

My heart was hard as stone when it was over;
When finally I'd had my fill of blood.
(And knew I was too old to be a soldier.)
Nothing left for me to do but just
Go back home and make myself a name
In ways of peace, forgetting war and Saul.

In ways of blood he made himself a name
(Though he was just a mercenary soldier)—
I loved Saul before it all was over.

2.

A mercenary soldier has no future;
Some say his way of life is hardly human.
And yet, we had our own small bloody world
(Part aches and sores and wrappings soaking blood,
Partly fear and glory grown familiar)
Confined within a shiny fence of swords.

But how I learned to love to fence with swords!
Another world, my homely past and future—
Once steel and eye and wrist became familiar
With each other, then that steel was almost human
(With an altogether human taste for blood).
I felt that sword and I could take the world.

I felt that Saul and I could take the world:
Take the whole world hostage with our swords.
The bond we felt was stronger than mere blood
(Though I can see with hindsight in the future
The bond we felt was something only human:
A need for love when death becomes familiar).

We were wizards, and death was our familiar;
Our swords held all the magic in the world.
(Richard thought it almost wasn't human,
The speed with which we parried others' swords,
Forever end another's petty future.)
Never scratched, though always steeped in blood.

Ambushed in a tavern, splashing ankle-deep in blood;
Fighting back-to-back in ways familiar.
Saul slipped: lost his footing and our future.
Broad blade hammered down and sent him from this world.
In angry grief I killed that one, then all the other swords;
Then locked the doors and murdered every human.

No choice, but to murder every human.
No one in that tavern was a stranger to blood.
(To those who live with pikes and slashing swords,
The inner parts of men become familiar.)
Saul's vitals looked like nothing in this world:
I had to kill them all to save my future.

Saul's vitals were not human, but familiar:
He never told me he was from another world:
I never told him I was from his future.

Most of my poems are conventionally free verse, or they keep their rhymes safely out of sight *à la* cummings. But I do think rhyme reinforces story, and so don't feel like apologizing for the use of it in these three tales.

"Saul's Death" doesn't exactly rhyme; it uses a variant of the Italian sestina form. (Maybe it would rhyme in Italian: they say almost everything does.) The sestina takes the last words of the first six lines and repeats them in an inside-out permutation in each succeeding verse: if the first verse has the end words 1-2-3-4-5-6, then the next one goes 6-1-5-2-4-3, and the next 3-6-4-1-2-5, and so forth. It's more complicated to explain than it is to do.

I had the story of "Saul's Death" for a couple of years before I wrote it down. It was going to be my Elsmere poem; the plan was to go back to Wordsworth's town and spend a month writing and hiking. I saw the poem as a long lyrical narrative along the lines of "The Rime of the Ancient Mariner"—commercially un-publishable, but I didn't much care. (The model was geographically appropriate; Coleridge was a neighbor of Wordsworth's.)

What happened was that my wife, Gay, and a friend and I took off for a month of camping in Maine. Gay was driving toward our next campsite while I lounged in the back drinking beer and flipping through a new book of poetry. Suddenly I came upon Ezra Pound's brutal and beautiful "Sestina: Altaforte"—and before I reached the last line, I knew I had my form. I grabbed a tablet and started sketching it out.

Our campsite for the next couple of days was to be Baxter State Park, a primitive mountainous area that's rather difficult of access; the bears outnumber the people. It turned out to be the perfect place.

In those latitudes, in June, it starts getting light very early, which suits my constitution. Ever since I started writing it's been my habit to roll out of bed around three or four in the morning, and do the bulk of my work while the rest of the world is still asleep. The sides of the tent started to show light around three thirty, so I quietly struggled out of my sleeping bag and slipped out to say hello to the mosquitoes.

It was raining slightly, sort of a Scottish mist, bracing cool. I'd stowed wood and newspaper under the car to stay dry and in short order had a crackling fire chasing the cool, the coffeepot starting to perk. I rolled a log in front of the fire and sat down and tried to slow my thoughts to where I could start to pick out the lines of the poem. It was hard to do because the beauty of the place was like a loud song distracting.

Anybody with eyes to see and the luck to travel knows what painters mean when they talk about the "quality of light" that inhabits a given place. It can't really be said accurately, but there's a dry lambence that belongs only to Spain; a naked ferocity to the light that bakes the plains of Africa; an aching glister that's dawn's promise on the streets of Paris; a peculiar gritty kind of light that energizes Manhattan. On that mountain in the park, on a misty summer morning, the light came from everywhere and nowhere; the woods simply glowed. I'd never seen anything like it before and haven't since, and it held me hypnotized. I sat in it for a moment that was probably an hour, heart hammering with the terrible delicate beauty of it, and when I was finally empty of thought and full of the light I wiped my face dry and got the tablet out of the car.

It was a big artist's tablet, eighteen by twenty-four inches, and by hunching over it I could just keep it dry in the shadow of my shoulders and Stetson. I'd made notes the previous afternoon as to the key words and general outline of the poem; I threw out most of them. I wrote the last three lines and proceeded to work backwards and forwards.

There's a mechanical aspect to writing the sestina that's attractive to me—like the satisfaction you get when you've done an accurate drawing, or when you jury-rig a repair to a machine and it works. That kind of fun aside, though, the form is unforgiving, and if you aren't careful with your choice of end words you'll wind up with something about as poetic as a grocery list. The beauty and challenge is to find words that do double and triple duty— verb, noun, adjective—and have them slam home at the ends of the lines in surprising yet inevitable ways. Not every line can be perfect, because of the tension between the logic of the poem and the necessity of using the required terminal words. But when it works it's like the ringing of the bell when a strong man brings the hammer down hard enough at the county fair. When it works several lines in a row there's nothing quite like it.

Which has everything to do with the way I want to end this book. I want to tell you why people keep writing when it would be easier just to get a job and live like a normal person.

When you start out writing, most of the kicks come from a succession of "firsts." You send out stories and eventually get your first encouraging letter back from an editor. Then you get your first check and see your name in print for the first time. You write your first book and, sooner or later, sell your first book. You see it on the stands in front of God and everybody. You get your first reviews; your first review in the *New York Times.* Your first five-figure deal; your first six-figure deal. First movie option. First time you hear actors saying your lines; first time you hear the audience laughing in the right places. Somewhere in there, your first talk show, the first academic paper on your work. The first letter from a reader and the first time a stranger knows who you are. There's even a wry kick the first time someone thinks you're important enough to vilify in print and (for me, at least) the first time a committee of well-meaning citizens has a book of yours banned.

It's all fine. But you know something? There's no kick the second time.

You get a good review and the guy liked it for the wrong reasons. You get a pretty big advance and wonder if you should have held out for a bit more. You get an interview in the local paper and every jerk in town wants to sell you aluminum siding.

And writing doesn't get easier with practice. It gets harder, partly because your standards mature; partly because you use up all the easy stuff, all the natural material, in the first years. You don't want to repeat yourself even though you must know, if you're honest with yourself and not stupid, that every writer has only one story, the one big story, and if he could live forever he would tell it a million different ways and never get it quite right. Yet you persist.

Maybe I'm breaking a code here, an unspoken lodge law. We don't talk about this for the same reason that people who are really in love don't talk about love.

You do it for the language.

Nobody writes who wasn't pushed and pulled by the language since childhood. If you didn't have your heart broken and opened repeatedly by it—whether it was Shakespeare and Milton or Heinlein and Bester—you wouldn't feel the debt that has to be discharged. You wouldn't feel the need to pay them back by trying to beat them at their own game.

This is what it distills to, the real satisfaction. It isn't seeing your name, cashing the checks, reading the reviews and fan mail. It's loving the language and wanting to do right by it.

Most of the time you fail. The constraints and tensions I referred to in talking about the sestina are only more easily described than the different ones that wait hidden in other forms. Whether you're tackling a villanelle or an adventure novel, the language is your ally and your enemy at the same time. You fight it and embrace it and come up with something. It's almost always a bad translation of the thing that was in your head.

But often you come up with a word that is just the right word. Some golden times you write a sentence and you know—you *know*—that nobody else could have done it as well. Some rare times, a whole paragraph. A few times in a life, maybe a whole chapter without one word out of place. Nobody has ever written a perfect book.

But you keep trying. That's what it's about.

JOE HALDEMAN
Florida, 1984